# FADE TO BLACK

# F A D E
# TO BLACK

## WENDY CORSI STAUB

Kensington Books
http://www.kensingtonbooks.com

KENSINGTON BOOKS are published by

Kensington Publishing Corp.
850 Third Avenue
New York, NY 10022

Library of Congress Card Catalog Number: 97-074360
ISBN 1-57566-285-X

First Kensington Hardcover Printing: May, 1998
10  9  8  7  6  5  4  3  2  1

Printed in the United States of America

For my dear friends:
Mike and Lisa, Gabrielle and Drew

And for Mark and Morgan—again

# prologue

It's raining.

Of course it is.

Mallory Eden tears her concentration from the dark, slick highway to smile grimly at the irony.

A stormy summer night, a deserted mountain road, a frightened blonde driving alone . . .

It's like a scene from a movie—not, of course, one of *hers*.

Mallory Eden does romantic comedy. Period.

"The new Meg Ryan" they'd called her when she'd burst into mainstream America a few years back. Just as Meg had once been called "the new Goldie."

Mallory swerves slightly to avoid a water-filled rut. She peers ahead through the windshield, looking for the bridge.

Not yet. A few more miles to go.

In a few weeks—no, days—they'll be calling some perky blond actress "the new Mallory Eden."

And as for the *old* Mallory Eden . . .

She clenches the wheel more tightly.

The old Mallory Eden will be dead.

Not Hollywood *dead*, as in washed up.

Dead as in . . .

Dead.

Out of habit, Mallory glances into the rearview mirror to make sure nobody's following her. The road stretches behind her, empty as far back as the last curve. She hasn't seen another car since Dry Fork, the tiny town seven miles back through the mountains. She's alone out here . . . at least, she thinks she is. But after what she's been through, she can never really be sure someone isn't lurking just beyond the shadows.

Mallory wonders how the tabloids will break the news to the world. The *New York Post* will, undoubtedly, come up with a short, clever headline. They always do.

They're big on alliteration. Maybe they'll go with *Mallory Meets Her Maker*. Or *Eden's End*.

"You're sick," she says aloud—not that she's the type of person who goes around speaking to herself.

Not like Gran.

Her grandmother, who had raised her after Mallory's teenage mother left, had been a big self-talker. If Gran wasn't carrying on a spirited one-way conversation as she baked a strudel or dusted the tidy bedrooms, then she was singing to herself. Loudly. Show tunes, mostly.

Gran had loved the theater. And movies. Even television.

Over the past few years, hardly a day had passed when Mallory hadn't thought wistfully how proud Gran would have been if she could see her now. See what a big star she'd become, how the whole world loved her.

But all Gran had known, when she'd died the week Mallory graduated from high school, was that her wayward granddaughter had been running around with Brawley Johnson, a redneck gas station attendant who was seven years older than she was.

Gran had loathed Brawley from the moment she met him. Her pursed-lipped reaction had driven Mallory right into his arms. When Gran tried to forbid her to see Brawley, she'd threatened to run away with him.

"The second they hand me my diploma Sunday, I'm outta here!" she'd screamed at Gran that horrible night.

"And where do you think you're going to go?" Vera O'Neal had shouted right back, her fleshy face blotchy from the oppressive heat and her own fury.

"Away to . . . California. With Brawley."

She'd blurted that out on impulse—all of it. But the instant she'd said it, she'd known it was a perfect plan. She'd always wanted to see the West Coast. Santa Monica and San Francisco. Hollywood and Haight-Ashbury.

Oh, there had been a time when she'd been perfectly content to be wholesome and stay put in her heartland hometown. A time when all that mattered was becoming runner-up in the local Dairy Princess pageant, and snagging a part-time job at Burger King, and going out with upright boys named Chad and Brett.

But sometime before her seventeenth birthday she'd entered what Gran had called her "rebellious stage." It seemed that she and Gran—who had always been warm and affectionate with each other—were suddenly butting heads at every turn.

The worst part was, Mallory had known all along exactly what Gran was worried about.

*Like Mother, like daughter*—that was what she was thinking every time Mallory missed her curfew or got a D on a test.

*Like Mother, like daughter.*

Vera's only child, Becky O'Neal, had run wild—then, had simply run away. For good.

Gran, worried that Mallory was going to become her mother, had attempted to impose a series of ridiculously strict rules. And Mallory, who knew she had her mother's looks and her genes, had decided she might as well live up to her legacy.

On that final muggy June night when Gran had attempted to forbid Mallory to go out with Brawley, she had been filled with rage. Not just at Gran, but at her mother for getting herself pregnant at fifteen and then abandoning Mallory when she was a toddler; at her father, whoever he was; even at Brawley, for refusing to attempt winning Gran over by ditching the sullen attitude he always flaunted around adults.

When Mallory had grabbed an overnight bag and stormed out of the house, Gran was crying. And she had gone anyway, even though she had known that Gran was thinking of how her own daughter had left the same way . . . and never come back.

Gran couldn't have known that Mallory had no intention of really leaving town that night.

And Mallory couldn't have known Gran would drop dead of a heart attack a few hours after Mallory slammed the door in her face.

Now, as she drives around a sharp, sloping curve, the car's headlights pick up a sign up ahead in the road.

ROCK RIVER FALLS BRIDGE.

This is it.

She takes a deep breath as she slows the car, checking again in her rearview mirror for headlights.

There's no one there. No one up ahead either, on the opposite side of the water.

No one to see her drive onto the wet two-lane bridge high above the swift currents of the Rock River Falls.

No one to see her pull over halfway across and turn off the lights, and then the engine.

No one to see her fumbling, with violently trembling hands, for the envelope she had stashed earlier in her Italian leather purse.

No one to witness Mallory Eden, this year's buoyant Hollywood blonde, propping a suicide note on the dashboard, stepping out into the pouring rain, and walking over to the rickety railing to stare, mesmerized, at the foaming black water below.

# chapter

# 1

It's a white sweater that catches Elizabeth Baxter's eye today.

Yesterday it was the most minuscule pair of jeans she had ever seen; last week, a small straw sun hat with a navy and white polka dot bow at the back.

But today it's a teeny white sweater edged with lace, not ruffly, strictly feminine lace, but scalloped lace, the kind that would suit a boy or a girl. On the sweater's little pocket, a pale yellow duck has been embroidered.

Elizabeth stands staring at the sweater in the window of the shop.

Wee World.

That's the name of the shop.

Elizabeth has never ventured inside.

She never will.

Because she'll never have a baby.

Tears threaten to flood her eyes, and she does her best to drag her gaze away from the exquisite white sweater she will never have reason to buy.

If only—

"Hey, Liz!"

In the plate-glass window she sees a reflection of Pamela Minelli waving at her from across the street.

She groans inwardly and rolls her eyes behind her sunglasses but turns away from the window, pastes a smile on her face, and waves back. She starts walking again, slowly, pretending to be engrossed in flipping through the mail she's just removed from her post office box.

Maybe Pamela, who's loaded down with shopping bags and

toting her newborn in a Snugli and pushing her toddler in a carriage, will just stay there on the other side of North Main Street and be on her way.

But no, being Pamela, she won't.

Even as Elizabeth jabs her key into the driver's side lock of the red Hyundai parked in the ten-minute zone, Pamela's making her way across the street, flipping her blond pageboy around and calling, "Liz, hang on a sec!"

Elizabeth turns and pretends to be surprised to see Pamela approaching.

"Hi, guys,' she says, smiling down at two-year-old Hannah, who rewards her with a drooly smile.

"What's going on?" Pamela huffs and adjusts the straps of the Snugli.

"Not much."

"We've been shopping," Pamela informs her, holding up the bags she's clutching in one hand.

"I see that. How's this little fella been?" Elizabeth peeks over the fabric pouch to see the precious sleeping baby, trying to ignore her stab of envy for what breezy Pamela seems to take for granted.

Children.

Two beautiful children of her own.

"Jason? He's a handful, that's how he's been. All he wants to do is nurse. And he weighs a ton. He's gaining weight a hundred times faster than I did when I was pregnant. On him it looks good. But look at me. I can't seem to take off this last twenty-five pounds." She pats her ample hips, then eyes Elizabeth, who's wearing a baggy white T-shirt and denim shorts. "You know, Liz, you're one of those people who looks good with curves."

Not sure whether it's a sincere compliment or a veiled insult, Elizabeth murmurs, "Thanks."

"I've got to go on a diet," Pamela declares, then hollers, "Hannah, don't put that in your mouth!" She swoops down over the carriage and wrestles something out of her towheaded daughter's grasp.

Hannah promptly starts screaming.

Elizabeth shifts her mail from her left hand to her right, looks at her car, and says, "Well, I'd better hit the road. I'm in a ten-minute spot."

"They won't ticket you if you're standing right by your car,"

Pamela announces with the authority of a woman who's married to a Windemere Cove policeman.

"They won't?" Elizabeth tries to think of another reason to make a quick getaway.

"Nope." Pamela hands an animal cracker to the howling Hannah, who promptly shuts up and shoves it into her mouth. "Even if they tried to ticket you, you're with me and everyone on the force knows I'm Frank's wife. Listen, were you planning to go straight home?"

"I—yes," Elizabeth says, thinking that Pamela might want her to go over to the Sailboat Cafe for coffee, and that's the last thing she wants to do.

"Great. Would you mind doing me a huge favor?"

"What is it?" Elizabeth tries not to sound wary, but it isn't easy. Pamela's a nice enough person, but there are times—a lot of times—when Pamela doesn't seem to respect the boundaries Elizabeth is doing her best to establish.

"My back and my arms are breaking and I can't fit these bags in the rack under the stroller. Would you mind . . . ?"

"Of course I'll take them for you," Elizabeth says, relieved, opening the car door and motioning for Pamela to put the bags in.

"Not just the bags, actually. Would you mind taking the stroller too?"

"I guess I—"

"And Hannah?"

Elizabeth blinks.

"It's just that I have a few more errands to run—there's a sale on diapers over at Carmen's Drugs—and then I have to take Jason to the doctor for his two-month shots, and it'll be so much easier to do it if Hannah's not with me. She screamed as soon as she saw the syringe when I took him for his two-week shots, even though I promised her she didn't have to have one this time. Did you ever try to wrestle two screaming kids down a flight of stairs and into their car seats?"

Elizabeth can only shake her head and open her mouth to protest, but before she can, Pamela continues talking.

Pamela always does this—asks for some huge favor and then rattles on and on so that Elizabeth can't get a word in to refuse.

"I was going to leave Hannah with Ellie Hanson from our play group, but her daughter's got one of those nasty summer colds and the last thing I need is for Hannah to catch it and give it to the baby. Did you know that colds are linked with crib death?"

Elizabeth helplessly shakes her head again, fully aware of Pamela's insinuation that if she doesn't baby-sit Hannah, and Jason subsequently succumbs to crib death, it will be entirely her fault.

"I read that in some magazine article the last time I was at the pediatrician's office," Pamela goes on, bending and unstrapping the cracker-munching Hannah, then pulling her out of the stroller. The little girl reaches out with a soggy-crumb-covered hand and grabs a handful of Elizabeth's long, dark hair.

"Let go of that, sweet-pea," Pamela says, and unpries her daughter's fingers. "Sorry, Liz. She loves to pull hair. I'm practically going bald."

"My name isn't Sweet-pea. It's Babe," Hannah announces, lifting her chin stubbornly.

Pamela rolls her eyes and informs Elizabeth, "She's been telling everyone that lately. Babe has always been Frank's nickname for me, and I guess she just—I don't know, maybe she's jealous. You know how little girls love their daddies."

*No, I don't know that,* Elizabeth thinks. *I've never had a daddy to love. Or a mom.*

"Anyway," Pamela continues, "you'd think I wouldn't be as worried about SIDS this time around, but every night, there I am, hopping out of bed a thousand times to check and make sure Jason's still breathing."

Pamela plops Hannah in the passenger seat of the car and pulls the seat belt snugly over her, continuing to talk. "I think I'm worse than I was after Hannah was born, but you know, boys have a higher risk than girls do. Frank said that if I don't stop being so neurotic about Jason, he's going to start sleeping on the couch—Frank, not Jason—but I can't help it."

"Shouldn't she be in a car seat?" Elizabeth asks when Pamela pauses for a breath. "I mean, isn't it illegal to—"

"The seat belt is fine for now. She's big for her age. Anyway, you're driving only a few blocks, and you're a safe driver. I trust you. If you get stopped, just tell them she's Frank's child, and they won't fine you."

"But I don't—"

"No big deal, Liz," Pamela assures her. "Trust me."

"But it's not—"

"I'm her mother. I wouldn't do anything that would put her in

danger, would I? There you go, sweet-pea. Listen to Aunt Liz."
Ignoring Elizabeth's protest, Pamela plants a kiss on Hannah's
head, sticks another cracker into her hand, and delivers the box
and a bedraggled stuffed skunk to Elizabeth.

"She's had her nap and she'll be fine without a snack since she
has her crackers, although if you happen to have any fruit or juice
around, she'll probably love it. But not bananas. I'm positive she's
allergic to bananas, even though the doctor says she isn't. I should
be back at around four. Are you sure you don't mind?"

Elizabeth numbly shakes her head.

"You're a sweetie. Anytime you need a favor, you just ask,"
Pamela says, collapsing the stroller with a single practiced move.
"Want to open your trunk? I can just shove this in there. Or I can
put it in the backseat, but the wheels might be kind of yucky. I
think we rode right through a pile of doggie you-know-what on
Front Street."

"Dog poopie," Hannah clarifies, bouncing in the front seat. "Pee-
eeuh. Dog poopie stinks."

"I'll pop the trunk," Elizabeth says hurriedly, and hits the button
on the door handle.

"She's at that age when all she wants to do is talk about you-
know-what," Pamela confides, putting the stroller into the car.

"Poopie," Hannah announces happily. "Poopie, poopie,
poopie."

"If I tell her not to say it, she does it even more, so I just ignore
it," Pamela whispers to Elizabeth, then says, "Hey, this is a new
car! I just realized it. It's really nice. Look how clean the upholstery
is. Hannah, don't smear anything on Aunt Liz's seat."

Elizabeth glances inside the car to see that the toddler has already
left a sticky cracker-colored smudge beside her dimply leg.

Pamela doesn't seem to notice. She's running a fingertip along
the hood of the car. "I love the color, Liz—very sporty. You know
what Frank says? That there's a better chance of getting stopped
by the cops if you're driving a red car."

"Really?" Elizabeth keeps her voice carefully neutral, thankful
for the sunglasses that shield her eyes from her neighbor's scrutiny.
"Why's that?"

"I don't know. Maybe they think people who drive red cars
are more daring—the types who might be smuggling drugs or
something. Who knows? Frank's not on traffic patrol anymore.
Well, we've got to run, don't we, Jason-boy? Thanks again, Liz."

"No problem," she lies, and gets into the car beside Hannah.

"Where Mommy go?" Hannah asks in alarm, watching as Pamela and Jason stroll off down the street.

"Your mommy and Jason have to go someplace, sweetie, but I'm going to take you home with me," Elizabeth says, fastening her seat belt, putting the key into the ignition, and smiling reassuringly at the child.

Hannah contemplates that for a moment, then opens her mouth and lets out a screech.

"Hannah want Mommy!"

"No, it's okay, Hannah," Elizabeth says, reaching over and catching the little girl's hands, which are clawing at the door handle. "We're going to have such fun together, you'll see."

"Hannah want Mommy!"

"But if you go with Mommy, you'll have to go to the doctor's office. That's where she's taking Jason."

"The doctor?" Hannah stops clawing, but she's still sobbing.

"Yes, and you'll have to have a shot."

"A shot? No! No! Hannah don't want a shot!" Hannah cries harder, shaking her little head back and forth so quickly that she's a blur of bobbing blond curls.

"If you come with me, you don't have to have one," Elizabeth says, and Hannah calms down. She picks up her skunk from the seat and cuddles him against her cheek, sticking her thumb in her mouth.

Breathing a sigh of relief, Elizabeth starts the car and backs out of the spot. She heads down busy North Main Street through the heart of Windemere Cove, past the white clapboard Congregational church and the redbrick town hall and the row of green awnings that front a cluster of shops.

At the end of North Main she makes a right onto tree-lined Center Street, which runs along the waterfront. It's dotted with bait and tackle shacks and fish markets and a few small, no-frills pubs and cafes. Beyond the street and the shops, the deep blue sailboat-dotted waters of Narragansett Bay sparkle in the August sunshine.

"Daddy!" Hannah announces, taking her thumb out of her mouth and pointing.

Elizabeth glances in that direction and sees a white police car at the intersection of Center and Pine. The officer behind the wheel has a shock of white hair and he's wearing glasses.

"That's not your daddy, Hannah," Elizabeth says, glancing at the speedometer as she passes the cop. She's only going five miles above the speed limit, but, remembering what Pamela just said about red cars—and with Hannah not in a car seat to boot—she half expects a siren to sound behind her.

It doesn't, of course. She's noticed that here in Rhode Island, people seem to drive at breakneck speed without getting stopped.

"Hannah's daddy," Hannah insists, looking over her shoulder and sounding like she's on the verge of tears.

"That's not your daddy. Your daddy has dark hair, Hannah, remember? And a mustache. And he's young. That man was old."

"Daddy!"

"Hannah, when we get to my house, would you like some juice?" Elizabeth asks.

"Juice? Need juice. Okay."

"What kind of juice?" She is mindlessly trying to distract Hannah, trying to relax, trying not to keep glancing in her rearview mirror as she drives two more blocks down Center.

What if the cop really had come after her? What if he asked to see her license?

It isn't the first time she's gone over that terrifying scenario.

She'll have to say that her license is expired and that she doesn't have it with her—which, in a sense, is the truth.

She thinks of the license back at home, the expired one from Illinois that bears the name Elizabeth Baxter and a photo that looks strikingly like her.

She should probably get rid of it. If ayone ever found it and connected her . . .

"Need juice," Hannah says urgently.

"I know you do, Hannah. But what kind? I have apple . . . and orange . . ."

She turns right onto Green Garden Way, following the road as it curves past the dead end sign.

Hannah has decided on apple juice by the time Elizabeth pulls into the driveway of the small gray-shingled, white-shuttered Cape Cod she's been renting, fully furnished, for nearly five years.

When the middle-aged woman who lived there passed away shortly before Elizabeth came to town, she left the place to her only son, who is overseas in the military. He presumably plans to return someday, having chosen not to put the place on the market.

Elizabeth doesn't like to think about what she'll do when that happens. It wasn't easy to find a suitable house in her price range, and an apartment or town house is out of the question. The last thing she wants is close daily contact with neighbors.

The house is set way back from the street and fronted with three tall maple trees and a row of shrubs that offer considerable privacy—not that Green Garden Way is exactly teeming with activity. It's a hushed, pleasant neighborhood of small ranch houses and one-story Cape Cods, populated mostly by retired people with grown children.

Janet Kravinski, the local Realtor who had rented the house to Elizabeth, had promised peace and quiet when Elizabeth told her she would be working from a home office.

"In the back and on one side, your neighbor would be the woods," she'd told Elizabeth over the phone the day she'd called about the listing. "On the other, there's an eighty-year-old woman who's very sweet. I don't think she'll be having wild drug parties," she'd joked, and Elizabeth had forced a laugh.

"In any case," Janet had gone on, "New Englanders tend to pretty much keep to themselves, so I don't think there will be a problem."

That Yankee disdain for outsiders was one reason Elizabeth had chosen to move there, but Janet Kravinski didn't know that.

Another thing Janet Kravinski didn't know was that the eighty-year-old woman next door would die only a year after Elizabeth moved in, and that her house would be sold to Frank and Pamela Minelli.

Pamela may have been born and raised in Massachusetts, but she never, ever kept to herself. The day they'd moved in, she'd come bouncing across the yard to introduce herself and Hannah, who was a month old then. She'd asked all kinds of personal questions too.

About Elizabeth's work as a writer—a lie—and about why she'd gotten divorced from her husband—another lie—and about where she'd grown up, and so on and so on.

If Pamela noticed Elizabeth was reticent about answering her countless queries, she hadn't let on.

And since that first day, Pamela hasn't asked many more questions. She's the kind of self-absorbed person, Elizabeth has discovered, who talks endlessly about herself and her husband and her kids.

"Hannah go home now," Hannah says as Elizabeth pulls up in front of the garage and shuts off the car.

"No, you're coming to my house, Hannah. Remember?"

"Home!" Hannah insists, pointing at the yellow aluminum-sided house beyond the hedge.

Elizabeth sighs and gets out, then goes around and unbuckles Hannah's seat belt. She tucks her mail under her arm and picks the child up before she can escape across the yard. "Come on, Hannah, let's go get your apple juice."

"Hannah don't like apple juice!"

"How about grape?" Elizabeth suggests, unlocking the door and hurrying Hannah inside before she can start screaming again.

"Grape?" The child considers it for a mere second before nodding agreeably and saying, "Okay."

As she settles Hannah at the kitchen table with a small glass of grape juice, Elizabeth wonders what kind of mother she would be. She used to do a lot of baby-sitting back when she was in high school, and the kids always seemed to like her, cuddling up to her and begging her to stay and play even after their parents were home.

*I probably would be a great mom,* she tells herself, patting Hannah's white-blond hair. *Not that I'll ever find out.*

And it's just as well. Always, in the back of her mind, is the knowledge that she might not have inherited only her mother's looks. What if she'd also inherited her mother's . . .

Violent tendencies?

She has very few memories of Becky O'Neal, who had left the Nebraska farmhouse not long after her daughter's third birthday. But she remembers certain things about her mother—bits and pieces of scenes that occasionally run through her mind even now, like the rough cut of a film in the hands of an overzealous editor.

Her mother yanking her out of her high chair by her hair . . .

Screaming at her for messing her diaper right after being changed . . .

Smacking her across the face.

Slamming her into the wall.

Throwing her onto the floor.

Kicking her.

Elizabeth squeezes her eyes shut to block out the images and finds Hannah watching her with solemn eyes, a thumb in her mouth.

*I could never hurt a child,* Elizabeth tells herself, reaching out to stroke Pamela's daughter's silky blond hair.

*Never.*

*I would never be the kind of mother she was.*

She feels a sharp sense of loss at the thought, because she'll never have the chance to prove that to herself, or anyone else.

No, she'll never be anyone's mother.

"I'll be right back, Hannah," she says, shaking her head to rid herself of the disturbing truth, of lingering images.

She goes back down the hall to the front door and pulls it closed, then locks both bolts and the chain.

She glances into the living room out of habit, to make sure everything is as she'd left it. Yes, there's her needlepoint sitting on the Shaker pine coffee table in front of the floral print couch, and there, on the hardwood floor beside the navy recliner, is the copy of *People* magazine she'd been reading the night before. The drapes are carefully closed.

She decides to open them, since Pamela will be coming over to get Hannah and might think it's odd to have everything shut in the middle of a sunny summer afternoon.

Pamela's been inside her house only a few times, and every time she made Elizabeth nervous. It wasn't as though she'd snooped through the cupboards or asked a lot of questions, but she'd looked around with a shrewd eye that didn't miss anything. And she'd asked to see Elizabeth's office.

"I'd love to see where a real writer works," she'd insisted when Elizabeth had protested that her office was a mess. "And anyway, our house is always a mess and I've basically gotten over caring. You need to lighten up a little, Liz. Don't be such a June Cleaver."

What could she do but lead Pamela to the spare bedroom, where she kept her computer, desk, and books? She'd half expected Pamela to point out that the room was in perfect order, but for some reason she'd kept her mouth shut about that.

She *had* examined the rows of titles on the bookshelf. They were mostly poular fiction, and a few reference books.

And she *had* asked, "What is it that you write, again?"

Elizabeth told her, even though she'd said it several times in the past. "Technical stuff. I freelance. I do annual reports and newsletters and articles for trade journals, that kind of thing."

She'd hurried Pamela out of her office before she could pry further, and distracted her by asking whether she'd gotten a haircut.

Pamela loves to talk about her hair. She's always relating details about how she has it dyed and cut and styled.

The few times Pamela has been inside Elizabeth's house were never by invitation. She seems to have a way of seeping in, especially in the summer, when she and Elizabeth bump into each other outside more often.

Elizabeth opens the curtains in the living room and in the small dining room, then goes down the hall to shut the doors to her bedroom and the office. When she returns to the kitchen, she finds that Hannah has spilled grape juice all over herself, her pink and white sunsuit, and the white ceramic tile floor. A river of purple is running across the red Formica tabletop and has soaked the pile of mail she just picked up from the post office.

"Oops," Hannah says guiltily when Elizabeth comes in and sees the mess.

"It's okay," she tells the child.

She picks up the mail, which she has yet to examine, and sticks it into one half of the double stainless steel sink. Then she grabs a pile of wet paper towels and cleans the floor and Hannah's sticky hands and face.

"Yucky," Hannah comments, then adds, "Poopie."

Remembering what Pamela said, Elizabeth ignores that. She surveys the purple-streaked sunsuit and says, "You know what? If we don't get that into the washing machine, it's going to stain really badly. Will you let me take it off you?"

Hannah nods, looking bored.

Elizabeth wrestles her out of the sunsuit and leads her, clad only in her training pants, into the living room. "Do you want to sit here and watch television while I go down and put your outfit into the laundry?"

"TV," Hannah agrees, climbing onto the couch.

Elizabeth turns it on, finding a late-afternoon cartoon show. "Here you go, sweetie. Is this good?"

"Good."

Elizabeth smiles and leaves Hannah in the living room, thinking that as much as she dislikes Pamela's taking advantage of her, it's kind of nice to have a little child around the house.

*You'll never have one of your own,* she reminds herself. *You'll be alone for the rest of your life.*

Sighing, she unlocks the door in the hallway that leads down to the basement. It's unfinished, and filled with cobwebs and junk left behind by the woman who lived there before and died in the house.

Elizabeth flicks on the light and makes her way gingerly down the steep steps, ducking to avoid a shred of spiderweb dangling near the bottom of the stairs. She puts the sunsuit into the washer that sits in one corner, near an old, deep laundry sink.

"Cold, delicate," she murmurs aloud as she sets the controls.

She turns to go back up to the kitchen and jumps, gasping at the sight of someone moving in the shadows under the stairs.

She opens her mouth to scream, then realizes that it's nothing. Just an old wooden coat stand, some boxes, and her imagination.

But her heart is still pounding as she hurries back upstairs.

"Were you a good girl for Aunt Liz?" Pamela asks when she returns an hour later and scoops a squirmy Hannah off the couch.

"She sure was," Elizabeth lies, wishing she could tell Pamela about how she'd found Hannah—whose "poopie" comment was apparently meant to be a warning—smelling to high heaven and shredding the *People* magazine when she'd come back up from doing the laundry. She could also mention how Hannah had, in one swift movement, shattered her favorite crystal candy dish that had been sitting on the coffee table.

She wished, too, that she knew how to tell Pamela she didn't want to be called "aunt" or "Liz."

"What happened to her clothes?" Pamela balances Hannah on her hip and steadies the crying baby in his carrier. "Did she throw up on them or something?"

"Oh, I almost forgot." Elizabeth tells her about the grape juice incident. "I forgot to get the sunsuit out of the washing machine and put it into the dryer." More like, she hadn't been able to leave the little monster alone for another minute because she'd undoubtedly destroy the house. "Let me run down and get it for you now, and you can—"

"Actually, I'm kind of in a hurry right now, Liz. We're running late and Frank likes dinner to be ready when he gets home. I'll tell you what, just throw it into your dryer and run it over whenever you have a chance, okay?"

"Sure," Elizabeth says reluctantly, following Pamela to the door. She watches as her neighbor hurries down the driveway and across her own front yard, still carrying both of her children.

Then she carefully double-bolts and chains her door again, and goes around closing the blinds and curtains. When she gets to the kitchen, she spies her grape-juice-soaked mail still in the sink.

She spreads a layer of paper towels on the table, then carries the wet, sticky pile over and sets it down. She sits cross-legged on a chair and starts going through it.

Since she hasn't been to the post office since late last week, there's quite a bit of mail. Some of it is junk, most of it bills, and a few catalogues and magazines.

An envelope catches her eye as she crumples a supermarket flyer into a ball.

A pink envelope, poking out from beneath her phone bill.

She frowns and pulls it out. It's square and stiff; the kind of envelope that might contain a greeting card.

Her name and post office box address are typed neatly on the outside.

There's no return address.

But the postmark is Windemere Cove.

For a moment Elizabeth only stares at it, her hands trembling.

*It's probably just more junk mail,* she tells herself. *It looks like a card and there's no return address, so they can get people to open it out of curiosity.*

Slowly, she slides her index finger beneath the flap and starts to rip the envelope open. The stiff edge catches her flesh, and she winces.

"Just a paper cut," she says aloud, sticking her finger into her mouth and sucking the metallic-tasting blood away before opening the envelope the rest of the way.

She pulls out a greeting card.

On the front is a photo of a teddy bear with a sad face.

Inside, a scrawled message reads, *I know who you are.*

The card is unsigned.

Elizabeth's heart is pounding. Shaking her head in disbelief, she tosses the card onto the table and backs away from it.

*I know who you are.*

There's only one person who could have sent it.

Unless it's some kind of joke,

"It has to be," Elizabeth whispers. "It's a joke, or a mistake. . . . It can't be . . ."

*It can't be him.*

# chapter

## 2

Elizabeth bends to smooth the mauve duvet cover and tuck it beneath the pillows, then winces. She twists to rub the burning spot between her shoulder blades, a telltale remnant of her sleepless night. The few times she had managed to doze off, nightmares had tormented her.

She had been hurtled back to another August night, to the sprawling rented mansion high on the cliffs above the beach at Malibu, to the vast king-sized bed in the master bedroom there. The hot, dry Santa Anas stirred the filmy white draperies on the floor-to-ceiling windows and set the wind chimes on the stone terrace to an eerie, mournful tolling.

And there, beyond the landscaped pool area, a dark silhouette crept toward her, moving stealthily through the shadows.

In that impossibly convenient manner of dreams, she could see the figure clearly though she was inside the house, in bed, tossing in a restless sleep. She sensed that danger was closing in; she knew that in a matter of moments, she would be dead. . . .

*No!*

*Stop thinkinq of that. It was only a dream. . . .*

*Only a nightmare.*

Elizabeth lets out a shuddering sigh and abruptly shoves the quilt beneath the edges of the pillow shams. She turns and surveys the room, not reassured by its sun-splashed order or by the faint strains of an old Billy Joel song playing on the easy-listening radio station in the next room.

The day Janet Kravinski had first shown Elizabeth this house, she had pointed out how spacious the master bedroom was, how bright with "all those windows"—three-paned, high rectangles overlooking the asphalt driveway and chain-link-fenced backyard.

Elizabeth had nodded mutely as the Realtor rattled on. She had been remembering the skylit vaulted ceiling and three full walls of glass in that other, long-ago master bedroom that overlooked a lush, landscaped terrace and kidney-shaped swimming pool, and, off in the distance, the blue Pacific Ocean.

How she had loved that expansive view. She distinctly remembered instructing the interior decorator not to cover those windows. When the woman—one of those ubiquitous designer-clad, Mercedes-driving Beverly Hills blondes—had pointed out that the room might feel too stark without some kind of draperies to soften the boxy lines, Elizabeth had insisted on simple white sheers so that she would never feel closed in.

In the beginning she had rarely bothered to draw the drapes at night, wanting to feel as though she were sleeping outdoors, just as she had so long ago as a midwestern Girl Scout. It was comforting to open her eyes and see the moonlight filtering through the lush, blooming shrubs, reflected in the crystalline aqua waters of the pool.

How could it have never occurred to her that the windows worked both ways?

That someone was looking in on her as she lay alone in the wee hours of the morning?

How vulnerable she had been. . . .

How utterly reckless.

Now she glances at the heavy, lined curtains and sturdy venetian blinds she has installed at every window in this small bedroom, where only flimsy vinyl shades existed before. She had forced herself to open the blinds and curtains this morning, refusing to allow herself to give in to the terror that has threatened to send her over the edge ever since she opened that card yesterday afternoon. . . .

*I know who you are.*

The scrawled message has been continuously running through her mind.

Even the teddy bear illustration haunts her, the creature's black button eyes seeming to follow her with menacing intent.

*It has to be a mistake. Somebody meant to send the card to someone else. . . .*

But it was addressed to her. . . .

To Elizabeth Baxter.

Well, maybe it hadn't been meant in a threatening way. Maybe someone sent it as a joke.

There's only one problem with that scenario.

There is no one in Elizabeth Baxter's past who would play a joke on her, because she *has* no past.

This is it, this solitary life in this quiet New England town. There are no old boyfriends, no long-lost friends, no far-flung family members.

Whoever sent the card has figured out who she really is.

And they meant to scare the hell out of her.

They have succeeded.

Whoever sent it is right here in town, or they were as recently as a few days ago.

Do they know where she lives? Or did they trace her to Windemere Cove through the post office box address she uses for everything, another attempt at keeping her exact location a secret, should anyone figure out the alias she's been using.

And apparently, someone has.

Oh, God.

All at once her body gives in to the panic, involuntarily releasing it to surge from her gut and course through her veins. Urgent warnings screech in her brain, and her heart launches into a violent pounding.

Trembling, she strides to the nearest window and jerks her jittery hand toward the white plastic rod that controls the blinds.

Only when all three windows are darkened and the curtains drawn again does she shakily release the breath she has been holding.

She has succeeded in shutting out the bright morning sunlight.

She is once again alone and safe in the shadows. . . .

Alone.

Safe.

For now.

By early afternoon the frantic feeling has subsided enough so that Elizabeth is able to leave the easy chair in the living room, where she has been warily huddled for hours, her arms wrapped so tightly around her bent knees that her whole body now aches with tension.

She fixes herself a tuna sandwich, which she barely touches, and then decides to throw in a load of laundry. Anything to keep busy.

In the cellar she quells the thought that someone might be hiding in the dark corners that aren't quite reached by the light from the bare overhead bulbs.

She forces herself to move efficiently to the washing machine and open the lid.

Inside, plastered against the side, she sees a damp scrap of pink and white ruffled fabric, and she remembers. . . .

Hannah Minelli's sunsuit.

Elizabeth sniffs it, but there's no hint of mildew, though it's been sitting there, damp, for nearly twenty-four hours. She puts it into the dryer and turns it on low.

Then she fills the washer with bath towels and washcloths, measures the liquid detergent, dumps it in, turns the dial, and pulls the knob so that water starts gushing into the machine.

Hannah's sunsuit.

When it's dry, she'll have to bring it next door.

She promised Pamela that she would.

And if she doesn't, Pamela will come over to get it.

Venturing out of her protected nest seems too perilous to comprehend. . . .

Yet, the thought of having her privacy needlessly invaded by her neighbor's prying eyes and nosy questions is unbearable.

Outside, she can hear the birds singing, and the faint sound of a neighbor's lawn mower.

*Nothing's going to happen to you in broad daylight, with people all around*, she tells herself firmly.

No. He would wait until after dark—after midnight, when she was alone in her bed and there was no one to hear her scream. . . .

Just as he had before.


"Elizabeth!"

Frank Minelli's brown eyes widen in surprise and he opens the screen door wider.

"Pamela's not home," he tells her. "She went to some play group with the kids."

"That's okay. I just wanted to return this." She hands him the neatly folded pink and white sunsuit, still warm from the dryer.

Frank holds it up by the ruffled shoulder straps, then shakes his head and looks at her. "Must have been pretty skimpy on you, but Hannah's always glad to share her clothes."

She forces her mouth to smile, knowing he can't see that her eyes aren't smiling. They're hidden behind the sunglasses she wears whenever she leaves the house, even just to cross the yard.

"Actually, Hannah has about a hundred of these little pink outfits," Frank tells her. "I don't think anyone would have realized this one was missing."

Elizabeth nods stiffly, wanting only to go, feeling trapped in this neighborly suburban encounter.

"Then again," Frank says with a chuckle, "knowing my wife, Hannah's closet is probably alphabetized and labeled. She loves playing dress-up with Hannah, poor kid, like she's one of those Barbie dolls. But my daughter doesn't seem to mind, you know? Still, I'm telling you, the day I find Jason in a pink bonnet, I put my foot down."

She smiles, relaxes slightly.

He's nice, Frank. He must be a good cop. With his easygoing manner and sense of humor, he's the kind of person you'd want around if you were in trouble.

Not that Elizabeth has any intention of confiding her troubles to him. That's not even an option.

She takes a step backward, bumps into the black wrought iron railing at the edge of the small cement stoop.

"Want to come in?" Frank asks, still holding the door open with one hand, clutching the sunsuit in the other. "I can offer you that diet iced tea that Pam drinks, or a cold beer. I was just about to have one myself. Cutting the lawn always makes me thirsty as hell."

"No, I should get back. I have—"

What?

*Work to do?*

*Calls to return?*

*Company coming over?*

She can't think of a single excuse that wouldn't sound like a feeble lie. So she simply trails off with a shrug, and puts a foot down on the top step.

"I noticed your grass is getting a little overgrown," Frank says, leaning his shoulder against the door to prop it open, and casting a glance over at her yard next door. "You want me to take care of it for you?"

"Oh, no, that's okay," she tells him quickly. "It's fine. I mean, I'll get to it as soon as I have a chance. It hasn't needed mowing that much this month since it's been so dry. I, uh, had planned to do it today, but . . ."

*But I'm too terrified to leave my house for the amount of time it would take me to mow the grass.*

"Are you sure you don't want a hand? I'd be glad to help you out," Frank says. "Pam told me she owes you a favor, anyway, for you taking Hannah off her hands yesterday afternoon. That really was nice of you to go out of your way like that."

"It was no problem, really," Elizabeth assures him, and moves down another step.

Frank shrugs. "Well, we owe you one, then. Just let us know what you need. And if you get too lonely later, feel free to drop by. We're always around on weekend nights when I'm not working, 'specially now that the baby's here too. It isn't easy to find a sitter for two kids."

"No, I'm sure it's not," she agrees conversationally.

Suddenly, it occurs to her that maybe he expects her to volunteer to stay with the kids so that he and Pamela can have a night out.

Then she realizes he doesn't seem the type to drop a broad hint like that. His wife would do it, but—

Correction. Pamela would come right out and ask if she needed a favor like that.

Well, Elizabeth isn't about to offer her baby-sitting services to Frank, whether he's hinting or not. She has enough to worry about.

Still, as she looks into his friendly face, she feels a pang of regret. He's been so nice, offering to help her with her lawn and inviting her inside for a beer. . . .

*You're just feeling guilty because you can't be neighborly in return,* she tells herself.

Once upon a time, reaching out to people had been second nature to her.

But that had ended many years ago, long before she had come to Windemere Cove.

She had learned, once she had made it big back in Hollywood, never to trust anyone outside of a very select circle of friends. Everybody else, it turned out, wanted something from her— wanted her money or her connections or her body, or simply a share of the limelight.

"You all right, Elizabeth?" Frank Minelli asks, seeming to lean forward a little, his brown eyes concerned.

"I'm fine," she says hastily, and nearly stumbles moving down the last step to the sidewalk. "I have to get going. Tell Pamela I said hello. . . ."

"Will do."

She turns and just stops her foot from landing smack in the border of red and white impatiens along the sidewalk. She takes a giant step over the flower bed and crosses the lawn, tripping over a garden hose along the way.

She feels Frank Minelli's eyes on her and knows he must be thinking she's a clumsy, jittery fool.

But when she turns back, the screen door is closed and he's not watching her after all.

*You're totally paranoid. Everyone in the world isn't caught up in watching every move you make.*

Not anymore.

Not like the old days, when she couldn't step out her door to get the morning paper without paparazzi jumping from the bushes, when she couldn't go to the ladies' room in a restaurant without being trailed by a barrage of fans and press and curiosity seekers.

Those days are over.

Now nobody's watching her.

Nobody except the shadowy stranger she had thought she'd escaped for good five years ago . . .

Today.

Five years ago today, she realizes with a start as she jabs the key into the lock and opens the back door to her house.

She hadn't realized it was the anniversary until now, when the date had suddenly popped into her head.

That's it, then.

There goes the last glimmer of hope, hope that the card she had received yesterday had been some kind of fluke, that it hadn't been meant for her or that it hadn't been from the person who had made her life a living hell five years ago.

She knows, now, that it arrived yesterday for a reason.

Whoever had sent that card knows exactly what day it is, and he knows that Mallory Eden isn't dead.

But she has no doubt that he's going to make sure that she will be soon.

*  *  *

The child sits cross-legged on the scarred rust-colored linoleum floor in front of a small color television set. His neck is craned uncomfortably as he looks up at the screen, because the set isn't at eye level. It sits high atop the rickety white-painted table his grandfather picked out of someone's trash last year.

Grampa's always doing stuff like that. It's embarrassing.

So is the way Grammy's always going around in that same green cotton dress and shoes so worn, the soles slap against her heels like beach flipflops—and the fact that she often hunts for greens in the vacant lot behind the house.

She flours them, salts them, and fries them in oil, and they taste pretty good, but they're still weeds. They don't serve weeds in the school cafeteria or at the free day camp run by the town. None of his friends eat weeds at home.

And Elizabeth, he's positive, doesn't eat weeds, though he never asked her about it.

There are a lot of things he's never asked her.

The screen door in the kitchen bangs, and he hears footsteps in the hall, then voices speaking in Portuguese.

His grandfather's, then his grandmother's. Then a third voice. It's *her*.

He moves closer to the television set, stretching his arm to turn up the volume. It's just some stupid cartoon, but he focuses on the screen intently, as though there are no distractions.

No stupid golden oldies music blasting from his grandfather's small radio in the next room.

No simmering teapot building to a whistle, forgotten, on the gas range down the hall in the kitchen.

No voices bickering, then hollering from the bedroom in a language he understands but has never chosen to speak.

Money.

She's come for money.

She always comes for money.

Doesn't ask to see him, or even about him.

Her child.

Her father hollers that he has no money to give her, especially not for what she'll spend it on. Crack.

Her mother screams at him to shut up, or the whole neighborhood will hear.

Then, open windows clearly forgotten, they rant at their daughter; she rants back at them.

She knows they have money; do they want her to starve?

"What about your son?" her mother shouts. "We can barely afford to feed him now that your father's out of work on disability. Do you want to take food out of your son's mouth? Do you want him to starve? Do you care?"

"He won't starve," comes the reckless reply. "He's got that lady. She must give him money."

The child squeezes his eyes closed and bends his head, shaking it. Elizabeth. But how does she know?

"What lady?" his grandmother asks, sounding slightly less angry. Curious.

"That lady who takes him out for ice cream all the time. I have friends. They see her with him. She's trying to take my place. She's trying to take over as his mother."

"What the hell are you talking about?" his grandfather demands.

"She's hallucinating again," his grandmother says, as if that's the only possible explanation. "Calm down, Rafael. You don't want to get worked up. Your heart—"

"My heart is fine."

"I'm not hallucinating," says their daughter. "You two don't even know what he's up to half the time, do you? What the hell kind of guardians are you?"

"Don't you curse at us!" Manny's grandfather bellows. "What kind of mother are you? What kind of daughter? What kind of person leaves her own flesh and blood without looking back? Except when you need money for—"

"Rafael, your heart!"

"Forget it! I don't need your money. I don't need anything from you."

Footsteps again, retreating quickly down the hall toward the back of the house. The door creaks open, slams closed.

His grandmother makes her way down the hall into the kitchen and the teapot makes a deflating, moaning sound as it slowly ceases to whistle.

His grandfather mutters something to himself, then curses and throws something against the wall in the next room.

And the child opens his eyes just in time to see a large brown roach the size of a small mouse scurrying across the linoleum inches from his bare leg.

* * *

Had she actually thought she could escape the fear, escape the memories, even for a short time?

Elizabeth draws a deep breath and forces herself to look back at the headline that has caught her eye in this evening's edition of the *Harbor Times*.

It's a major story, located on the second page, opposite a piece about the ongoing reservoir water shortage in the East Bay, compounded by the hot, dry August they've had.

### Five Years Since Mysterious Death of America's Sweetheart

Even the dinky local paper has marked the anniversary with a full-length feature story off the wire, accompanied by several photographs.

One is a flattering shot of Mallory Eden taken, according to the caption beneath, in the March before her suicide.

In it, she is standing on the red carpet at the Shrine Auditorium just before the Oscar ceremony. Her golden hair is upswept in a mass of curls to reveal dazzling jewels at her throat and ears. Her blue eyes are bright with anticipation, and her lithe figure is clad in a slinky black Dolce & Gabbana midriff-baring gown.

She is on the arm of one of Hollywood's most eligible bachelors, one of the five nominees for best supporting actor that particular year. Though the tabloids practically had them married off the following morning, the date was in truth a publicity stunt, arranged by their mutual manager.

Two years later, the actor would finally win the golden statuette that had eluded him the night Mallory had been his date; in the year following that he would be forced out of the closet by a militant gay tabloid, only to fade to near obscurity soon afterward.

*You and me both,* Elizabeth tells him ruefully, laying a fingertip on his newsprint image.

The next photo is a grainy candid that had been published in the tabloids early that terrible summer, showing her drawn and pale, leaving the hospital in a wheelchair. She remembers how she had tried to hide her bony frame beneath a baggy sweatshirt and jeans, but now she realizes that the sagging clothes only emphasized that her once-celebrated curves had given way to skeletal proportions. One of her hands is thrown up in front of her face, as though to shield herself . . . from the photographer? Or from the bullets she had suddenly found herself expecting at every turn?

The final picture shows the desolate Rock River Falls Bridge—a rickety structure looming high above the raging white water that had, presumably, swallowed Mallory Eden's battered body.

Elizabeth looks away again, clears her throat. The sound seems deafening in the quiet room.

She wraps a strand of long, dark hair around her index finger and glances at the loudly ticking mantel clock above the yellow brick fireplace—how she loathes yellow brick. In her Malibu mansion there were three huge, rustic stone fireplaces.

She notes absently that according to the clock, it's twenty after eight.

Almost time to turn on the television and watch a rerun of *Family of Foes*, the sitcom starring Kenny Abner, one of her old Hollywood pals. Every time she sees his familiar freckled face beaming at her from her television screen, she finds herself battling the impulse to pick up the phone and call him.

Of course, that's impossible.

She continues to twist her hair and look around at the room that suddenly, somehow, seems foreign to her—to Mallory Eden. None of this belongs to her—the blue-and-green-striped couch, the boxy coffee table with its scarred wood veneer, the peach-colored silk flowers in a basket on the television console. The room could desperately use a paint job, and the area rug beneath the coffee table, a cheap polyester Oriental, is worn. Shabby—it's all so shabby.

*But it isn't mine, so it doesn't matter,* she tells herself.

It's rented; the house is rented; even her identity is rented. Stolen, rather, from the real Elizabeth Baxter, who won't be needing it anymore.

Finally, she reaches up, beneath the shade on the floor lamp beside her chair, and clicks the switch so that the bulb is a touch brighter.

It was actually bright enough before, but she needs another moment of reprieve before reading the article about her life—and death.

For a moment she considers tossing the paper away without reading it.

Why put herself through more torture?

Then she realizes that she has no choice. She has to read it; has to know what the press is saying now, five years later. Has to know what kind of stuff *he's* been reading; whether there are any clues in the article that could tip someone off—not just that Mallory Eden didn't die, but where she is, and who she has become.

And so she takes a deep breath and begins to relive the nightmare one more time.

## Five Years Since Mysterious Death of America's Sweetheart

*In countless films earlier this decade, Mallory Eden portrayed the perky, pretty girl-next-door who captured the leading man's heart—and the hearts of her audience. But five years ago today, August twenty-second, the twenty-four-year-old actress took her own life when she jumped from the Rock River Falls Bridge in a rural, mountainous region of northwestern Montana. Her body has never been found.*

*What led a woman who had everything to such a tragic end?*

*There is no question among those who knew her.*

*"It was the stalker, pure and simple," maintains Flynn Soderland, the late star's flamboyant agent, who has since retired.*

*"The stalker" refers to the anonymous fan who became obsessed with Mallory Eden at least six months before her suicide. Star stalking is certainly nothing new, but the death nearly a decade ago of* My Sister Sam *actress Rebecca Schaeffer, murdered at the hands of an obsessed fan, thrust the syndrome into the public eye.*

*According to Roger Boyd of Boyd Security, a Los Angeles firm with many of tinseltown's top names on its client roster, "Highly visible show business professionals are certainly accustomed to overzealous fans, and everyone, even the most universally popular stars, receives threatening mail occasionally. But once in a while you have a situation where the fan is a true psychopath, where the threats start to cross the line, and where the victim is in real danger."*

*That is precisely what happened to Mallory Eden.*

*At first she was reportedly not even aware of the menacing letters that had been addressed to her and received at her publicity office over a period of several weeks during the spring before her death. When the messages became increasingly ominous and threatened violence, however, the actress was alerted. She hired a security consultant and was rarely seen thereafter in public without a bodyguard at her side. Yet despite the unsettling problems in her personal life, Eden continued to display the sunny, breezy California-girl demeanor that made her famous.*

*It is rumored that the letters gradually gave way to threatening telephone calls, and that Mallory Eden arrived at her rented Malibu mansion one evening to find that her beloved pet dog had had its throat slashed. According to Soderland, there was a note accompanying the corpse, written in the* animal's blood that read, "You're next." Los Angeles police have consistently refused to comment on that report.

The cunning stalker somehow managed to continue to elude both the star's security advisers and the police. Finally, in July, after several months of harassment, the gun-toting intruder broke into the house and attacked Mallory Eden herself. The actress was shot as she slept in her bedroom, hit by a single bullet in her stomach.

The plucky actress survived the wound and the subsequent surgery, which left her unable to bear children. Despite that traumatizing condition, she released a statement thanking the medical professionals, Los Angeles police, and friends who had stood by her, and requesting that her fans allow her a private recovery.

Just days after Eden's release from the hospital, as her personal assistant, Gretchen Dodd, sorted mail and gifts sent by well-wishers, a floral arrangement exploded. Dodd was disfigured in the blast. She has since dropped from public view and could not be reached by this reporter for comment.

Meanwhile, the injury to Eden's assistant seemed to drive the actress over the edge. Reclusive in the weeks that followed the explosion, she ultimately eluded the press and her bodyguards, apparently fleeing alone in mid-Auqust to a secluded wilderness area of northern Montana. Little is known of how she spent the days before her black Lexus was found abandoned at the Rock River Falls Bridge, a suicide note on the dashboard.

The text of the note has never been released, but the motive behind her death is no mystery to loved ones left behind.

"Mallory loved life. She was always upbeat, always laughing and joking around," says Rae Hamilton, Eden's closest friend and former roommate who was until recently seen as a semiregular on the daytime soap opera Morning, Noon, and Night. "She had hoped to marry one day and have children. That possibility was cruelly stolen from her."

Another Eden confidante, former stand-up comic Kenny Abner, who now stars in the popular NBC sitcom Family of Foes, declined to be interviewed for this article. He did release a statement through his publicist, calling his late friend "a superior human being. She is still missed every day, not just by those who knew her, but by the fans who worshipped her."

Rae Hamilton concurs. "She was a rare commodity in Hollywood. I don't know a soul who didn't think she was a great person, and that doesn't happen very often in this town."

The golden-haired, azure-eyed Hamilton, chairwoman of the Mallory Eden Foundation—which according to the actress's will provides scholarship money to single mothers—bears an almost eerie resemblance to her late friend. In fact, the two met at an audition when both were struggling actresses, up for the same role—a sexy, slightly ditzy blue-eyed blond con woman in director Cal Lansing's comedy smash, "Wrong Side of the Tracks."

*In an interview, Eden once cited the audition as "the turning point in my life. Not just because it helped to launch my career, but because it was how I met Rae. My first thought when I saw her was that it was like looking into a mirror—only a trick mirror, the opposite of one of those funhouse kinds. In this mirror, everything looks slightly better than in real life. I mean, Rae is gorgeous. My second thought, when I learned I was to audition directly after her, was 'uh-oh.' I never thought I'd measure up."*

*Eden, of course, won the role, a small part that nonetheless captured the attention of critics and audiences alike.*

*Meanwhile, Hamilton and Eden went on to share more than a striking resemblance. For two years they shared a house in L.A.'s San Fernando Valley. And they shared a genuine friendship, rare by Hollywood standards.*

*Meanwhile, Hamilton admits that they look so much alike that fans have always mistaken her for Eden, and it continued even after her suicide.*

*"People would stop on the street and do a double take," she said recently. "It's like they thought I was a ghost, or that Mallory was still alive after all. But that doesn't happen so much anymore. I guess after so many years, people start to forget."*

*Not everyone. The Mallory Eden Fan Club has an active Web site and continues to publish a semiannual newsletter filled with facts, photos, and tributes to their fallen idol.*

*"Just because she's gone doesn't mean she's not still on our minds and in our hearts," says Elise Sweet, a San Diego housewife and president of the fan club. "She was truly special—so different from other successful actresses. She never minded signing autographs or stopping to chat and kid around with fans."*

*Sweet refuses to acknowledge that it might have been that very accessibility that triggered Eden's stalker's obsession. She comments, "Mallory was a kind and loving person, and there's no way that what happened to her was her fault."*

*Hamilton sheds additional light on the true character of the late actress. "When this nutcase began stalking Mallory, threatening her, and finally physically attacking not just her, but someone close to her, she fell apart. She simply couldn't go on that way. She felt that it was only a matter of time before the stalker again hurt somebody she cared about, and this time fatally. And then there was the knowledge that she could never bear a child because of what that bullet wound had done to her. Mallory adored children."*

*Growing up in the tiny town of Custer Creek in rural Nebraska, the future actress—born Cindy O'Neal—had often displayed that caring nature, not to mention her trademark sense of humor. She was loved by everyone she met, though according to those who knew her, she displayed a wild, restless streak not surprising for an overprotected small-town girl with lofty aspirations.*

*After being abandoned as a toddler by her unwed teenage mother, she was raised by her maternal grandmother. Vera O'Neal kept a strict rein on young Cindy, who began entering—and winning—local beauty pageants as an adolescent.*

*According to hometown legend, on the night she graduated from Custer Creek High School, Cindy O'Neal ran away from home with her then boyfriend, Brawley Johnson, seven years her senior. Hours later, her grief-stricken grandmother died of a heart attack.*

*"She always blamed herself [for her grandmother's death]," says Johnson, 36, now a Los Angeles limousine driver, and still single. "If that hadn't happened, she probably would have gone back home after we had our taste of freedom. I know I would have. I always figured we'd go back to Custer Creek, get married, and have a bunch of kids. But when Vera died, Cindy had nothing to go back to. So she turned to acting. She was determined not to let anything get in the way of her dream."*

*According to Johnson, he and Eden stayed together for several years, and he supported her financially while she, like countless other midwestern runaways, struggled to make it in Hollywood. Unlike the vast majority of nubile young hopefuls, Mallory Eden made it.*

*And like other suddenly successful stars, she didn't waste time in severing her relationship with the hometown lover who knew her when.*

*By some accounts, the split between Eden and Johnson was a bitter one. But the man who is, by all accounts, the only serious lover the famed actress ever had, refuses to comment on the end of their relationship.*

*He will say only, "She was a great lady, and I will always be grateful for the time we had together. She taught me a lot, and no one knows how much I miss her to this day."*

*After performing bit parts in high-profile, big-budget movies, the actress, just after her twentieth birthday, landed a lead in Oscar-winning director Langdon McKay's romantic comedy* Stars in Her Eyes, *opposite veteran actor Tom Hawes. She became an overnight sensation and leading lady, appearing in a number of well-received films in the years that followed. Among them are the blockbusters* Mommy's Boyfriend, *and* Monday in the Park, *the latter her final film, which was released shortly after her death.*

*"She had an incredible amount of potential, and she had only begun to tap into her thespian skills. Had she lived," says Soderland, her agent, from his retirement home in Pacific Palisades, "I have no doubt that Mallory would have become one of the greatest dramatic actresses of our time. I continue to mourn her loss."*

*As do legions of fans—some of whom, it is said, believe that the actress's untimely death wasn't a suicide.*

*Some of those who have speculated that Mallory Eden didn't take her own life theorize that she was abducted to Montana by her stalker, then forced to write the suicide note before being thrown or pushed from the bridge into the deadly rocky gorge.*

*Still others believe that the actress never jumped, or was forced, off that bridge at all. Their assumption is that she faked her death to escape her stalker, and is presumably alive and well somewhere in the world, perhaps still living in fear of the crazed fan who shattered her fairytale life.*

*Subscribers to this speculation point as evidence to the fact that Mallory Eden's body has never been found.*

*However, Allen Macy, the sheriff of Dry Fork, Montana, a remote town not far from the fateful bridge, contends that the failure to recover a body from the raging Rock River is hardly unusual.*

*"This is one of the fastest-moving, most treacherous bodies of water in the country," Macy said. "First, you have the waterfall just downstream from the bridge. There is a deep vault underwater in the rock beneath the falls that has been known to temporarily—and maybe permanently—trap debris and bodies that go over."*

*Beyond that point, according to Macy, the river travels primarily through rugged wilderness, where very few humans have ventured. Therefore, it would be not only conceivable, but highly likely, for a body to travel downstream and become snagged in the rough terrain along the way.*

*As an example, the sheriff cited the case of three Canadian fly-fishermen who drowned a decade ago in the river, not far from the bridge in question, after being swept over the falls. Two of the bodies were recovered thirteen miles downstream several weeks later, and the third has never been found.*

*It is understandable that some of her fans prefer to believe that the effervescent Mallory Eden escaped such a grisly fate.*

*Meanwhile, the stalker who tormented the actress and ultimately destroyed her remains at large. There have been no leads and no suspects in the case, which remains open to this day.*

Elizabeth crumples the newspaper and tosses it to the hardwood floor beside her chair. She rises abruptly, crossing restlessly to the window to part the dark green brocade draperies. She lifts one of the slats in the venetian blinds to peer out into the night.

The light from the room behind her obscures the view until she presses her face right up to the glass. Only then does she see that the quiet, curving dead-end street is seemingly deserted.

She drops the blind and steps back from the window. . . .

Then leaps into the air and cries out as a sudden shrill sound pierces the air.

*The phone . . .*

*It's just the phone. . . .*

She clasps a trembling hand against her mouth and turns toward the telephone, which sits on an end table across the room.

It rings again.

And again.

There are only two people who might be calling her.

One is Manny Souza, the eight-year-old boy she befriended in the local park a year ago. He alone possesses her unlisted telephone number; on the rare occasions when her phone rings, it's been him.

Until now.

There's only one other person who might be calling—who might somehow have gotten hold of her number.

But how?

And why?

Why is he doing this to her again?

She lets the phone ring, clamping her hands over her ears to shut out the persistent noise, until it finally ceases a full minute later, leaving her alone in the room with the crumpled newspaper and the ticking clock.

"We'll be ready for you in about five minutes, Mr. Johnson," calls a bespectacled production assistant, sticking her close-cropped dark head into the small glassed-in cubicle.

Brawley Johnson nods at her.

She's what he privately refers to as fashionably ugly. He knows it's a stylish look; still, he wonders why women want to do that to themselves—wear boy-shorn hair and horn-rimmed glasses and boxy, baggy clothes that reveal not a hint of flesh or a womanly curve.

Not his kind of woman at all.

*His kind of woman . . .*

No.

Not *kind* of woman, as if there is an entire class of available, perfect specimens all ripe for the choosing.

There had been only one woman for him.

Cindy O'Neal.

*The bitch.*

He absently thrums his fingertips on the Formica tabletop, then realizes he probably appears nervous to anyone watching from the other side of the glass.

The last thing he needs is for anyone to think he's uncomfortable about the prospect of appearing on camera. He has to show them that he's utterly relaxed, a real pro at this television stuff.

He straightens his posture and tries to appear at ease, wishing he had a magazine to leaf through casually.

He resists the urge to jiggle his leg impatiently, licks his lips, and finds that they taste strangely waxy, thanks to the lipstick the makeup woman insisted on applying.

"You don't want to look washed out on camera," she had said, peering into his face as she applied the lipstick. She was decent-looking and he had almost opened his mouth to flirt with her the way he flirts with anyone attractive, before he realized that she smelled faintly of garlic. There was a telltale white paper bag from an Italian restaurant on the counter behind her.

It was all he could do not to wrinkle his nose in distaste as she breathed into his face while she worked on him. He was so eager for it to be over that he hadn't even protested the makeup she'd applied.

Now, here he is, about to go on national television, wearing rosy pink lipstick. He won't look washed out—he'll just look like a freakin' fag.

He fumbles in his pocket for something to wipe it on, but comes up with nothing.

*Washed out.*

Yeah, right.

With this tan, he's going to look washed out. He's spent every day this week roasting at the beach, just so he'll look his best today.

Not that, at the beginning of the past week, he'd even had any interviews set up. But with August twenty-second looming on the horizon, he figured the press would come sniffing him out. They do it every year.

Only it's not always television.

Back when it first happened, five years ago, he was on every talk show and newsmagazine program that existed, not to mention the actual network news.

But ever since, he's done only some local television news spots whenever they commemorate Mallory Eden's death with scholarship presentation.

Mostly, it's print reporters who ask him for comment. A couple of times he's been interviewed by legitimate newspapers, and the tabloids always want to talk to him.

But today it's *Scoop Hollywood*, a live half-hour entertainment news program with millions of regular viewers.

And here he is, bronzed and buffed, and dressed in head-to-toe Versace.

She taught him to dress, Cindy did.

*Mallory*, he corrects himself.

That was a subconscious slip. He rarely thinks of her as Cindy anymore. She had, of course, officially stopped being Cindy when she started calling herself Mallory Eden, but it took him a while after that to stop thinking of her as Cindy O'Neal. Because at home, with him, away from the glare of the cameras, she still acted like her.

At least, for a while.

Still asked for his opinion, still laughed at his jokes, still gave him blowjobs whenever he asked. Maybe not as eagerly as she once had, but at least she made an effort. At least she was there for him.

Especially when he reminded her that he had been with her from the beginning.

He was her one remaining tie to her past life.

And he knew her deepest, darkest secrets. . . .

One in particular.

Whenever he brought that up, she started acting nice to him again.

But gradually she had changed so much, he barely recognized her. Her emotional distance from him had grown in direct proportion with her success. The more she got caught up in all that Hollywood crap, the less attention she gave to him.

And if she was worried that he would reveal her big secret, she didn't let on.

Finally, one day, just after they had returned from a week-long vacation *he* had paid for—even though he was making far less money than she was by that time—she fucking moved out of their one-bedroom Long Beach apartment. She relocated to a rented house in the Valley with her friend Rae, a real phony whom Brawley had never liked.

And from there Mallory went straight to Malibu, to the Mediterranean-style beachfront mansion with the fancy gates and the picture-perfect landscaping and the professional decorating inside.

Not that he'd ever been inside—as an invited guest anyway.

How many times, in the years that followed, had he threatened to reveal her deep, dark secret to the press?

"Go ahead," she would say, looking at him with those fake blue eyes, making him wonder whether she was as undaunted as she appeared.

But he had never been able to bring himself to do it. He was saving that secret as a last resort. He couldn't use it to win her back—only to destroy her. He hadn't had the chance.

*But it's never too late. . . .*

"Mr. Johnson?"

It's the production assistant again, smiling and gesturing. She has a speck of something dark caught between her front teeth.

"We're ready for you," she says.

He nods and gets up, following her into the adjacent dimly lit studio, where he will once again tell the world, in a halting, grieving voice, how much he still misses his dead lover, Mallory Eden.

"Rae darling."

"Hello, Flynn."

They embrace, the golden-haired starlet and the flamboyant retired agent, beside the table at Mitsuhisa, the trendy nouveau Japanese restaurant on La Cienega Boulevard in Beverly Hills.

Flynn Soderland casts a shrewd eye over her well-sculpted features and thinks that she has aged; well, who hasn't? His own hair is fully white-gray now, he reminds himself, and his hairline seems to be shrinking back from his face at an alarming rate.

Still, he is no longer in the business—at least, not technically.

But Rae Hamilton is still a working actress—for the most part. Until recently she had played the role of dim-but-adorable Rainbow Weber on the soap opera *Morning, Noon, and Night*. But poor Rainbow had been hacked to death by a machete-wielding serial killer during May Sweeps.

"How have you been, really?" Flynn asks Rae after they've ordered—sashimi and salad for her; a shrimp dish in wasabi butter sauce for him. He leans forward and lays a gentle hand over hers, finding it icy.

"Do you mean since my character was killed off?" she asks, her blue eyes narrowing at him as she sips her club soda.

"I mean since your best friend was killed off. Five years ago today, to be exact. Isn't that why we're here?"

They get together for lunch every year on this date—at first to console themselves over her lost friend; his lost client. Now that the grief has waned and they have little in common, they continue the tradition out of habit. He suspects Rae is as reluctant as he is to let go entirely.

"Oh. I didn't realize you were referring to Mallory." She shakes her head and echoes, "God. 'Killed off.' You always were blunt, Flynn."

"Well, it was your phrase."

"I was talking about Rainbow Weber, who, in case you aren't a soap fan, met her maker a few months ago."

"I'm not a soap fan, but I watched."

"What did you think?"

"You were very good."

A white lie never hurt anyone in Hollywood, that's for damn sure.

And anyway, it wasn't that *she* was so awful. It was the writing, the melodrama . . . just not the kind of scene that's conducive to an actress's reputation.

He can tell, by the world-weary expression in her blue eyes, that she's perfectly aware of that truth.

He continues. "But I was more concerned that you might be upset over Mallory, even after so many years. I'm just . . . worried about you."

"Why?"

"Because you're out of work, and because you look . . ."

"What?" she presses when he trails off.

*Never criticize an actress on her appearance.*

He may have retired, but he hasn't lost the Hollywood touch.

"You look sad," he says. "Or tired. In your eyes. They're not sparkling."

"Well, hell. I was up before dawn this morning to tape a live interview with one of those New York morning shows."

"Good for you," he tells her, thinking maybe, contrary to local gossip, she isn't out of work after all. Has she landed a role without his hearing about it?

Maybe he's more out of the loop than he realizes. He still lives right there in the Hollywood Hills; he continues to subscribe to the trades and to dine with his friends in the industry. But it's not the same as being in the business.

He asks tentatively, "What are you publicizing, Rae?"

"Are you kidding? You just said it yourself. Today's the fifth anniversary."

"Ah, yes." He nods, surprised at his own momentary lapse. Of course she had been interviewed about Mallory.

Even after all these years the media wants to rehash her life, her death, as though some new detail is going to pop up and stun the world.

"I'm surprised they don't come after you," Rae remarks. "After all, you were her agent."

"But you were her best friend." He pauses, then admits, "And anyway, they *do* come after me. I've talked to several print journalists recently about Mallory, but I've decided not to do television interviews any longer."

"Too emotional?"

He nods, though of course that isn't the case at all. He's perfectly capable of controlling his emotions, particularly on camera. It's just . . .

Who wants to have their balding head and wrinkled, liver-spotted face broadcast to millions of people?

"You always were a proud SOB."

He looks up, startled, at Rae's comment.

"And you're a lot sharper than you look," he responds.

"Touché." She smiles and shakes her head so that her long blond hair flips back, behind her shoulders.

She tells him, "I'm glad you've noticed. It's taken me a long time to shake that pesky dumb-blonde image."

He doesn't tell her that sometimes it's better not to try too hard. Not everyone likes a smart cookie—not here anyway.

Mallory knew that instinctively, without his having to tell her. She knew just how to play it, the role of the sweetly sexy, slightly zany girl-next-door. She never worried, the way Rae always has, about being seen as a bimbo.

Not that anyone—within the industry or beyond it—perceived Mallory Eden as a bimbo. Far from it. Her superb comic timing was pure genius, and she had always been quick-witted with the press, tossing off quips with the aplomb of a shrewd professional. She was able to laugh at anything—including herself—a rare trait in Hollywood.

Rae, on the other hand, for all her beauty and intellect, isn't nearly as sure of herself.

And why would she be?

She hasn't had anywhere near Mallory's success. There have been a few minor movie roles in recent years, and a lead in a quickly-canceled television sitcom last season before *Morning, Noon, and Night* came along.

Flynn wonders, as he has many times over the years, whether he could have made a difference in Rae Hamilton's career had he signed her on as a client. She had approached him almost a decade ago, and he had met with her on Mallory's recommendation.

Years in the business had taught him to recognize instantly whether an actress had potential. He had seen that star quality in Mallory the moment she had walked into his office.

He hadn't seen it in Rae.

He had turned her down for representation, softening the blow by telling her his client list was simply too crowded at the time.

He never knew whether she'd believed him.

But they remained casual acquaintances, both before and after Mallory's death.

And she is still with Buddy Charles, the agent to whom he had referred her. Charles is a decent agent who has made a name for himself over the past few years managing the careers of middle-of-the-road performers.

"She's going to be my breakout star," Charles had crowed to Flynn years back when he'd called to thank him for sending her his way.

"I hope so," Flynn had said sincerely, though he was fairly certain that Rae Hamilton wasn't destined for cinematic greatness.

She, like Mallory Eden, is beautiful, and smart, and funny.

But her pale beauty is considerably less accessible than Mallory's fresh-faced loveliness had been; it's almost too deliberate, as though she has spent the last hour and a half applying makeup and styling her hair.

And her Ivy League background is a little too apparent; get her talking about a classic novel and she'll go off on a tangent about themes and metaphors and leave everyone in the dust.

Meanwhile, her quick wit is a little too direct; some comments too barbed for comfort.

*Sharp.*

Yes, that certainly does describe the actress sitting before him.

There will never be another Mallory Eden.

Flynn Soderland clears his throat and lifts his glass.

Rae Hamilton follows his cue.

"To Mallory," he says quietly. "Wherever she is."

# chapter

## 3

"Manny?"

The child, who had been running across the small gravel-paved playground toward the swingset, turns at the sound of his name.

"Elizabeth," he says happily, doing an about-face and making a beeline in her direction.

She is reminded of the first time she ever laid eyes on him, a few years ago. She had been strolling through the small park in the winter dusk, huddled into a down parka, her head bent against the wind that whipped off the bay. She had assumed she had the place to herself until she followed the path around a bend, through a grove of evergreens, and came upon the child. There was something so desolate about the way he sat in the swing, barely moving, his feet scuffing the worn, muddy spot in the gravel beneath him.

He had looked up, spotted her with those enormous brown eyes, and offered a halfhearted smile that melted her heart.

From that moment on, Manny Souza has been her sole friend in Windemere Cove. Just as she is his.

And she had fallen in love with the child long before she realized that his background was nearly identical to her own. That merely sealed the bond.

"What are you doing here?" he asks, obviously thrilled to see her.

He hugs her, knocking her large sunglasses askew.

She hurriedly rights them, then says brightly, "Visiting you. How have you been?"

"Good."

She nods but looks him over, taking in the frayed cutoff jeans, the ripped, stained white T-shirt, the dark circles under his big ebony eyes. He hasn't been sleeping. That's nothing new. But there are no new bruises; none that she can see. The mark on his right cheek where his grandfather bashed him with a fist has almost faded.

"How are your grandparents?" she asks him.

He shrugs, knowing what she means; that she's not merely inquiring after their health, though ever since his grandfather's heart attack, that has been a family issue. But Elizabeth wants to know how they, as his legal guardians, have been treating him this week.

"They're okay. . . ."

"Manny, is everything all right at home?" Elizabeth persists, reaching out to ruffle his thick straight black hair.

"Yeah . . . "

She knows him too well to believe that's all there is to it.

"What happened?" she asks him.

"Nothin'."

She waits.

"My mom stopped by yesterday," he says at last, kicking at the gravel with a worn sneaker. "She wanted money. My grandfather threw her out."

"Did you talk to her?"

"Nah. I was busy watching TV."

*Sure you were, Manny.*

She pictures him, huddled in front of the television set, trying to shut out the screaming voices of his mother, the crack addict, and her poverty-stricken parents, who have been saddled with the care and feeding of an asthmatic grandchild who might as well be an orphan.

Elizabeth has never met Manny's family, though there have been times when she has almost felt compelled to confront them.

But she has always held back, primarily for his sake, yet partly for her own.

After all, his grandparents are all Manny has, and they do love him—even Manny has admitted as much. His grandmother, who is nearly crippled from arthritis, still manages to make him his favorite devil's food cupcakes with fudge frosting every chance she gets, and his grandfather, whose heart is growing weaker every day, painstakingly built him a polished wooden sled from second-hand scrap lumber last winter, carving the boy's initials into the underside, along with the phrase "made with love by Gramps."

But the Souzas believe in old-fashioned discipline, which in

Elizabeth's opinion sometimes seems to qualify as borderline child abuse. She knows from experience.

Her own mother had beat her, yes. Not to discipline her, but out of teenage rage against the child she perceived as having tied her down, ruined her life.

But Vera, her grandmother, had been quick to spank her behind or smack her across the face. When Elizabeth talked back, Vera had often snatched up the nearest object—a lamp, a toaster, the vast leatherbound family Bible—and sent it sailing toward her impudent granddaughter. The physical discipline wasn't the same as what Becky had done to her. But to a child, the line between discipline and abuse might as well not exist.

Oh, yes, Elizabeth can relate to Manny.

Still, she's aware that the alternative to his grandparents' custody—a foster home—might be no better for him.

She knows this, too, from experience. There was a time, when she was around Manny's age, when her grandmother was hospitalized for over a month after a sudden, serious heart attack—a prelude to the massive one that came later, ending her life.

There was no one to look after Elizabeth in Vera's absence, and she had been temporarily placed with a foster family. It wasn't an experience she had ever wanted to repeat, or would wish on anyone else. The foster parents made no bones about the fact that they were in it for the subsidy money, and the place was overcrowded with problem kids who lied and stole, including a teenage boy whose leering glances gave her the creeps.

No, she doesn't believe Manny would be better off in a foster home.

Nor does she want to file a report against his grandparents and risk attracting the attention of the authorities. She won't do that unless she absolutely has to—if she feels the child is truly at risk.

So when Manny turns up with a fresh slap mark on his cheek or a halting walk due to an aching behind, she simply nurses him tenderly and listens as he pours out his heart.

More than once, he has asked, "Can't I come live with you, Elizabeth? Can't you be my mom?"

What can she say to that but a gentle, wistful *no*? She certainly can't admit to the child that she has often fantasized about taking him in, about raising him with the maternal love and affection he so sorely needs . . . things she, too, had once sorely needed.

But that's impossible—more so now than ever before.

Now that she is no longer sure of her obscurity.

"Did you call me last night, Manny?" she asks abruptly, switching gears.

"Did I call you? Unh-unh. How come?"

A chill steals over her, despite the hot August sun beating down from the cloudless sky.

"I just . . . I heard the phone ringing and I couldn't get to it in time," she says, trying not to give away her inner alarm.

Because if it hadn't been Manny, then it must have been . . .

"Well, it wasn't me," Manny says. "I was real busy last night. I had a special day camp meeting to go to."

"On a Saturday night?" she asks absently, her mind careening over a thousand and one terrifying scenarios.

She can't stay here and let him come after her like a hunter closing in on a pathetic animal snared helplessly in a trap. She has no choice but to get away. . . .

"It was about the Labor Day play," Manny is saying.

"Hmmm?"

"The meeting last night," he reminds her, and adds proudly, "I got the lead role."

That captures her attention. She knows how desperately Manny, a child who has never had any kind of attention or encouragement at home, longs to be in the spotlight.

She has been coaching him with his lines for the audition, and has noticed that he seems to have a flair for acting.

"You got the lead?" she squeals, and gives the little boy a hug, lifting him off his feet. "Oh, Manny, that's fantastic."

"No, it isn't," he says dejectedly when she sets him down. "I can't do it."

"Why not?"

"I would need two different costumes—a frog one and a prince one. Grammy says there's no money to buy them, and she doesn't know how to sew."

"Well, I do," Elizabeth says spontaneously.

"You do?"

"Sure."

Of course she sews.

Sort of.

Hadn't she taken home economics classes back at Custer Creek High? Hadn't she been graded a respectable C-plus on her junior project? It was a ruffled prairie blouse that had been a real pain because of all the gathers, but she had not only completed it, she had actually proudly worn it—until two of the buttons simultaneously popped off one day as she was lifting her arm to wave to the mailman.

"Then, Elizabeth, would you make me my—oh—" Manny interrupts his own excited question.

"What's wrong?"

"Grammy doesn't have any money to buy the stuff for the costume even if someone else makes it. She doesn't have any money at all."

"I'll buy the fabric, Manny. Don't worry. I'll take care of it for you."

Even as she says it, she knows it's a mistake. She's boxing herself into staying here, when only minutes ago she was planning her escape.

But his young face is already lit up. "You'll do that for me?"

She hesitates only briefly before saying, "Sure I will. I'll have to stitch it by hand because I don't have a sewing machine, so it'll take some time, but it's no problem."

"You sure? Because the show's in two weeks, and—"

"Manny, I'll have the costumes ready for you by then. I promise."

Vera taught her, so many years ago, never to break a promise. *"If you don't intend to do something, Cindy, then don't ever give your word to someone that you will."*

And so she had learned, very young, never to make promises. Because you never knew what life was going to toss your way.

Like with Brawley. "Don't ever leave me, Cindy," he used to say, usually late at night, in the dark, as they lay in the sagging full-sized bed in the apartment they shared. "Promise you won't ever leave."

She never promised him that. Never promised him anything. She knew better.

*So what's happened to you now?* a disdainful inner voice demands. *What makes you think you should start making promises now, to a little boy who's depending on you because he has no one else?*

Cindy O'Neal didn't make promises.

Nor did Mallory Eden.

But apparently, Elizabeth Baxter does.

Whether she keeps them remains to be seen.

\* \* \*

"What's the matter, Jason-boy?" Pamela Minelli reaches into the bouncy seat that sits in the middle of the kitchen table and picks up her whimpering son, hugging his little body close. Then she makes a face.

"Oh, Christ, did you go again? I just changed you," she says with a groan. "Why couldn't you wait until later, when Daddy gets home? Maybe I could have talked him into doing diaper duty for a change."

Jason coos, looking at her with his solemn, infant-blue eyes.

"Yeah, you're right," she mutters. "He probably would have come up with a good excuse to get out of it, as usual."

He looks so much like his daddy, Jason, with all that dark hair and the quick, dimpled grin.

Maybe that—and the fact that this one's a boy—will help Frank to take more of an interest in parenting this time around, Pamela thinks hopefully as she balances the baby in one arm and goes back to the sink to turn off the water she'd left running into the bowl of chip dip she'd just polished off.

Maybe the reason Frank has left so much up to Pamela in the past is that he simply doesn't know anything about girls.

How would he? After all, he'd been raised single-handedly by his father after his mother had died giving birth to him.

That happened to people, back in the fifties.

Of course, it happens now too, but hardly ever. You rarely hear of a woman going into the hospital to have a baby and not coming out.

Still, a few weeks before Pamela had Hannah, she had seen an episode of that television program, *E.R.*, where a woman had died having a baby because of something the doctor did or didn't do— she can't remember how it went now.

At the time, she hadn't wanted to watch it; she had read somewhere earlier that week that pregnant women shouldn't see that particular episode. But Frank loved the show; he had insisted on turning it on that night in bed, and she had been too tired to get up and go into the next room. So she had watched it. And it had been a nightmare.

That program—combined with the knowledge that her own mother-in-law hadn't made it through childbirth—had made her a basket case over the next couple of weeks before giving birth to

Hannah. She had been terrified that something would happen to her and the baby, or just to her, or just to the baby.

Frank had tried his best to calm her down, she supposed—by trying to shrug the whole thing off. He had told her that she was paranoid, that it was those crazy pregnancy hormones, that hundreds of women had babies every single day and there wasn't a thing to worry about.

He made it sound so easy.

A flicker of anger darts through her even now, almost three years later, as she remembers his laid-back attitude.

The nurses had commented, as she went through labor with him as her coach, at how remarkably unruffled he was. And Pamela, huffing and writhing and wailing as eight-pound Hannah ripped into the strained, tender flesh of her perineum, had wanted to scream, "Of course he's unruffled! I'm the one being tortured!"

In retrospect, she figures it's probably a good quality, being unflappable, when you're married to someone as high strung as she has always been.

Frank makes everything sound easy, shrugging off problems with a wave of his hand and a calm, "it'll be okay." He's casual about the kids, the house, their marriage . . .

Especially their marriage.

Especially lately.

Her obstetrician gave her the green light to resume their sex life weeks ago, and the new birth control pills—prescribed at Frank's insistence—had become effective immediately after she started them.

Still, Frank has shown absolutely no interest in sleeping with her.

*It's a wonder we managed to have you,* Pamela tells Jason silently, planting a kiss on his still-tender head, feeling a tuft of downy baby hair tickle her lip.

It's been nearly a year since they made love.

And it hadn't been easy convincing Frank to make love to her back then—let alone, to have a second child. He had been adamant that he wanted only one.

"Let's quit while we're ahead" was how he put it every time she brought up the subject. He would remind her of how freaked out she had been before, during, and after giving birth to Hannah, and how he didn't ever want to put her through that again.

"You said yourself that one was enough, Pam," he would tell her over and over again.

It was true. She *had* said that . . . in the delivery room while she was in agony, pushing, and again when the doctor was stitching her episiotomy, and even days later, when she was home, attempting to go to the bathroom again, like a normal person, without crying from the acute, irrational fear that her insides were somehow going to drop out into the toilet bowl.

But the more time that passed after Hannah's birth, the more she longed for another child.

Motherhood is the greatest fulfillment she has ever known. It is intensely pleasurable to be the center of someone's world, to see how your child lights up when you come into a room, to hold that warm little body close in your arms and know utter contentment.

Unfortunately, Frank doesn't seem to see it quite that way. Pamela knows he loves his kids. He just doesn't have much time to spend with them, after putting in so many hours at work, especially now that he's a detective. And anyway, maybe men in general just aren't great with diapers and spit-up and sleepless nights.

Jason was an accident, at least as far as Frank was concerned. He had been too out of it that night to realize she hadn't put her diaphragm in when they'd come home from the policeman's ball, where she had fed him martinis and made suggestive comments in his ear as she rubbed up against him on the dance floor.

She had known from a slightly crampy feeling in her lower belly that she was ovulating that night, had realized it was the perfect chance to conceive another child, since they rarely got a romantic night out alone together.

They had left Hannah with the teenage girl down the street, who has since gone off to college, and they had gotten dressed up and gone out to the ball. It was almost like old times, that night— like when they were dating.

Back then he had never been able to get enough of her. Frank had always had a strong sex drive. Their encounters would leave her feeling sore and achy, but certain that her man was crazy about her.

When was the last time he even touched her, Pamela wonders now. Maybe, if she hadn't been pregnant for the past year . . .

But . . .

"I wanted you so badly," she whispers into Jason's small, perfect ear as she carries him through the dining room and down the toy-cluttered hallway. "I'm so glad you're here."

He gurgles happily.

"Shhh," she whispers as they pass Hannah's closed door. "Don't want to wake up your sister. Lord knows she needs her nap these days, now that she's hit the terrible twos. Here we go."

She uses her shoulder to shove open the door to the nursery, which used to be two closets before they knocked the dividing wall down and added a window last spring. Now the house is without a coat closet and linen closet, but so far they've managed.

Of course, it's summertime. Pamela doesn't know where they're going to keep their jackets and hats and boots once the weather changes—which, in New England, could be any day now that August is winding down.

She has painted the tiny room white and pasted up a wallpaper border: yellow ducks splashing cheerfully through bright blue puddles. She sewed the yellow and blue madras changing table pad and cradle comforter herself, and painted the white knobs of a wicker yard-sale dresser to match.

The room is bright and lively, if a little cramped. It's big enough for a crib—almost time to pull Hannah's out of the basement—but not for a bed.

"Don't worry, Jason-boy," she tells him. "By the time you're ready for that, maybe we'll be moving into a bigger house. Maybe your daddy will get a nice raise now that he's a detective."

She lays the baby down on his table and begins to unfasten the snaps that run up the legs of his stretchie. Her fingers work automatically, and she hums absently as she works, her mind on what to make for dinner. Frank will be home late—she hates when he works on Sundays, but that's the way it is when you're married to a cop. Weekends, holidays, midnights—she's used to being alone with the kids.

She hears a sound and looks up, out the window. It faces the yard and the house next door.

She sees Elizabeth Baxter quickly getting out of her car. The woman, who appears to be in a hurry to get inside, as usual, is wearing large sunglasses, along with a pair of worn jeans and a cropped pink top. Her long hair is braided and hangs down her back.

Envy darts through Pamela as she watches her neighbor stride quickly from her car to her door.

Suddenly, she's conscious of the fact that her hair needs to be washed, and of the yellowed breast milk stain on her own white T-shirt, and the uncomfortably snug fit of her maternity jeans.

She hasn't been able to get back into her regular jeans yet. . . .

Oh, hell. Who is she kidding? She never got back into them after she had Hannah. She had lost only fifteen of the forty pounds she had gained with her first pregnancy. And with Jason, she gained another thirty-five.

He had weighed nearly nine pounds at birth.

When she came home from the hospital, she had lost seven.

"Relax . . . it's fluid" was what the nurse had said when Pamela called in a panic. "It'll come off gradually. Don't be so hard on yourself. You just had a baby."

But now, two months later, she has lost only two additional pounds.

No wonder her husband isn't interested in sleeping with her. No wonder he'd rather spend nights on the couch, pretending he's all caught up in watching boxing matches and baseball games on ESPN. But Frank has never been much of a sports fan; she knows he's just avoiding her.

Again she looks at Elizabeth, who is unlocking her door, looking so damned good from behind in those tight, faded jeans.

"God, how I hate you," Pamela says aloud, watching her neighbor intently.

Then she sighs and looks away, unfastening the tapes on Jason's smelly diaper.

Elizabeth eats her solitary dinner in front of the television set.

A grilled cheese sandwich and Campbell's tomato soup.

Gran often used to make this supper on rainy days. The two of them would sit together at the old round wooden table in the cozy kitchen with the rain pouring down outside. The television would be on in the living room, of course, even though no one was watching it—Gran hated a silent house.

That was why she was always singing and talking to herself, Elizabeth supposed, although Brawley later told her that a lot of people in town thought her grandmother was a little nuts.

That hurt, even though Gran was dead by then; even though Elizabeth herself realized, in retrospect, that her grandmother had certainly had her eccentricities.

But back in that comfy, rambling Nebraska farmhouse, Gran

was all she'd had, and Elizabeth had loved her fiercely despite her old-fashioned method of discipline.

*Spare the rod and spoil the child.*

How many times had Gran said that?

And yet . . .

How many times had she pulled her granddaughter onto her ample lap, stroked her hair, and said, "I love you, little girl. Don't you ever forget it."

She spoons some of the creamy red soup from her bowl to her mouth and swallows it, hard, as a sudden wave of longing comes over her.

*Oh, Gran, I miss you,* she thinks, staring unseeingly at Mike Wallace, who is grimly discussing a political scandal on *60 Minutes.*

What she wouldn't give to have her grandmother there with her now. The memory of Vera O'Neal's loving companionship fills her with an unbearable ache.

Lonely . . . she is so damned lonely.

Not just for Gran, for *anyone.*

How much longer can she go on like this, living every day in solitary confinement, afraid to smile at a stranger or greet a neighbor?

*How much longer? Forever. You have no choice, especially now,* she reminds herself, remembering again the chilling card she'd received in the mail.

And the phone call she hadn't dared to answer.

*But that could have been a wrong number, or a telemarketer. . . .*

She shouldn't, *couldn't,* jump to conclusions.

Because if she does, she will become so frightened that she won't be able to stay in Windemere Cove another day. She'll have to flee, once again, taking nothing but the bundle of money in her safe deposit box down at the local bank.

Hundreds of thousands of dollars in cash she'd hidden from the tax man back when she was a big Hollywood star, on the advice of her business manager.

"You'll never get caught. Everyone does it," he had told her, puffing glibly on a fat, illegal Cuban cigar.

And Mallory Eden had been around that town long enough to believe him. That didn't mean she had to do it too, but she had, recklessly, giddy with her incredible financial success.

Again Gran's voice comes echoing back to her over the years. . . .

*"I don't care what everyone else is doing. If everyone decided to jump off a bridge, would you do it too, Cindy?"*

The irony in that oft-repeated grandmotherly pearl strikes her now, and she has to smile.

*No, Gran,* she thinks, *I wouldn't jump off a bridge.*

*And I didn't jump off a bridge.*

*The world just thinks I did.*

Well . . .

Not the *whole* world.

Apparently, there are people who believe that Mallory Eden, like Elvis, is alive and well.

One person in particular.

And he has found her again . . .

Or has he?

What else could that eerie greeting card mean?

*I know who you are.*

*Don't start thinking about it,* she commands herself once more. *If you think about it, you'll want to get out as fast as you can. . . .*

*And Manny needs you here, to make his costume.*

But the card . . .

And the phone call . . .

*Think about something else. . . .*

*Anything else.*

*Think about eating your soup and sandwich, and about Gran. . . .*

She picks up her spoon again and forces herself to eat, to remember how she and Gran would chat about movie stars and TV shows as they ate their supper—at least, in the early days.

Gran always knew who all of the big stars were, and she gossiped about them like they were neighbors right there down Orchard Lane.

"Did you hear about Farrah and Lee? She left him for another man," Gran would report, shaking her gray head.

Or, "I don't know why that nice Rock Hudson doesn't get married again. He's such a good catch, don't you think?"

Later, when things had grown strained between them and Gran went around with perpetually pursed lips over Cindy's wild ways, the channel six newsanchor in the next room would be the only one talking at suppertime.

And, typically, Gran would be the only one eating, especially when the meal consisted of grilled cheese and tomato soup.

"Do you know how fattening that is?" the teenage Cindy would ask, poking at the buttery golden sandwich oozing gooey cheese on her plate.

"Well, you could use a little meat on your bones," Gran would invariably retort.

She had always thought Cindy was too thin, God bless her.

But Cindy had known, even then, that you couldn't be too thin if you planned to be an actress.

And Lord, how she had wanted to be an actress.

She had dreamed of it ever since her first ballet recital, when she was five and gawky and dressed, like the other little ballerinas, in a pink leotard and white apron, clutching a wooden spoon as a prop for the big finale, 'If I Knew You Were Comin' I'd'a Baked a Cake."

The audience had applauded like crazy, and, of course, there was Gran in the front row, jumping up and down and yelling her name.

Afterward, Gran had taken her, still in her costume with rouge on her cheeks, to Friendly's for an ice cream sundae. The waitress and all the other customers there had noticed her, making a big fuss over her. She had lapped up all that attention and praise right along with the sumptuous chocolate-peanut-butter ice cream, feeling special for the first time in her short life.

"If only your mama could have seen you tonight," Gran had whispered as she tucked Cindy into bed after they got home.

Those words would haunt Cindy long afterward, as she had often wondered what her grandmother had meant by that.

*If only your mama could have seen you ... what?*

*She would be so proud?*

*She would wish she had never taken off without a backward glance?*

*She would change her mind and come back to raise you, the way a mama should?*

Elizabeth will never know what Gran had meant by that cryptic statement, and it doesn't matter anymore anyway.

Last she knew, her mama was an alcoholic junkie living on the streets in Chicago.

She sighs and picks up her grilled cheese sandwich. The toasted bread has grown cold and leaves a grease mark on the paper plate, but is still, somehow, appetizing. She made it with a smear of full-fat Hellman's mayonnaise, and she buttered each slice of bread on both sides, just the way Gran used to.

She takes a big bite and thinks of all the grilled cheese sandwiches she could have eaten with Gran back in Nebraska but didn't because she was watching her weight.

And of the times, when she was living on the ubiquitous Beverly Hills diet of salad greens and sushi, when she would have killed for a crusty, gooey sandwich to dunk into a big bowl of tangy, rich tomato soup.

But Mallory Eden was a goddess, and everyone knows goddesses come in a size three.

It's been a relief, these past five years, to let her body fill out to its natural shape. . . .

To stop counting fat grams and not stress about finding time for the gym . . .

Funny—now she has all the time in the world to work out if she wants to. But she never, ever *wanted* to do it. It was simply an occupational hazard, just like having her teeth capped and constantly visiting tanning salons against her better judgment.

How she used to hate all those hours spent sculpting her body on the treadmill and Stairmaster and stationery bike as her personal trainer, Jack, hollered commands and advice and encouragement. He was almost more famous than she was, and has recently been making the talk show rounds, having just come out with his own line of exercise clothes, workout equipment, and fat-free frozen desserts.

*Good for him.*

Elizabeth dunks the last bite of her sandwich into her bowl of soup and pops it into her mouth.

Delicious.

What a pleasure it has been to rediscover sinful treats—barbecue potato chips and cream-filled chocolate cupcakes and lasagna.

She had always assumed that if she stopped her stringent dieting and ate whatever she wanted to, she would blow up to two hundred pounds, the way Gran had.

Luckily, that hasn't happened. She isn't bone thin, but she's not overweight either—unless you're talking Hollywood standards.

She's a perfect size nine.

A perfect size nine with brown hair—her natural color, which she had started bleaching in junior high—and brown eyes—sans the blue contacts she had constantly worn as Mallory Eden. She never needed the contacts for vision purposes, just as she doesn't need the nonprescription glasses she wears in public these days, whenever she can't hide behind a pair of sunglasses

She's hardly movie goddess material now, she thinks ruefully. Elizabeth Baxter bears very little resemblance to the woman whose face had graced dozens of magazine covers all over the world.

Still, *he* has managed to find her.

How?

Though she had never stopped looking over her shoulder, she hadn't ever really expected him to track her down after she left Montana without a trace on that stormy summer night five years ago.

Her plan had been simple, but foolproof.

Step one had been slipping past the reporters camped outside her gate to get to the Beverly Hills bank where she had stashed enough hundred-dollar bills in her safe deposit box to last her a lifetime—if she was frugal.

How thankful she had been, then, that she had gone against her own conscience and cheated the government out of all that tax money. All that cash was ultimately her salvation.

She had left her home by the back gate in the middle of a steamy August night, letting the black Lexus roll down the short, hilly drive in neutral, not wanting to risk starting the engine until she was safely down the street.

Before getting into the car, she had sheared off her long blond hair with a pair of kitchen scissors, then dyed it a mousy brown with one of those cheap over-the-counter box kits. Her Beverly Hills stylist, Arnaud, would have gone ballistic had he seen the result. For some reason, that knowledge had filled her with a prickle of grim satisfaction as she looked in the mirror.

She carefully swept the hair into a plastic bag, along with the hair dye box, and brought it with her when she left. She didn't want the household staff, or Rae, who was staying with her, to suspect that she had changed her appearance.

She even left a note for Rae, saying she had to get away for a few days and was going up to Big Sur. They had often done that together, the two of them, staying at a windswept resort high in the mountains, overlooking the ocean.

And she had gone there alone too, so it wouldn't have been that unusual. There had been times when she needed to escape the chaos of her life in L.A., to be alone with her thoughts and the soothing rhythm of the waves.

She had, of course, felt terrible about lying to Rae, her closest friend. But she had made up her mind to tell no one of her plan, not just for her own protection, but for the protection of her friends. The last thing she wanted was for the stalker to turn his attention to Rae, suspecting that she knew something.

She had seen her friend's tear-ravaged face on television in the days after Mallory Eden's suicide. The world could see that her grief was real—and that was what Elizabeth had been counting on. Rae was a decent actress—no matter what the critics said— but she certainly couldn't be counted on to play the part of the grieving friend for the rest of her life.

What if she slipped to someone, someday?

Or what if she insisted on keeping in touch?

Or coming along?

That was a distinct possibility, knowing Rae, whose loyal friendship had sustained Mallory through the breakup with Brawley, the pressures of superstardom, and the terrors of stalking. She had always insisted on taking care of Mallory, on being at her side even when Mallory insisted she would be better off alone.

"Being alone isn't healthy," Rae would say in her blunt upbeat manner. "I'm coming over."

Mallory had fought the impulse to look in on her friend, sleeping in the guest room, that August night before she left. She was afraid that if she saw Rae one last time, she would be tempted to wake her.

No, there had been no question about telling her the truth.

The only way Mallory could save her own life was to cut every tie to the past.

And she had done it.

She had driven from L.A. to Helena, with her shorn brown hair and her newly brown-again eyes, wearing no makeup, an old T-shirt and jeans, and a pair of clear, horn-rimmed glasses that had been a prop for a long-ago movie role.

No one had recognized her in the few stops she had made to get gas and food, and twice to sleep in cheap motel rooms when she grew so bleary-eyed she could go no farther. She had reveled in the sudden anonymity—the ability to come and go like a normal person, without strangers' eyes trailing every move she made.

Still, she had been edgy the whole trip, keeping a constant eye on the rearview mirror, expecting to see a car tailing her.

Just outside Boise, as her plan took solid shape, she bought a bicycle and camping gear as well as protective clothing.

By the time she had crossed into Montana, she knew exactly what she would do.

She'd had the Rock River Falls Bridge in mind all along, remembering it from a vacation she and Brawley had taken years before, when she was poised on the threshold of fame—and going it solo. He must have sensed that their relationship was in serious trouble when he suggested that they go away for a week, just the two of them, to his friend's cabin in that remote corner of northwestern Montana.

Rather than bringing them closer together, the trip had only made it clear to Mallory that what she and Brawley had once had was over. It had long been over, in fact, but she had been afraid to officially end it for a number of reasons.

She felt sorry for him in a way.

And she was partly afraid of how he would react when she broke it off.

And then there was her deep, dark secret . . . the one that only he knew.

She had spent a lot of time alone during that week in the wilderness, gathering her thoughts and her courage as she hiked the rough terrain while Brawley moodily fished and whittled back at the cabin. She had come upon the bridge one misty, gray afternoon, finding the scenic gorge deserted except for a lone fisherman who was about to make his way down to the water.

It was he who had told her about the three Canadians who had drowned in the river the summer before, two of their bodies swept miles downstream and battered beyond recognition against the jagged rocks and boulders, the third swallowed forever by the foaming white water.

At the time she had shuddered at the very idea, thinking that it was a shame that the third man's family would have no one to bury.

In the years that followed, Mallory had done her best to try to and forget that difficult week in Montana, when she had struggled to end that spent relationship as Brawley tried desperately to salvage it.

It wasn't until years later, when she realized she had to fake her death in order to save her life, that the bridge came back to haunt her.

It had looked the same as she remembered it, as daunting and remote in reality as it had seemed in her memory.

There had been a moment, that rainy August night, as she stood at that rickety railing high above the rushing river, when she had actually considered jumping for real, ending it all right there.

But only for a harsh, fleeting moment or two.

Then she realized that her life was worth living, even if she had to permanently abandon everyone she cared about, and the career she had worked so damned hard to build.

It still hurts, she thinks as she stares vacantly at the television, where Andy Rooney is commenting on some inane topic. She desperately misses acting, if not the media circus that surrounds a successful performer's career. She always relished stepping into character, savoring the challenge of transforming herself into somebody else, somebody whose mannerisms and speech and body language were utterly different from her own.

*Well, the challenge is still on,* she tells herself with an inner sigh. *You get to be somebody else for the rest of your life.*

And hopefully, it will be a long performance.

It's steamy out here tonight, especially for New England in late August.

Yet despite the unusually sultry night, her house is sealed as tightly as leftover fish under Saran Wrap. Every window on the small Cape Cod house is tightly closed.

And she definitely doesn't have central air-conditioning.

*She* being Elizabeth Baxter . . .

Who's so sure that nobody knows her true identity.

Well, she's wrong.

It's time to circle the house again, cautiously, sticking to the shadows amid the foundation shrubbery. Maybe this time something will have changed. . . .

But no.

The blinds are drawn in every window, leaving not even the slightest crack that someone might peer through.

She's a clever, cautious woman, this so-called Elizabeth Baxter. She's not taking any chances, is she?

Doesn't want anyone to figure out who she really is.

A car door slams in the distance, somewhere down Green Garden Way, and an engine starts.

There's little chance that it's going to head in this direction, toward the end of the cul-de-sac.

Still, it's not a bad idea to crouch low behind a rhododendron bush until the sound of the car has faded in the opposite direction—and for a while after that, just for good measure.

Finally, it's safe to stand again and look up at the darkened window above.

What is she doing in there, beyond the closed blinds and locked doors?

Imagining the possibilities is almost as interesting as actually spying on her would be.

*Almost.*

There's no need to stay out here sweating in the mosquito-infested, overgrown grass on the off chance that she'll slip up on her security measures. It's getting late.

She might even be asleep already, her dark hair tousled on the pillow, her breathing deep and even.

Wouldn't it be something to see her that way? To tiptoe up to the bed, to reach out and touch that famous flesh, to . . .

*No.*

*Not tonight.*

*But soon . . .*

# chapter

## 4

"Wow, traffic jam," Elizabeth murmurs, braking for the light at a North Main Street intersection. Several cars are in front of her, which is unusual.

The small town is certainly teeming with activity for high noon on a Monday. Most restaurants aren't even open on Mondays in Rhode Island. Maybe the bustle is due to tourists spilling over from the Newport Jazz Festival this past weekend—although Windemere Cove isn't usually a tourist destination. It's generally a quiet, sleepy place where people keep to themselves in typical Yankee fashion.

Which, of course, is precisely why Elizabeth chose to live there.

That, and its proximity to the Atlantic Ocean.

She had so loved living by the beach in California.

The coast is rockier; the water far colder here. But there's still that salty-fresh smell in the air, the distant sound of waves crashing, and the cry of gulls overhead. And sometimes, if she closes her eyes on a warm summer day as she sits by the bay, it's almost like being back in Malibu.

*But you'll never see Malibu or the Pacific again,* she reminds herself. She'll never be able to go back to the West Coast . . . or to travel anywhere beyond this relatively isolated strip of eastern Rhode Island. She hasn't dared to venture beyond the ten-mile radius surrounding Windemere Cove since she arrived in the East Bay nearly five years before.

She adjusts her dark glasses so that they sit higher on her nose and glances at the people strolling past the old sea captains' mansions, most now converted to stores, that line the tree-shaded street.

What is up with this crowd?

Then she sees a white banner stretched across the street ahead, and realizes why there's so much action here today.

FIRST ANNUAL BACK-TO-SCHOOL SIDEWALK SALE DAYS,
AUGUST 24–29

No wonder.

The sooner she gets home, the better.

She eyes the crowds of strangers with trepidation.

Not that a stalker seems likely to be hunting for back-to-school bargains.

The thought nearly makes her smile before she catches herself and remembers that there's nothing funny about a stalker. Nothing funny at all about the premise of her would-be killer lurking somewhere in this innocuous small-town street scene.

The light changes and the cars in front of her move forward. Elizabeth makes a right onto Center Street, breathing an audible sigh of relief as she leaves the business district behind.

She notices whitecaps out on the water today. How she longs to roll down her car window and let that brisk ocean breeze whip through her hair, the way she used to back in California.

But that would be far too dangerous.

It would leave her vulnerable to anyone who wanted to reach inside the open window and grab her.

Even before the card and the phone call, she had never gone anywhere with the windows rolled down or the car doors unlocked. She isn't about to start now, not after what's happened.

She chews her lower lip as she continues along Center Street, not willing to let the fear suck her in again.

She had been doing so well all morning, at the fabric store on Route 136 in neighboring Warren. It had been fun, picking out the fabric for Manny's costumes, along with purple sequins to jazz up the prince outfit and black felt to make into spots for the frog suit.

She had taken a course in costume design back when she'd first arrived in L.A., young and eager to learn the business from the ground up. Of course, Brawley had been irritated about that, and she hadn't enrolled in any other classes after the costume one was over. It was too expensive, he said, and it cut into their time together. Then he talked her into earning some cash to help pay her share of the rent. . . .

*God, why did I ever listen to that jerk?* she wonders now, then shakes her head.

Brawley Johnson is long ago and far away, literally part of

another lifetime—the one *before* Mallory Eden, even. It's amazing that she can still look back on their time together and feel so angry, so frustrated, at the way he had treated her—and the way she had put up with him for so long.

But he had been her first love—her only love, really. There had been no one after him; at least, no one serious. She was too caught up in her career by then, and besides, where did a wealthy, famous woman meet a nice, normal man?

Lord knew, she needed *nice* and *normal* after Brawley, with his jealous rages and accusations and smothering attention.

But he was all she had after Gran died. They were two kids alone together in a strange place, and she had clung to him in the beginning as fervently as he had clung to her in the end.

Brawley Johnson.

God.

What got her started thinking about him anyway?

She makes a right-hand turn onto Green Garden Way and frowns, filled with a growing sense of uneasiness as she follows the curving street around toward her house.

*Something's wrong.*

The knowledge takes hold despite the reasonable voice in her head that says there's nothing to worry about.

It's broad daylight, a beautiful, sunny summer afternoon.

She passes a neighbor hanging clothes on the line in her side yard, and another putting his garbage cans by the curb. Children are romping on a front lawn, and an elderly woman is walking her black Labrador retriever in the street.

Still . . .

*Something's wrong.*

She pulls into her driveway, knowing that she should be reassured by the sight of her house looking exactly the way she left it two hours earlier.

She really should mow and water the lawn, she thinks vaguely, noticing that it's looking straggly and brown. She'll do it later . . . if she can convince herself to leave the safety of the house again.

She can't shake the feeling of apprehension as she parks the car in her usual spot, grabs her shopping bag with a shaking hand, and opens the door to step out.

She glances toward the Minellis' house, almost hoping to see Pamela bounding toward her across the grass.

But it appears deserted, though the windows are open, as always, and the back door is probably unlocked, as Pamela has told her it often is.

"Frank's always bugging me about leaving it open, but Windemere Cove couldn't be any safer. And I just don't like to bother bringing keys with me when I go out. I have enough stuff to lug around with the two kids," Pamela has said to Elizabeth.

Pamela would be at the sidewalk sale if anyone would be. She loves to shop.

And Frank must be at work.

Normally, she's thrilled when she can come and go without risking a run-in with her neighbors.

*And you are today,* she tells herself firmly. *The last thing you need is for Pamela to come buzzing around, chattering about this, that, and the other. For all you know, she'll mention one of those newspaper articles or television segments about Mallory Eden and then what will you do?*

Well, okay, *that* isn't very likely. Her neighbor's conversation always revolves around herself, her kids, and her husband.

Pamela has never shown the slightest interest in current events or the entertainment industry. For all Elizabeth knows, she doesn't even know who Brad Pitt or Sharon Stone are, and she's most likely never even heard of Mallory Eden.

Her sandals make a hollow clicking noise on the blacktop as she moves from the car to the door, her key ready in one hand, her purse and the shopping bag tucked under her opposite arm. She unlocks the first dead bolt, then sticks a second key into a second dead bolt with expert efficiency. Finally, she puts the last key into the knob, turns it, and pushes the door open.

She's taken several steps into the kitchen before she realizes that she was right.

Something is very, very wrong.

Elizabeth lets out a high, shrill, involuntary scream.

Manny's worn sneakers practically skip along the cracked sidewalk of Pine Street as he hurries home from day camp.

He can't wait to call Elizabeth and tell her about his first day of rehearsal for the Labor Day play. It went great, and afterward, two of the teenage drama counselors told him he was doing a fantastic job. He promised them he'd know all his lines by the weekend and have his costume ready in time for dress rehearsals next week.

He still can't believe he will get to be the star of the show after all—and it's all because of Elizabeth.

He wishes he could do something nice for her, to show her how grateful he is . . . not just because she's making his costumes, but because she really cares about him.

Maybe he should pick her some flowers in the vacant lot behind the house. There used to be a factory there, but it burned down a few years ago. Manny was glad when that happened. The factory was a big ugly yellow brick building with broken windows, and it blocked the view of the water from Manny's bedroom.

Now he can see, in the distance beyond the rooftops of Center Street, Narragansett Bay. And in the vacant lot, growing among the scattered bricks and shards of glass from the factory, are the most beautiful wildflowers. They continue to grow even though the ground is getting dry and dusty because it hasn't rained in weeks.

Elizabeth would probably like a nice bouquet, Manny decides. She always smells like flowers, so she must like them.

He never knows when he's going to see her, but he'll pick some flowers just in case she shows up at the park later today.

He wishes he knew where she lives, but she has never told him, and he hasn't dared to ask. There are a lot of things she doesn't seem to want to talk about, and Manny knows enough not to be nosy about her life.

Sometimes he wonders if she's some kind of magical fairy god- mother who appears only to him, like the one in the Labor Day play. He wonders about it even though he knows it's not true, because after all, he doesn't believe in magic.

If magic were a real thing, he would be able to make a wish, snap his fingers, and, poof! Elizabeth would be his mom. She would find him a nice daddy, and they would take him away somewhere, to some beautiful tropical island, where they would kiss him all the time and tell him how much they love him, and give him lots of brothers and sisters—but only after he's had them, his parents, all to himself for a while.

Manny sighs.

Too bad he doesn't believe in magic.

He's almost in front of his house, but instead of continuing on along the sidewalk, he turns and scoots down a dark alley lined with garbage cans and rusty car parts. He pops out at the edge of the vacant lot and scrambles over a crumbling stone wall, dropping to the dusty, weed-choked ground on the other side.

A huge rat scurries out of his path as he heads for the prettiest patch of wildflowers.

Manny doesn't mind rats as long as they're not in the house, and they haven't been, except for once, before the exterminator came, a few summers ago. But they're common in the rubble from the factory, and along the rocky waterfront beyond Center Street, where he and his friends used to play pirate.

Manny picks some purple flowers with yellow centers, then some feathery white things on long stems. He's making his way toward a low-growing patch of deep pink blossoms, when he hears a noise behind him.

He turns and sees *her*.

His mother.

"Hi, Manny," she says, coming a little closer, then stopping a few feet away.

She's wearing a grimy-looking tank top, rubber sandals, and cutoff black shorts. Her bony white arms and legs are covered with red marks. Her face is all discolored and sunken, especially beneath her eyes, and her dark hair hangs in limp clumps around her shoulders.

He says nothing, just stares at her.

"What are you doing?" she asks, taking another step toward him. She smiles, revealing a mouthful of crooked teeth.

"Picking flowers," he mumbles.

"For who? Grammy?"

He shakes his head.

His mother walks closer, her face less friendly. Her dark pupils are oddly big and round.

"Who are they for?"

He shrugs.

"They're for that lady, right? Elizabeth?"

"How did you know her name?"

"I heard you talking to her at the playground."

"You were spying on me?"

"You're my son, Manny. It's not spying. I'm keeping an eye on you. Somebody has to."

He takes a step backward, still clutching the flowers.

"You know, Manny, I'm still your mother. I feel real bad that I haven't been around much for you . . ."

*You've never been around for me.*

". . . and I'm working real hard to get myself together so that I can come and get you."

*Come and get you.*

The words sound ominous, and he forces back a shudder.

"Pretty soon you and me are going to be together, Manny. Won't that be nice? I'll get us a place to live, someplace nice. Would you like that?"

"No," he says, taking another step backward. "I don't want to live with you."

Her eyes narrow.

"What are you talking about? I'm your mother. You're my son. You belong with me."

"No." He shakes his head stubbornly and kicks his toe against the dusty ground.

"Who are those flowers for?"

Something keeps him from telling her the truth. He bites down hard on his upper lip with his lower teeth to keep from blurting it out.

"They're for Elizabeth, aren't they." It isn't a question.

"No."

"Yes, they are. You're giving her flowers. You never gave me flowers, Manny. And I'm your mother."

*Oh, yeah? Well, I'm your son. You never gave me anything.*

He just looks at her, unwilling to let his angry thoughts escape aloud.

She stands there, watching him, for a long time.

Then she says, "I'm coming to get you, Manny. As soon as I can."

"Grammy and Gramps won't let you take me away."

"So? You're my son. I can take you if I want to."

"They won't let you," he repeats.

*And neither will Elizabeth.*

"Who says I'm going to ask them for their permission?"

"You have to. You can't just take me. Grammy and Gramps are my guardians."

"They won't be for long. Your grandfather's pretty sick, Manny. He can't work anymore, and neither can your grandmother, with her hands all mangled from that arthritis. They're going to lose their house. And you're not going to have a place to live, except with me."

"I don't want to live with you."

"Too bad."

He glares at her.

She glares back.

With a sudden, impulsive movement, he reaches out and flings the wildflower bouquet squarely in her face, so that the stems hit her and then scatter on the ground.

"There!" he yells, hating her. "There! I gave you flowers. Are you happy now?"

And he turns and runs toward home as fast as he can.

"Do you have any idea who would have done this?"

Elizabeth shakes her head mutely, sitting on the couch with her head buried in her hands. She can't bear to look at the living room, with the open drawers and toppled lamps and cushions tossed haphazardly on the floor.

It's no better than the rest of the house. Every inch of it has been disturbed by the intruder, who got in by breaking a basement window, then kicking in the door leading up into the house, which she has always kept locked.

Frank Minelli's footsteps come closer, and she feels him sitting beside her.

"Don't worry, Elizabeth," he says, his voice calm. "You already said nothing has been stolen. You're lucky. Some people come home to a break-in and every valuable thing they own has vanished."

She nods, unable to stop the trembling that has seized her whole body.

"There's been a rash of break-ins like this in Windemere Cove lately," Frank goes on. "It's probably kids."

She lifts her head, looks at him. "You mean people's houses are being ransacked without anything being stolen?"

"Well, most of the time, something is missing," he admits. "Jewelry, or spare cash . . . you're sure everything is here?"

She nods. She has no jewelry. She left all her diamonds and rubies and emeralds behind in Malibu.

And her cash . . . it's in the safe deposit box at the bank.

There's nothing of value in the house.

And, fortunately, nothing that reveals her true identity. So if it really was just a random break-in, she's safe.

But it wasn't.

She knows it wasn't.

It was her stalker, making himself known. He's come back to torment her before he kills her.

Her teeth are chattering and she clenches them together so Frank won't hear.

He's still talking. "It's a good thing I was home and heard you scream, Elizabeth. Otherwise, you'd be here all upset and alone until a patrol car could get here. Are you sure you don't want me to call them and have someone come over and file a report?"

"I'm positive," she says emphatically. "Nothing is missing, so—"

"You really should file—"

"I said no. I appreciate that you came running over, but I didn't call you here officially. You're my neighbor, Frank, and you're not on duty. You happen to be a cop, but that doesn't mean you—"

"I know, I know. Look, Elizabeth, this is your business. I just want to make sure you feel safe. A woman living all alone . . ."

"I'm fine. I feel safe."

Does she sound unconvincing?

She must.

He's looking dubiously at her, rubbing his lip beneath his mustache between his thumb and forefinger, as though he's trying to think of something he can say that will help to make her feel better.

"If you want me to stay here tonight, I'd be glad to" is what he comes up with.

She blurts out, "No!"

Looking only slightly taken aback, he goes on. "I meant so you wouldn't have to be alone here tonight, after what happened. After all, I am a cop. I have a gun. And I'm sure Pamela wouldn't mind. . . ."

"No," she says again less vehemently, "it's okay. I don't need you to do that. I'll be fine."

"Elizabeth—"

"Frank?"

It's Pamela's voice, coming faintly from outside, in the direction of the Minellis' yard.

"She's back," he says.

"She's looking for you," Elizabeth tells him. "Go ahead."

He stands. "Are you—"

"I'm fine." She can't help being irritated with his persistence, though she knows he's only trying to help.

Can't he understand she just needs to be left alone, as soon as possible?

"Frank? Where are you?" Pamela's voice is growing louder.

"Okay," he says, heading for the door. "As long as you're okay, I'll go. But if you need anything, or if you notice anything unusual, I'm right next door. And I'm off tonight, so I'll be around. If you want me to fix that basement window, I—"

"It's okay. I'll take care of it." Then, realizing she's bordering on rude, she forces herself to add politely, "But thank you. I appreciate it."

Finally, he's gone.

She's alone.

She gets up and locks the door behind him, then begins to move through the rooms, surveying the damage.

Mostly, things are just moved around on tables and countertops, with drawers and doors and cupboards left open as though someone went through everything, looking for something.

Her bedding is tossed on the floor in the bedroom, and the contents of the bathroom hamper have been dumped into the tub. She checks all the windows to ensure that the intruder didn't unlock one for easy entry later, after dark.

They're fine.

And the plain white envelope in the drawer of her desk in the spare bedroom—the envelope containing the expired Illinois license for Elizabeth Baxter—is still there.

Still sealed.

*Thank God.*

The only thing is . . .

Is it her imagination, or does the flap seem slightly damp, as though it were recently sealed?

Is this the same envelope she sealed herself so long ago?

Or did someone rip that one open, steal the license, and replace the envelope with a new one from the supply in the bottom drawer?

Is someone out there somewhere, looking into the real Elizabeth Baxter?

Is someone going to connect her to . . .

*You're just paranoid,* she tells herself, inhaling deeply, then exhaling, trying to calm down. *The flap feels damp because it's August, and it's humid. Everything in the house feels damp.*

She runs her fingers over the rectangular bump inside the envelope. *Anyway, here's the license, right here.*

But she rips the envelope open just to be sure it isn't just a dupe, a square of plain old cardboard the thief left in a dummy envelope to fool her. . . .

No, the license is there.

Elizabeth Baxter's face stares back at her.

She hasn't seen it in a while, that face. It's eerie how much it looks like her own. Eerie, in a way, that so many of the vital statistics match her own.

*Hair: Brown.*

*Eyes: Brown.*

*Height: 5'9".*

Only the weight is different.

Elizabeth Baxter had been a scrawny hundred and fifteen pounds.

And, of course, a few years younger, though her expression in the picture reveals a woman who has seen a lifetime's worth of trouble.

So the license is still here.

She takes another plain white envelope from the bottom drawer of the desk and seals the license into it, thinking she really should destroy it. It expired years ago; it's dangerous keeping it around for anyone to find. It's the only thing in the house that, if stolen, would be a serious problem.

She puts it back into the drawer, telling herself she'll deal with it later.

Then, suddenly, she remembers.

There's one other thing that would be dangerous if someone got their hands on them.

Her keys.

The spare set, to the house and the car and the safe deposit box.

She keeps the ring on a nail high inside the kitchen cupboard where she keeps her cups and plates.

Frowning, she hurries back to the kitchen and opens the cupboard door, which had been left ajar and which she had closed on her last pass through the room.

She stands on tiptoe and reaches up to feel for the key ring.

For a second she can't find the nail.

Then her hand brushes across the tip of it, and she moves her fingers along it, knowing, with chilling certainty before she reaches the spot where it meets the cupboard wall, that it's empty.

* * *

The woman in the dirty T-shirt scurries along State Street in the blazing summer sun, muttering to herself.

About the child she'd abandoned.

The child who has never been far from her mind, especially lately.

No matter how she tries to push the image away, it comes back to haunt her as soon as her guard is down.

She sees the child's enormous, frightened eyes. . . .

Hears the small voice whimpering . . .

*Please, Mommy, please don't hurt me. Please don't hurt me.*

"Shut up! I never meant to hurt you!" she yells aloud to quiet the voice.

Then she realizes that she's startled a passing middle-aged couple who are walking a perfectly groomed, ridiculously small black dog.

"What are you looking at?" she yells at them. "Can't I talk to my kid without everyone trying to listen in?"

She sees that the lady, a tall and impeccably dressed redhead, is casting a furtive glance over her shoulder as they retreat, as though fearing an attack.

"Don't worry about her, Felice," the man is saying, his voice carried back despite the noise from the traffic. "She won't hurt us. She's just a crazy street person."

*Just a crazy street person.*

The woman in the dirty T-shirt sighs and keeps walking.

Keeps thinking bitterly about the child she abandoned.

The child who later abandoned her.


"What were you doing next door?" Pamela asks Frank as he comes walking back across the lawn, hands casually thrust in the front pockets of his khaki shorts.

She tries not to allow suspicion to creep onto her face as she waits for him to come near enough to answer her. He's not the type to yell across the yard.

"Somebody broke into Elizabeth's place," he says, coming to a stop a few feet away.

"You're kidding." She does her best not to reveal her relief that it's not some lame excuse. He wouldn't lie about something like a break-in. "When?"

"This morning, I guess, while she was out."

Pamela switches the baby to her other hip and calls to Hannah, who's wandered over to the green turtle-shaped plastic sandbox, "Hannah! Look! Daddy's here!"

Hannah ignores her, picking up a shovel and poking it into the sand.

To Frank, Pamela says, "So who broke into her place?"

He shrugs. "Must have been kids."

"What was stolen?"

"Nothing."

"Nothing?"

He shakes his head. "She must have come home when they were in the act, scared 'em away before they could take anything."

"Did she see anyone?"

"Nope."

"Huh. That's too bad. Did you water the lawn?"

"I didn't get a chance." He reaches out and tickles the baby's belly. "And anyway—"

"Here, take him," Pamela says, starting to hand Jason over.

"I can't. I'm filthy from working in the basement. I'm going to take a shower."

"The grass looks like it's really dry."

"Well, there's a ban on outdoor water use in the East Bay. Didn't you hear?"

"Then why'd you say you would water the lawn when I asked you this morning?" she asks, annoyed.

"I forgot about the ban."

"Well, the grass is dying."

"It's not dying, Pam. It'll be fine. Maybe it'll rain tonight or tomorrow."

She looks up at the cloudless blue sky. "I doubt it. It hasn't rained in weeks."

"Well, that's why there's a ban on water use. The reservoir levels are dangerously low."

"Running one garden hose for ten minutes won't put the whole East Bay in jeopardy, Frank."

"It's against the law, Pam. And I can't go around breaking the law. I'm a cop, remember?"

He brushes past her, going into the house and letting the screen door bang shut behind him.

"Hannah, come on," Pamela calls, turning just in time to see her daughter lying sprawled on her back in the sandbox, dumping shovels full of sand over her blond head. "Oh, God, Hannah, cut that out!"

"Sand," Hannah says gleefully, dumping another scoop of it over her head. "Sand."

Pamela goes over to her and bends to grab her daughter, careful not to jostle Jason too much.

Hannah, still holding the shovel, reaches down, scoops up some sand, and flings it all over Pamela and the baby.

"You little—" Pamela breaks off and tries to control her temper. "Hannah, that's bad! You're going to sit in time-out."

"No!"

"Yes."

She reaches down and grabs her daughter, somehow managing to get hold of her squirming little body while still balancing the baby on her other hip. She lugs both children into the house, then deposits Hannah on the kitchen floor.

"Go over to that chair," Pamela says angrily, "and sit in time-out."

"No!"

"What's going on?"

Pamela looks up to see Frank standing in the doorway, naked from the waist up.

She feels a pang at the sight of his familiar, tanned, hairy chest, remembering how she used to run her fingers over it as they lay in bed after making love. . . .

"Daddy!" Hannah calls, running toward her father.

"Get back over to that chair, Hannah!" Pamela orders.

"Why? What 'd she do?" Frank wants to know.

"She threw sand at me and Jason," she tells him, wishing the kids were both asleep, so she could go over to him and put her arms around him and stroke his naked skin the way she had so long ago.

"Hannah, did you throw sand at Mommy and your baby brother?"

"Yeah."

"Did you mean to do it?"

"No. It was a accident," Hannah announces, casting a smug glance in Pamela's direction.

"It wasn't an accident," Pamela says firmly as Jason starts to fuss.

"How do you know?" Frank asks.

Pamela frowns at him. "Because I'm thirty and she's two."

Jason cries out. She bounces him up and down to soothe him and says, "It's okay, Jason-boy. Mommy will feed you in a minute."

"If it was an accident, you don't have to sit in time-out," Frank tells Hannah. "As long as you tell Mommy you're sorry."

"I'm sorry, Mommy," the little girl says promptly.

"Now go play," Frank says, and Hannah makes a beeline for the toy box in the living room.

"Frank, why did you do that?" Pamela asks, patting Jason's little head and bouncing him on her hip as he wails again. "I was trying to teach her right from wrong."

"She said it was an accident."

"Well, it wasn't. Trust me. She was being a b-r-a-t." She didn't like to use words like that in front of Hannah, who had a way of picking things up and adding them to her vocabulary.

"Is that any way to talk about your own child?"

"Frank, come on. She's two. She's going to be a b-r-a-t now and then. Every kid is. I'm just being truthful. And anyway, you can't just go around and undo my discipline."

"I can't do anything right these days, can I?"

"What's that supposed to mean?"

"Never mind." He turns and walks away, down the hall toward the bathroom.

"Come back here and talk to me!" Pamela calls after him.

He shakes his head and says, with his usual, maddening calm, "You're too unreasonable to talk to these days."

"Unreasonable?" she practically shrieks, causing Jason to burst into tears in her arms.

She follows Frank down the hall. "How dare you call me unreasonable! I'm exhausted from single-handedly taking care of two kids and this house morning, noon, and night. I don't get more than two hours of sleep at a stretch, and I don't get a minute to myself, and my own husband isn't interested in talking to me or looking at me or touching me!"

"For Christ's sake, keep it down, Pam. The whole neighborhood will hear you" is all he says before disappearing into the bathroom and closing the door behind him.

A moment later she hears the shower water running.

"Be quiet!" she yells at Jason, who's sobbing loudly in her arms. "Be quiet!"

"Mommy, why are you yelling at everyone?"

It's Hannah, in the doorway of the living room, looking upset.

Pamela takes a deep breath, feeling like she's going to lose it. She really is.

She counts to ten.

Then she tells Hannah, "I'm not yelling anymore. See? Go back and play now."

And she takes Jason into the living room, sits in the rocking chair, and unbuttons her blouse.

She stares at the wall, her jaw clenched painfully in fury as she nurses her baby son.

"Are you Elizabeth Baxter?"

She clears her throat. "Yes. Come on in."

She steps aside and holds the door open wider to allow the stranger to enter her house.

It's dusk, and she doesn't get a good look at his face until he's standing in the brightly lit kitchen.

Her first thought is that he's gorgeous, with the kind of rugged features that are usually reserved for leading men in adventure films. He has a strong, square jaw, high cheekbones, and wide-set green eyes beneath full, dark brows. His skin is tanned and somewhat weathered-looking, and his wavy brown hair touches the collar of his jean jacket. He's big and broad-shouldered, and the scent of the chilly salt air seems to cling to him as she closes the door behind him.

Her next thought, as she steals another look at his handsome face, is that she's seen him someplace before.

The thought jars her.

"I'm Harper Smith," he's saying, shaking her hand. His fingers are cold and his grasp is sturdy.

"Thanks for coming," she murmurs, her thoughts spinning.

Why does he look so familiar? How does she know him?

She wouldn't forget meeting someone like him. . . .

"So your house keys were stolen?" he's asking, his hands hooked on the back belt loops of his jeans now that he's set his toolbox down.

She nods. "I want you to change all the dead bolts on the front and back doors, and put one on the basement door—the lock on that one is broken. Can you do that?"

"I sure can." He grins. "That's why they call me a locksmith."

She almost forgets to smile in response, so caught up is she in trying to place him.

She must have simply seen him around Windemere Cove. After all, his locksmith shop is right on Center Street, though she never heard of it until she found him in the yellow pages.

"Have we met?" he suddenly asks, peering at her more closely.

"Have we . . . ? Oh. No. No, I don't think we have," she says stupidly.

"You look sort of familiar."

"Oh . . ."

*Of course he thinks you look familiar. You're Mallory Eden.*

*But why does he look familiar to you?*

"People say that to me all the time. I guess I have one of those faces," she tells him, moving away toward the doorway to the hall. "You can start on the back door, there. If you need anything just holler. I'll be in there." She gestures down the hall, toward the master bedroom.

"Okay, thanks."

She must have seen him on the street in town, she decides, walking down the hall and into the bedroom. Although she's surprised she doesn't remember exactly when and where. A man that good-looking would be hard to forget.

Especially when you're a woman who hasn't been touched even casually by someone of the opposite sex in almost half a dozen years.

She can't help wondering what it would be like to be held in Harper Smith's strong-looking arms, then breaks off her fantasy in disgust with herself.

*He's the locksmith,* she reminds herself. *You called him here to change your locks, not to feed your sexual fantasies.*

She busies herself putting fresh sheets and blankets on the bed, but still, she is filled with an acute awareness of the man in her kitchen.

She hears the clanking and banging of tools as he works, and the faint sound of him whistling some nameless tune.

She finds herself trying to think of some excuse to go back to the kitchen, though she knows it's pathetic and nothing can come of her attraction to him, even if he were interested.

She can't get involved with a man—especially now, when she's making plans to leave this town just as soon as she's taken care of Manny.

But that doesn't mean she can't catch an up-close glimpse of the good-looking locksmith at work, and maybe see him flash that wide, white smile at her again.

Finally, just as she's about to give in and go and fetch herself a glass of water, she hears him calling her name.

Not "Ms. Baxter," as one might expect . . .

But "Elizabeth."

And she finds herself admiring the sound of her name on his lips. . . .

Even though it's not her name at all.

"Yes?" she responds, stepping into the hall and seeing him in the kitchen doorway. "Do you need something?"

"I don't suppose I could bother you for a glass of water?"

"Sure . . . that's fine. Help yourself. The glasses are above the sink. . . ."

*But if he helps himself, you can't go into the kitchen and talk to him.*

"Or," she continues, "there's some iced tea made, if you'd like some of that."

"Iced tea would be great," he says, and there's that grin again, with a dimple popping up at each side of his generous mouth.

"Okay," she says, and walks toward him. "It's in a pitcher in the fridge."

As she passes the doorway to the living room, she glimpses the disarray and remembers, all at once, why Harper Smith is there.

He's there to change her locks because someone broke into her house while she wasn't home.

Someone who stole her keys and obviously had intended to come back later.

It might have been a bunch of harmless kids, as Frank Minelli had suggested, planning to rob her when she isn't home.

Or it might have been someone who schemes to come back when she *is* at home, to catch her unaware, in her bed, asleep, the way he had last time. . . .

"How are the locks coming along?" she asks Harper Smith tersely as she joins him in the kitchen.

"So far, so good. The back door's done and so is the basement. I had a bit of trouble removing one of the cylinders on that broken lock, but now you're all set. I can work on the front door as soon as I finish my iced tea."

She nods, taking down two glasses, then changes her mind and puts one back. If she pours some tea for herself, it'll seem too chummy, like she's planning to sit and visit with him while he drinks his.

"Aren't you having any?" he asks.

She starts to shake her head, then, inexplicably, finds herself nodding and saying, "Yes." She takes out another glass, fills them both, and hands him one.

"Thanks," he says, and takes a long drink. He leans against the counter and sets the still-half-full glass down, keeping his hand around it as if to prove he's not dawdling and will finish it in a moment.

At least, that's what she thinks he's doing. As if he knows that she's wary about them standing there together, in this suddenly semisocial setting.

"How did you find me?" he asks, and she blinks.

"What?"

"Did someone refer you to me, or . . ."

"Oh. Oh, I found you in the yellow pages. Aaron's Locksmith. Who's Aaron?"

"Nobody. I just figured, when I came to town last year, that there were quite a few locksmiths already established here in the East Bay. I wanted to be the first one listed in the yellow pages, to help bring in some business. You can't get ahead of a name that begins with a double A."

"No, you can't," she agrees, smiling. "And it worked. I called you because you were the first listing I came to."

"See? Pretty smart, huh?" He taps his forehead with a fingertip and grins again. Then he asks, "How about you?"

"Yeah, I'm pretty smart too."

He laughs. "I don't doubt that, but I meant . . . what do you do? For a living?"

"Me? I . . . I'm a writer."

"A writer?" He's all interested. "What do you write?"

"Just . . . technical stuff. Not . . . screenplays or anything."

"Screenplays? Is that what you want to do?"

*Damn, where did that come from?*

"No," she says quickly, and it's the truth. She had never wanted to write screenplays. Just act them out.

"Then why . . . ?"

"I just said that because whenever you tell someone you're a writer, that's the conclusion they jump to. People think everyone wants to get rich and live in Beverly Hills."

"Not everyone wants that," he says, wearing a veiled expression she can't read. "What kind of technical stuff do you write?"

"Annual reports . . . company newsletters . . . that sort of thing."

It had seemed the perfect fictional occupation when she'd first moved there five years before. What else would keep her at home, alone, seven days a week?

But now she realizes that he might ask to see something she's written. What will she do then?

She quickly changes the subject, asking him, "Where did you move here from?"

"Me? West Coast," he says, his tone suddenly terse. He lifts his glass to his lips and drains it, giving her the distinct impression that he doesn't want to talk about himself any more than she wants to talk about herself.

She finds that unsettling for some reason.

"Well, I'll get busy on the front door," he tells her, setting his glass in the sink and running water into it.

"You can leave that. I'll put it into the dishwasher," she tells him.

He nods, picks up his toolbox, and leaves the room.

She's standing at the sink, when she hears a knock on the back door. She jumps and sees Frank Minelli standing there.

"Just checking in," he says when she opens the door. "Is everything okay?"

"Everything's fine. I'm having the locks changed."

"Why?"

She decides not to mention the stolen keys. He might press her into reporting the incident, and the last thing she wants is a big commotion with the police involved.

She shrugs and says, "I just feel safer that way."

"You're using the guy from Aaron's Locksmith down on Center Street?" His voice is low, as though he doesn't want Harper to overhear.

"How'd you know?"

"I saw the truck in the driveway."

She nods.

Something in his expression makes her ask, "Is there something about him you don't like?"

"Not per se." He leans against the door frame, his hands in the front pockets of his khaki Dockers. "He's new in town though. I don't know if a stranger is the best person to trust with your locks."

A chill sneaks over her.

"There are a number of locksmiths in town who have been established for years," Frank says quietly. "I would have been glad to recommend one."

"It's okay. This is fine," she tells him in what she hopes is a convincing tone.

Inside, the uneasy feeling she'd had earlier today is back full force.

"If you need anything, I'm right next door," Frank reminds her. His brown eyes are so reassuring, so kind and caring that she almost asks him if his earlier offer—to spend the night—still stands. Suddenly, she finds great comfort in the thought of having an armed police officer under her roof tonight.

But now Frank is no longer leaning; he's heading for home, calling over his shoulder, "Have a good night, Elizabeth."

"I will," she calls after him. "Thanks for coming by."

She returns to the bedroom and finishes making the bed, then straightens the bottles of lotion and perfume on her dresser top. By the time she's finished with that, she hears him repacking his toolbox and his footsteps in the hall.

"All set," he calls when she pokes her head into the doorway.

"Already? That was fast."

He nods. "It isn't very complicated."

He shows her how the new locks work, and hands her two sets of keys for them. "Do you need any more, or do you live here alone?"

"Oh . . ." It hadn't occurred to her that he didn't know that. But how would he? For all he knows, she has a husband and a bunch of kids. She contemplates telling him that, but only briefly, before she admits, "I live here alone."

He nods.

She's trying to read his expression, when the phone rings, abruptly cutting into her thoughts.

Her heart begins to pound.

"Aren't you going to get that?" Harper asks when it rings again.

"I—yes. Of course." She goes into the living room and picks up the receiver, grasping it so tightly that her hand hurts.

"Hello?"

"Elizabeth?"

"Manny!" She lets out a shuddering sigh of relief. "Is everything okay?"

There's the slightest pause before he says, "Uh-huh."

"Manny . . . are you sure about that?"

"Yeah. But I was just wondering, um, if you had a chance to get the material and stuff for my costumes?"

"I bought it this morning, but I haven't had a chance to start working on them yet. I'll get busy first thing tomorrow morning."

"Oh, good," he says, sounding a little distracted.

"Manny, are you sure you're all right?"

"I'm positive."

But something's wrong. She can hear it in his tone.

"How are your grandparents?"

"They're fine," he says quickly.

"What about your mother? She hasn't been there again, bothering them for money, has she?"

Again the slight hesitation before he answers. "No, she hasn't been around. Well, I'll be seeing you, Elizabeth. Thanks again for making my costumes."

"No problem, Manny. And remember . . . you call me if you need me. Okay? If you need anything at all. I'm here."

"Yeah, I know. Are you going to the park tomorrow for a walk?"

"I'm . . . not sure yet."

"If you do, I'll probably be there."

"I'll keep that in mind," she says with a smile.

"Thanks, Elizabeth. For the costumes, I mean," he says before hanging up.

She replaces the receiver, wondering what happened to him. Something caused that hollow tremor in his little-boy voice.

A sound from the hallway causes her to look up and see Harper Smith, still standing there with the keys in his hand.

"Oh," she says, "sorry about that. It was just . . ."

What business is it of his who it was? Why is she about to tell this stranger her personal business?

She cuts herself off, saying only, "Two sets of keys will be fine, so how much do I owe you?"

"I'll send you a bill."

"But I can pay you right now. Just tell me—"

"I have to figure it out when I get back to my shop. It's okay. I'll bill you. You can send a check or drop it off at my place. It's on Center Street, just past Pine."

"All right," she says reluctantly. But she won't be dropping by his shop. She'll send a check.

"So, I'll be going . . ."

She nods. "Thanks again." Had she thanked him before? She suddenly feels awkward, torn between wanting him to go and needing him to stay for some reason she couldn't fathom.

She can't trust him.

He is a stranger, new in town, from the West Coast. . . .

What if . . . ?

No. He can't be the one.

She turns and walks to the door, opening it for him.

He has no choice but to walk out, turning on the step to look back at her. "It was nice meeting you, Elizabeth. You give me a call if you have any trouble with those new dead bolts."

"I will."

"Or you can page me . . . I can give you the number—"

"That's okay. I'm sure everything will be fine."

"I'm sure it will," he agrees.

Then he leaves, getting into his white van and driving away with a wave.

She secures the locks on her door, the locks he just installed. . . .

Locks he would have keys to open.

# chapter

# 5

Rae Hamilton gets into her one-bedroom Burbank apartment at four in the morning to find the red message light blinking on her answering machine.

She kicks off her high heels and pauses to turn on a lamp before padding over to the phone in her bare feet.

Just a moment earlier she had been exhausted from a full night of club hopping.

Now she feels renewed energy at the thought that there might be a message from her agent, calling to say someone from one of her dozens of recent auditions wanted to see her again.

Sure enough, Buddy Charles's recorded voice greets her ears after she presses the button.

"It's me, sugar. I wanted to be the one to tell you before you heard it somewhere else—it'll be all over the papers in the morning. The part in that new TriStar comedy is going to Gwyneth. Cameron decided to go with a Name after all. Sorry, sugar. Something else will pan out though. Hang in there."

There's a double beep, meaning not just that the message has ended, but that it's the only one.

*Cameron decided to go with a Name. . . .*

She curses and savagely yanks first one, then the other of her clip-on earrings from her earlobe.

That's how it's always been. They've always wanted a Name. But not hers.

*Sorry, sugar.*

"What the hell kind of agent are you?" she mutters at an invisible Buddy Charles.

She's had it with him. Everyone in the business knows that he's antagonized one too many influential directors with his abrasive personality. For all she knows, he's the reason she lost this latest role to a Name.

First thing tomorrow, she's going to get rid of him, as she's been promising herself for months, years now. She's on a freelance basis anyway these days, having refused to renew her contract with him. He simply hasn't helped her career lately. If anything, he's hindered it.

So it's settled. She'll go on her own for a while, until she can land a decent agent. Maybe Flynn can recommend someone.

She strides back across the room to the door, which she'd left ajar in her haste to get to the answering machine.

Not a good idea in this neighborhood, in a building that doesn't have security.

She thinks longingly of the old days, a few years back, when she was living in a rented house behind electronic gates in Pacific Palisades.

Roles had been easier to come by back then.

She likes to think it was her youth and talent that had made her more sought after then than she has been lately.

But it doesn't take a genius to figure out that her erstwhile success was primarily due to her association with the legendary Mallory Eden.

During the first year after her friend's death, she had found herself with enough work so that she could actually be a little choosy. Nothing major had come her way—certainly no leads in blockbuster films or even decent roles in indies.

But in two big-budget movies she had played Nicole Kidman's loyal friend, and Glenn Close's loyal sister—thankless background roles, really, but she was working. Then she had been cast—for a few blissful weeks, until the project's financial backing fell apart— as the suicidal war bride of Gary Sinese for a high-profile period picture, in what had promised to be a challenging, career-making role.

After that, things went downhill.

There were more bit parts with waning visibility, and then the lead as the long-suffering wife of a stand-up comedy buffoon in that quickly canceled television sitcom, and finally, her role as Rainbow Weber on *Morning, Noon, and Night.*

An out-of-work soap opera actress—that's what she is now.

Just a down-and-out loser whose only value to the Hollywood-hungry media is her connection to Mallory Eden.

*It isn't fair. She's not even dead when she's dead,* Rae thinks grimly, going into her small bedroom and turning on the bedside lamp.

Her gaze falls on a framed snapshot of Mallory on her dresser, and she feels a stab of guilt.

But then she thinks of a guy she dated briefly last year, the one who had actually seemed interested in *her,* until she realized that he kept telling her how much she looked like Mallory Eden. He spent their first and second dates asking her what the famous actress had really been like, and whether Rae thought she had actually killed herself.

She couldn't get rid of the jerk, who clearly didn't know or care who Rae Hamilton is.

Not many people ever have.

Not even her own parents, stuffy East Coast professionals who sent her to Yale, expecting her to become a doctor like her father or a lawyer like her mother. Instead, she had majored in drama.

They had always been distant toward their only child, but once she drifted from the path they had chosen for her, she might as well have fallen off the face of the earth.

She hasn't heard from them in months. They call to check in every once in a while, ostensibly hoping to hear that she's decided to give up on this show business foolishness, come home, become a doctor—or marry one.

She sits on the edge of the bed and peels off her black sheer stockings, then stands again and strips off the halter-top cocktail dress.

In the bathroom she removes her eye makeup, washes her face, and brushes her teeth, all the while cursing Buddy Charles for not landing her better auditions.

If only Flynn Soderland had signed her on when she'd approached him years ago. By now he could have done for her what he did for Mallory.

But he had given her some lame excuse about his client list being too full, not giving her enough credit for knowing a classic agent brush-off.

It's a wonder she keeps in touch with him after all these years, especially now that he's retired. Well, all that ties them together is Mallory's ghost.

Mallory's ghost . . .

She shudders at the very idea, and it isn't the first time it's crossed her mind.

They'd had a conversation about it once, her and Mallory. They were drinking wine up in Big Sur, lounging lazily at dusk on the porch at some remote inn, when somehow the conversation had turned to the death of Mallory's grandmother, who had raised her.

"I used to lie in bed at night and wait for her spirit to appear to me," Mallory had said so solemnly that Rae had burst out laughing.

"You don't believe in ghosts, do you?" she had asked her friend.

"I don't know, Rae. If anyone was going to come back as a ghost, it would have been Gran. She had a real flair for drama, and she used to love to sneak up on people, see them jump. She would probably enjoy going around as a ghost. But then, maybe she's so peaceful wherever she is that she doesn't feel the need to come back. I hope that's the case."

"Well, I wouldn't want anyone's ghost coming around to haunt me."

"Not even if it were me?" Mallory had asked, the teasing sparkle back in her impossibly blue eyes. "You wouldn't be afraid, would you, Rae?"

"Of a ghost? You bet I would."

"Not if it were my ghost."

"I'd be afraid of anyone's ghost, Mallory. Ever see *The Shining?*"

"Ever see *Beetlejuice?* I would be a fun ghost, Rae. And I could fill you in on all the details about what's waiting on the other side. Aren't you curious?"

"Okay, maybe a little."

"Well, if I die before you do, I'll come back and fill you in. I promise I won't spook you with chains or make stuff float around or anything. I'll just pop in and say, 'Hey, Rae, it's me.' "

They had started laughing at the idea of Mallory casually dropping in on her as a ghost, and had gone on drinking their wine.

But Rae has never forgotten her friend's promise.

And it has never ceased to disturb her.

So far, Mallory hasn't made an appearance.

But it doesn't mean Rae isn't always a little on edge when she's alone at night, waiting and wondering. . . .

Elizabeth stretches and looks at the clock.

Nine A.M.

She's been hunched over the green felt fabric for three hours already.

She hadn't risen at dawn intentionally, even though she'd been concerned about not getting started on the costume yesterday.

The fact is, she hadn't slept at all last night, and it had nothing to do with the uncomfortably humid weather and the fact that she couldn't open her windows for whatever slight relief that might offer.

Finally, when she heard the birds starting to sing outside her window, she figured she might as well get up and get busy on Manny's costumes.

Now, as she sets her sewing aside and goes into the kitchen to make a cup of tea, she allows her mind to wander back to Harper Smith.

He was in her thoughts throughout the restless night.

She had alternated between wishing she could see him again because she's so attracted to him . . .

And being terrified that he's the one who's been terrorizing her all along.

After all . . .

He's new in town.

He's from the West Coast.

He was noticeably cagey when she asked him about his past.

And what about her strange feeling that she had seen him someplace before?

For some reason, she keeps thinking that it hadn't been here in town, or recently.

She keeps thinking that it had been a long time ago, in California.

But that might just be her paranoia creeping in.

Then again, it might not.

What if the reason she recognizes him is that he's the obsessed fan who was stalking her?

She has often wondered over the years if her attacker was someone whose face she had glimpsed in the throngs of people who were always crowding around to see her. Maybe she had talked to him, smiled at him, even signed an autograph for him, feeding his sick fantasies.

And maybe he's Harper Smith.

The evidence points in that direction, though all of it's circumstantial.

And she can't quite convince herself that she has anything to fear from the man whose presence attracted rather than repelled her when they were alone together here yesterday.

Besides . . .

He's a locksmith.

A locksmith wouldn't break into someone's house by smashing a basement window and kicking in a door.

A locksmith would know how to get in undetected.

A locksmith could probably come and go without anyone knowing he had been there, if he wanted to.

So . . .

If he's not the stalker, then Harper Smith is simply a man whose mere presence aroused feelings of lust that she had long ago buried.

And Harper Smith just happens to be new in town, cagey about his past, from the West Coast. . . .

And vaguely familiar.

*Why?*

She knows she should stay as far away from him as possible in the next few days, before she leaves town.

And she will leave town.

She has no choice.

Her only regret is that she won't be able to tell Manny why she's going, or even say good-bye.

No, that's not her *only* regret.

She regrets, too, that if Harper Smith really is simply a nice, normal man—just a nice local locksmith who makes her lonely heart go pitter-patter—she will never see him again.

"Are you all done eating, Hannah?" Pamela asks the two-year-old, eyeing the untouched half-slice of peanut butter toast remaining on her plastic Barney plate.

"All done."

"You didn't eat your toast."

"Hannah eat bananas."

"I see that you ate your bananas. And you drank all your milk too. But what about your toast?"

"Hannah no like toast. Watch Elmo now?"

Pamela sighs. "All right."

She settles her daughter in the living room in front of *Sesame Street,* then returns to the kitchen.

She fights the urge to go to the cupboard and get a Pop-Tart. She buys them for Frank, but finds herself sneaking them herself, even though they're not the low-fat kind. She's constantly hungry lately. It has to be because she's nursing.

As soon as she weans Jason, she'll go back to having a normal appetite.

She'll be able to eat slimming foods like salads. Lettuce and tomatoes are off limits to nursing mothers, according to the pediatrician. Lettuce gives the baby gas through the breast milk, and tomatoes make the milk too acidic.

Pamela turns away from the cupboard, telling herself she doesn't need to eat a Pop-Tart right now. She'll only be angry with herself later.

A rare private moment, she realizes, sitting at the table and picking up the barely touched mug of coffee she'd poured an hour earlier. Coffee is something else she's supposed to be avoiding while she's breastfeeding, but one cup now and then can't hurt.

She'd poured some for Frank too, hoping they could sit at the table together for five minutes before he left for work.

But he'd dumped his into a plastic Dunkin' Donuts travel mug and taken it with him, saying he was late.

He had left without kissing her good-bye.

*Well, he was in a hurry,* she tells herself, trying not to think about the early days of their marriage, when they would eat breakfast together after making love and showering together, when he would leave her at the door with a lingering kiss.

*This is what happens when you have children,* Pamela decides. *The romance vanishes.*

But it can't happen to everyone, can it? There must be parents out there who are still crazy about each other, who still kiss passionately and make love every night. . . .

Every night.

*Try once a year. If I'm lucky.*

She clutches the mug in both hands, elbows propped on the table, pondering the problem. It can't be as bad as it seems. Maybe she just has a touch of postpartum depression.

*But you had the baby over two months ago.*

*So?*

*Is there a cap on the postpartum depression period?*

Anyway . . .

*Our marriage isn't abnormal. We're both just exhausted, and busy. Once things settle down . . .*

But when will that be? When Hannah and Jason are grown and living on their own? How do other couples manage to keep the passion alive?

Pamela decides to bring up the topic at Wednesday's play group, then just as quickly decides against it. The last thing she wants to do is admit to the other moms—all of them nearly as slim and beautiful as damned Elizabeth next door—that her sex life is less than perfect.

Elizabeth.

That's the last thing she wants to think about.

She pictures Frank hurrying across the lawn last night, looking guilty.

And no, it hadn't been her imagination.

He had looked guilty as sin.

He was supposed to be out there watering the grass—an intention he had suddenly announced during dinner.

"But what about the watering ban?" Pamela had asked.

"You were right this afternoon. It won't make any difference if I give the grass a little water. It is getting pretty brown."

And so he'd gone outside to water the grass.

And, at some point, while she was giving Jason his sponge bath or reading Hannah *Good Night, Moon* for the zillionth time, he had gone over to Elizabeth Baxter's house.

She had glimpsed him through the nursery window, hurrying back to their own yard.

He'd resumed watering the grass, not coming inside for nearly another hour. When she asked what took him so long, he'd merely said, "You were right. It was really dry."

Hmmm.

Pamela's eyes are narrowed as she takes a sip of her coffee. . . .

Then makes a face.

It's cold, dammit.

Before she could drink it earlier, Jason had needed to be nursed, and then, just after she'd gotten him changed and dressed for the day, had spit up all over his outfit. By the time she put him into something clean, Hannah was up and clamoring for breakfast.

Pamela rises, sticks the coffee into the microwave, and turns it on for a minute.

While she waits for it to heat, she removes the Barney plate from Hannah's high chair and carries it over to the trash. But instead of dumping the untouched piece of toast in, she grabs it and takes a bite.

The next thing she knows, she's sitting at the table, finishing it off with her now-steaming coffee—and glad Frank can't see her.

She's noticed the little disapproving glances he sends her lately whenever she eats something fattening. He hasn't actually *said* anything about her weight, but that doesn't mean he isn't disgusted by her appearance these days.

No wonder they no longer have sex. Who wouldn't be turned off by the quivering jellylike flesh that covers her once-slim belly, hips, and thighs?

Had there really been a time when her husband had told her, every day, how wildly attracted he was to her? He used to tell her daily that she looked great, used to buy her sexy outfits so that he could show her off, used to call her "babe."

She thinks back to when they met, nearly five years ago at Redondo Beach.

That was Pamela's first trip to California; she and her friend June were spending a blissful two weeks sightseeing up and down the coast.

She distinctly remembers what she had been wearing when she met the man who would become her husband. It was a red bikini. Though she had been in California for only a few days, her lean, hard body was already evenly tanned, thanks to a head start in the tanning booths back home.

Frank had struck up a conversation with her and June as they waded in the surf. It turned out he was from the East Coast too— from New Jersey. He was there on vacation, visiting his brother, Rick, who lived in Pasadena. Back home he lived with his widowed father, and he had recently been laid off from the factory where he had worked since high school graduation.

"I've always been a sucker for skinny, beautiful blondes," he had told Pamela before asking her out.

Their first date was dinner at a restaurant in Marina Del Rey. Joining them were Frank's brother, an ex-marine who had earned a medal in the Gulf War, and June, a fervent pacifist who had marched in Washington to protest it. Naturally, the two had taken an instant dislike to each other before the drinks even arrived on the table. They did their best to cut the evening short, but their bickering hadn't dampened Pamela's and Frank's ardor in the least.

She slept with him that night, in his car parked outside the motel room she shared with June. It was reckless and raw, that first time, but incredibly satisfying. When Pamela returned to her room at dawn, she woke June and announced that she was going to marry Frank.

"I really hope you don't," June had said, "because that would mean I have to see his brother at the wedding, and I never want to lay eyes on that SOB again."

As it turned out, Rick had been the best man and June the maid of honor a year later, and they had reluctantly called a truce in honor of the happy occasion.

Pamela and Frank had honeymooned at the Cape—misty mornings, deserted dunes, dazzling falling leaves.

They moved to an apartment in Windemere Cove, a picture-perfect seaside town only an hour away from her parents in the Boston suburbs and twenty minutes from Frank's first place of employment, working the night shift at a toy factory in Pawtucket.

By day, he attended the police academy, pursuing his dream of entering law enforcement. She toasted him with champagne when he landed the job on the local police force. They bought the house soon afterward; Pamela got pregnant, and she fully expected to live happily ever after.

She licks a glob of peanut butter off her finger and stares off into space, wondering what happened.

How fortuitous that the Windemere Cove Public Library had chosen last week to finally leap into the nineties by acquiring two brand-new computers with on-line services that can be accessed by the public.

That little tidbit of information had appeared in Saturday's edition of the *Harbor Times*. According to the librarian, Vivian Saunders, the computers would be available on a first-come, first-serve basis, although a sign-up sheet would become necessary once school is back in session next week, when, presumably, local students would be jostling one another in their eagerness to surf the Net.

But at this hour on a hot, sunny Tuesday morning in late August, the library—a historic federal-style brick building conveniently located on North Main Street between the post office and the police department—is, thankfully, all but deserted.

And luckily, the librarian is busy in the book stacks, helping an elderly, hard-of-hearing man who's looking for an obscure book about World War I, in which he served. Neither of them seems to notice the person who scurries straight over to the computers, sliding furtively into a seat behind the one closest to the window, farthest from prying eyes.

A crumpled scrap of paper is removed from a pocket, smoothed so that the scrawled notes can be read.

A few commands are entered on the keyboard, and then a name is typed in. . . .

*B-A-X-T-E-R, E-L-I-Z-A-B-E-T-H.*

Along with other pertinent information that was copied off the driver's license that had been so conveniently left in that envelope in her desk drawer.

She had even been so thoughtful as to have left a supply of identical envelopes in the desk.

How simple it had been to jot down the necessary data from the license, then slip it into a new envelope. The ripped, original envelope had been easily disposed of later—burned so that no one would ever trace it.

As if anyone would ever have a reason to try.

"Perhaps, if you're interested in World War One, Mr. Collins, you would be interested in learning to use one of our new computers," the librarian is suggesting in a hushed tone as she and the elderly man emerge from the bookstacks.

*Damn!*

*Don't come over here now.*

*I need only a few minutes. . . .*

"Eh? Use one of the new *whats?*" asks Mr. Collins, his voice booming through the silent library.

"Computers. We just got them last week, through a special grant . . . you won't believe how much information is available on the Internet."

"The Internet? Is that what you're talking about? What the hell would *I* need with the Internet? I wouldn't even know what it was if my grandson didn't make a mint working on some software program."

"That's wonderful. Then you must be curious about—"

"Do you know how old I am? Guess how old I am."

"Um . . . well, if you served in the first World War, you must be . . . uh . . ."

"I'm ninety-eight years old. That's how old I am. What does a ninety-eight-year-old man need with the Internet?"

"Well," the librarian says feebly, "you could find out about people you used to know. You know, maybe look up your old war buddies, find out where they are today."

"I'll tell you where they are. They're all dead," says Mr. Collins.

"Everyone I ever knew is dead, except my kids and grandkids and great-grandkids, and none of them want anything to do with me."

The librarian makes a *tsk-tsk* sound and listens sympathetically while Mr. Collins relates his miserable existence, and how his family is just waiting for him to die so that they can inherit the old captain's house with a water view, the house he's lived in from the day he was born, the house that's been in the family for two centuries. They don't want it to live in, but to sell so it can be turned into an antique shop, like most of the others in the historic district. Or, worse yet, a bed and breakfast, so that a bunch of strangers can run roughshod over the place.

*Tsk-tsk* goes the librarian over and over again.

Meanwhile, the computer has come up with some fascinating information about Elizabeth Baxter.

Previous addresses, all of them in the Chicago area.

And previous arrests, all of them for drug possession—or prostitution.

But most interesting of all is a short blurb from a Chicago paper, dated six years earlier, when Elizabeth Baxter—purportedly the same Elizabeth Baxter who now lives in Windemere Cove—had been found in a fleabag hotel, dead of a drug overdose.

Brawley Johnson pops the tape into the VCR and stretches out on the bed with the remote control. The blinds are drawn against the bright midday sun, leaving him alone in the shadows.

He fast-forwards past the opening credits and the early scene showing the nerdy, bespectacled male star walking out on his fat, ugly wife to find "a real woman."

Brawley has seen the film so many times, he can recite the dialogue.

Sometimes he does, taking the role of the male star, rewinding certain scenes so that he can repeat stimulating snatches of conversation with the youngest of the half-dozen female actresses.

Babie Love.

That's what she called herself when she filmed this movie back in the mid-eighties, wearing a red wig and so much makeup it's difficult to recognize her teenage face—which is rarely on camera anyway—unless you freeze the frame and study one of the few close-ups very carefully.

Even her voice was different back then—higher-pitched, with remnants of a little-girl squeal. She had barely been eighteen.

He presses play when the tape reaches her first scene. In it, the man goes to a seedy strip club and she's one of the exotic dancers.

Brawley presses the control and watches her dance scene in slow motion, wanting to prolong the shots of her nubile young body writhing and strutting, her bare breasts jiggling provocatively, and her slightly fleshy stomach and hips still bearing the last remnants of adolescent padding.

He watches the dance three times, then fast-forwards again, past the graphic sex scene where two older female stars seduce the nerd in the alley behind the club, leaving him naked and stealing his wallet.

He presses play again for the scene where Babie Love comes along, giving him a ride in her jalopy.

The naked nerd has no place to go, so she brings him home with her, to the suburban house where she lives with her unsuspecting parents, who think she's at cheerleading practice every night while she's dancing.

She sneaks him up to her room, a frilly little-girl room with an eyelet-covered canopy bed.

She puts on her see-through nightie, then climbs into bed with him, running her hands over his tense body.

"It's all right," she tells the quaking nerd. "Don't be afraid. I won't hurt you. I just want to make you feel better."

"But . . . I'm married. I have children."

"Married men with children really, *really* turn me on," she purrs.

She takes off her nightie and does a dance of seduction just for him, stopped just short of making love to him by her angry parents, who suddenly burst into her room.

Babie Love protests tearfully as her father grabs her hapless would-be lover and tosses him out of the house. . . .

And that's the end of Babie Love's role in the movie.

Brawley presses stop.

He has never bothered to watch the end.

He rewinds to the point where the precocious redhead first slips the nightie over her head.

That body.

He knows every inch of it.

It had belonged to him back when she made the film.

The whole thing had been his idea. They were three months behind in the rent, and he was out day and night, busting his ass busing tables and pumping gas while she sat around the apartment, crying about her dead grandmother and talking endlessly about becoming an actress.

"You want to become an actress? Well, I got you an audition," he had announced one night when he got home, his hands black with grease from the gas station.

"An audition?" She looked up from her copy of *Premiere* magazine. "For what?"

"A movie," Brawley told her truthfully, adding that he had met the director, Jazz Taylor, just that afternoon at the service station. They got to talking as Brawley filled the gas tank of his Range Rover.

"Jazz Taylor—that sounds like it should be the name of a director. But I've never heard of him," she said, not suspicious, just intrigued.

"Oh, he's terrific. It would be a big honor to work with someone like him."

What Brawley didn't tell her was that it was the director's first film—and it was porn.

She didn't find that out even when she got the part, following a brief audition during which she was asked to dance seductively, wearing a skimpy bathing suit.

Brawley had insisted on being present at the audition.

It was he who convinced her to take off her clothes when Jazz Taylor asked her to.

"This is Hollywood—the big league," he told her, pulling her aside for a pep talk. "You've got to be realistic. Every actress does nude scenes."

So she took off the skimpy bathing suit for the director, whose careful, semileering appraisal of her nude body made even Brawley a little uncomfortable.

But when she landed the role, he took her out to dinner to celebrate.

And he was there with her, at her insistence, while she filmed it, helping to coach her performance until Taylor told him to shut up or get out.

She had ultimately acted the part like the pro that she later became—unaware, still, that the film was pornography. She didn't realize it until months later, when she saw the finished product.

In retrospect, he is astonished at her naïveté—even considering her age at the time, and the fact that she was fresh from Nebraska.

When she discovered the truth, she was horrified, of course.

Brawley had feigned shock, telling her that no, of course he hadn't realized what kind of production it was.

"But look at it this way," he told her. "You didn't do anything but dance around naked. And you made a hell of a lot of money . . . and there's a lot more where that came from. Taylor's loaded."

"I'm never doing that again, Brawley! What's going to happen when everyone back home sees it?"

"Don't worry. They don't show X-rated stuff at the Custer Creek Cinema, remember?"

"Well, what if someone—"

"Don't worry! Even if somebody sees it, they won't know who you are. You look completely different now."

The red wig had been her idea—she had been experimenting with different looks back then. And on Brawley's advice, she hadn't used her real name on the contract or in her billing.

And the director, a shady character who wasn't big on legal details and whose own real name wasn't even Jazz Taylor, knew her only as Babie Love.

He hadn't asked or seemed to care about her real name.

Cindy O'Neal.

The future Mallory Eden.

To Mallory's dismay, the film had been released on video in the late eighties, along with dozens of other relatively obscure porn movies. But apparently no one had ever picked up on her presence. Presumably, only she and Brawley were aware that she was Babie Love.

And Jazz Taylor, wherever he is, is obviously still unaware that he's sitting on a potential gold mine.

If the world ever discovers that Hollywood's long-dead girl-next-door had appeared, nude and provocative, in a porn movie . . .

But that will remain Brawley's little secret.

For now.


Elizabeth hesitates on the sidewalk in front of the post office. She should go in and check her mail; she hasn't since Friday.

Friday, when the card came.

*I know who you are.*

Earlier, filled with trepidation, she had checked her mailbox back at home—a mailbox that is always empty except for the occasional flyer or junk mail addressed to "resident." But she was almost startled to see that there was nothing in it today.

After all, somebody broke into the house. If it had been the stalker, then he knows where she lives. If he wants to frighten her again, to make his presence known, then he could do it by sending another card or a letter right to her home.

But . . .

If he knows where she lives, why would he have bothered sending something to her at the post office address in the first place?

The card had been sent from Windemere Cove sometime last week.

Is he in town now, watching her every move?

Or was the break-in a fluke, totally unrelated?

Just kids, the way Frank had said . . .

Someone jostles her.

She gasps, looks up to see two pudgy middle-aged women, both clad in nylon jogging suits and sneakers.

"Sorry," one of them calls over her shoulder as they continue to race-walk by her.

Her heart is pounding and her feet seem rooted to the ground.

She can't just stand there in the middle of the sidewalk, scared out of her wits, obstructing pedestrian traffic all day.

*Go,* she tells herself. *Go get the mail. It's just mail; it can't hurt you.*

She tries not to remember the flower arrangement that had exploded and maimed her assistant, Gretchen.

That hadn't come through the mail, of course. The police hadn't even been able to trace it to a florist. Nobody had a clue where it had come from or how it had arrived; there had been so much confusion back then, so many gifts and flowers and cards from well-wishers.

*Don't think about that,* Elizabeth tells herself again, but it's all there in her mind, the sound of Gretchen's scream intermingling with the thunderous blast; the sight of blood spattered everywhere. . . .

*Get the mail,* she commands herself, *before you have a nervous breakdown here on the street.*

But what if . . . ?

Well, if there's a package waiting in her box, she won't open it. She won't even accept it.

If there's a package, she'll leave town immediately.

*What about Manny's costume?*

If there's a package, she'll leave town immediately, *but* she'll bring the fabric and sequins with her, and she'll finish the costume on the road, and she'll mail it to Manny with an explanation.

Except . . .

What explanation does one give to an eight-year-old boy upon deserting him?

"Elizabeth?"

She jumps at the sound of her name, turning to see a man standing behind her.

He's big and tall enough to easily overpower her, and his face is partly hidden behind a pair of sunglasses.

Her impulse is to scream, to run from the stranger . . .

But then she realizes that it isn't a stranger after all.

It's Harper Smith.

Harper Smith, whose sex appeal was partly responsible for her sleepless night.

"Hi," he says, grinning so that those familiar dimples appear on either side of his generous mouth.

And all she can think about, suddenly, is what it would be like to feel those lips on hers.

Then she manages to say "Hi," trying to sound casual.

As though she isn't consumed by lust.

And fear.

As though she isn't a fugitive movie star being stalked by the psycho who forced her to fake her death five years ago.

"How did those locks work out for you?"

"Locks . . . ? Oh, um, they . . . you know . . . they're fine."

"How did those locks work out. God, that was a stupid question," he says with a slightly sheepish grin.

"Not for a locksmith." She can't help grinning back.

She finds herself wishing she weren't wearing this worn pair of jeans and a simple white Gap T-shirt, and that her hair wasn't pulled back in a casual ponytail fastened with a plain old elastic band.

"On your way to the post office?" he asks.

She nods.

"I'm just coming from there. Actually, I just sent you your bill."

"You could have saved yourself a stamp if we'd run into each other two minutes earlier," she tells him.

"Oh, well. It won't break me." He shrugs good-naturedly, then adds, "and neither will two cups of coffee at the Sailboat Cafe. What do you say?"

It takes her a moment to realize he's asking her out, more or less.

She's so taken aback that she can't think of a single thing to say but "Okay."

"I'll wait here while you go into the post office, if you want."

"Um . . . no. No, that's all right. I can come back later."

She doesn't want anything to delay this . . . this . . . whatever it is that's happening between her and this man.

And she doesn't want to risk letting anything ruin it. If there's another sinister greeting card in her post office box, or a package without a return address . . .

Well, she doesn't need to know about it until after.

She will allow herself this one stolen interlude with Harper Smith. A cup of coffee in the Sailboat Cafe. And that's it.

After that he'll be out of her life, and she'll be leaving town. . . .

She finds herself walking beside him along North Main Street, laughing as he jokes about the eager, bargain-hunting crowds at the sidewalk sale down the block.

How long has it been since she laughed out loud?

Years?

God, it feels good to walk down a sun-splashed street with a good-looking man at her side and the salt breeze in her hair.

She can almost forget that she's there on borrowed time. . . .

That someone wants her dead.

Dark thoughts keep trying to shove their way back into her mind, but for once she won't let them intrude.

She sits at a small, round table and watches Harper go up to the counter for two coffees. He returns with a couple of shortbread cut-out cookies.

"Mmm, you have to try this," he says after taking a big bite of one.

"No, thanks, I'm really not hun—"

"No, I mean you *have* to taste it." He offers it to her, holding it right in front of her mouth, and she bites into the crumbly, butter-rich cookie before stopping to think.

About the wisdom of accepting food from a man who, though she's instinctively all but ruled him out, could be the person who tried to kill her five years ago . . .

Or about the intimacy in the gesture—that he, a virtual stranger, is sharing his cookie with her, as though they've known each other forever, as though they're . . .

Lovers.

"What do you think?"

"Excuse me?"

"Is that a great cookie, or what?"

"It is," she says belatedly, chewing, swallowing. "It's delicious."

"I've been hooked on them ever since I moved to Windemere Cove. I come in here every day and buy a couple. Nellie won't give me her recipe."

"Nellie?"

"The owner—see the lady wearing the glasses and the red T-shirt, back behind the counter? That's Nellie. I'm surprised you haven't met her. She's the kind of person who knows every customer by name. How long have you lived here again?"

Has she told him? She doesn't remember.

Her guard goes up.

"A few years," she says cautiously, "but I hardly ever come in here."

"Well, I bet you'll start, now that you've tasted that cookie. Here, take the rest of it."

She smiles stiffly and accepts it, taking another small bite.

She has left her sunglasses on though they're inside; if he thinks anything odd of that, he doesn't say it.

His own sunglasses are off, and she notices that his green eyes are the color of the ocean on an overcast day. They're honest eyes . . . aren't they? Kind eyes.

Not the eyes of a murderer.

"What's the matter?" he asks, and she realizes he's caught her staring at him.

"Nothing," she says quickly. "I was just thinking . . ."

"That I look familiar? Because I keep thinking the same thing, ever since I saw you last night. And I still can't figure out where we've seen each other before."

"Probably on the street. It's a small town."

"I guess," he muses in a tone that makes it clear he isn't quite convinced that's the case.

And she's reassured by that, because if he were the one who has been stalking her, he wouldn't sit there telling her she looks familiar. He wouldn't want her to suspect that he knows her true identity.

She realizes he's asking her something.

"Pardon?" she says stupidly, then says, "I'm sorry. It's not that I'm deliberately not paying attention, it's just that I'm . . . I guess I'm really tired."

"Didn't sleep well last night?"

Her head snaps up.

How did he know that?

Oh.

*Because you just told him you're really tired, you idiot.*

*Relax and talk to him like a normal human being.*

Well, that would be a lot easier if she *were* a normal human being, instead of living the life of a paranoid recluse.

"What I asked before," Harper is saying patiently, "is what you like to do in your spare time."

"Oh . . . read. And . . . sew. I sew. . . ." She tries to think of something else, something that won't be a total lie.

"So you're not the outdoorsy type?" he asks. "Not into Rollerblades or sailing or hiking or anything?"

Long ago . . .

So long ago, she had enjoyed all of those things. But now . . .

"Me? No. No, I guess I'm not really the outdoorsy type. Are you?"

"I like to work out, yeah. I ski . . ."

"Water or snow?"

"Both."

She nods.

"And I run a few miles every morning, to stay in shape from all these cookies."

She smiles.

There's a pause.

"Do you go out much?" he asks.

"What do you mean?"

He gives her a slightly puzzled look, then clarifies, "You know, with friends, out dancing, or playing pool . . . that kind of thing."

"Not very often." She does her best not to sound wistful.

It's just that the way he's talking to her, the way a man talks to a woman when he's interested in getting to know her . . .

It's making her remember exactly what she has given up in her life. There was a time when she had friends, when she went out, when she loved to drink margaritas and flirt and dance until the wee hours. And then there were the gala events, the glitzy Holly-wood fund-raisers, the premieres . . .

"What about the movies?"

"What about them?" she asks, startled, like he's read her mind.

"Do you go?"

*I used to star in them.*

"Sure, I go. . . ."

*Just not in the past five years.*

"What kind of movies do you like?"

"Oh . . . all kinds, I guess," she says warily, taking a drink from the hot mug of coffee.

"Have you seen *The Invasion* yet?"

She shakes her head, thinking she must be the only person on earth who hasn't seen the extraterrestrial blockbuster hit of the summer; she's been reading about it for two months now.

"You're kidding," he says, but not like he's suspicious, rather . . . pleasantly surprised. "How about going with me, then, Elizabeth? Later on tonight? We could—"

"I can't," she cuts in before she can find herself doing something absolutely insane . . .

Like saying yes.

Because his invitation is so incredibly tempting, and she realizes that she would like nothing more than to sit in a darkened movie theater with this man, munching popcorn and watching a movie—*not* at a premiere or a private screening, but at a regular movie theater with regular people. People who aren't bitter because they weren't cast in *The Invasion*, who haven't worked with the director, who didn't have a hand in financing the picture.

It would be so different to see a movie now that she's no longer in the industry, such pure pleasure, but . . .

"Another night, then?" Harper asks, looking only slightly disap-pointed at her refusal.

"Why not," she says with a shrug, sipping her coffee.

Because it's easier than telling him the truth—that there will be no other night.

"Great. I'll call you."

She realizes that he has her number; she gave it to him when she first called him about changing her locks.

But it doesn't matter. She won't be there when he calls.

"Unless," he says, as though he's suddenly realized something, "you're seeing somebody else?"

Her stomach flutters, dammit. He's romantically interested in her, and she wishes, oh, how she wishes . . .

"No, I'm not seeing anybody," she tells him because he's waiting.

"Good. Then I'll call you," he repeats.

"You know," she blurts out, shoving her chair back and bracing her hands on the table, about to stand, "I have to get going."

"No, you don't." He places a hand on hers.

Taken aback, she flinches, looks at him to see whether he meant it ominously.

Because despite his kind green eyes and her own fierce attraction to him, she still can't shake the fear that he isn't what he seems, or the memory of the way he hedged when she asked him about his background last night.

But his grip on her hand is gentle, and he's smiling. "Don't go yet, Elizabeth. At least finish your coffee."

"I really can't. I have a lot to do." She had told Manny she would look for him in the park, though now she desperately wants only to go home, to hide.

"Are you sure you have to go?"

"I'm positive," she tells Harper, and adds vaguely, "We'll get together again soon. . . ."

*But only in my restless dreams.*

"Damn," he says, releasing her hand, snapping his fingers, and shaking his head. "I'm never going to see you again, am I?"

*How does he know?*

A chill slips down her spine, though she realizes again that he hasn't read her mind. He can't know that she's about to leave town.

"You finally meet a beautiful woman and you want to get to know her better," he says as if to himself, "and you can't seem to get it through your thick head that she's not interested."

Elizabeth doesn't know what to say.

"I'm sorry," he says, looking at her. "It's just that . . . I guess I read you wrong. It's obvious you want nothing to do with me—"

"That's not true. I—"

"Look, you don't have to—"

"No, really," she says, somehow unable to help herself. "It's not that I don't—I mean, I *do* want . . ."

She trails off, wishing he'd interrupt her again.

But this time he's waiting for her to finish her sentence, and when she doesn't, he prods, "You do want . . . what?"

"I want to see you again," she says in a small voice, not looking at him.

"You do?"

She nods, still afraid to meet his gaze.

"Maybe it's just me, but I can't help feeling like you really have a funny way of showing your affection."

She smiles. "I'm sorry. Like I said, I didn't get much sleep last night, and . . . I don't know. I guess I'm just not myself."

*Truer words have never been spoken,* she thinks ruefully.

"Oh, right," he says, nodding. "The break-in. I forgot all about that. No wonder. Did the police find out who did it?"

She shakes her head.

"Are you afraid to be alone tonight? Because I can . . ."

*Don't tempt me, please.*

". . . give you some pepper spray, if that'll help you to feel safer."

Oh.

For a moment she had thought he was going to volunteer to come spend the night, the way Frank had.

But Frank is a neighbor, and a cop.

This man is a virtual stranger. It would hardly be appropriate for him to offer to stay at her place. . . .

Even if the merest notion of spending the night with him has already filled her mind with disturbing images.

Images of Harper Smith naked, in her bed, of herself lying in his bare, muscular arms, feeling safe for the first time in years . . .

"I can tell by the look on your face that you're not exactly turned on by the idea of pepper spray," he comments.

She feels her cheeks grow hot. If he only knew what *is* turning her on . . .

"Well, that's understandable. The problem with any weapon is that the attacker can turn it on you."

*Or they can surprise you so that you don't have time to reach for your weapon,* she thinks, remembering the pistol she'd had tucked in the drawer of her nightstand back in Malibu.

"Well, maybe you can get a dog," Harper suggests.

She freezes.

A dog.

She'd had a dog once, a big, lovable black Lab named Gent.

That was short for "Gentleman." Because that was the dog's

nature. He never jumped on the furniture or slobbered or got in the way. He was a perfect dog.

And she had come home one day to find him lying stiffly on the living room floor, his throat slit, his blood soaked into the white carpet. . . .

"What's the matter? You don't like dogs?" Harper is asking.

She forces herself to look at him, to shake her head mutely.

"Personally, I love them. Anyway, listen, Elizabeth," he says, "I know you're probably jumpy after what happened . . ."

*Jumpy.*

The understatement of the year.

". . . but chances are that whoever broke into your place yesterday won't try it again. And even if they do, those new locks I installed are the best you can buy. Nobody's going to be able to force their way in now."

She finally manages to speak. "I know."

He goes on, telling her more about the dead bolts he installed, about how they work, obviously trying to reassure her that she has nothing to worry about.

She can't help thinking, *if you only knew* . . .

And then, for some bizarre reason, it crosses her mind suddenly that maybe she should simply . . .

Tell him the truth.

All of it.

About who she is, and what she's doing here, and why she can't let herself go out with him . . .

Or fall in love with him.

*No. That's impossible. You can't tell him anything. You've got to get out of there. . . .*

She bites down hard on her lip to quell the crazy instinct to spill her secret, and the second he pauses in his conversation, she stands and tells him she has to go.

This time he doesn't argue.

Just tells her he'll give her a call, and they'll catch that movie some night this week.

"That sounds great," she says simply. "Thank you for the coffee. And the cookie."

"My pleasure. I'll be seeing you."

*No,* she thinks as she heads for the door, *you won't.*

And she realizes, as she hurries back down North Main toward the post office, that she's filled with an inexplicably profound sense of loss.

The nightmare has come back.

It always does.

The woman tosses on the lumpy mattress, moaning in her sleep, trying to escape the image of the child.

Her child.

A child with large, pleading eyes . . .

A child with a frantic, sobbing voice . . .

*Please don't hurt me anymore, Mama. Please don't hurt me. I didn't do anything bad. Why are you hurting me?*

She stands over the cowering child, her body taut with anger, her throat raw from screaming curses.

But gradually, the fury melts away, and she can't remember why it was there in the first place.

She opens her mouth to speak, to say that she never meant to hurt anyone, especially this beautiful, vulnerable creature, her own flesh and blood.

But her voice is gone.

She can't make a sound.

And then the tables are turning.

And she's the one on the floor, trying to shrink into a corner as the child's cruel fists beat down violently on her own tender flesh.

She's the one sobbing; yet still, nothing is coming out of her mouth.

And now the child is turning away, walking away, without a backward glance.

And the woman is left behind, desperately trying to call out, to stop the child from leaving her.

Alone.

Abandoned.

# chapter

# 6

"You're doing a great job, Manny. Keep it up."

The child smiles at his day camp counselor, Rhonda, a pretty high school girl with long, shiny brown hair. She's not as pretty as Elizabeth, and her hair is a lighter shade, but Rhonda kind of reminds Manny of her anyway.

She always takes the time to talk to Manny, and she told him she was rooting for him to get the lead in the play. She's the assistant director, and today, all through rehearsal, she kept catching his eye and nodding her approval.

"How are your costumes coming along?" Rhonda asks him, still in step at his side as they head away from the park pavilion where rehearsals are held.

"Fine," Manny says. At least, he's sure they're coming along fine. Elizabeth said she would make them for him, and she would never say it if she didn't mean it.

She's the only person Manny has ever trusted not to let him down.

He's keeping his eye out for her as they walk along the path. She had said she might come to the park yesterday, but she hadn't shown up. Maybe she'll be around today. He'll come back a little later to look for her if it doesn't rain.

It's been cloudy all day, for the first time in weeks, and everybody's been saying that it's supposed to storm out this afternoon. Manny is praying that it won't, because if it rains, Elizabeth won't come, and he really needs to see her.

"So, is your grandmother using a pattern to make the costumes?" Rhonda asks, brushing a damp tendril of hair away from her flushed cheeks. It's uncomfortably warm today, the kind of weather where you don't feel like moving around much.

"Uh, my grandmother isn't making them," Manny tells her. "My friend is doing it for me."

"Oh. That's nice."

"Yeah." Manny can't think of anything else to say to Rhonda, but that's okay, because they've reached the fork in the path, and she says good-bye and heads in the opposite direction, just as he'd known she would.

A girl like Rhonda wouldn't live in Manny's neighborhood. She probably lives in The Bay, a gated community outside of town, by the water.

Or maybe over in the historical district downtown, in one of the big three-story houses with a plaque by the door saying what year it was built. According to those plaques, some of the houses in Windemere Cove have been around for three hundred years.

Manny's grandparents' house is old too—but not in a *good* way, like so many New England landmarks. It's pretty much falling apart, and last night he heard Grammy telling Grampa that the front steps are all rotted and they need to be fixed, or someone's going to break their neck.

But Grampa can't fix the steps now that his heart is so bad. And Manny heard him telling Grammy that he can't afford to hire someone to do it either.

Manny wishes he had some money to give them.

He wishes, too, that he didn't have to live with them, because he knows that the money they spend taking care of him could be used to fix up their house and maybe even to hire a better doctor to take care of Grampa's heart and Grammy's arthritis.

He wonders how they would really feel if his mother came and took him away.

He figures they might miss him a little, because they do act like they care about him. But maybe they would mostly be relieved that they wouldn't have to take care of him anymore. Maybe, if his mother asked them, they would say she could take him away.

The last thing he wants is to go live with his mother. The very image of her scary, bony face makes him shudder.

He keeps remembering what she said—that she's his mother and she can take him anywhere she wants.

*Well, you don't have to go with her. You can run away before she comes to get you.*

But what about Elizabeth?

He could never leave Elizabeth.

She's been so kind to him. How would she feel if he disappeared? That wouldn't be fair to her.

So running away is out of the question.

Manny walks slowly toward the house he shares with his grandparents.

When he gets there, nobody's home.

A note on the table says that Grammy has taken Grampa to the doctor for a checkup.

Manny opens the refrigerator, hungry.

He finds half a piece of cheese left in the meat compartment, and a jar of Grammy's home-made pickles. He wishes they could have regular store-bought pickles, the kind he's had at his friends' houses. But Grammy cans her own, from cucumbers she buys by the bushel at the farmer's market. They're soggy and too sour, but Manny's stomach is so hollow that he eats four of them, along with the cheese and a big glass of water.

Still feeling hungry, Manny goes out back to his grandfather's shed for some scrap wood, a hammer, and some nails.

Then he sets to work, determined to fix the front steps.

"Gretchen? I'm home, honey."

She looks up from the murder mystery she's reading and murmurs, "Hi."

"How was your day?"

"Fine," she says tersely, and asks, because she knows it's expected, "How was yours?"

"Not so great. I lost a patient. Mrs. Alderson."

"Isn't she the woman who just turned a hundred and one years old?"

"That's her."

"Well, I guess she had to die sooner or later, don't you think?"

Her mother shrugs, opens her mouth as if to say something, and then closes it again.

She turns and goes down the long hall to her own room, the white shoes of her nurse's uniform almost silent on the hardwood floor.

Gretchen looks back at her book, then sticks her finger between the pages and closes it, staring out the window at the cloudy August afternoon.

Outside, in the next yard, the neighbors' three kids are playing on their wooden swingset despite the oppressive heat. They've been out there all day, every day, ever since school got out in June. You would think kids would get tired of the same thing day in, day out.

Lord knows, Gretchen does.

Every night when she gets into the twin bed in her childhood bedroom, she thinks that she'll go crazy if she has to face another day just like the one before.

Her mother will flutter around her, trying to interest her in some inane conversation about the garden or the weather or one of her patients at the nursing home.

Gretchen will listen politely, eager for her mother to go off to work so that she can be left alone.

Alone to stare out the window, or at the television, or into the pages of a book . . .

To look at anything but a mirror.

Her room at home is almost exactly the way Gretchen left it when she moved to Los Angeles after high school graduation back in eighty-eight. The walls are still a pale lemon color, the carpet still off-white. The same frilly white priscillas hang at the two windows; the same yellow-rose-flowered chinz spread is on the same too-soft mattress on the same maple bed.

Only one thing has changed.

On the wall between the closet door and the window is the faint outline of a rectangle where the paint is a slightly deeper shade of yellow than the rest of the walls.

That's where the full-length mirror used to hang—the antique mahogany-framed looking-glass that had once belonged to Great-Grandmother Dodd.

Over the years, that mirror had reflected Gretchen in her Brownie uniform and in prom dresses and in her cap and gown on graduation day.

Now it's gone.

Where it is, Gretchen has no clue. Nor does she care whether her mother sold it at a yard sale or stashed it in the drafty old attic.

The rest of the slightly ramshackle Queen Anne Victorian is the same as it was when Gretchen left it nearly a decade ago.

Except, again, for a few minor changes.

Down the hall, in the bathroom, the mirrored door has been removed from the medicine cabinet over the sink.

And in the foyer downstairs there is no longer a large mirror hanging on the door of the coat closet.

Gretchen's mother is taking no chances.

The curtains are drawn throughout the house long before dark so that the windows won't accidentally betray a reflection.

Even the trusty old stainless steel toaster that always sat on the kitchen counter has been replaced, so that there's no possibility of Gretchen accidentally glimpsing herself in its shiny surface.

Gretchen looked into a mirror once, about five years ago, not long after it happened. She was still in L.A. then, still in the hospital where she had been rushed from Mallory Eden's Malibu mansion after that basket of flowers had exploded in her hands.

She had gotten out of her hospital bed in the middle of the night, and she had shakily wheeled her IV stand into the small adjoining bathroom. She had peeled off the bandages in the dark, wincing at the raw, stinging pain but unwilling or unable to stop until she saw what had been done to her.

Finally, the bandages removed, she had turned on the light, and . . .

*Screamed.*

Screamed so long and so loud that nurses had come running from every direction, screamed so hysterically that they had sedated her.

They must have, because she later remembered someone rushing at her with a needle, and then blessed silence and darkness for a long time afterward.

If only she didn't remember the rest of it . . .

What she'd seen in the mirror.

Her face . . .

The face that had once caused a stranger on a bus in L.A. to hand her a business card and tell her to call about modeling opportunities . . .

Her face was . . .

*Gone.*

She had become a monster, a hideous monster doomed to live the rest of her life in seclusion. There is no money for the kind of plastic surgery this kind of damage would demand.

Gretchen knows. She had met with Dr. Reed Dalton before she'd been released from Cedars Sinai. Rumored to be the finest plastic surgeon in the world, he had brusquely told her what it would cost for him to even attempt to reconstruct her face.

If she and her mother had saved every penny they'd ever earned in their lives, they would still have only a fraction of the money.

Her mother had written a letter to Mallory, asking if she would consider helping pay for the plastic surgery.

There had been no response.

And then, not long after the letter had been sent, Mallory had taken her own life.

And so Gretchen had allowed her mother to take her back to her eastern Connecticut hometown. There was no place else for her to go. Nothing left for her in Los Angeles, where beautiful faces are as common as palm trees and cellular phones.

She had hoped to become an actress.

She was well on her way, when that bomb destroyed her life.

She had already done a couple of commercials—one for toothpaste and two for hair products. She'd landed a decent agent and hired a reputable acting coach; she had a terrific apartment in West Lake Village, loads of friends, and a boyfriend.

She also had the most amazing job a would-be actress could hope for.

Personal assistant to Mallory Eden.

She had gotten the job through her agent, who had mentioned to her that the client of a colleague was looking to hire a new assistant, and was she possibly interested?

Great pay, flexible hours. Was she interested? Was he kidding?

She didn't find out until she went on the interview that the client was one of the most prominent actresses in Hollywood.

Malloy Eden had been barefoot and makeup-free that day. Gretchen later discovered that her new boss was always that down-to-earth at home, away from the spotlight. She had grown not only to respect her, but to really like her.

That was *before* the explosion that changed everything.

*You should have known better.*

How many times has Gretchen cursed herself for continuing to work for Mallory after the violent attack on her boss?

*You should have known that anyone connected to her might be in danger, that the Eden household couldn't be the safest place in the world in those days after Mallory was shot.*

How could she have been so blind, so stupid?

*It wasn't your fault.*

*Mallory should have warned you that you might be in danger. She should have sent you home when you showed up for work that day.*

*Mallory's fault.*

Rage courses through Gretchen as the familiar refrain fills her tormented mind.

*Mallory's fault.*

It's all Mallory's fault. . . .

The last thing Elizabeth wants to do is go to the park.

But she didn't show up the day before yesterday, even though she had told Manny she would try.

She just couldn't.

After leaving Harper Smith, she had impulsively gone straight home.

No post office.

No park.

She had found her house just as she had left it, but that doesn't mean the threat has gone away. It doesn't mean someone isn't watching her every move, waiting until the time is right to . . .

So.

Today, the park.

And afterward, the post office.

She hurries along the path toward the playground, wishing the sun were shining and the sky were blue. Nice weather would be reassuring somehow.

But the late-summer afternoon is humid and overcast, with ominously dark, low clouds way out on the horizon over the water. It's one of those New England days when the whole world seems depressingly monochromatic. Nothing but gray, no matter where you look.

The meteorologist on the radio that morning had said there's actually a chance of thunderstorms today.

"And to all you folks who are disappointed about missing a ball game or a picnic: Remember that this is one of the driest summers on record. Heaven knows we need the rain," she had commented brightly before the program went back to the news announcer, who had followed up with a story about the severe water shortage in the East Bay area.

Elizabeth rounds a bend in the path and sees that the playground is deserted.

That's not surprising on a day like this.

Except . . .

One of the swings is swaying slowly back and forth, as though someone had been there just a moment before.

But that's impossible.

Nobody passed Elizabeth on the path, and it's the only route into and out of the playground area, which is surrounded by dense woods.

The swing is still moving, its chain making a slight squeaking sound.

Maybe it's the wind, Elizabeth thinks, staring at it.

But there's no wind; the muggy air is hushed with the kind of stillness that precedes a summer thunderstorm.

And besides, only one of the swings is moving.

Her heart begins to pound.

Maybe, since she saw no one on the path, a child jumped off the swing and ducked into the woods.

Her eyes flit slowly along the overgrown screen of foliage surrounding the edge of the playground.

And slowly, an eerie sensation steals over her.

Someone is watching her from behind those trees.

She's certain of it.

"Manny?" she calls, her voice sounding hollow to her own ears. "Is that you?"

*Please let it be Manny. Please let him be playing a little joke on me. . . .*

But Manny isn't a mischievous child, and he's never hidden on her before.

*It's your imagination. There's no one there.*

Elizabeth turns abruptly and starts walking away from the playground and the swing, her sneakered feet crunching loudly on the gravel path.

So loudly that she doesn't hear the footsteps behind her until a split second before an icy hand grips her bare arm.

*       *       *

### Casting Director Seeks the New Mallory Eden!

The bold headline leaps out at Flynn Soderland.

He sits upright in his chaise longue and adjusts his prescription sunglasses, scanning the full-page ad in today's issue of *Variety*.

It's a publicity gimmick, of course, for a new romantic comedy to be directed by Martin de Lisser. The man had been a virtual unknown until last year, when his low-budget independent caused a sensation at Sundance, then wound up winning several Golden Globes and, ultimately, an Academy Award for Best Picture.

Now Hollywood's newest golden boy, who's rumored to be all of thirty-two, has a deal with Paramount, and, according to the ad, is hoping to cast an unknown in the lead role of his new film.

Flynn has heard the buzz about this particular casting call for weeks; it's the same old story.

There'll be all kinds of media hoopla showcasing the hopeful unknowns who will storm the auditions, and in the end some fairly well-known Name will be cast . . . if she hasn't secretly already been.

"Mallory Eden would have been perfect for this film," de Lisser is quoted as saying. "I need someone who can somehow fill her shoes—someone who has that rare combination of dazzling beauty and zany sense of humor."

Flynn shakes his head, folds the paper, and tosses it onto the flagstone poolside patio.

He lights a cigarette, leans back, and closes his eyes, enjoying the warmth of the sun on his face.

It's amazing that in a town where today's hottest starlet will be yesterday's news at midnight, his former client hasn't been allowed to die a natural death after five years. Mallory Eden has been transformed into a true Hollywood legend, along with Monroe, Dean, and a handful of others who died young, at the height of their fame.

*I need someone who can fill her shoes.*

"Don't we all," Flynn mutters.

If she had lived, Mallory Eden would have been his ticket to immortality. . . .

Or, at least, to a very cushy retirement.

Just another year or two of Mallory Eden commissions, and he could have bought himself a villa in Monte Cristo or perhaps a small island in the South Pacific.

*You could have had it all, anyway, if you had played your cards right,* he reminds himself.

If not for those weekly trips to Vegas, he would now be wealthy beyond his wildest dreams.

But he had thrown away millions over the course of his career, thanks to gambling and booze.

Flynn drags deeply on his cigarette.

That last year of Mallory's life—his most successful ever, financially—had mostly been a blur.

He hadn't even realized he was in deep trouble when his star client took him aside and told him that if he didn't straighten out, she was going to fire him as her agent.

"But you can't fire me," he had told Mallory, bewildered. "I got you to where you are today."

*And you got me to where I am today*, he had added silently.

They both knew that if she fired him, it would be all over for his career.

"I'll do what I have to do, Flynn," she had said grimly. "You're going down fast, and believe me, you're not going to take me with you. I've worked too hard to get where I am."

He had begged her for another chance, and she—caught up in her own personal drama created by the stalking—had given it to him.

Still, he somehow hadn't realized how serious his problem was.

Not then, and not when rumors started circulating in Hollywood that Mallory was secretly shopping around for a new agent.

Not even when he started waking up in strange places, with memory blanks. There were entire weekends, at times, when he simply couldn't account for his whereabouts or his actions. There were times when he knew he'd been beaten or robbed by the men he'd picked up, and still he didn't stop.

That was a long, hot, harrowing summer.

But by mid-August he had finally started to believe that maybe it really was time to turn himself around, to get people to take him seriously again.

Mallory's death had been the catalyst he needed.

He had joined AA and Gamblers Anonymous the week after her funeral. Got himself tested for HIV and found, miraculously, that he'd managed to escape the virus.

He'd been clean and behaving himself for five years now, with just occasional lapses . . .

Until recently.

"Back on the sauce, huh? I knew it was only a matter of time." That was how one of his favorite Vegas bartenders had greeted him the first time he ventured back to his beloved town last winter.

Since then he's made the trip across the desert at least a dozen times. But Flynn has promised himself that it won't be a regular thing—that he isn't going to revert to his old ways. He never wants to see his life spin out of control that way again, with the endless booze, the reckless gambling, the dangerous random sex.

But just yesterday he woke up in a dumpy apartment in West Hollywood, a gorgeous stranger asleep next to him. He was a beautiful boy, couldn't have been more than twenty, his cheeks baby smooth, without the slightest hint of a bearded shadow.

*Just how you always liked them.*

Flynn still hasn't the foggiest notion where he and the stranger had found each other or what they had done—and he hadn't stuck around to find out. He knows only that he'd had a monster hangover, and that his wallet is missing the two thousand dollars in cash he'd had when he'd gone out the night before.

If he isn't careful, he's going to lose everything this time.

Everything.

He turns his head and opens his eyes to look up at his sprawling stucco Spanish-style house with its red tile roof and arched windows and doorways. Perched high in the Hollywood Hills off Mulholland Drive, on impeccably landscaped, terraced acreage, his home had once belonged to a silent film star, a forties screen goddess, and the lead guitarist of a world-renowned heavy metal rock band.

There's the customary pool and tennis courts, but also a private screening room, a gym, and a greenhouse where Flynn used to grow his prize orchids. The property has a majestic view of the city off in the distance—and, in the foreground, of the infamous mansion that had formerly been owned by Madonna. Parked in Flynn's three-car garage are his Jaguar convertible, his Mercedes, and his Bentley.

Not bad for a kid who had grown up in a cold-water walk-up in the midst of Depression-era Baltimore.

After spending the war years stationed at some dinky Texas naval base, he had moved to Los Angeles intent on becoming an actor, until a casting director did him a favor after his first audition and told him, bluntly, that he sucked.

Flynn had bounced back from that the way he'd bounced back from his mother's death in a car accident when he was ten, and from his alcoholic father's brutal beatings throughout his childhood.

He had simply, quite resourcefully, set aside his illusions of how his life should be, and he had gone on.

If he couldn't be an actor, he would find some other way to get rich in Los Angeles.

Because he sure as hell wasn't going to be poor the rest of his life, and he wasn't going to spend it in Baltimore.

His destiny was sealed the day he answered an ad and landed a job in the mail room at the famed William Morris Agency.

*Maybe you should go back,* he tells himself idly, closing his eyes again.

Not, of course, back to William Morris. Decades earlier, he'd had a highly publicized falling out with the agency's powers-that-be. After that he had branched off on his own, amid insiders' predictions that he would never make it.

*You did it once . . . you can do it again.*

Maybe it's time to come out of retirement, get back into the swing of things. Lure back a few former clients and start collecting commission checks again.

*Anything you can make now would be a drop in the bucket compared to what Mallory could have brought you. . . .*

But the whole world knows Mallory has been dead for five years now.

Didn't he commemorate her death just the other day at his annual lunch with Rae Hamilton?

Rae Hamilton.

*Casting agent seeks the new Mallory Eden.*

Hmm.

Flynn reaches toward a glass-topped table at his side, stubs out his cigarette in the crystal ashtray, and picks up his cellular phone.

Harper hears a rumble in the distance, puts down his roast beef sandwich—rare, and dripping mayonnaise and ketchup, just the way he likes it—and goes to the small kitchen window to look outside.

There's a decent view of the bay from this apartment above his small shop on Center Street—which is one of the few positive things the ramshackle place has going for it. Aside from the view, there's a fireplace in the bedroom—not that it works—and a built-in bookshelf in the living room, which would be useful if he had any books.

But his books are in storage in Los Angeles, along with most of his worldly possessions. He had left abruptly, no time to sort through his belongings to decide what should stay and what should come with him. He had arrived in Windemere Cove with little more than the clothes on his back and the tools to set up his locksmith business.

The fewer reminders of L.A., and what had happened there, the better.

Harper notes that the water has gone from a pale bluish-gray to a dark greenish-gray, and a slight breeze seems to have kicked up, driving the dark clouds closer to shore.

Can it be that it's actually going to storm, after what seems like years without rain?

Harper remembers that he left the windows open on the van when he returned from that morning's job over in Warren, where he had fixed the lock on a church collection box that had been tampered with.

With a sigh he heads down the steep staircase leading from the kitchen to a small vestibule behind his shop. He steps out the back door and crosses to his van, which is parked on the dirt driveway that runs alongside the building.

Another rumble of thunder causes him to look up at the darkening sky.

No rain yet, but it looks like it's coming.

There's no discernible breeze yet either.

The air is motionless; it's as though everything around him is poised—the thirsty trees and parched grass and dusty earth—waiting for the promised torrents of cool, cleansing water.

Harper swiftly rolls up the windows on the van and heads back to the house. Just before stepping inside, he pauses with his hand on the knob and looks up at the sky again.

Rain would be a refreshing relief from these dog days of August.

Yet he feels apprehensive.

And it isn't because of the approaching storm.

He wonders where Elizabeth Baxter is now, whether she, too, is watching the darkening sky with a sense of trepidation.

Harper goes up the stairs, lifts the receiver of the old-fashioned rotary-dial wall telephone in the kitchen, and dials the number he's committed to memory.

It rings once, twice, three times.

He frowns.

She isn't home . . .

Or she isn't answering.

He continues to let it ring long after he's sure she won't answer, staring absently out the window, his hand clenched on the receiver.

\* \* \*

"Looking for someone?"

Elizabeth spins to see a stranger, a woman, whose painful grip on her arm tightens as they come face-to-face.

Too numb to speak, Elizabeth can only look at her. She sees the woman's skeletal frame, her gaunt features, her lifeless hair that appears to have been hacked off without regard for consistent length, much less style. Her eyes are bottomless black, and filled with wrath.

"What are you doing here?" the woman asks, her question punctuated by a distant roll of thunder.

Elizabeth struggles to find her voice, to respond somehow, and all the while her mind is racing.

Who is this person?

Was this woman the masked attacker who shot her in her Malibu bedroom five years ago?

Is she the one who sent the flowers that maimed Gretchen Dodd . . .

And the card that just days ago had plunged Elizabeth right back into her nightmarish past?

Or is she just some deranged homeless person who's going to demand Elizabeth's wallet or rough her up?

"You know, he isn't here." The woman practically spits the words at her.

And all at once Elizabeth is carried back over the years to the Nebraska farmhouse, to a time when she had huddled on the floor as an angry, bitter woman stood over her, cursing her, hurting her with words and then with fists.

Could this woman be . . .

Her mother?

"He isn't here," she bites out again, her nails digging into Elizabeth's flesh.

"Who isn't here?" Elizabeth finally manages to ask, surprised that her question comes out coherent. Fear is screeching through her mind, drowning all reason.

*It's my mother. It's her. She's back. She's going to hurt me again. . . .*

*Please, please don't hurt me,* begs the little-girl voice in her mind.

"Don't play dumb with me, you bitch."

"I'm not—"

"He *was* here, you know. Waiting for you. But then I came along, and do you know what he did?"

She shakes her head, trembling.

"He ran away. And it's all your fault."

"I don't know what you're talking about," Elizabeth says, trying desperately to keep her tone level, reasonable.

Trying to convince herself that this isn't her mother. It can't be. This woman is too young, too short. . . .

But who is she, then?

And what is she talking about?

Elizabeth glances frantically around the deserted clearing.

If only someone would come along . . .

But no one is going to show up at the playground now, when it's about to rain.

"I *said*, don't play dumb with me. I know who you are. I know what you're up to."

*I know who you are.*

What does she mean by that?

Elizabeth focuses on the woman's face, searching her ravaged features, finding blatant animosity.

"You listen to me," she says, tightening her hold on Elizabeth's aching arm. There is surprising strength in her bony hand. "You stay away from my son. Do you hear me?"

"Your . . . your son?"

"He's *mine*. Leave him alone. If you don't, you'll be sorry. I mean it, bitch. You'll be sorry."

Slowly, the truth dawns on Elizabeth.

"Are you talking about Manny?" she asks the hostile stranger, and the glint in the woman's eye answers her question before she speaks.

"What the hell is the matter with you? Of course I'm talking about Manny. You stay away from my kid! You can't take him away from me, you got that?"

She nods, and, taking a chance, jerks her shoulder in an abrupt, twisting motion. To her surprise, the woman releases her grasp on Elizabeth, who impulsively, in that instant, decides against running away.

"I didn't hear you say anything," the woman says. "You understand what I'm saying?"

"I understand," Elizabeth says, rubbing her throbbing arm. "But I'm not trying to take him away from you. I'm just his friend. That's all."

"Don't you stand there and lie to me. You can't fool me."

"I'm not—"

"Shut up!" The bony hand reaches out again, this time cracking Elizabeth across the cheek.

"Remember what I said. If you don't leave him alone, you'll be sorry, and he'll be sorry," the woman snarls, then turns and starts to run, disappearing into the woods at the edge of the path.


Manny steps over a gaping hole on the front steps on his way to the door. His earlier attempt to fix them had been futile. He simply had no idea how to go about it.

"Manny? Is that you?"

So they're home.

He had been hoping they would still be at the doctor's office so he wouldn't have to talk to anyone. He needs to be alone, to calm himself down after what happened at the playground.

"Hi, Grammy." He pokes his head into the kitchen.

His grandmother is standing at the stove. She's wearing a plaid sleeveless housedress that reveals her flabby white arms and her vein-covered legs clad in knee-highs and those shoes with the broken soles. She's poking a spatula at something in her battered old cast-iron pan. More weeds, probably.

"Do you want some cardoon?" she asks, confirming his suspicions.

"No," he says, though he's so hungry, his stomach has been grumbling. He's always hungry. Always.

He had been hoping to see Elizabeth in the park, hoping she would take him out for an ice cream cone the way she often does, urging him to get the triple scoop, asking if he wants anything else afterward. Sometimes, if she presses him enough, he'll order a strawberry-banana milk shake to go, even when he's so full, he's bursting.

A milk shake, after all, can be stashed in his grandparents' old frost-layered freezer to be finished later, or even the next day.

Today he hadn't had the chance to see Elizabeth.

When he'd arrived at the playground, *she* had been there.

His mother.

Sitting in one of the swings, like she had been waiting for him to show up.

He turned and ran when he saw her, ignoring her hollers to stop, to *come back here, you little shit.*

He shudders at the memory of her shrill voice.

He had been certain she would chase after him, but she hadn't. Now he wonders why.

She had said she was going to get him, to take him away with her.

Well, maybe she's changed her mind.

Or maybe she's not ready yet.

Maybe she's waiting . . .

*Waiting for what?*

Has she asked his grandparents for their permission to take him?

Are they thinking it over?

Manny glances at his grandmother, who has her back to him as she fries the greens at the stove.

"Grammy?" he asks tentatively.

"What?" She reaches for the plastic salt shaker she keeps on the ledge above the stove, shaking it over the pan.

He watches as she takes a fork, spears a wilted, oil-slicked green stem, and pops it into her mouth.

She chews, swallows, and reaches for the salt again, then turns toward him and asks impatiently, "What is it, Manny? What do you want?"

*I want to know if you care enough about me to keep me even though you and Grampa can't afford me.*

*I want to know if you'll make sure my mother doesn't come and take me away with her.*

*I want to know if she's asked you if she can take me, and if you told her "no way."*

*I want to know . . .*

*Do you love me?*

"What do you want?" his grandmother repeats.

"Nothing," Manny says, and leaves the room.

# chapter

## 7

*". . . another hot, sunny day with temperatures climbing into the mid-nineties. Yesterday's potential for rain may have passed us by, but the long-range forecast shows that there may be a chance of thunderstorms closer to the weekend."*

Elizabeth turns off the clock radio and sits up in bed, rubbing her eyes.

It's seven-thirty on the nose.

She had set the alarm in the middle of the night, after tossing and turning for hours. She figured that if she did manage to drift off to sleep, she might not wake up in time to catch Manny on his way to day camp.

She really needs to talk to the child.

She gets out of bed and goes into the bathroom, stretching before reaching for her toothbrush.

She sees in the mirror that her eyes, not surprisingly, are underscored by dark trenches.

Well, at least she slept a few hours.

And she must have been so exhausted that she didn't even dream, for a change. No nightmares about being back in L.A., no sinister letters or threatening phone calls, no bullets flying or flower arrangements exploding.

Yesterday's confrontation with Manny's mother had left her feeling unsettled. . . .

Yet, on some level, almost . . .

Relieved?

The woman has obviously been watching her; most likely, she was the one who broke into Elizabeth's house.

It could mean that she's safe, after all . . .

Safe, that is, from the stalker who had terrorized her in Los Angeles.

Safe.

And still anonymous.

Manny's mother doesn't seem to know that the object of her jealousy is the supposedly dead Mallory Eden.

Nor, Elizabeth suspects, would that knowledge make a difference.

The woman is apparently furious with her because she thinks Elizabeth is trying to "steal" her son.

Elizabeth squeezes a glob of toothpaste onto her brush.

This isn't something that she intends to take lightly.

Yet she can't help feeling as though a good portion of her recent troubles have been alleviated.

Manny's mother, she can deal with.

She has no idea how, but she's certain the situation is manageable.

It certainly isn't life-threatening, even if the woman is a crack addict.

Regardless of her threats, Elizabeth knows she isn't in the kind of danger she would be in if the shadowy stranger who had driven her into hiding had suddenly resurfaced here in New England, aware of her true identity and intending to make her life miserable once again—before ending it.

So the stalker is no longer an issue.

Although . . .

There is the card.

The card she received in her post office box last week, the one with the Windemere Cove postmark.

The one that reads, "I know who you are."

Could Manny's mother have sent it?

Why?

It doesn't make sense for her to have done it. . . .

Although, the woman is a drug addict, and drug addicts can be delusional. Drug addicts do a lot of things that don't seem to make sense, don't they?

But why, assuming that she doesn't know who Elizabeth really is, would she have sent that particular card? What significance would that message have for someone who isn't trying to escape her past?

It could simply be a threat, meaning that she knows that Elizabeth has been spending time with her son.

It could simply mean that she's been watching her, following her—which, apparently, she has.

So Manny's mother *could* have sent the card, and the message *could* have nothing to do with Elizabeth's past as Mallory Eden.

But what if Manny's mother isn't responsible?

What if her menacing involvement in Elizabeth's life is simply a coincidence?

What if someone else really did send it?

Who?

Elizabeth had lain awake for hours the previous night, trying to come up with a likely scenario, one that would make the message—*I know who you are*—seem innocuous rather than ominous.

She had done her best to convince herself that the card was some sort of marketing gimmick, just junk mail.

That the same unsigned card was sent out to hundreds of thousands of people in the area.

But . . .

What does it mean?

There was no enclosure advertising a product, no return address, no follow-up.

Unless . . .

She never had checked her post office box yesterday.

Maybe her post office box holds the key to the mystery. Maybe the card was some sort of teaser, like a newspaper ad that reads *Watch this space.*

Maybe whoever had sent it—a local printing company, perhaps, since it was a greeting card?—had mailed her another card since, containing information that would explain the product they were selling.

Maybe—if the card was a fluke and Manny's mother is behind the break-in and the stalker hasn't found her after all—then, maybe Elizabeth will be able to have some semblance of a normal life.

Until now, she had assumed her existence in hiding would mean spending every day alone, barricaded inside her house, or looking over her shoulder every time she's forced to leave.

That's how it's been for five years.

No friends, no fun, no career, no . . .

Romance.

But now there's Harper Smith.

And for the first time, Elizabeth dares to allow herself to hope . . .
No, *hope* is too strong.

To fantasize . . .

About . . .

Companionship.

About someone to talk to, someone to care about, someone to touch, to kiss, to love . . .

*But you know that can't happen.*

*Don't get your hopes up.*

*Nothing has changed since last week, before you got the card. The reality is, you're still in hiding. You always will be. You have to be careful, and being careful means keeping a low profile. It means trusting no one.*

Or does it?

Maybe she had been wrong when she decided how she would have to live her life as Elizabeth Baxter.

There had been no question but that she would have to erase her past as Cindy O'Neal, and Mallory Eden. . . .

And the past of the real Elizabeth Baxter.

But maybe enough time has gone by.

Maybe, if she dares to venture slowly out of her sheltered, lonely world, she'll be okay.

Some things won't change.

She'll never get her career back.

She'll never, God help her, realize her fondest childhood dream and become a perfect mommy.

She'll never forget the horrors she has experienced, or what happened to Gent, and to Gretchen, and she'll never see her old friends again.

But maybe the stalker has forgotten all about Mallory Eden, and maybe no one in town will recognize her if she dares to remove her sunglasses and stop scurrying around with her head down, and maybe . . .

*You should have checked the post office box yesterday,* Elizabeth scolds herself again, spitting toothpaste into the sink and rinsing her brush. *If you had, you might already know what that card was all about. That it wasn't meant as a threat. And that no one knows your true identity, or that Mallory Eden is still alive. . . .*

After the run-in with Manny's mother in the park, she had come straight home, so jittery about what had happened that she had almost considered going to the police.

Or maybe just to Frank Minelli.

Considering her state of mind yesterday, if he had been outside working in his yard the way he sometimes is, she might actually have gone over to talk to him.

She might have explained that she had been threatened by the mother of a local child she had befriended, and she might have asked if Frank could look into it for her.

Just to make sure that the woman wasn't going to harm Manny . . .

Or Elizabeth.

But Frank hadn't been outside, and by the time she saw him pull into his driveway a few hours later, she had decided against talking to him, or reporting the incident to the police.

The only person she will tell, just as soon as she can find him, is Manny.

She reaches over, turns on the water in the tub, and slips off her nightgown.


Pamela stands with her hands on her hips, staring at the stack of magazines she just discovered, tucked way at the back of a shelf in the basement.

Upstairs, Hannah is chattering and banging her spoon in her high chair, and Jason, perched in his bouncy seat on the kitchen table, occasionally adds a high-pitched, happy gurgle.

Pamela knows she should get back up there; she can't leave them alone longer than a minute or two.

But she can't seem to make herself do anything but stare at her husband's cache of reading material.

It's not as though she had been snooping, looking for incriminating evidence against Frank.

She had gone down there looking for Hannah's old bottles, which she had packed away about a year ago.

Last night she made the decision that it's time to wean Jason so that she can stop breastfeeding and start seriously concentrating on getting back into shape.

She discovered that the bottles weren't where she'd thought she'd put them, on the shelves inside a cupboard at the foot of the stairs.

What *is* there is this stack of magazines . . .

Pornographic magazines.

*Playboy, Penthouse, Hustler,* and several others with raunchy titles she has never heard of.

According to the dates on the spines, they're all fairly current. The issues on top of the pile are for next month, September. He must have just bought them.

Up in the kitchen, Jason is starting to fuss.

Hannah yells, "Mommy? Mommy, where are you?"

Pamela calls, "I'll be right up."

She narrows her eyes at the thought of Frank spending what little extra money they have on this filth. Money they could be using to put into the bank for the kids' educations.

Isn't he the one who's always harping on her to watch the budget? Not to spend so much on groceries, on the kids' clothes, on things for the house . . .

When was the last time she ever bought anything for herself? Anything—makeup, an outfit, a new summer purse to replace the one with the broken strap, the one Frank stapled together and pronounced "good as new, you can get a few more years out of it, easy."

*Damn you, Frank.*

*I've been putting in all these hours, even though I'm already exhausted, on clipping grocery coupons from the Sunday paper and sewing curtains for the nursery because it's cheaper than buying them.*

*Meanwhile you've been throwing away hundreds of dollars on these disgusting magazines.*

She picks up the one at the top of the pile. It promptly falls open to a dog-eared page featuring a spread-eagle, naked blonde with the most enormous breasts Pamela has ever seen.

"Damn you, Frank," she mutters aloud, flipping through it and noticing that the corners of certain pages are folded down, and that those pages invariably picture beautiful blondes in impossibly provocative positions.

Up in the kitchen, she can hear Jason starting to wail, and Hannah is banging on her high chair tray, angrily shouting, "Mommy! Mommy!"

Pamela flings the magazine back into the cupboard, closes the door, and starts stomping up the stairs.

By the time she reaches the top, she knows she can't do what she *wants* to do.

That is, she can't storm into the living room, wake her husband—

who spent the night on the couch, as usual—and demand to know what's going on.

Whether he's having an affair.

*A stack of porn magazines in the basement doesn't mean anything,* she reminds herself.

He always liked that sort of thing, she remembers. A few times, when they had stayed in hotels, he had insisted on renting X-rated movies from Spectravision. Though she had feebly protested, she had found them titillating herself. The sex she and Frank shared during and after those movies was incredibly hot.

What she wouldn't give to have him make love to her that passionately again . . .

Even though back then, in those hotel rooms, she had often wondered—as her husband panted above her, pounding into her, his eyes screwed tightly closed in concentration—whether he was imagining that she was someone else, one of those buxom porn actresses.

Now she wouldn't care what he was imagining, just as long as he still wanted to make love to her.

Which he doesn't.

But the stack of dirty magazines in the basement aren't evidence that he's cheating on her.

Even though she's positive that he is.

All she has to do is catch him in the act.

She's been waiting.

Watching.

A blind, white, violent rage fills Pamela at the thought of her husband with . . .

*Her.*

She pauses at the top of the stairs and takes several deep breaths before going calmly back into the kitchen, where both her children are now sobbing loudly and Frank is hollering, "What the hell is going on? I'm trying to get some sleep!"

Pamela takes Hannah out of her high chair, sets her on the floor with a hug, and reaches for Jason, who silences the moment she picks him up.

Then she turns to her husband, who is standing in the doorway, wearing only a pair of shorts.

"Everything's fine. Go back to sleep," she tells him sweetly, then turns away, seething inside.

* * *

Manny spots a figure standing at the edge of the clearing around the park pavilion, and freezes on the path.

For a moment, with the sun glinting into his eyes, he thinks it's his mother again.

But then the person takes a few steps closer, waves, and he realizes it's her.

"Elizabeth!" he calls out, running toward her.

She looks so pretty, he thinks, in her blue and white sundress. She has sandals on her feet, and her hair is hanging down loose today. She hardly ever wears it like that.

"Hi, Manny." She smiles as he draws near.

But he can tell something's wrong, even though he can't see her eyes behind the dark sunglasses.

"What's the matter with your face?" he asks, spotting a faint red mark, like a bruise, on her cheek.

She reaches up, her fingers touching the skin, and says, "Oh, this? I just . . . I bumped into a door."

He thinks she might be lying, but he can't imagine why she'd do that. "How come you're here?"

"I knew you'd be going to rehearsal for the play . . . do you have a minute before you start?"

He nods, glancing over his shoulder at the stone pavilion. He sees Rhonda and a few other counselors and kids gathered around the picnic tables, but not everyone is there yet.

"I looked for you yesterday afternoon at the playground," Elizabeth tells him.

"You did?" A bad feeling steals over him as he remembers what happened yesterday.

His mother.

At the playground.

"You weren't there," Elizabeth continues, "but somebody was. I met your mom, Manny."

"She isn't my mom," he says quickly.

Elizabeth pauses, looking puzzled.

"She's my *mother*, but not a 'mom,' " he explains, and somehow she seems to understand.

"I know how you feel, Manny. And I want to help you."

"Help me what? Did she tell you she's taking me away?"

The expression on Elizabeth's face reveals that no, his mother didn't tell her that.

"What are you talking about? She threatened to take you away, Manny? When was that?"

He shrugs. "The other day. She said she's going to take me, no matter what my grandparents say."

Elizabeth frowns. "Did you tell anyone? Did you tell your grandparents?"

"Nah."

He doesn't tell her that he's afraid they won't mind—that maybe they'll want his mother to take him so that they won't have to take care of him anymore.

He wants so badly to ask Elizabeth to help him—to let him live with her. To be his new mom.

But he doesn't.

He can't.

He already knows, somehow, what her answer will be.

No.

She'll find some nice way to say it, but no matter what, it would still be no.

And he can't stand the thought of hearing that from her.

Because she's the one person in the world who has never hurt him.

And if she does, he doesn't know how he'll stand it.

"What did my mother say to you yesterday?" he asks her, shuddering at the thought of his dear Elizabeth meeting up with that terrible, scary woman at the playground, the way he had.

"She wanted to know if I was trying to steal you away from her," Elizabeth says. Again her hand flutters up to touch the red mark on her cheek, then back down again as though she's realized what she was doing.

"But she doesn't have me!" Manny feels sick to his stomach; the dry, stale toast he'd eaten for breakfast threatens to come up in his throat.

"Manny, I know she doesn't have you." Elizabeth places both her hands gently on his shoulders. "I know she hasn't been a mother to you."

He's shaking. "What did you tell her?"

"Nothing. Just that I'm your friend, and that's all."

*That's all.*

Just a friend.

If he had been wondering whether she might want to be his

mom—and he hadn't been wondering, because he knows the answer, but still—

*If* he had been wondering, he wouldn't be anymore.

Elizabeth is just his friend.

*Friends are good things to have,* he tells himself, trying to be positive despite the sinking feeling in his stomach.

But friends don't live with you.

They don't adopt you.

"Manny," Elizabeth is saying, "I'm worried about you."

He looks up. "You are?"

She nods. "You need to tell someone what's going on, Manny."

"Tell who?"

"Your grandparents."

He shakes his head. "I can't. There's nothing they can do."

"They can tell the police that your mother's bothering you, making threats."

"Can't you tell the police for me?"

Elizabeth hesitates, then says, "I could tell them. But I think that's up to your grandparents. Why don't you want them to know?"

*Because I'm afraid they won't do anything about it.*

*I'm afraid that if I tell them my mother wants me back, they'll be glad. That they'll say that she can take me.*

"Manny . . . ?"

"Elizabeth, it's okay. I'll tell my grandparents," he lies.

She looks doubtful. "Are you afraid they'll get angry at you? That they'll hurt you?"

"No."

"Because this isn't your fault, Manny. And no one is going to get angry at you."

She looks as though she's trying to convince herself of that, along with him.

And anyway, that isn't it. He isn't afraid that his grandparents will hurt him physically. That, he could take.

He's afraid . . .

"Manny, you really should tell them. They need to know what's going on."

"I will. I'll tell them." He nods at her. "You're right. They need to know. They can tell the police. I'll let them know tonight."

"Okay," she says after watching him carefully for a moment. Though he can't see her eyes behind her sunglasses, he knows they're focused intently on his face.

"I have to go to my rehearsal," he says, squirming under her probing gaze. "They're probably waiting for me."

He looks over at the pavilion. He can tell that not everyone is there yet, but he doesn't want to stand there, lying to Elizabeth, any longer.

"Okay, go ahead. I'll meet you at the playground tomorrow and you can tell me what's going on. And, Manny, don't forget that you have my phone number. You can call me if you need me."

He nods, turns, and starts walking away, toward the pavilion. Then, remembering something, he looks back over his shoulder.

She's still standing there, watching him.

"Hey, Elizabeth?" he calls. "How are my costumes coming? Have you had time to—"

"They're almost ready for you, Manny," she calls back. "The frog is just about done."

"Thanks," he says, giving her a double thumbs-up, as though he doesn't have a care in the world.

He continues walking slowly toward his rehearsal, wondering why he's wasting his time.

When the curtain goes up on the show next week, somebody else will be playing the lead role. . . .

Because he'll be long gone.

He can't stay and wait for his mother to come and take him away.

He has no choice but to go on his own.

As soon as he figures out where to go, and how to get there, he'll be out of there.

Rae Hamilton has been to the Skybar at the Mondrian Hotel dozens of times, but never with Flynn Soderland.

So many people stop by to greet him despite the relatively sheltered seats they've chosen, off in a corner on a big white cushion, that it takes nearly an hour before he is finally able to turn his attention to her and get straight to the point, without interruption.

"Do you know Martin de Lisser?" he asks, watching her over the rim of the glass as he takes a sip from his second martini.

A wispy cloud of cigarette smoke around his face seems to suit the ethereal setting, shrouding the once-high-powered agent in an aura of mystique.

"Know him personally? No. But of course I know who he is. Who doesn't? Why do you ask?"

"He's holding an open casting call for his new film. He's looking for the new Mallory Eden." He reaches into his Armani blazer, pulls out a folded piece of paper, and hands it to her.

She scans the ad from yesterday's issue of *Variety*, which is still sitting, unread, on her table at home.

"I spoke with him last night."

"I didn't know you knew him."

"We've never met. I got in touch with him through a mutual friend."

She nods. Flynn Soderland may be retired, but his name still opens seemingly impenetrable doors in this town.

"He was honest with me about the casting call, which, of course, is a publicity stunt," Flynn is saying. "De Lisser isn't interested in casting a nobody from Podunk, no matter what he's telling the press. And he hasn't secretly cast the role yet either. He wants to meet with you, Rae."

Her heart begins to pound. She doesn't betray her excitement, merely takes a sip of Perrier before asking, "Why?"

"He wants you to read for the lead role." He exhales twin streams of smoke from his nostrils and adds, "Tomorrow. At his house in Napa. Are you interested?"

"Are you kidding? Sure, I'm interested, but . . ." She leans forward, resting her chin on her hand, struggling not to seem over-eager. She doesn't want anyone, not even Flynn, to know how desperately she needs a break. "Has he seen any of my work? Is that why—"

"He's never heard of you. I called him and told him about you."

"Oh." Her disappointment is fleeting. "What did you tell him, exactly?"

"That you're a talented actress. That you're currently available. And that you're a dead ringer for Mallory Eden, and you were her closest friend."

"I see."

"I pointed out that as he so clearly already knows, Mallory is still a bankable commodity in this town, and her popularity doesn't seem to be waning even after five years. I also reminded him that the press has been lending considerable coverage to the anniversary of her death last weekend, which means she's on people's minds."

"What did he say?"

"He knew all of that, of course. He's not just a talented director,

Rae. He's a shrewd businessman. Why do you think he chose now to search for the new Mallory?''

"He wants *me* to be the new Mallory?'' she asks, careful to keep her tone level, not to give anything away.

"He isn't opposed to the idea. The press would go nuts. Mallory's lookalike best friend stepping into the spotlight as Hollywood's newest film goddess . . . It's ideal.''

"I see what you mean.''

"There's only one problem.''

"What?''

Flynn holds up a finger, indicating for her to wait while he stubs out his cigarette, tilts his glass, and drains the last of his martini.

She watches, wondering when he started drinking again. She's familiar with his past bout with alcoholism—not because he's opened up to her about it. Even if she hadn't been privy to Mallory's concerns about her agent's drinking, it's been common knowledge in Hollywood for some time now that Soderland is an AA veteran.

At their lunch the other day he'd had a club soda.

Now he's motioning the bartender for a third martini.

"What's the one problem?'' Rae asks him impatiently.

"Your image.''

"What image?''

"That's the problem. You need to create a new Rae. You need to loosen up a little, laugh a lot, be a screwball.''

"You want me to re-create the old Mallory, not create a new Rae.''

"Exactly.''

She nods coolly, sipping her Perrier.

"Do you know what I mean?''

"I think so.''

"De Lisser's looking for the new Mallory Eden, Rae. That's what you've got to give him.''

The waiter sets another martini in front of Flynn, and he reaches for it greedily. He takes a gulp, then says, obviously feigning nonchalance, "Oh, and there's another little potential problem.''

She sighs. "What is it, Flynn?''

"Your agent.''

"Enough said. I'll ditch Buddy today. I had been planning on doing it anyway.''

"What about your contract?''

"What contract? There hasn't been a contract in a few years

now. He hasn't gotten me anything decent, Flynn. I need someone like you to represent me."

Flynn nods. "I'll represent you, Rae."

"What about retirement?"

"Screw retirement," he says, lifting his glass again and lighting another cigarette. "It's no fun."

The phone is ringing.

Elizabeth, sitting on the floor surrounded by purple fabric and sequins, is looking at it.

She can't answer it.

What if it's that voice, the eerie, guttural voice from five years ago?

The one that said, "Prepare to die, Mallory Eden."

But she had told Manny to call her if he needed her.

It could be him.

Or it could be Harper Smith.

Or it could be the voice.

There's only one way to find out.

Elizabeth stands and moves slowly toward the phone, reaching out with a shaking hand.

She lifts the receiver . . .

Just in time to hear a click.

Whoever it was had hung up.

What if it was Manny?

Or Harper?

What if it was the voice?

She stands there, trembling, wondering what to do.

Should she take advantage of modern technology and press *69?

If she does, she knows, her phone will automatically dial the number of whoever just called her.

And she'll know.

So . . .

*Do it,* she commands herself.

*Just do it.*

But before she can move, the phone rings again.

Her heart pounds wildly as, still holding the receiver, she takes her thumb off the talk button and says in a whisper, "Hello?"

"Hello, I'm calling on behalf of *Bay View* magazine. Are you familiar with our publication?"

Elizabeth can't speak, can't move.

"You're not? Then please allow me a moment of your time to tell you a little bit about *Bay View*," the friendly but detached female voice goes on, as if reading from a script. "We are a local environmental magazine devoted to—"

"I'm sorry, I . . . I don't have time right now," Elizabeth cuts in.

"But it will only take a—"

"I have to go!" Elizabeth says almost frantically, and hangs up.

Then realizes she should have asked the woman if she had tried to call a minute earlier.

Had she been the one who hung up when Elizabeth answered?

But why would she do that?

And if she hadn't . . .

Who had?

*You'll never know*, Elizabeth tells herself, realizing that now it's too late to press *69.

She goes back to her sewing, forcing herself to stop thinking about the phone call.

The television is on. *Entertainment Tonight*. Even after all these years, she's still curious about the industry news and gossip.

Every once in a while, she'll see one of her old friends doing an interview.

Good old Kenny Abner is always popping up, hyping his successful network comedy, *Family of Foes*.

And Rae had been on last fall when she got the lead in that sitcom. Too bad it had been canceled after only one episode.

Elizabeth feels a pang of regret at the thought of the friends she will never see again. It wasn't easy to find true, loyal friendship in cut-throat, back-stabbing Hollywood. But she'd had Kenny and Rae and Flynn and . . .

Gretchen.

She wonders where her former assistant is now.

One of her final acts as Mallory Eden had been to arrange for all of Gretchen's medical bills to be sent to her. That way, she could cover anything that wasn't covered by the insurance policy Mallory had supplied the year before, when she first hired Gretchen as an assistant.

But what could her money heal, in the end?

Gretchen would be disfigured for the rest of her life.

And Elizabeth would carry the guilt with her for the rest of her life.

If only she hadn't been so out of it, recovering from her own surgery and the grim news that she would never bear children.

As a child in Nebraska, she used to dream about the kind of mother she would be. So different from her own mother. She would never hurt her children, she would never even have to raise her voice. They would be little angels, the children she would have one day.

She wanted lots of children; at the very least, two boys and two girls. That way, each boy would have a brother and each girl would have a sister.

She had always longed for a sister. She used to dream that one day, her mother—transformed, of course, into a smiling model citizen—would come back to Custer Creek and present her with a baby sister.

Funny how dreams, when they came true at all, could be warped versions of what you imagined.

But she doesn't want to think about that now.

Nor does she want to remember the aftermath of the stalker's attack, and the surgery that had ensured that one of her fondest dreams would never come true in *any* form.

But it's too late.

She's already journeying back to the day of the explosion . . .

She had been lying glumly in her bed, unaware of what was going on in the rest of the house. She had no idea that her assistant was even there, let alone going through cards and gifts from well-wishers.

Her security people had later said they had instructed everything that arrived to be placed in her detached office out behind the pool, to be inspected by police first. But somehow there'd been a mix-up, and the flowers and a few other items had gotten through, into the house, where—

Elizabeth jumps to her feet, clapping a hand over her mouth to muffle her own startled cry.

She just heard a faint sound outside.

*It's probably just the wind . . .*

Except that there is no wind.

She stands, frozen, in the middle of the living room, frantically wondering what to do.

Then she hears it again . . .

A footstep.

Followed by the doorbell.

*Would a stalker come right up and ring the bell?*

*Would Manny's mother come right up and ring the bell?*

There's no window in the front door, no way to look out and see who is standing there.

Then she hears someone rapping, and a voice calls, "Elizabeth? Are you in there?"

Harper Smith.

She lets out a sigh and moves automatically to the door, fumbling with the dead bolts, then throwing it open.

"Are you all right?"

"I'm fine," she tells him, noticing how attractive he is in his snug black jeans and a white T-shirt that reveals his muscular, tanned arms.

"I just tried to call you, and there was no answer. I got worried—"

"I just got home," she tells him.

She sees that he's looking past her, at the fabric spread out on the floor, and the half-finished cup of herbal tea on the coffee table, and the television, where Roseanne is telling an *Entertainment Tonight* reporter about the new series she's producing.

Harper only nods. He doesn't believe her—she can see it in his expression. But to his credit, he says nothing more than "I'm glad you're okay."

"I'm fine," she says again. "Really."

"So, did you ever get to the post office?"

Her guard goes up. Why is he asking about that? Just casual interest, or something more? Could he possibly have sent her that card?

No.

No.

*No!*

"Yeah, I got there," she says cautiously, refusing to suspect him of anything other than making conversation.

She doesn't tell him that she hadn't gotten to the post office until just that morning, after leaving Manny.

Or that her box had been blessedly empty except for a telephone bill.

"That's good," he says, again looking past her into the living room. "What are you up to tonight?"

"Just busy sewing."

"What are you making?"

"Costumes," she says briefly.

"Isn't it a little early for Halloween?"

"They're . . . for a friend. For a play." She isn't about to compli-
cate the explanation with any more detail than that.

"So you hang around with theatrical types?"

"Once in a while," she says, managing to keep the irony out of
her voice.

*I used to live in Hollywood. I used to be an actress.*

"Pretty muggy out tonight, isn't it?" he asks, shifting gears,
leaning against the step railing.

She nods, noticing the faint glisten of sweat on his forehead.
Her own hair is sticking to her scalp in the heat.

"Too bad we didn't get that big rainstorm yesterday," he comments.

"I know. It passed right over."

"We could use rain."

"We could."

She's wondering how long he's going to hang around, discussing
the weather, when he surprises her with a question.

"You wouldn't happen to have any more of that iced tea, would
you? I'm awfully thirsty from the heat. . . ."

Startled, she looks into Harper's eyes and sees that he's smiling.
Hopeful.

There is more iced tea. A whole pitcherful, freshly made. With
lemon.

But she can't offer it to him. Can't invite him in. Can't start
taking risks . . .

Then again, it would be heaven to sit at the kitchen table with
him, to get to look into those sexy green eyes for just a little while
longer.

How much harm could that do?

"Actually," she says impulsively, opening the door wide, "there
is more iced tea. Why don't you come in and have some with me?"


"Hey, aren't you the guy who was on TV the other night?"

Brawley Johnson turns to see a gorgeous brunette standing
behind his bar stool.

She's wearing a white vinyl miniskirt and matching boots, a
little too heavily into the retro seventies look for his taste. And
when she smiles at him, he sees that her tongue is pierced. She

probably has a tattoo too, he thinks, trying not to wrinkle his nose in distaste.

Still, her breasts are poking provocatively from the V neckline of her red blouse, and her thighs above her boots are taut and shapely.

"You used to go out with Mallory Eden, right?" she's saying, leaning toward him so that her breasts are practically tumbling out of her shirt.

"Yeah, I did." Brawley pastes on an expression of sorrow, the same one he'd worn for the interview about his dead girlfriend.

"I'm so sorry about your loss," the woman says, slipping onto the next stool, which is empty.

It's still early, not even six o'clock yet. But it's his night off, and he can't stand sitting around at home, endlessly thinking about *her.*

"You must really miss her," the stranger says to him, laying a perfectly manicured hand over his.

But her nails are polished in that trendy shade of black, and he frowns slightly at the sight. So many women in this town don't know what the hell they're doing when it comes to style.

No one has Mallory Eden's class.

"You have no idea how much I miss her," he tells the woman, fighting not to pull his hand away.

"Are you an actor too?"

"Nah. I drive a limo."

"Oh."

He waits for her to get up, make some excuse, and leave. Sometimes they do.

But she doesn't.

"Is that how you met Mallory?" she asks him. "Driving a limo?"

"Nope." He resents the way she's called her by her first name, Mallory, as though they were acquaintances. So many people do that—act as though they know her, just because she was a big movie star.

But nobody really knew Mallory.

Nobody but him.

"How did you meet her, then?"

"We're from the same hometown."

He doesn't go into the details.

How he had spotted Cindy one steamy summer's day back in Custer Creek, Nebraska, when she was a mere high school girl and he was a grown man. How he had fallen in love with her the moment he'd set eyes on her, giggling in the backseat of her friend's battered station wagon when they pulled up at the service station where he worked.

Her brown hair was pulled into a bouncy, high ponytail and she was wearing a pair of cutoff dungarees with a white halter top that left her stomach, arms, and back bare, revealing too much sun-kissed skin for him to ignore.

He had caught her eye and she had winked at him.

And the next day she came back alone, on her beat-up bicycle, riding three miles from her grandma's house just to flirt with him, not caring that he was twenty-three or that his father was in jail over in Boone County.

"So you knew her before she was rich and famous?" the woman in the miniskirt is asking him, lighting a cigarette.

"Yeah. We moved out here to L.A. together. We were planning to get married and have a bunch of kids."

"But then she killed herself. That's so sad."

"Yeah."

He doesn't tell her about what had happened in between the time they moved to L.A. and her suicide. He doesn't mention that Cindy—that *Mallory*—left him long before she killed herself. That he had tried everything to win her back, to make her love him the way he still loved her.

Will always love her.

He just buys her a drink, and he lets her comfort him—first at the bar, and then, later, in his king-sized water bed back at his apartment, where she does incredible things to his body with those black-manicured hands and that pierced tongue while he closes his eyes and pretends that she's his young, sweet Cindy O'Neal and that she's hopelessly in love with him again.

"So what's your favorite food?" Harper asks after a brief silence, and Elizabeth smiles.

He smiles back, pleased to see that his innocuous question seems to have jump-started the conversation.

They've been sitting at her kitchen table for over an hour, talking about their various likes and dislikes when it comes to music— he's crazy about classic rock; she likes alternative. He's into jazz; she likes show tunes.

The lull in the conversation had occurred only when he asked her what her favorite movie is, and she told him that she doesn't have one.

Then she clammed up, started fiddling with her glass, lifting it and setting it down over and over again so that it has left a wet, ringlike pattern on the tabletop.

"My favorite food?" she repeats, resting her chin in her hand and seeming to ponder his question. "Hmmm. I like just about everything."

"Even squid?"

"I love squid."

"Not me. My least favorite food is squid. Tastes like rubber bands. Yech."

She grins, a rare sight, and asks, "What about your favorite?"

"That's easy. A big juicy steak, so rare it's cold and bloody, with mushrooms and onions sautéed in butter on the side."

She makes a face. "Didn't anyone ever tell you that red meat isn't healthy? Especially 'cold and bloody.'"

"Yeah, yeah, I've heard all about it. Rare red meat is practically a death sentence. Not to mention butter. But I happen to like to live a little now and then. How about you? Are you a vegetarian or something?"

"Nah. But steak is far from my favorite food."

"Which is . . . ?"

"I can't pick just one. I guess it would have to be a tie between lasagna and pizza."

"Yeah? You like Italian food?"

She nods.

"Have you ever been to Momma Mangia's?" he asks, naming a cozy little family-owned restaurant over on Center Street. He's been there just once, alone. The food was delicious, but he'd had to fend off a waitress who asked too many nosy questions about his past.

Still, he would go back.

With Elizabeth, this time.

They can sit at one of the cozy booths way back in the corner, and he can watch the candlelight flickering on her beautiful face, and maybe put some money into the tabletop jukebox and play an old love song or two.

"I've never been there," she tells him, and again there's that veiled expression.

"Maybe we'll go," he says, watching her carefully. "Maybe tomorrow night."

"I can't," she says quickly.

"Why not?"

"I ... I can't remember." She rubs her temple, knitting her brows, as if trying to recall a previous engagement. "But there's something I have to do ..."

"You're making that up," he says, unable to keep his voice from hardening. "You said you wanted to see me. Now you're obviously giving me excuses."

"I—"

"And earlier," he cuts her off, "you didn't answer the phone when I called. Were you afraid it was me? Were you trying to avoid talking to me?"

"I was out."

"Whatever." He shrugs, folds his arms on the table, leans toward her.

She watches him, silent.

"I don't play games, Elizabeth," he says finally. "You said you would go out with me. I told you I'd call. This is the last time I'm going to ask. Can I take you out to dinner tomorrow night?"

For a long time she simply watches him from beneath her long, dark lashes, her head tilted downward, her leg jiggling nervously under the table.

He waits for her reply, and when it comes, he's surprised.

"All right," she tells him in a muted tone. "I'll go to dinner with you."

It's all he can do not to jump up in victory, to shout, "Yesss!"

All he says is "I'll pick you up at eight. We'll go to Momma Mangia's."

"I'll meet you at the restaurant," she amends quickly.

He starts to protest, but her eyes narrow at him, and he realizes she's on the verge of backing out.

So he agrees to her meeting him there, and starts to give her directions.

"I know where it is," she interrupts quietly.

"Oh. Okay. Then I'll see you there at eight tomorrow night."

"Good."

"I'll make a reservation. I bet the place gets crowded on a Friday."

"Probably."

Sensing she wants him to go, he pushes his iced tea glass away and shoves back his chair.

"Thanks for stopping over," she says quietly, surprising him again.

"Like I said, I was worried about you."

She nods. "Well, like I said, I'm fine. But it was nice of you anyway."

"I'm a nice guy, Elizabeth."

"Yeah."

He can't read the tone in that single word, or the expression on her face.

She walks him to the front door, stepping around the fabric spread out on the floor.

"Guess you have to finish your sewing, huh?" he asks.

She nods and opens the door for him.

He looks down at her lovely face. "See you tomorrow night, Elizabeth."

"See you tomorrow night." Her voice is soft; her brown eyes collide with his.

He wants desperately to take her into his arms, to crush her lips beneath his in a blistering kiss.

Somehow, he restrains himself.

*Patience*, he tells himself as he turns away, walking out the door and down the steps.

*You'll have her soon enough.*

*And you don't want to scare her away. . . .*

# chapter

8

Pamela smears a glob of white Daily Care diaper ointment on Jason's bare bottom, her eyes focused on the window.

Outside, Elizabeth is mowing her lawn. She's wearing her usual outfit of shorts, a T-shirt, and sneakers, but somehow, the casual clothes seem to emphasize her exquisite figure. There seems to be a bounce in her walk as she pushes the mower over the grass, as though she's lighthearted.

In the years since Pamela has been her neighbor, Elizabeth has never seemed lighthearted.

No, she's always been skittish, withdrawn, uptight.

The kind of woman who, as Frank would say, could use a good— *Don't even think it.*

That's the last combination of ideas Pamela wants running through her mind.

Her husband, and Elizabeth, and sex.

Unfortunately, that's all that's been on her mind for the past twenty-four hours.

Discovering the porn magazines may not have been proof of Frank's affair, but they are proof that he hasn't lost interest in sex. And if he's not getting it from Pamela, then he must be getting it someplace else. A few girlie magazines would never provide enough stimulation for a man whose sex drive is as strong as Frank's has always been.

Anyway, she had caught him sneaking back from Elizabeth's house the other night, when he was supposed to be watering the grass. Who knows how many times he's crept next door under cover of darkness, even in the middle of the night, after she and the kids are asleep?

That has to be why he's been sleeping on the couch—so that he can come and go as he pleases.

And all those midnight shifts he's been working lately . . . has he really been out on patrol? Or has he been snug in Elizabeth Baxter's bed, yards away from his unsuspecting wife?

The thought of it makes her sick.

"Mommy?"

Hannah's in the doorway of the nursery, chocolate smeared all over her face, along with a guilty expression.

"Hannah, what are you *doing?*"

"Eating choc-o-late. Mmmm. Yummy chocolate, Mommy. Get more for Hannah?"

"No, I'm not going to get you more. Where did you get it?"

She hurriedly slips a fresh diaper beneath Jason's bottom, lifts the tapes, and expertly attaches the sticky strips to the cartoon-illustrated front panel.

"Where did you get the chocolate, Hannah?" she repeats.

"In Mommy's room. Under Mommy's pillow."

So Hannah had discovered Pamela's secret stash. Had she also eaten the snack-sized package of Raisinettes? Pamela had been saving them for tonight, planning to eat them while watching *20/20* on television.

What a thrilling way to spend a Friday evening.

"Hannah, that was a very bad thing to do." Pamela begins snapping the crotch of Jason's onesie. "You need to ask Mommy before you go around eating things."

"Can Hannah eat more chocolate, Mommy?" the toddler asks obediently.

"No."

Hannah makes a face, pouts, reaches a sticky hand out toward the pale yellow wall of her brother's room.

"No! Stop that!" Pamela hollers, but it's too late.

There's a streak of chocolate on the wall.

Pamela dashes over, grabs her daughter's hand, and fights the urge to smack it.

She has never hit her child.

Never.

But she's about to.

Only a sound from the changing table stops her.

She turns in time to see Jason making a movement, appearing as though he's about to roll over, off the table.

"No!" Pamela dashes over, grabs him.

Her heart is pounding.

He wasn't in danger.

He can't roll over yet. He can't. He's only two months old, and Hannah hadn't rolled over until she was in her fourth month.

Still, she hadn't been thinking when she'd left him alone on the table.

*You're losing it* she tells herself, clutching the gurgling baby to her breast. *You left Jason on the table without thinking he could fall—*

But he couldn't have fallen.

*And you almost slapped Hannah.*

She lets out a shuddering sigh.

"What's wrong, Mommy?" Hannah asks, sucking on her chocolate-covered hand.

"Nothing, Hannah."

*Your mommy's just losing her mind.*

*And it's all Daddy's fault.*

She glances at the window, sees her shapely neighbor pushing her lawn mower up a slight incline in the lawn.

*Frank's fault, and Elizabeth Baxter's fault.*

Elizabeth puts the mower and rake into the shed at the back of her property and turns to survey her work.

The grass is still brown, but at least it's no longer straggly. It took her two hours to mow it and rake up the clippings.

She closes and locks the shed, then starts toward the house, wiping a trickle of sweat from her neck. It's another hot, humid day, but the sun isn't shining as brightly as usual and the sky is a milky color. The weather forecast had called for rain tonight and tomorrow.

Good. Maybe the grass will turn green again.

It looks pretty bad, in contrast with the Minellis' lawn next door. They must have been watering it—maybe the ban has been lifted, though she hasn't heard anything. Frank is a cop. He wouldn't break the law, would he?

She had seen Pamela leave a while ago, driving off in a hurry with the two children in their car seats, but her neighbor hadn't so much as waved. She was lugging her usual diaper bags and other paraphernalia out to the car, looking preoccupied.

Elizabeth had been partly relieved to have escaped a meaningless conversation . . .

And maybe a little disappointed too.

Having Harper around last night made her realize how much she's been missing, cutting herself off from the world the way she has. Maybe it really is time to venture out, to allow herself contact, maybe even friendship, with other people.

Of course, Pamela isn't Harper.

And the contact Elizabeth wants with him isn't necessarily just friendship.

That's why she found herself saying yes when he asked her out for tonight.

She had done it against her better judgment, had done it even though she had fully intended to say no.

It's too late to back out now.

That's the thing about Harper.

Every time she tries to disentangle herself from him, he manages to snare her further into his beguiling web.

"Elizabeth! How goes it?"

She turns to see Frank Minelli stepping out of his patrol car in the driveway, wearing his police uniform.

"Hi, Frank," she calls, waving.

"Your lawn looks good." He walks over, jangling his car keys in his hand as he inspects the grass. "Did you cut it?"

"Just now."

"Looks like it could use some water too."

"Is the watering ban still on?"

He nods. "But maybe things will start getting back to normal if it rains tonight and tomorrow the way it's supposed to. They're predicting severe thunderstorms for the coastal area."

"Sure, the one night I'm going out," she murmurs, mostly to herself, but Frank lifts a brow.

"Hot date?" he asks, flashing his good-natured grin.

She shrugs.

"Where are you going?"

"To dinner."

"Who with?"

She'd rather not tell him, but can't figure out how to get around it.

So she says, "Harper Smith."

"The locksmith?"

She nods, suddenly feeling wary. She thought she saw some

fleeting, unsettling expression in Frank's eyes when she mentioned the name, but it's gone, and she isn't sure what it was.

"What's wrong?" she asks him.

"Nothing," he says, but she knows with a sudden, chilling certainty that he's hiding something.

Something about Harper.

"Do you know something about him?" she asks Frank, watching his face carefully.

"Nothing concrete . . ." The reluctance in his tone and the cagey expression in his brown eyes makes Elizabeth's stomach turn over with a sickening thud.

"Look, it's nothing," he says. "You just be careful tonight, okay?"

"What is it, Frank?"

He hesitates, clearly uncomfortable.

"Listen, this is off the record. I could get into big trouble for saying anything about official police business. But you're my neighbor, and—"

"What?" Her voice is high-pitched now, almost shrill. "What do you know about Harper?"

"I don't want to scare you, Elizabeth. But he hasn't been in town for very long, and . . . well, we're just keeping an eye on him. That's all."

"Why?"

Again Frank hedges, looking over his shoulder as though afraid he's going to be overheard. "This isn't something I'm supposed to talk about."

"You've got to tell me, Frank. Please."

"Okay. I'll tell you. And remember, it's probably nothing . . ."

"What is it?"

"Harper Smith matches the description of a fugitive from California, that's all. And he showed up here last year right around the time the guy disappeared from L.A."

"L.A.?"

Frank nods.

"What's he wanted for?" she manages to ask even as she thinks this can't be happening.

"Violating a restraining order, officially. It was filed against him by some actress, someone I never heard of—I can't remember her name. Not anybody you would have heard of. But he's also wanted for questioning in a murder case. He's suspected of killing his former girlfriend and threatening her fiancé. He went off the deep end when he found out she was engaged to someone else, that he couldn't have her."

"Oh my God."

"Take it easy, Elizabeth." Frank lays a hand on her arm. "I'm not saying Harper Smith is the same person. In fact, we're doing our best to rule it out. It's just that there's a resemblance, and the timing is right. And our locksmith tends to keep to himself, which isn't helping matters. Neither is the fact that his last name is Smith. Hardly a creative alias, if it is one."

She's shaking her head, a trembling hand pressed against her lips .

"Don't get all upset, okay? Oh, man, I shouldn't have said anything. Look at you." Frank peers into her face. "Are you going to be okay?"

"I'm . . . fine. I'm glad you told me. Frank—"

She hesitates.

Part of her wants to confess everything to him. She'll tell him who she really is, and that Harper Smith must be the stalker who terrorized her in Los Angeles five years ago. He must have followed her here, posing as a locksmith, and . . .

Oh, Christ. She had played right into his hands.

The break-in had to be a carefully orchestrated part of his plan—he'd broken the lock on her basement door and stolen her spare keys, knowing she would need a locksmith, that she would be nervous and frantic enough to call the first one listed.

And now he intends to make his move, as soon as he gets her alone tonight.

If she tells Frank, Smith can be taken into custody.

Or can he?

She has no evidence against him.

And neither do the police, or they would already have arrested him.

The fact that he's asked her out means nothing.

Telling Frank her secrets won't help to save her life.

The only thing that will save her is leaving town.

Immediately.

She turns abruptly and heads for the house.

"Elizabeth?" Frank calls behind her.

She had forgotten all about him standing there.

She pauses, turns to see him looking distressed.

"I didn't mean to spoil your date. Please don't get all bent out of shape about this. Chances are, Smith isn't the guy they're looking for. Go out with him. Try to relax and have fun. Just don't let him get you alone until you know him better."

She nods, clears her throat, tries to sound normal. "I'll be careful. Thanks for the tip, Frank."

"And don't forget . . . please don't say anything to anyone. I could get into a lot of trouble for telling you."

*But I could have gotten into far worse trouble if you hadn't.*

It's raining.

The storm clouds that have hovered over the Connecticut town all afternoon have finally opened up, sending fat, wet drops toward the parched earth.

Gretchen Dodd sits in the window of her room as always, her elbows resting on the windowsill as she watches the rain starting to fall, wishing it had brought cooler air with it.

But the day is still hot, without the slightest gust of breeze to stir the frilly white priscillas at the window.

The children next door are still frolicking on their wooden swingset, undaunted by the precipitation.

Finally, their mother opens the back door and hollers, "Ashley! Jennifer! Ryan! Get in here! Can't you see that it's pouring out?"

It's hardly pouring.

Not yet.

But a rumble of thunder in the distance promises that this won't be merely a passing shower.

Gretchen listens, rolling her eyes as the three children protest that they're not ready to come inside yet, then watches in amusement as they scramble toward the house when their mother threatens not to let them watch *Pinky and the Brain* tomorrow morning.

Only when they're safely inside, the back screen door slamming shut behind them, does she stand and turn away from the window.

She moves slowly across the room, stopping to pull a slicker over the plain gray athletic T-shirt she wears every day.

There had been a time when she wouldn't be caught dead in either this T-shirt or the cheap yellow vinyl slicker. She had always been impeccably dressed, painstakingly building a wardrobe the way her mother had built her collection of Lladro figurines.

"They're an investment, Gretchen," her mother would say each time she splurged on a new piece to display in the lighted glass shelves of the hutch in the dining room.

Just as Gretchen's wardrobe had been an investment.

An investment in her future as an actress.

She had prudently stockpiled her baby-sitting money as a teen-ager, spending it on classic designer clothing purchased at the upscale mall over in Stamford. When she moved to L.A., her luggage was filled with cashmere sweaters, velvet skirts, Italian leather shoes—every item meticulously chosen to flatter Gretchen's figure, compliment her complexion, and coordinate with the rest of her wardrobe.

Now it's a sloppy gray T-shirt, day in and day out, worn with plain cotton elastic-waist shorts in the summer, jeans in the winter.

Wearing anything else would be a joke.

Like decorating a Christmas tree whose top has been raggedly hacked off.

Gretchen leaves her room, moving down the familiar staircase, past the ticking grandfather clock in the foyer and through the silent parlor, dining room, kitchen. In the sunroom at the back of the house she slips her feet into a pair of sandals and opens the door.

She steps out into the yard, tilting her head up, toward the sky.

Raindrops splatter against her ravaged face, and she closes her eyes and breathes deeply, inhaling the scent of damp earth.

How she had loved the outdoors . . .

But that was so long ago.

She used to jog, and Rollerblade, and go to the beach.

Now she spends day after day shut upstairs in her bedroom, venturing out only under cover of darkness, or on stormy days like this, when—

A nearby shriek abruptly interrupts her thoughts.

She opens her eyes, spins around . . .

And sees one of the little towheaded girls who lives next door.

She's standing by a bush that separates the two yards, clutching a soggy rag doll that had apparently been inadvertently left out in the rain.

Her eyes are wide, terrified, focused on Gretchen's face . . .

Rather, on the battered purple mess that had once been Gretchen's face.

"Mommy!" the little girl screams, turning and running toward the house. "Help! Help! There's a terrible scary monster next door! I told you I saw it before, in the window! I told you it was real! Help!"

Gretchen turns and scurries back into the house, slamming the door behind her with an anguished curse.

Elizabeth stands at the edge of the woods, gazing at the pavilion, where the children of Windemere Cove's day camp are rehearsing next weekend's big play.

From where she's standing, with her sunglasses on and staring into the hazy sun, she can't seem to spot him.

She takes a few steps closer, away from the shelter of the trees, one hand in her mouth as she nervously bites her nails.

The other hand is clutching a plastic shopping bag that holds the two costumes she hurriedly finished that afternoon.

She can't leave town without giving them to him. She had promised.

And anyway, she needs to see him one last time, to make sure he told his grandparents about his mother's threats, the way he promised he would.

She scans the children in the distant shadows of the park pavilion, seeking the familiar, slightly built figure with the cap of glossy dark hair.

He isn't there.

Her gut twists, her hand tightening on the plastic handles of the bag.

Where is he?

Maybe he's already on his way home. Maybe his part is over.

Except he has the lead role. And the rehearsal appears to be in full swing.

Well, maybe his grandparents kept him home that morning because they're worried his mother will show up at the park and abduct him.

Or maybe she already has.

*Please, Manny . . . please don't do this to me now. You have to be all right. I can't worry about you too.*

She turns away, heading back toward the path through the woods, uncertain of her destination.

She could go by Manny's grandparents' house, just to—

"Excuse me! Excuse me, miss?"

She realizes someone is calling after her, and turns to see a pretty teenaged girl with light brown hair hurrying toward her.

"You're Manny's friend, aren't you?"

Elizabeth is unable to speak, her mind racing.

"I've seen you with him," the girl adds, coming to a halt a few feet away from her.

Elizabeth nods, then finds her voice and says, "I'm his friend, yes. I was bringing his costumes for the show." She lifts the bag in her hand, shows it to the girl, vaguely needing to justify her presence there.

Because the girl is looking at her with what appears to be suspicion.

"Where is he?"

They have uttered the same question, perfectly in unison.

Startled, Elizabeth stares into the girl's worried, slightly accusing brown eyes.

"You don't know where he is?" Elizabeth asks, a surge of panic rising in her throat.

The girl shakes her head. "He hasn't shown up for rehearsal all day. We called his grandparents' house, and they said he's supposed to be here. He left home before eight this morning, on his way to the park."

"Oh, God. Oh, Manny ..." Elizabeth clutches the bag to her chest, against her racing heart.

The sun goes behind a thickening cloud, and Elizabeth glances up at the sky, wondering if it's a sign.

*Where's Manny?*

*Is he in trouble?*

"You mean you don't know where Manny is?" The distrust has vanished from the girl's face as she stares at Elizabeth, who shakes her head.

"I'm Rhonda," the girl says abruptly, as though to make up for what she had been thinking.

Elizabeth doesn't volunteer her own name, and the girl stumbles on with the rapid-fire speech of a teenager who's terribly upset.

"I can't believe this is happening. I mean, I thought maybe ... I've seen him with you in the park, and I, you know, I knew you weren't his mom or anything. When he didn't show up today, and his grandparents said he's missing, I thought—God, I'm sorry. I can tell you're really worried about him."

Elizabeth nods, distracted. She asks, "What did his grandparents say when they found out he hasn't shown up here? Did they call the police?"

"They were going to look for him, I guess. I don't know if

they've reported it yet. We're all just really worried about Manny, and when I spotted you hanging around over here, I thought—"

She cuts herself off, then continues. "He's a great kid. He was working so hard on the show, learning his lines. What if some psycho child molester grabbed him and—oh, God. I can't even think about it."

*Or what if his crack-addict mother intercepted him on his way to the park and abducted him?*

Elizabeth is seized by a vivid memory of Manny's mother's drug-crazed, hateful eyes.

She swallows hard, turns away from Rhonda's concerned young face.

"I have to go," she murmurs, taking a step away, then turning back abruptly, remembering. She thrusts the bag containing the two finished costumes into Rhonda's hands. "Take these, okay? And if Manny shows up, give them to him. Tell him . . ."

*Tell him I said good-bye?*

*Tell him I'll call?*

She won't be able to call him. She can't possibly dare to take that risk, to make any connection to Windemere Cove once she's gone . . .

And so she'll never know where Manny is, whether he's all right.

Unless . . .

Unless she doesn't leave until she finds him.

"Where are you going?" Rhonda calls behind her as she takes off, practically running.

Elizabeth doesn't answer, just keeps fleeing along the path leading through the woods, toward the edge of the park.

Harper stands in front of the mirror, shaving cream lathered on his face, a towel wrapped around his waist.

He isn't meeting Elizabeth for a few hours, but figured he might as well get ready now.

*You're not too anxious for tonight,* he thinks wryly, reaching for his razor.

It's just that it's been so long.

He tilts his head forward and moves the blade over his skin, wondering how long it's been since he has held a woman, *any* woman, in his arms.

Then he realizes he doesn't have to wonder.

He knows exactly when the last time was.

Over a year ago, back in Los Angeles, before . . .

No.

He doesn't want to ruin his exhilarated mood by thinking about *that*.

Instead, his mind conjures Elizabeth Baxter, with her big brown eyes and her skin that looks so soft and smooth, skin that is faintly scented with subtle perfume that reminds him of a glorious spring bouquet.

He smiles, wondering if she's found his little surprise yet . . .

Then winces as his blade slips, slicing into his flesh so that a stinging trickle of crimson runs down his neck.

The traffic on I-95 is snarled as usual. What else would you expect on a Friday afternoon before the last true weekend of the summer, especially outside a coastal city like Boston?

It'll get better when the traffic for the Cape branches off in a few miles, she thinks, moving her foot from the brake to the gas and inching the Toyota forward a few feet before braking again in sync with the red pickup truck in front of her.

On the radio, the traffic copter reporter says blithely, "And it's a snail's crawl into and out of the city this afternoon, with a slow go on the Mass Pike and routes 128 and 93. And if you're unfortunate enough to be out on 95 south of the city, it's bumper to bumper all the way to the split, with a serious car–tractor-trailer accident tying things up at Exit 11. Back to you, Steve."

Pamela reaches out and turns off the radio, which she had turned on a few minutes earlier to drown out Hannah's whining from the backseat.

Sure enough, as soon as the car is silent, her daughter cranks it up again. "Hannah's hungry, Mommy. Hannah needs something to eat. Eat *now*."

"Hannah, when we get to Nana and Papa's, then you can eat something." *If they're around.*

She had tried to reach her parents before leaving home earlier, but there had been no answer. She hopes they're only out to lunch or shopping, that they haven't decided to go up to their house in Maine for the weekend. Not wanting to wait until she'd spoken to them, she had left a message on the machine telling them that she and the kids were coming for the weekend, but hadn't told them why, of course.

She isn't about to let them know that she's left her husband—maybe temporarily, maybe for good. That depends on his reaction to the note she'd left him on the kitchen table.

*Dear Frank,*
   *I'm taking the kids to my mother's for the weekend. Call or come if you want to talk to me.*

*Pamela*

That's it. No further information. And not *Love, Pam* the way she usually signs notes to him.

Had the note been straightforward enough?

She hadn't mentioned how upset she's been, or that he's the reason she's left. But he'll have to know. He'll have to come after her. After all, she's never left town to visit her parents without first discussing it with him.

He probably found the note when he stopped home, as he often does, while out on patrol.

She used to think it sweet that he did that—that he would check up on her and the kids during the day, to say hello and make sure everything's okay.

But now she wonders about his true motive for coming around like that.

Is he hoping for a glimpse of their beautiful neighbor?

Hoping to impress her with his patrol car, his uniform?

Is it Pamela's imagination, or have his visits home become more frequent lately?

*It's not your imagination. You saw him sneaking back from her place the other night,* she reminds herself.

The pit of rage ignites in her stomach once again.

She stares out the windshield, realizes they've been at an absolute standstill for several minutes now.

In the backseat, Hannah's whining has turned to crying, and, of course, Jason has awakened and has joined in. The din is deafening.

"Cut it out, you guys," she yells. "Quiet down. I'm trying to drive!"

"Mommy not driving. Mommy park car," Hannah stops crying long enough to observe.

"We are *not* parked!"

Pamela jams her hand down on the horn.

"Move, dammit!" she yells vainly at the cars clogging the road in front of her. Her voice is tight with frustration, despair. "Move!"

Elizabeth drives slowly down Green Garden Way, wondering if she should have stopped at Manny's grandparents' house.

She had driven by several times, looking for a sign of . . . Something.

A sign of Manny, a sign of a police investigation, anything that would tell her what's going on.

But there was nothing to see.

She has to do something. There has to be some way of finding out if Manny's okay without involving herself with the authorities.

Now, of all times.

"Manny, where are you?" she mutters aloud.

On the seat beside her is a large zippered canvas bag, a bag she brought to the bank so that she could empty out her safety deposit box.

The bag is bulging now.

She rounds the curve at the end of the street and sees her house up ahead.

*This is it—the last time you'll ever do this.*

*The last time you'll ever come home here.*

And it has been *home,* she realizes

Not the one she would have chosen for herself years ago, nothing like Gran's big, cozy Nebraska farmhouse or as grand and comfortable as the Malibu mansion she had abandoned.

But this little Cape has sheltered her for half a decade; within its simple clapboard walls she has felt as safe as she ever could have under the circumstances.

Now she'll be cast adrift once again, roaming in search of a new refuge.

She doesn't *feel* like going, dammit. She doesn't want to run again. She's tired of running, exhausted from fear, weary of the tedium, the loneliness of her existence.

*But you have no choice.*

*If you don't go, you'll die.*

She'd been so damned wrong about Harper Smith.

How could she have imagined that he might be someone who could rescue her from the nightmare, when in reality he's the one who has caused it?

How could she have been imagining what it would be like to

kiss him while he, most likely, had been fantasizing about killing her?

She pulls into the driveway and looks at the house.

Something has captured her attention, something she glimpsed just now, out of the corner of her eye.

For a moment she can't put her finger on what it is.

Then she sees it.

On the front step.

Some sort of package, wrapped in green tissue paper.

The kind of tissue paper florists use.

She jerks the car to a halt, staring at it, a roaring in her ears as panic rushes through her veins.

"Elizabeth?"

She gasps at the distant sound of her name, turns to see Frank Minelli poking his head out his front door.

She can't reply, only looks at him, one hand still clenched on the steering wheel, the other on the gearshift.

He's saying something else, but she can't hear him through the glass. She should roll down the window, but she can't move.

She can't move . . .

*You have to roll down the window,* she commands herself. *You have to pull yourself together.*

She reaches for the lever, cranks it so that it opens halfway, enough for Frank's voice to reach her ears.

"Have you seen Pam?"

*Have you seen Pam?*

*Have you seen Pam?*

It takes an eternity for her to decipher the question, to find her voice, to conjure the correct response.

*Have you seen Pam?*

"Earlier," she manages to say in a strangled tone. "With the kids. Leaving."

"Did she say anything to you about where she was going?"

Elizabeth shakes her head, looks back at the ominous package on the front steps.

"She left a note saying she went to her mother's in Boston, but I've been trying to call and I keep getting the machine. She should have been there by now."

Elizabeth tries to focus on what he's saying.

"Hey, are you all right?" he asks, coming closer to the car, peering at her face. "You look terrible."

"I'm . . ." She can't seem to speak coherently.

"You're not still spooked by what I told you about Harper Smith, are you?"

She can't reply.

"Listen, relax," he tells her. "You're only going to dinner with him, right? You weren't planning to be alone with him, were you?"

Planning to be alone with him?

Wishing, yes.

Hoping, yes.

Yes, she had allowed herself to imagine that dinner at Momma Mangia's would lead to something more . . .

Until Frank had told her that Harper Smith is suspected of stalking an actress in L.A., and killing two other people.

*You don't know it, Frank Minelli, but you've saved my life,* she thinks, looking into his warm brown eyes.

*No. You're not safe yet. You won't be until you get out of here.*

But she still has a few hours until she's supposed to meet him at the restaurant.

He won't realize she's on to him until she doesn't show up, and by then she'll be . . .

"Elizabeth?"

She shakes her head, focuses on Frank again.

"You look very upset. Do you want to come over to talk? I took the rest of the day off, and I'm waiting to hear from Pamela, so I'll be around."

She shakes her head, again looks at the flower arrangement on the step.

He follows her gaze.

"What is that?" he asks, looking at her.

She shrugs. "I have no idea. I guess . . . he sent it. Harper."

"Aren't you going to check?"

She shakes her head, numb.

"Do you want me to go look at it?" Frank asks kindly.

"No! No, don't touch it!" she calls, but he's already striding across the lawn.

She leaps out of her car, calling, "Frank, don't—"

But he's already picking up the green tissue-wrapped package . . .

And nothing's happening.

No explosion.

No screams of pain.

No blood.

He walks back over to her, holding the package in one hand, and offering her a small square cardboard rectangle with the other.

"This card was attached. It's a floral arrangement. See?"

He tilts it toward her, and she flinches.

She takes the card gingerly, turns it over, sees the printed note and signature.

*Looking forward to tonight. Harper.*

"This is a woman's handwriting," she tells Frank, studying it in disbelief.

"He must have ordered them over the phone. Whoever took the order at the florist shop wrote the card. The delivery person must have left them there when you weren't home."

"Oh . . ."

Of course.

The person in the shop had written the note. A woman.

And there is no bomb planted among the fresh summer blooms.

Not this time.

*Looking forward to tonight . . .*

She's filled with foreboding.

Just, she's certain, as he had intended.

He wanted the flowers to trigger the memory of what had happened in L.A.

He had known she would be paralyzed with fear at the sight of that arrangement sitting on the steps.

*You bastard,* she thinks, and thrusts the card at Frank.

"Take this," she says, "and the flowers. Get rid of it for me, will you?"

He looks hesitant. "Elizabeth, I told you, when I said that about Harper I didn't mean to—"

"No," she says emphatically, "get rid of it for me. Please, Frank."

He shrugs. "Okay, sure. No problem."

"Thank you."

He turns toward his house, then looks back at her. "You sure you're going to be all right?"

She nods.

"Well, if you need anything, you holler. I'll be around all night, so if your date tries anything funny . . ."

She nods again, thanks him.

She isn't going to tell him that she's not going on any date with Harper Smith.

That she's leaving town as soon as possible . . .

*Now.*

She can't even stick around to find out what's happened to Manny.

Her life depends on getting out of there as fast as she can, and not looking back.

# chapter

# 9

Martin de Lisser's Napa Valley home is modest by industry standards. It's nice, but not the spectacular digs one would expect from a director of his ranking.

*This'll be on the market soon* was Rae's first thought upon seeing it; he would trade it for an estate on Stone Canyon Road in Bel Air, a penthouse on Central Park South in Manhattan, a mansion on Miami's Star Island—the customary real estate for a man of his stature.

Though she's fully aware that a year ago no one had ever heard of him, Rae had found herself disappointed—by both the setting and the director himself.

She had been expecting evidence of vast power, yet the man mirrors his unassuming home.

Martin de Lisser's current residence, a two-story wood-frame house at the end of a meandering, oak-shaded drive, is simple and rustic, adorned with window boxes and white-railed porches. It sits on a dozen scenic acres dotted with redwood and eucalyptus groves and bordered by vineyards, with the Vaca Mountains looming in the distance.

Meanwhile, the bespectacled, somewhat paunchy de Lisser is shorter and balder than he appears in photographs she's seen, and he has a slight, but disconcerting, speech impediment.

He speaks as though he's slurping through a mouthful of saliva, and after their short, introductory conversation, Rae had found herself wanting to grab him by the shoulders, shake him, and shout, "Swallow, why don't you?"

Now, as she finishes her reading from the script, with de Lisser's girlfriend, a model named Lita, woodenly playing the other role, Rae glances at the famed director to gauge his reaction.

He's sitting sprawled on the burgundy leather couch, his legs straight out in front of him, crossed at the ankles, and his hand rubbing his goatee thoughtfully.

Beside him on the couch is an impeccably dressed studio executive who happened to be in town for a meeting and came by to hear her read.

In a matching wing chair off to the side sits Flynn, and he nods encouragingly at Rae when she catches his eye.

She's careful to maintain her Mallory-sparkle, to give a flippant little curtsy the way Mallory might, to casually toss her hair—worn in Mallory's signature style, blown straight and swept back from her face with a side part.

"Thank you," de Lisser says at last, rising, along with the studio exec, whose name escapes her.

Bob, or Tom, or Jim—something like that.

She knows she should have been more careful to make note of it; it's just that she had been so nervous when she was introduced earlier.

It hadn't helped that they'd been forced to fly up here on a tiny twin-engine plane that kept shuddering and lurching, or that the landing at the Sonoma County Airport had been a perilously bumpy one, thanks to the wind.

Rae has never been crazy about flying; she avoids it whenever possible.

But damn, she would have personally taken the controls of Wilbur and Orville's original glider in a hurricane if that were her only means of getting here for this audition.

She can hardly believe de Lisser agreed to see her, or that the studio exec—what the *hell* was his name anyway?—happened to be in town.

"It was a pleasure—the script is very amusing," Rae tells them, her voice a perfect echo of Mallory's distinct cadence and accent. She has worked painstakingly on it over the past twenty-four hours, reconstructing it not just from memory, but from videos of her late friend's movies.

She had a French manicure, Mallory's signature style. And she doused herself in Mallory's favorite perfume, a buoyant floral fragrance that's much lighter than Rae's usual scent.

She's even wearing Mallory's clothing—a navy linen shift and matching pumps that her friend had lent her for an audition just a few weeks before her death. It's been hanging in the back of

Rae's closet ever since, neatly pressed, its classic style pleasingly current.

"Would you mind stepping outside for a few moments?" de Lisser is asking Rae.

"No problem."

"Lita will show you the way to the sunroom. It was nice meeting you."

"You too, Mr. de Lisser." The words are more casual than any Rae would have spoken; this is Mallory's breezy, chummy style.

She goes over, shakes his hand, again in a laid-back, easy manner. She moves next to the executive whose name she has forgotten, shaking his hand and saying warmly, "I'm so glad you happened to be in town."

"I am too," he says, casting a glance at de Lisser, a glance that sends a chill of apprehension down Rae's spine.

Are they interested?

She'll know soon enough, she thinks as she follows the bony, black-clad Lita from the room, leaving Flynn Soderland alone with the director and studio suit.

They head down a long hall that runs the length of the house, lined with rooms that appear, from the glances Rae sneaks, to be impeccably furnished and decorated in California modern.

"You can wait here," Lita says as they reach the end of the hall. She opens a pair of French doors, and Rae sees that they lead to a glassed-in room at the back of the house.

It's large, airy, and sun-splashed, with a white and dark blue ceramic tile floor and white wicker furniture that's pleasantly accented by plump cushions in navy and white ticking fabric. There are lush tropical plants everywhere. The cheerful chirping from several caged tropical birds and the steady trickling of water from a stone fountain in one corner adds to the illusion of being outside.

"Have a seat," Lita offers in her vague monotone.

"Thanks."

Rae perches stiffly on the edge of an armchair.

Then, belatedly remembering that she's still Mallory, she crosses one bare, tanned leg over the other and leans back, as though she hasn't a care in the world.

"So . . . good luck." Lita's voice is detached.

"Thanks."

The model nods, drifting out of the room with a gesture that's really more of a shrug than a wave.

*Bitch,* Rae thinks. *You don't wish me luck. You couldn't care less whether I get this role. You probably want it for yourself.*

She lets out a nervous, quiet sigh and checks her watch, wondering whether she's in for a long wait.

Manny looks around the Providence bus terminal, trying to appear to anyone who might be watching as though he hasn't a care in the world.

Everyone seems to be minding their own business, reading the *Journal News* or chatting with a companion—except for an elderly lady who's seated against the wall, sipping coffee in a paper Dunkin' Donuts cup and munching on a muffin. She looks right at Manny when he glances at her, and she frowns slightly, as though wondering what a boy his age is doing alone in a big, busy bus terminal.

He's wondering the same thing himself.

Running away might not have been such a good idea, he now realizes. For one thing, the local bus he'd ridden just to get this far had eaten most of the money he'd had with him—which, actually, was the few dollars' worth of change he'd found when he opened his piggy bank that morning. He'd been stuffing spare dimes and nickels into it for so long that he'd been certain he'd find a fortune, but when he'd added it all up, he was sick.

How far is he going to get?

He's decided to go to California, because it's as far away as you can get from Rhode Island and still be in the same country. He figures that he'll go to Hollywood and become a big movie star. They're always looking for talented kids now that Macauley Culkin's voice has changed, and besides, Rhonda said Manny is one of the best actors she's ever seen.

He feels a pang at the thought of the play he'll never get to star in. He had been looking forward to getting up there onstage; he'd even dared to imagine that Grammy and Grampa might be in the audience. He had told them about it, and Grammy had said they'd try to come.

There's only one person he'd been certain would attend his big night. Elizabeth. He knew he could count on her to be there; she had said she was looking forward to it.

As soon as he gets to where he's going, he'll call her and let her know he's all right. He has her phone number in his pocket.

Maybe she'll even come out and visit him. If he gets a big movie right away, he'll even buy her plane ticket, to pay her back for all the stuff she's done for him.

Manny glances out the big plate-glass window at the Bonanza bus pulling into the spot marked Lane Two.

An announcement over the loudspeaker tells him that it will be boarding in five minutes, and it's headed for New York City via Hartford and White Plains.

New York City.

There are a lot of movie stars there too—aren't there?

Besides, New York is a lot closer to Rhode Island than Hollywood is. Maybe he should . . .

He hurries up to the ticket counter and waits impatiently while the man behind the desk tries to explain to some old guy who doesn't speak English that he just missed the bus to Logan Airport and the next one doesn't leave for almost two hours.

Finally, it's Manny's turn to step up.

"How much is a ticket to New York City?" he asks.

The man looks him over, opens his mouth like he's going to ask Manny if he's traveling alone.

"My grandma can't remember how much the fare was, and I think she dropped her ticket somewhere," Manny says quickly, motioning behind him in the general direction of the waiting area, where there are at least five vaguely confused-looking old ladies who might be mistaken for his grandmother.

"It's twenty-nine ninety-five one way," the man says, still appearing doubtful.

"*Dollars?*"

The man narrows his eyes, says, "Yes, dollars."

"Okay, thank you," Manny tells him, trying to hide his dismay.

Conscious of the guy's eyes following him, he walks across the terminal and sits next to the muffin-eating, nosy old lady.

He decides he'd better talk to her, in case the counter guy is still watching.

"Are you going to New York City?" he asks her.

She tightens her grip on her handbag in her lap. "Yes," she says, not unfriendly, but not grandmotherly warm either.

"So am I," Manny tells her in a conversational tone.

"Alone?" She frowns.

"Yeah. I have to go visit my . . . sister. My mother's dead." Those last words, an afterthought, give him a great deal of satisfaction.

"That's too bad," the woman says.

"Yeah." He shrugs.

The loudspeaker clicks on and a voice announces that the bus for New York City is now boarding in Lane Two.

The old woman stands, brushes the crumbs off her double-knit pink pants suit.

"Do you want some help carrying your bags?" Manny asks, an idea forming in his mind.

"No, I—"

"I can help you. I'm going on the same bus."

All he has to do is walk next to this lady, and sneak past the guy standing in front of the open luggage bins in the side of the bus, collecting the tickets.

*But that's against the law!*

*So? You can't afford a ticket. Someday, when you're a rich, famous movie star, you can pay the bus company back.*

*Besides, if you go back home now, you'll get beat by Grampa for running away, and your mother will come after you.*

"All right, you can carry that suitcase," the old lady has decided.

He obediently picks it up, finding it impossibly heavy. What does she have in there, giant rocks?

He starts lugging it toward the door, noticing that there's a good long line waiting to board the bus.

He's just a short little kid in the crowd. They'll never notice him.

He and the lady wait in line.

"You go ahead of me. Ladies first," he says as they get closer to the driver collecting the tickets.

The old woman actually cracks a smile and steps in front of Manny.

Finally, they reach the head of the line.

"Ticket, please?" the man says to the old woman.

She fumbles for it in the pocket of her jacket.

That's Manny's cue.

Still lugging her suitcase, he sidesteps her, then scoots around the ticket collector, who doesn't seem to notice.

*Home free,* Manny thinks, putting one foot on the step.

Then he feels a hand clamp down on his shoulder, and a stern voice says, "Where do you think you're going, son?"

Rae doesn't ask Flynn for the news until they're in the limo, heading down the long, winding drive away from Martin de Lisser's house.

She tries not to give away her anxiety, but realizes that her perfect French manicure is tapping a furious staccato against the tinted window of the car.

"Well?" she demands, turning to her new agent. "What did they say?"

"First of all," he says, turning to her, "can I tell you that you were fabulous?"

She smiles.

"You *are* Mallory Eden," he informs her. "If I didn't know better, I'd be spooked by you. You look like her, you sound like her, you even have her walk—that slow, nonchalant way she used to move around. How did you do it, and overnight, Rae?"

She doesn't tell him about the tacks she placed inside the toes of the linen pumps, that every time she sets her feet down, she must do so gingerly, thus naturally slowing her gait and refraining from her usual, more purposeful stride.

"I'm an actress, remember?" is her slightly haughty reply to Flynn, who raises an appraising eyebrow.

"You certainly are," he agrees mildly. "And your performance absolutely grabbed Martin's attention. He's interested, Rae. He and John are going to discuss it . . ."

Oh, *John. That* was the studio executive's name.

". . . and he'll get back to us later on today, or tomorrow. But I really think that it's possible that you might be cast. De Lisser commented on your reading. He said that it was like watching Mallory Eden's ghost."

*Mallory Eden's ghost.*

A shiver runs down Rae's spine, once again, at the persistent image.

*Mallory's dead,* she reminds herself.

And she isn't coming back. . . .

No matter what she promised that long-ago day in Big Sur.

Rae smiles at Flynn, and she gestures at the stocked limousine bar opposite her. "Why don't you open that bottle of champagne, Flynn, and we'll celebrate?"

He hesitates.

"Or are you on the wagon again?" she asks, remembering his three-martini lunch just yesterday.

"It's not ... it's just ... I'm trying not to—oh, what the hell. You're right. We should celebrate. I'll open the champagne," he says with a careless laugh.

Elizabeth freezes with her hand on the back doorknob.

The phone.

It's ringing.

Now.

She was just about to leave.

She falters, turning back to look at it.

What if it's Manny?

Or ...

What if it's Harper Smith?

Either way, she should answer it.

She's longing to put her mind at ease about Manny before she leaves; it was an agonizing decision, choosing to go without knowing whether he's all right.

And if it's Harper—

She has to act as though nothing's wrong. As though she's still planning on meeting him at Momma Mangia's restaurant at eight o'clock.

She has to thank him for the flowers, even, so he won't be suspicious.

She can't make him suspicious.

She needs a few hours to make a head start, to get far enough away from Windemere Cove so that he won't be able to trace her.

She moves quickly through the kitchen, through the house she just bade farewell.

Grabbing the receiver, she lifts it and says breathlessly, "Hello?"

"Elizabeth?"

"Manny!"

"Elizabeth, I need you. I'm in trouble. . . ."

"What is it? Where are you? Are you with your mother?"

"No."

He's sobbing, she realizes, and her heart constricts.

*Elizabeth, I need you.*

"Where are you, Manny?" she repeats, clenching the receiver in one hand, and in the other, her heavy canvas bank bag, the bag filled with hundreds of thousands of dollars in escape money.

"I'm at the bus station in Providence . . . in the security office . . . I need you to come and get me."

"I'll be right there, Manny. Just hang on, okay? I'll be right there," she promises.

And she never, ever breaks a promise.


Harper picks up the telephone, listening to the ringing on the other end of the line.

He's about to conclude that no one's going to answer, when he hears a click, and a voice.

"Momma Mangia's, can I help you?"

"Yes, please, I need a reservation for this evening."

"What time, sir?"

"Eight o'clock."

"How many?"

"Two," he says, then adds, "and can we have one of the booths, please? Preferably toward the back of the dining room?"

It's darker there. More private.

"A booth toward the back? I think we can arrange that for you, sir."

Harper thanks him and hangs up, a smile playing over his lips.

He glances at the clock.

Just a few more hours to kill.


Pamela can tell by looking at the big two-story brick house from the driveway that her parents aren't home.

Still, she gets out of the car, then opens the back door and unstraps first Hannah, then Jason from their car seats. Holding Hannah's hand and balancing the baby on her hip, she makes her way slowly up the drive, noting that the garage is closed and neither the Honda nor the Pathfinder is parked in the driveway. Since her parents rarely go out separately, that means one of their vehicles is in the garage.

And *that* most likely means they've gone up to Maine for the weekend.

Pamela has never been to the vacation home they purchased almost a year ago, when her father retired. She doesn't even know what town it's in, only that it's someplace near Camden. She has the address and phone number written down back at home.

She also knows that the place needs a lot of work. Her parents have spent nearly every weekend this summer up there, painting, shingling, and refinishing the hardwood floors.

"You'll have to come up," they've been saying since they bought the place. But it was out of the question during the rugged winter; it was too far for her to travel in her pregnancy; and when she brought it up to Frank in late July, he had said he couldn't get the time off.

"Why don't you and the kids go up?" he had suggested amiably. "Hannah would love the beach, and your parents keep complaining to you about how they've seen Jason only a couple of times since he was born."

Now she realizes he was obviously trying to get rid of them for a long weekend, so he could have his fun with the tramp next door.

"Where's Nana?" Hannah asks as they stand helplessly in front of the back door, which is locked up tight, the blinds on the window drawn. "Where's Papa?"

"I think they're up at their new house in Maine," Pamela tells her daughter.

Now she wishes she *had* taken Frank up on his suggestion and visited them there with the kids over the summer. If she had, she would at least know where the house is, and she could drive up and stay with them there.

As it is, she has no place to go.

No place but home to Windemere Cove, and Frank.

"Are you sure I need to go back home?" Manny asks Elizabeth as she pulls over to the curb a short distance down the street from his house.

"I'm positive," she tells him, glancing nervously at the digital clock on the dashboard.

It's seven-thirty.

She has just enough time to dash back home, find Frank Minelli and tell him about Manny's situation, then grab her bag of money and get out of town.

She still doesn't know where she's going. It doesn't matter. She just has to get away, to start driving anywhere. She'll figure out her destination along the way.

Manny is looking doubtful, shaking his head. "But I don't want to go home, Elizabeth. What if my grandfather—"

"He promised when you called him that he won't hurt you, Manny. Remember?"

The boy nods; his eyes aren't convinced.

"We're going to do just what we discussed, okay?" Elizabeth takes a deep breath, struggling not to look again at the clock as she says patiently, "You're going to go back home to your grandparents' house, and I'm going home to talk this over with my policeman friend next door. He'll contact your grandparents, and they'll do something about your mother's threats."

"Grammy sounded angry at me when I talked to her."

*I know,* Elizabeth thinks. *She sounded angry at me too.*

She tells herself that the woman had simply been worried about her missing grandson, trying to dismiss the thought that the grandparents should have called the police when they first realized Manny hadn't arrived at his rehearsal. The grandmother said she figured he was off playing hooky somewhere and that he'd show up sooner or later.

These people shouldn't have custody of a child.

They simply aren't equipped, emotionally or financially, to deal with Manny, or with the threats their daughter has made.

*It isn't that they don't care,* Elizabeth thinks.

The grandmother *had* sounded relieved when Elizabeth had called them from the pay phone at the bus station, telling them that she was a friend of Manny's and that he had called her to pick him up there after deciding not to run away.

She didn't mention the threats his mother had made—that would be up to the police to discuss with them.

Nor did she get into the run-in Manny had had with station security. There was no reason to tell them that. The officer in charge had grudgingly released the boy to Elizabeth after lecturing him about the seriousness of his infraction.

"Providence? How did he get to Providence?" his grandmother had asked Elizabeth in her broken English.

She hadn't been very happy to hear that he'd taken the local bus alone, transferring at busy Kennedy Square in the heart of the city.

That was when the grandfather got on the phone.

"Put Manny on," he curtly instructed Elizabeth after she had briefly explained the story again—that the child had run away because he was afraid his mother was going to kidnap him.

And so Manny got on the phone, and started crying, and told

the man that he wouldn't come home until his grandfather promised not to beat him.

He had promised.

Elizabeth prays to God that he meant it.

She reaches out and pulls the little boy into her arms, squeezing him tightly, a painful lump strangling her efforts to speak.

"Will you come back with the police later?" Manny asks, clinging to her blue denim shirt.

She shakes her head, then finds her voice and says truthfully, "I can't, Manny."

"But why not? I need you . . ."

There it is again.

*I need you.*

"I would if I could. But I have something that I have to do," she tells him, swallowing hard around the lump. It refuses to subside. "You just make sure you tell the police officers everything, okay?"

"Is it your friend who's going to come and talk to me?"

"I'm not sure," she says, thinking that Frank had said he'd be off duty tonight.

"I want it to be your friend, Elizabeth. Okay? I'll talk to your friend, but not to anyone else."

"I'll try and make sure he's the one who comes," she tells him, "but I can't guarantee it, Manny. You have to cooperate though. Will you promise me that? No more running away."

He nods, lowers his gaze.

She studies his precious face, longing to reach out and run a fingertip down that tear-streaked brown cheek.

This is the last time she'll ever see this child who has grown to mean so much to her.

"Be good, Manny," she says, fighting not to blink and release the tears that are blurring her vision.

He looks up at her, and she sees that his own eyes are filled with tears. He nods.

And it's almost like he knows, she thinks, her arms still tight around his shoulders.

But he can't know she's leaving.

And he can't know what he has meant to her.

That he's been the child she has never had . . .

Will never have.

"Okay," she says, ruffling his dark hair and giving him one last, fierce hug, "you have to go inside now. Remember what I told you."

"I will," he tells her. "And I'll call you if I need you."

She doesn't reply, just watches as he gets out of the car and walks away, shuffling his worn-out shoes on the broken concrete sidewalk.

Flynn Soderland's car phone rings as he's turning his Mercedes onto Laurel Canyon Boulevard, having dropped Rae off at her Burbank apartment five minutes earlier. She'd been in a hurry to get inside, but before she went he told her again how pleased he had been with her performance.

To say that she had surprised him would have been an understatement. She had shocked him, not just with the way she had nailed the character during the reading, but with her apt impersonation of Mallory Eden.

It had been eerie, almost, the way Rae had captured her dead friend.

If he hadn't known better, he would have believed that Mallory Eden had come back to life, that the suicide really had been a fake. Rae had it all down pat—the sexy saunter, the animated speech, the wholesome sensuality that had sent Mallory from unknown to A-list practically overnight.

Star quality.

It's that simple.

Rae Hamilton had suddenly displayed the star quality he had failed to see in her back when she first approached him to represent her.

Flynn knows de Lisser had been impressed with her, and so had that studio exec.

Now his phone is ringing, and enough time has passed since they left Napa that he can dare to hope it's de Lisser calling with a response.

The flight back to the Hollywood-Burbank airport had been delayed by wind, and when they'd finally taken off, it hadn't exactly been a pleasant trip. Rae had been pale, her eyes wide with terror.

Even Flynn, who has always enjoyed flying, had found it necessary to keep guzzling champagne to numb the fear that the tiny plane was going to be struck by wind shear and go down in the Sierra Madres.

It hadn't, of course.

As he reaches for the phone in the console, setting his burning cigarette carefully in the ashtray before he picking it up, he hopes that the rough ride hadn't been an omen.

He keeps his eyes on the road as he flips it open.

"Flynn Soderland," he says efficiently, still feeling giddy with the exhilaration of survival, and being back in the business—or, maybe, simply from all the champagne.

"Please hold for Martin de Lisser," says a crisp, businesslike voice.

He smiles.

Christ, it's like he never left.

*Please hold for Martin de Lisser.*

He's back in the business he loves, wheeling and dealing with the best of them.

Why had he ever retired?

Oh.

Right.

He'd retired because he lost his star client.

Mallory Eden had ruined both their careers by jumping off that freaking bridge in Montana.

"Soderland?"

"I'm here."

"This is unofficial, got that?"

"Got it."

"We'll take her."

Sheer, positive energy surges through Flynn; he victoriously smacks the steering wheel with his palm and grins, tilting his head back and mouthing the word yesss.

Then he pulls himself together.

"I'm glad" is his cool, professional response to de Lisser. "What's the deal going to be?"

"We'll get back to you in a day or so with our offer. But remember, this is between you, me, the studio, and Hamilton. We're still holding that open casting call."

"Of course," Flynn says quickly, familiar with the intricacies of the business.

"The studio will be in touch with the particulars."

"I'll look forward to that," he says, knowing there will be very little negotiation involved.

Not like with Mallory, when everybody wanted a piece of her, when offers were coming in faster than the waves at Surfrider

Beach in Malibu. With Mallory he had mastered the art of the multimillion-dollar deal; with Mallory he was able to bleed them all dry to make it worth her while. She had died at the height of her career, and no matter what threats she made about firing Flynn because of his drinking, the truth remains that he had done right by her.

Rae isn't going to command anywhere near the kind of money or perks that Mallory had.

Not yet.

But soon . . .

Elizabeth sees that the house next door is dark when she pulls into her driveway, and her heart sinks.

Where's Frank?

He had said he'd be there all night.

And she had promised Manny she'd talk to him.

She supposes she could call the police, but that would mean complications that might delay her exit.

With Frank she can simply explain the situation and ask him to handle it from there. Manny will be safe in his hands. He's a law officer, and a father himself. She trusts him.

Not enough to tell him that she's leaving town, of course.

She'll just go.

She *has* to go, she thinks, her nerves on edge as she shifts her car into park and glances first at the Minellis' darkened home, then at her own.

It's almost eight o'clock.

There's no time to lose.

She gets out of the car and goes to the house, vaguely noticing that raindrops have started to fall . . .

And belatedly remembering that she'd left the zippered canvas bag right out on the counter.

Panic seizes her as she fits her key into first one, then the second dead bolt.

How could she have been so careless?

What if there's been another break-in?

What if her money, her ticket out of here, is gone?

She'll be trapped, like a helpless animal in a hunter's snare, waiting to become prey.

She throws open the door and heaves a sigh of relief.

It's there, right where she had left it.

She hurries over, grabs it, unzips it, and checks the contents just to be sure.

It's there, dozens of packets of big bills, enough to build a new life someplace.

She glances at the clock on the wall, which is edging perilously closer to eight.

What should she do?

*You have to get the hell out of there, before he realizes you've stood him up.*

*Before he comes after you. . . .*

But what about Manny?

She had promised him she'd talk to Frank.

A noise outside startles her.

Her heart racing, she turns toward the window, then breathes a sigh of relief.

It's Frank, having stepped out his back door to put something into the garbage can.

*Thank God.*

*Thank God.*

Never has she seen a more welcome sight.

She hurriedly shoves the pouch of money into a cupboard, then goes back to the door. It's raining more heavily now, with the familiar swishing sound a summer rain makes as it plops onto thankful foliage and grass.

"Frank," she calls across the dusky yard.

He looks startled, glances up. "Hey there."

"I didn't realize you were home."

"Oh . . . I was watching television in the dark. I like to do that sometimes, when Pam isn't around." He wipes raindrops from his face and continues. "She always has the house lit up like Sakonnet Lighthouse. You should see our electric bill. It's—"

"Can I talk to you for a minute?" Elizabeth interrupts, glancing again at the clock behind her, on the wall.

"Sure you can talk to me. Is everything all right?"

"Everything's fine with me, but . . . it's about a friend."

"Okay . . . I'll be right there. Let me just run in and turn off the oven. I had put a pizza in, and the buzzer's about to go off, so—"

"You don't have to do that. It'll take only a minute," Elizabeth says, fighting to keep the desperation out of her voice. "I won't keep you from your pizza—"

"It's no big deal," Frank tells her. "I'll be right there."

He disappears into his house.

Shaking, she returns to her kitchen and the ticking clock.

Outside, the rain falls steadily on the roof, gaining in intensity. There's a far-off roll of thunder, signifying that the promised storm is on its way, that they're in for a good soaking.

She paces across the floor, returns to the door to look for Frank, and sees that he's not yet on his way over.

"Damn," she whispers, pacing again.

She's got to get out of there.

Before it's too late . . .


"No, it's all right," Harper Smith tells the owner of Momma Mangia, a dapper man with slicked-back hair and a thick dark mustache. "I'll wait for her right here. I'm sure she'll be along any minute."

The man nods and turns to a young couple who's just arrived, shaking raindrops from their hair. They are without reservations. He tells them that he has nothing available, and they'll have to wait.

"How long?" the guy asks, glancing anxiously at his date.

They can't be out of college yet, Harper notes absently. The girl, a pretty blonde clad in a white summer dress and sandals, looks innocent and nervous. The boy, in his Polo shirt and carefully pressed chinos with perfect creases down the front, is obviously eager to impress her.

"It could be an hour, maybe more. On weekend nights we're very busy. We strongly recommend making dinner reservations," the owner tells the young couple.

"Sorry about this. I didn't know," the boy says to the girl, and then to the owner, "We'll wait, I guess."

The man nods.

Harper checks his watch.

Eight-oh-five.

Where is she?

He remembers how reluctant she'd been to agree to have dinner with him.

What if she's changed her mind?

What if she isn't coming?

Why had he agreed to let her meet him here, to let her drive to the restaurant herself?

He should have insisted that he pick her up, that it be like a regular date.

*That's all I wanted,* he thinks, irritated, glancing again at his watch, and then at the door. *Just a regular date.*

Was that too much to ask?

Maybe.

Maybe not.

It would all depend on Elizabeth.

He folds his arms grimly and leans back against the wall to wait, keeping a watchful eye outside, where the wind has picked up and the rain is falling harder.

The wipers are making a rhythmic squeaking against the windshield as Pamela wearily steers the Toyota off the exit ramp leading from 195 to 114 south, the divided highway that runs through the East Bay.

"The speedway" Frank calls it because of the winding curves and other drivers' tendency to fly along the road at seventy and eighty miles an hour.

*Make sure you never go over the speed limit on 114, Pamela. Especially with the kids in the car.*

How many times has she heard that from Frank, who as a police officer has seen countless fatal wrecks on the road?

How many times has she resented him for uttering that last part?

*Especially with the kids in the car.*

As though she would ever take a chance with her children.

As though he doesn't care how fast she drives when she's alone.

"Just a few more minutes, and we'll be home," she announces to Hannah, who's been whining ever since they left Boston an hour and a half ago.

The traffic hasn't been as bad on the journey home as it had been going in, but the roads around Boston and Providence were still congested enough to make it a stressful trip, especially with the rain and the cranky kids in the backseat.

"Hannah? We're almost there," Pamela says again.

There's no reply, and she glances briefly over her shoulder to see that her daughter's pale blond head is slumped to the side.

She, like Jason, is sound asleep.

*It's about time,* Pamela thinks, shaking her head as she accelerates onto the wet highway, eager to put an end to this trip from hell.

What had she been thinking, just taking off like that?

Why hadn't she waited to make sure her parents were going to be home, or at least thought to bring the telephone number and address of their summer home?

*Because you were too angry at Frank to think straight*, she reminds herself.

*All you wanted to do was get out of there, to make him worry about you and the kids.*

So.

*Is* he worried?

Or is he glad they're gone, eager to seize the opportunity to dash next door and into the willing arms of their single and available neighbor?

*We'll soon find out, won't we?* Pamela thinks as she presses down on the accelerator, Frank be damned, and steers out into the left lane to bypass the traffic that's sticking to the fifty-five-mile-an-hour speed limit.

"I'm really glad that you came to me with this problem, Elizabeth," Frank is saying.

He's seated next to her on the couch, the picture of a casual conversationalist with his arm stretched along the back and one ankle crossed over the opposite knee.

Outside, the storm has intensified, with booms of thunder occasionally punctuating the patter of drops on the roof. The lights keep flickering; it's only a matter of time before the power goes out. It happens often in electric storms like this.

"I figured you would know what to do about Manny's situation without his automatically being sent to foster care," Elizabeth tells Frank, doing her best to keep a hysterical edge from creeping into her voice.

The digital clock on the VCR across the room says that it's 8:22. Her mind is whirling.

Any second now, Harper Smith is going to show up here, looking for her. He'll be in a rage that she never showed up at the restaurant.

She has to get out of there. . . .

But Frank isn't showing any signs of imminent departure, probably because he isn't eager to go out into the nasty weather. Why, of all times, does it have to be stormy *now*?

"The situation is very serious," he's saying. "That poor kid must be going through hell, with a mother like that. I mean, I never had a mother—she died giving birth to me—but my situation was better than having some drug-addict mother coming around threatening to kidnap me," he concludes, shaking his head in an isn't-that-a-shame gesture.

Elizabeth shifts nervously on the couch cushion, looking again at the clock: 8:23.

"I agree with you that this situation will have to be handled very delicately," Frank goes on, rubbing his chin with his palm, as though in deep thought.

*Please, just go.*

*Please . . . I have to get out of here.*

But even as she wishes she'd never asked to talk to Frank Minelli, she's certain it was the right thing to do. She had promised Manny, and now he'll get the help he needs.

"Are you all right, Elizabeth?" Frank interrupts himself to ask, and she realizes that while she's been staring at the clock, he's been looking intently at her.

"I'm . . . fine. It's just that . . . I have to be someplace."

"In this weather?"

"I had . . . plans."

He raises an eyebrow, then slaps his cheek as though the light has just dawned.

"Your date," he says, "with Harper Smith."

"That's right." Does she sound as desperate as she feels? Can he hear her heart pounding, see her entire body trembling?

"I guess I thought you'd changed your mind about going out with him."

"I was going to back out of it," she says, "but then I realized it would be best not to jump to conclusions. To, you know . . . give him a chance, I guess . . ."

Frank nods, watching her, wearing an expression she can't quite decipher.

*He doesn't believe me,* she realizes. *He knows I'm lying.*

Again, she looks at the VCR clock: 8:25.

Oh, Christ.

Maybe she should just tell Frank the truth at this point. He's a cop, and Smith must already be on his way over here. Maybe Frank can get his gun and hide in the next room. That way, when Smith tries something, Frank can—

"Are you sure that's a wise decision, baby?"

She opens her mouth automatically, to reply to Frank's question, then blinks.

What did he just say?

Did he just call her . . .

Baby?

She frowns slightly.

But what . . . ?

Suddenly Pamela's voice echoes in her muddled mind.

*Babe has always been Frank's nickname for me.*

Hadn't she said that not too long ago, in one of those intimate confidences Elizabeth could have done without hearing, but must have filed away in her subconscious?

Frank must have slipped, Elizabeth realizes, glancing at his casual expression. He must have said *babe* out of habit . . .

Except that she could have sworn he'd said *baby.*

Not *babe.*

She forces her attention back to whatever it is that he's saying.

The lights flicker.

Thunder crashes.

". . . because it's not that I'm so sure that Smith is that fugitive we're looking for. But I didn't really think he was your type."

Again she's startled.

So startled that she forgets to check the clock again.

"What . . . what do you mean?" she asks Frank Minelli slowly, knitting her brows and trying to ignore the warning signals going off in her mind.

"I mean, I thought I knew your type, baby."

*Baby?*

She's unable to speak, just watches him, her mind racing, her hands clenching into fists at her sides.

"I thought that *I* was your type."

Her jaw drops.

This can't be happening.

Not now.

"What are you talking about?" she asks, her voice a ragged whisper.

"Remember? 'Married men with children really, *really* turn me on.' Isn't that what you said?"

She backs away, starts to rise. "Frank, I don't know what you're—"

A steely grip on her forearm forces her back down, and he pushes her backward on the couch, then leans over her.

"Isn't that what you said?" he asks again, his brown eyes boring into hers, suddenly gleaming with an expression she never in a million years expected to see there. "And then you took off your clothes, remember, baby? You took off your clothes, and you danced. Take off your clothes for me. Dance for me, baby . . ."

Baby.

*Babie.*

*Babie Love.*

It hits her all at once, with stunning clarity.

He's talking about that film, that horrible porn film she made back in the eighties, at Brawley's insistence.

*He's the one,* she realizes. *He knows who you are.*

Oh, Christ.

He's been right under her nose.

It was Frank all along.

"When did you figure it out?" she asks him weakly, feeling his breath hot against her face as he looms over her, pressing the hard length of his aroused body into her.

"Figure what out?" he asks, breathing hard.

"That I'm . . ." She trails off, feeling his hand moving over her belly, up to grope at her breasts.

"Say it," he murmurs, his eyes closing as if in ecstasy. "Say it. Say your name."

She can't speak. Sirens are screeching in her brain. She has to get away.

"Say it," he barks, his eyelids jerking open, his menacing gaze burning into her face. His hand lifts from her breasts, comes down to painfully seize her arm. "Tell me who you are. You aren't Elizabeth Baxter. Say your name."

"Mallory," she says in a whisper, struggling not to give in to the utter panic that threatens to overtake her.

"What? I can't hear you." He glares at her, shakes her impatiently, painfully. "Say it again. Say it louder."

She summons every bit of willpower not to struggle against him, every bit of strength to project her voice as he's commanding her to.

"I'm Mallory . . . Mallory Eden," she tells him.

As she speaks over the clamor of the storm outside, the lights give a final flicker and go out . . .

Just as she hears a faint footstep in the next room.


Rae Hamilton sits on the small, bare stone terrace of her apartment, a glass of Chablis in one hand, a framed photograph in the other. The one from her dresser.

In the distance she can hear the rush hour traffic on the Ventura Freeway and, close by, through an open window, the sound of her upstairs neighbor laughing on the telephone.

The blue linen shift is in the basket to go to the dry cleaner's; the matching pumps are back in her closet; the carefully applied makeup has been scrubbed from her face. Her hair is pulled back in a ponytail, her feet are bare, and she wears her black workout leotard.

She had been on her way down to the gym when Flynn called a few minutes ago with the news.

*Are you sitting down, Rae? Well, then sit . . .*

*You did it! You're going to be the new Mallory Eden.*

*The new Mallory Eden.*

She wipes absently at the sudden moisture in her eyes as she gazes at the woman in the photograph.

It isn't one of those posed head shots, but a regular snapshot Rae had taken during one of their long-ago trips up the coast to Big Sur.

It shows a beautiful blonde with dazzling light-blue eyes, eyes that laugh up at Rae as though they haven't a care in the world.

But Rae was Mallory's closest friend. Rae knows what her short life was really like, especially toward the end.

*You did it, Rae!*

*You're going to be the new Mallory Eden. . . .*

"I'm sorry, Mallory," Rae whispers softly, shaking her head and swallowing hard over the lump in her throat. "I really am so sorry. But . . . I need this. God, I need this so badly."

Then she puts the photo aside and raises the glass of wine to her mouth as tears trickle down her cheeks.


"Help! Please help me!" Elizabeth screams shrilly, frantically praying that she isn't in more danger from whoever is lurking in her kitchen than she is from Frank Minelli.

The only reply is a deafening clap of thunder outside, and the steady whoosh of blowing rain.

"Shut up," Frank says above her in the dark, clamping a rough hand over her mouth.

She lets out another muffled scream.

"Shut up! No one's going to hear you, so you might as well—"

He's cut off, then, by the figure that rushes into the room, leaping on him and tackling him to the floor before Elizabeth realizes what's happening.

She huddles on the couch, violently trembling, for only a moment before coming to her senses and focusing on the two shadowy silhouettes wrestling on the floor.

They crash into furniture and tip over a lamp, grunting and cursing.

Frank rolls over, landing on top. "You son of a bitch," he bites out, panting.

The thought seizes Elizabeth that he might have his gun with him, that he might use it, not just on his attacker, but on her.

She glances wildly about the darkened room, then leaps to her feet and gropes blindly in the shadows for the first possible weapon that's within reach.

Her fingers close over the heavy metal andiron sitting on the hearth.

She doesn't stop to think before rushing toward the struggling pair, triggered by adrenaline—and stark fear.

She brings the heavy andiron down on Frank Minelli's skull, becoming aware only in the moment after he crumples to the floor that she had used enough force to have killed him.

For a moment, the sole sound in the room is that of heavy breathing—her own, and Harper Smith's.

She can barely see the murky outline of the man lying on the floor, the man who has made her life a living hell.

"Is he dead?" she asks Harper.

She hears him move, dimly makes out his silhouette as he reaches down to feel for a pulse at Frank's neck.

He's silent for a moment, and when he speaks, his tone is matter-of-fact.

"No, he's alive. And apparently, so are you . . . Mallory Eden."

# chapter

# 10

Manny Souza is awakened in his bed by his grandmother shaking his shoulders.

"Get up," she says urgently in Portuguese, and then again in English.

"What?" He rubs his eyes. Why is she waking him up? She never wakes him up, not even when he asks her to, so he won't be late for day camp.

Something must be wrong.

"What time is it?"

"After ten," she says. "Get up."

He blinks up at her from his pillow, trying to erase the fog from his mind. Is it after ten at night?

She's wearing one of her shapeless sleeveless cotton nightgowns and her hair is in sponge curlers, but that doesn't mean anything. Sometimes she doesn't get dressed until afternoon.

His gaze darts around the small room and realizes that it's morning, though the light coming in the window is gray with the summer storm that continues outside, rain pattering against the house in the same comforting rhythm that had lulled Manny to sleep the night before.

"It's your friend," Grammy says hurriedly, pulling him by the arm. "They're talking about her on the radio. On the news."

"What friend?"

"The one who called here yesterday—the one who brought you home from Providence."

"*Elizabeth?*" he asks, incredulous.

Why would they be talking about her on the radio?

Unless . . .

Did she get hurt? Was there an accident?

*Please, don't let anything have happened to Elizabeth. I need her. . . .*
His heart pounds as he follows his grandmother down the stairs to the kitchen.

"Gretchen? Are you awake?"
She frowns at the sound of her mother's voice calling up to her room and continues to stare out the window, where the morning sky is just beginning to clear after the storm that passed through Connecticut overnight. A cool breeze from the west is finally fluttering through the window, blowing her hair back from her ravaged face.

"Gretchen?" There are footsteps on the stairs now, and her mother's voice is more persistent. The door bursts open and Gretchen jerks her head around to find her mother standing there on the threshold of her room.

"What's wrong?" Her irritation mingles with curiosity at the unsettling expression on her mother's face. She runs a hand through her sleep-tousled hair.

"Hurry—come downstairs. There's something you have to see on television."

"On television? But I was just going to take a—"

"Gretchen, hurry. Come on! You won't believe what's happened." With that, her mother dashes back down to the living room, where the volume on the television set moves up a notch, and then louder still.

Puzzled, Gretchen scurries down to join her mother and find out what the fuss is all about.

Brawley Johnson stares at the television screen, oblivious of the woman behind him on the bed. A naked woman, beautiful by some standards, but not by his. A woman whose name will escape him by afternoon, when he has left her behind and done his best to forget her, the way he has forgotten every woman since . . .
Cindy O'Neal.

"Brawley, what are you doing?" A pair of willowy arms snake around his bare chest from behind as she sits up and presses her full breasts into his back. "How can you just stop in the middle of—"

"Shhh!"

The woman falls silent, but still he reaches for the remote control on the bedside table, raising the volume until the news announcer's voice is deafening in the small bedroom.

Flynn Soderland stands motionless on his Alpine Walker, his gaze fixed on the television set built into the wall of his home gym.

He had been plodding through his workout, doing his best to overcome the throbbing in his head caused by too much booze and too little sleep the night before.

*Just this once,* he had told himself then, caught up in the celebration over his casting coup and his return to the business.

And when he woke up that morning, he had sworn it really was the last time. He can't afford to risk it all—not when he's poised on the brink of success once again. Not when he's responsible for giving the world "the new Mallory Eden."

In fact, when he heard that name from the television announcer's lips a moment ago, his first thought was that it was in reference to the open call for the de Lisser film.

But it wasn't.

No, that's not what's causing the latest media furor. Not by a long shot.

Flynn never moves his gaze from the screen as he dismounts his exercise machine and reaches for the phone.

Who can be calling at this hour?

At . . .

Rae lifts her head and glances at the clock radio on the nightstand.

. . . seven o'clock on a Saturday morning?

She pulls the quilt over her head and squeezes her eyes shut, hoping whoever it is will go away.

But the phone rings a second time . . .

A third . . .

A fourth . . .

And the machine picks it up, clicking on in the next room with her familiar recorded message.

"Hi, this is Rae, and I'm not in. Please leave your name, number, and the time you called, and I'll get back to you as soon as I can. Thanks."

A beep.

And then, "Rae, it's me. Flynn. Are you there? Pick up, Rae. You're not going to believe this . . ."

* * *

Harper Smith skipped his morning jog today, and not just because of the rain, which is still falling over coastal Rhode Island.

For one thing, he hasn't slept a wink, though he went through the motions of climbing into bed when he got home in the wee hours of the morning, after the police let him go.

For another, he's been waiting by the phone, thinking she might call. That she might want to talk to him.

Apparently not.

But the world wants to talk *about* her.

He sits on his futon with a cup of coffee in one hand and the television remote in the other, focused on the screen, where a breaking story has interrupted regular programming on every local network affiliate.

A story about *her*.

Elizabeth Baxter.

AKA Malloy Eden, who has just turned up alive and well and living in Windemere Cove, Rhode Island.

"Mrs. Minelli, how does it feel to discover that your husband is actually the man who stalked and tried to murder Mallory Eden five years ago?"

Pamela clenches her jaw and stares straight ahead, shouldering her way past the reporter who leapt at her out of nowhere as she got out of her father's car in the police station parking lot.

"Did you ever realize your husband was fixated on Mallory Eden?" someone else calls, rushing toward her with an outstretched microphone.

"What about you? Were you aware of your next-door neighbor's true identity, and that she was the reason your husband wanted to move to this particular town, to that particular house?"

Good Lord, the place is crawling with reporters, Pamela realizes, trying to move on, up the steps to the police department.

How many times has she been there in the past? she wonders vacantly, gazing at the familiar building. How many times, with the kids in tow, dropping off something that Frank forgot, or stopping in to say hello and show off her babies to the guys on desk duty?

The kids aren't with her today, of course.

They're at home with her mother, asleep and—hopefully—unaware of the furor that's erupted, surrounding their father.

Pamela takes another step, then realizes that her path is blocked by a camera crew that's up on the steps, shining an obnoxious spotlight right in her eyes.

She blinks, feels her father's arm coming around her.

"Ignore them, honey," he tells her, guiding her around the camera crew and into the building, where detectives are waiting to question her about her husband.

"I told you, I had no idea who she was until I happened to see her in that video," Frank Minelli says, keeping his voice steady and his gaze focused on the two grim-faced detectives seated across from him in the interrogation room.

They're more likely to believe you if your voice is steady, he knows, and if you look them in the eye.

But damn, it's nearly impossible not to find yourself shifty-eyed and warbling all over the place under tense circumstances like these.

He reaches up to wipe a bead of sweat from his brow.

"You're saying that you are *not* responsible for stalking Mallory Eden in California, for following her here to Rhode Island after she faked her suicide, and for resuming the stalking?"

"That's what I'm saying. Look, I already admitted that I sent the card to her post office box—"

"You had no choice. We've confirmed that the handwriting belonged to you."

"I didn't deny it.

"No, and you didn't deny that you broke into her house," one of the detectives puts in. "Or that you went to the library and used the computer there to investigate her background. Or that you were sneaking around at night, looking into her windows."

"No, that's not true. I couldn't see into her windows," Frank mutters. "The blinds were always down."

"Such a shame," the detective says in a mocking tone.

"You also admit that you were living in California five years ago when Mallory Eden was stalked and shot," adds the other. "I'd say it looks like—"

"I was *staying* there," Frank cuts in, careful not to let his voice rise. He clenches his fists beneath the table, away from their view. "I stayed there temporarily. With my brother, at his house. He lives in Pasadena. Check it out with him. I was out of work, so I went out there for a few months—but I swear I had nothing to do with stalking Mallory Eden. I didn't even know she *was* Mallory Eden until last night."

"Oh, come on. Then why send her the card?" asks one detective.

"A card that reads—" the other detective checks his notes, and continues—" 'I know who you are.' What did you mean by that if not—"

"I meant that I knew who she was—that she was Babie Love. Not Mallory Eden."

"Babie Love and Mallory Eden are the same person."

"But I didn't know that then. Look, I'm not the guy who stalked her in California and made her jump off a bridge. This whole thing is a coincidence."

"You mean your winding up as Mallory Eden's next-door neighbor?"

"Of course it's a coincidence. How could I have followed her here, the way you think I did, knowing that the house next door would suddenly go up for sale when the old lady died, and I would be able to buy it?"

"You tell me," one detective says.

"We're looking into the old lady's death," the other puts in.

Frank's heart starts beating even faster.

"You think I . . . ? But that's ridiculous," he says. "I swear this is a coincidence. I swear I'm just a normal married man, a *father*, for Christ's sake, who—"

"A normal married man who goes around stalking his next-door neighbor, breaking into her place, attempting to rape her."

"I didn't do anything she didn't want me to do, so—"

"And I don't think you and she are in agreement on that point."

Frank clamps his mouth shut.

There are a few moments of silence.

Then Frank says, "Look, I didn't know she was Mallory Eden. I didn't even know she was Babie Love until I saw that porn video a few weeks ago, and I happened to recognize her."

"So why stalk her? Why not go over to her like a normal person and say, 'Hey, I saw you in this video last night . . .'?"

"Because—have you *seen* the video?" Frank's face is hot; he knows he's flushed.

And flushed doesn't look good. Flushed indicates that a perp is lying.

The detectives shake their heads briefly.

"Well, after I saw that video, I figured she would go for that sort of thing," Frank begins.

He's interrupted by one of the detectives, saying incredulously, "You thought she would go for *stalking?*"

"I wasn't trying to stalk her. I was just trying to get her attention, trying to be . . ."

"Trying to be what, Frank?"

"I don't know . . ."

"What?"

"I don't know . . . mysterious," he blurts out.

He hates the smirks on their faces, loathes himself for being stupid enough to get caught.

And most of all, he's furious with Elizabeth Baxter—Mallory Eden.

So .

Mallory Eden.

She isn't dead after all?

Is it really such a surprise that the superstar actress never jumped off that bridge?

*You should have known . . .*

Mallory the golden girl would never have been able to take her own life—a golden life.

How clever she must have thought she was, to have escaped her stalker so easily, to have faded into obscurity.

How clever to have established a nice little life for herself, according to the television reporter now reporting live from the street in front of an unassuming Cape Cod house in a small Rhode Island town.

But not clever enough.

*The world knows you're alive, Mallory.*

*The world knows . . .*

*And I know.*

So . . .

What next?

*You'll have to see what she's going to do now.*

*And, depending on that . . .*

*You might have to get rid of her . . .*

The knowledge comes in an unexpected, yet oddly welcome surge of awareness.

*Get rid of her . . .*

Yes, that's right. It may have to be done.
*Get rid of her . . .*
This time for good, leaving nothing to chance.
But how?
When?
 The specifics can wait.
Step one can't.
The first thing to do is to get in touch with her again; to reestablish the connection; to win her trust.
*You had it before. You can get it back again.*
And after that, if the situation isn't satisfactory . . .
*Prepare to die, Mallory Eden. This time for good.*

# chapter

# 11

The ringing telephone jars Mallory's thoughts.

The police detective seated next to her on the couch glances at her and she gets up to answer it, knowing she doesn't have a choice.

Anything's better than sitting there, under police guard, staring at the television set, where her very existence is being trumpeted by the media in special live news reports that have disrupted the Saturday morning cartoons. Outside, reporters are swarming, and there are helicopters vibrating in the sky overhead.

She is once again a prisoner in her own home, dogged not by fear, as she has been for the past five years, but by the press, and her fans, and curiosity seekers.

Strange, how quickly the familiar trapped feeling has come rushing back at her, even after all these years. She can't even peer through the blinds at the hoopla in the street without feeling as though she's suffocating.

She reaches for the phone, lifts the receiver, sees the detective, a fleshy-faced, hard-eyed man, keeping a watchful gaze on her.

Presumably, he's there to keep her safe.

But she doesn't trust him.

She'll never trust anyone again.

"Hello?" she asks, bracing herself for a question zinged by a member of the press. They haven't gotten hold of her unlisted number yet, but she knows it's only a matter of time before they do, before they start calling and force her to take the phone off the hook.

"It's me."

She finds a faint smile slipping over her lips, catching her by surprise. How can she be smiling at a time like this?

"Harper," she says, unwilling to let him know how relieved she is to hear from him. "What do you want?"

"To make sure you're okay. Are you?"

"I'm fine."

"I figured you were. If you weren't, you would have paged me. Right?"

She hesitates. He had given her the number of his pager before they separated early that morning, telling her to use it if she needed anything. Anything at all.

She wasn't sure then, and still isn't, whether he was talking about needing a locksmith, or needing . . .

A man.

A friend.

Or . . .

Whatever Harper Smith has somehow become to her in the past twelve hours or so.

"Hello?" Harper prods.

"I'm here. I just . . . isn't your pager number for business purposes?"

"I'm self-employed. It's no big deal. Just like I said . . . if you need something, page me."

"I can't imagine what I would need, aside from some privacy."

"Privacy?" He makes a snorting noise. "I've been watching you on television. Finding out all sorts of things."

"Like . . . ?"

"Like, your natural hair and eye color is brown. Just the way it is now. You didn't say anything about that last night, to the cops that were there."

"There were a lot of things I didn't say last night. I was in shock."

"You and me both. I'm still in shock, Eliz—Mallory. I had no idea who you were. No wonder you seemed so familiar when I first saw you."

She frowns, the ringing doorbell momentarily distracting her.

The detective is looking out the window, apparently trying to figure out if it was rung by a member of the press, or by a fellow lawman. There's a pounding on the front door.

"I have to go," Mallory tells Harper.

"Wait. I'm coming over there."

"You . . . you can't."

"Why not?"

"You have no idea what's going on out there."

"I don't, huh? Let me tell you about it, then. It's a three-ring circus. I'm looking at your house right now, live on television. And by the way, there's a cop knocking at the door. He looks frustrated, and he's getting rained on. Maybe you should let him in."

She smiles, again unable to help herself, and calls to the detective, "It's okay, it's a cop."

He looks suspicious, but opens the door, one hand on the holster at his hip.

A uniformed officer steps in and the door is quickly shut behind him.

"I'm coming over," Harper repeats over the phone.

"Why?"

"Because I want to be with you."

"Because I'm Mallory Eden," she says, keeping her tone light.

"No. I'm not the star-struck type. I never even liked your movies all that much."

"Thanks a lot!"

"I'm trying to prove a point, Mallory."

"Which is . . ."

"That I wanted to be with you before I knew who you were. Remember?"

She smiles. He's right.

She wants to ask him where he was five years ago; why it's taken her so long to meet a man who would want her because of *what* she is, not *who* she is.

So, can I come?" he's asking.

"I don't think so," she tells him.

Old habits die hard.

"You shouldn't be alone, Mallory."

"I'm *not* alone. That's the problem. I've got security guards, camera crews, helicopters. I don't think I'll ever be alone again."

He doesn't argue with that.

"Tell them to expect me," he says calmly, "so they can let me in. I'll be there in ten minutes. I'll be wearing a yellow rain slicker, carrying a white umbrella."

"Sounds colorful."

"And a bouquet of roses."

She opens her mouth to protest, but he's already hung up.

She replaces the receiver, a bemused smile on her face.

It stays there until his words echo through her mind again.

*No wonder you seemed so familiar . . .*

Of course he'd thought she was familiar. He had seen every movie she'd ever made.

But what about *him?*

Why did *he* seem so familiar to her?

It has to be because she spotted him on the street here in Windemere Cove, she tells herself again.

Not because she saw him someplace in L.A.

Not because—

No.

She shakes her head.

*He isn't the stalker.*

Frank made that up, everything he said about Harper resembling some fugitive from L.A. According to his fellow local police officers, there *was* no fugitive from L.A.

Frank was simply trying to scare her off so that she wouldn't date Harper. Presumably, because he was jealous.

She shivers.

It still gives her the creeps, that Pamela's husband—her next-door neighbor—is the one who has made her life miserable for all this time. That he's been secretly watching her, lusting after her, making his plans . . .

*Christ,* she thinks with another shudder, remembering how she had decided to trust him about Manny; how she herself had summoned him over so that they could talk . . .

How could she have never suspected him?

How could she have suspected Harper?

Harper, who had saved her life?

Thank God Harper had shown up when he did, to find out why she hadn't arrived at the restaurant. Later he told her he'd been half angry at her for standing him up, and half worried that something had happened to her.

If Harper hadn't walked in the back door—which she had, in her agitated state of mind, carelessly left unlocked after Frank arrived—who knows what Frank would have done to her?

*She* knows.

He would have raped her.

Then killed her.

Instead, Harper had come to her rescue.

Then *she* had come to *his* rescue, knocking Frank out with that andiron.

Frank had been dazed when he'd come to last night, to find several of his fellow Windemere Cove police officers standing over him, their weapons drawn.

He had broken down and admitted to trying to force himself on her—and, when pressed, had also confessed to sending the card, breaking into her house, and stealing her keys in the hope that he could sneak in undetected.

The very thought sends a chill down her spine.

He had, however, refused to admit that he had followed her from California, establishing himself as her trusty next door . . . and a cop.

And that's the part that's giving Mallory some trouble.

She *wants* to believe that it's been Frank all along, all of it. That he's the one who tormented her in L.A., slashing her dog's throat, shooting her as she slept, sending the exploding floral arrangement.

That's what the detectives seem to believe, now that they've traced him to California that summer and established, through Pamela, that he's always had a "thing" for blue-eyed blondes.

"But what man doesn't?" Pamela had demanded tearfully.

Mallory had heard her, though she was in the next room, behind a closed door, with two detectives.

She had also heard Pamela protesting in one breath that her husband has to be innocent, and condemning him in the next, wailing that she *knew* it—she *knew* there was something going on, a reason why Frank had lost all interest in her. That she *knew* he was some sick, twisted psycho . . . and what about the children? How is she supposed to explain to them that their father is in jail?

Mallory doesn't like thinking about Pamela and the children. Doesn't like remembering how the three of them had arrived at the house moments before the police had come. Pamela had burst in the back door with Hannah and Jason in her arms, demanding to know where her husband was, calling Mallory a whore.

Then she had spotted Frank lying unconscious on the floor and started shrieking, "What have you done to him?"

Luckily, the police had arrived then.

And luckily, Harper had taken the by-then-crying children into the other room to calm them down.

*Harper to the rescue.*

The phrase has been running through Mallory's mind all through the sleepless night.

So has the knowledge that her life as she knew it is over once again.

She had seen it coming, had been certain that by that morning the news about her true identity would be all over the media.

She had even, for a few crazed moments, begged Harper not to call the police last night after she had knocked Frank out.

She had been frantic, realizing that if they called the police, she would have to reveal who she was . . .

And she would no longer be protected by anonymity.

It was Harper who pointed out that it no longer mattered.

That with Frank, her stalker, in custody, she's safe.

There's no reason to go on hiding.

No reason at all.

She can go back to being Mallory Eden.

Back to L.A.

Back to her career.

Back to everything she'd thought she must leave behind forever.

Everything she has missed so desperately over the past five years.

The only trouble is . . .

She's suddenly uncertain she *wants* to go back.

Manny is fixated on the television, and has been for the past two hours.

Ever since his grandmother called him down the stairs to listen to the radio report about Elizabeth . . .

About the fact that she's really that famous actress, Mallory Eden, who's supposed to be dead.

Before now, Manny had only vaguely known who Mallory Eden was.

He saw her in a movie Grammy was watching on TV one night a long time ago, a movie he wasn't supposed to be watching, because he was supposed to be in bed.

But he'd come downstairs and told Grammy he was having nightmares again. He no longer remembers whether he really was having nightmares that particular night, or whether he'd just said it so he could stay up late.

But he does remember that he'd watched the movie, called *Mommy's Boyfriend*, about a little kid who doesn't want his mother to remarry and does everything he can to sabotage her wedding.

Manny had thought, at the time, that if he had a mommy who

was as sweet and funny and beautiful as the mommy in the movie, his life would be perfect.

Just as he has often thought that if Elizabeth could be his mother, his life would be perfect.

And even though he's always known that would be impossible, he must have been holding on to a tiny piece of hope.

He must have been, because something inside him had shriveled and died that morning, the moment he had turned on the television to make sure that the lady they were talking about on the radio was the same Elizabeth who is his friend.

He hadn't even seen her face in the videotape footage, which showed her coming out of the Windemere Cove police station in the middle of the night, with police officers all around her. She had a coat draped over her head.

But it was her, all right.

The woman on television was wearing the same long-sleeved navy blue T-shirt Elizabeth had had on when she dropped him off at his grandparents' house last night.

And Manny had known, when he had recognized that it was her, that she would never be his mother after all.

No famous movie star is going to adopt a poor kid from a small town in Rhode Island.

Manny sighs, watching the television.

He barely recognizes Elizabeth in the lady they keep showing in old pictures and video clips. That lady has blond hair and light blue eyes, and she's always laughing.

Elizabeth has brown hair and brown eyes . . . and she never laughs.

Now he knows why.

Because of that bad man who wanted to hurt her.

The bad man who's now locked up in jail.

So she's safe.

And now she'll leave Windemere Cove and go back to Hollywood, where she belongs.

Maybe someday he can visit her there, Manny thinks hopefully.

The thought vanishes just as quickly as it had arisen.

Nah.

Movie stars don't invite little kids to visit them.

Movie stars have movie-star friends.

*But she really was my friend,* Manny protests, remembering the way she'd driven up to Providence to get him last night.

And how she'd stuck up for him when those bus station security guards had wanted to call the police.

And how she'd hugged him before he got out of the car at his house, promising that she'd make sure her policeman friend took care of his mother, so that she couldn't come and take Manny away.

Manny wonders now if the policeman friend she'd mentioned is the same policeman who had tried to hurt her at her house.

It makes him angry to think of anyone hurting Elizabeth.

Even though he'll probably never see her again.

Even though she'll never be his mother.

Tears roll slowly down his cheeks as Manny sits there, silently watching the television screen.

"Did you miss me?"

Mallory fights the urge to throw herself into Harper's muscular arms, to bury her head against his broad chest.

He looks so damn good to her, standing there with an armload of roses, dripping rain on the doormat.

*Yes, I missed you,* she wants to tell him. *Please don't leave me. Ever again.*

But this is a man she barely knows, a man she suspected—as recently as last night—of trying to kill her.

Besides, there are half a dozen cops and detectives in the room, keeping a wary eye on both her and the newcomer.

So she says simply, "Why don't you take off your raincoat? I'll take it for you."

He obliges, handing her the slicker and the roses.

"Careful," he warns, "they have thorns."

She sees that these roses, their prickery canes wrapped in several layers of damp paper towels, aren't the perfect, long-stemmed florist variety; rather, they're the rambling, sweet-smelling blooms that seem to grow wild over fences and trellises in Windemere Cove.

"I just cut them from my yard," Harper tells her, swiping at the water droplets that are clinging to his damp, dark, unruly hair.

"That was so sweet." Her casual tone doesn't betray the way her heart has leapt from its perch at his words.

*He cut them himself.*

*He did that for me.*

*This strapping man's man went out into his yard and he cut a bunch of roses for me.*

She hangs the coat over a chair, not caring that it will make a puddle on the hardwood floor.

"I've always liked to give a lady flowers. And you deserve them today, more than anyone I've ever known," Harper says with a shrug.

She remembers the floral arrangement he'd had delivered yesterday, the one she'd had Frank Minelli destroy.

She feels sick inside at the thought of how mistaken she'd been—about both men. Sick about what had almost happened . . .

"Have you heard anything about Frank Minelli?" Harper asks. "Did he confess?"

"Not to all of it, no. He's claiming he had no idea who I was—he just knew that I had been the actress in that sleazy movie. . . ." She trails off uncomfortably, shifting her gaze away from Harper's.

Babie Love. She told him at some point last night, as they sat on the uncomfortable bench at the police station, drinking cold, bitter coffee and waiting to be questioned again, about doing that film.

She had told him how uncomfortable she'd been with the nudity but how desperate for money and a "real" acting job. She had also told him about Brawley, how he had tricked her into making the film.

"Sounds like a really wonderful guy," Harper had said, shaking his head. "What kind of bastard would do something like that to a kid?"

"I wasn't a kid. . . ."

"You were eighteen. A kid."

Her reaction to the disgust on his face?

*Don't do this,* she had found herself begging him silently. *Don't show me how different you are from him. Don't make me wonder what it would be like to be with someone like you, someone who would look out for me, care about what happens to me.*

"So Minelli's claiming he didn't know you were Mallory Eden, huh? I wonder how long he'll hold out," Harper is saying.

She turns her attention back to the conversation, back to his handsome face, the concern in his green eyes.

"He's been trying to get through to me all morning, through his lawyer," she tells Harper. "I don't know what he wants to talk to me about."

"You haven't spoken to him?"

"No." She shudders. "I never want to see him again; I don't even want to hear his voice over the telephone. His lawyer keeps calling, telling me how bad Frank feels."

"Don't let it get to you," Harper says, briefly placing a hand on her arm.

When he moves it away, she fights the urge to grab on to it, to grab on to him.

"What?" he asks, staring at her as though he's read her mind.

"I . . . nothing," she tells him, looking away.

There's a knock on the front door just then, followed by a mad scrambling among the lawmen in the room before it's opened warily.

Another police officer enters, and Mallory sighs.

"Who else would they be expecting, now that Frank is in custody?" Harper asks her.

She looks incredulously at him. "The press."

"Oh. Right. Do you know how easy it is to see you standing there in a T-shirt and jeans and forget that you're this big movie star, that you're this huge, internationally significant story?"

"I wish I could forget."

"So . . . what are you going to do now? Go back to L.A., pick up where you left off?"

His tone is casual, but the expression in his green eyes is anything but that.

This is insane, Mallory thinks, that this man—a virtual stranger—means anything to her. She has known him only a few days, and had spent most of that time fearing him, trying to escape him.

But she can't forget the way he fought valiantly to save her last night; the way he comforted the children afterward; the way he submitted without complaint to the endless questioning from detectives; the way he insisted on waiting with her at the police station until close to dawn, when they allowed her to leave; how he had called after her as she was led out to a waiting squad car, flanked by several cops and holding her rain jacket over her head to hide her face from the dozens of press cameras, "I'll phone you in the morning."

And he *had* phoned.

And now he's there, standing at her side, making her feel safer by his very presence than any of this security force, with their watchful eyes and their ready weapons.

But there's nothing left to fear.

It's over.

As Harper said, Frank is in custody.

Why can't she get past the nagging sense of doubt that her worries are over?

*Because it's been so long,* she tells herself. *After so many years of living in fear, you're not going to just let go of it that easily.*

"Ms. Eden?"

*Ms. Eden . . .*

How long has it been since somebody called her that? The name comes zinging back from the past, making her pause momentarily before glancing up to see the newly arrived police officer standing before her, a sheet of paper in his hand.

"Yes?" she asks, a tremble in her voice.

"We've taken down several messages for you."

"What do you mean?"

"There have been calls for you at the police station. Your number is unlisted—"

"It is, but believe me—I know from past experience that it's only a matter of time before it gets out," she says, shaking her head.

"Well, calls are coming in from around the country. Apparently, quite a few people are trying to get a hold of you. Police headquarters is apparently the only place they can think of trying."

"Who's calling?" she asks, suddenly bone-weary, and not just from the lack of sleep.

"Mostly, the press," he tells her, confirming her suspicions. "We've fielded those calls. And there were dozens of fans—most of them men. But," he adds, "we did take down several names and numbers from people who claimed to be personal acquaintances of yours, people who said you'd want to hear from them."

"Who are they?" She reaches for the sheet of paper he's handed her, scanning the list of names from the distant past, names that whisk her back over the years to another time, another place . . . another life.

A life she isn't so sure she wants back.

*Flynn Soderland.*

*Brawley Johnson.*

*Rae Hamilton.*

*Gretchen Dodd.*
*Becky O'Neal.*

The phone rings, and Rae Hamilton jumps to answer it.
*Mallory . . . it has to be Mallory.*
But it isn't.
It's Flynn.
"Have you heard from her yet?" he wants to know, his voice edgy.
"No. Have you?"
"No."
Rae hears him exhale sharply and wonders if he's smoking a cigarette, or simply sighing.
"We should go to her," Rae says, and bites her lip. "If she doesn't call us. She shouldn't be alone through all of this."
"She's been alone for five years, Rae. By choice."
"I know, but . . . I just hate to think of what she might be going through, Flynn."
"Well, so do I."
Rae toys with the plastic ring on the neck of the bottle of spring water she'd been drinking from. "Do you think she'll call?"
"Eventually. When she's ready."
"Do you think she'll come back?"
"Back, what?" Flynn asks. "Back to L.A.? Back into our lives? Back to acting?"
She hesitates, then says, "All of the above."
Flynn is silent for a moment. "There's no way of knowing, Rae. We'll just have to wait and see."
What he doesn't say, what's on both of their minds, is that there'll be no need for Martin de Lisser to cast Rae as "the new Mallory Eden . . ."
Not if the old Mallory Eden comes back.

Gretchen sits in her window, staring out at the backyard, at the tiresome, familiar view that is all she's seen for five years now.
She's sick of the same old overgrown rhododendron shrubs, the drab chain-link fence, the whiny kids next door, their monstrosity of a swingset.
Sick of sitting there alone, day in and day out, while the world keeps spinning around her.
Sick of her mother's worried hovering, of the flavorless food

and halfhearted encouragement she tries to force on Gretchen, and her talk of the senior citizens wasting away in the nursing home where she works.

Gretchen has no sympathy for any of them, the ancient geezers who have lived long, full lives.

She doesn't want to hear—via her sympathetic mother—their complaints about being widowed, or about their children and grandchildren not calling, or about not being able to get around anymore, or about being wrinkled and gray.

Gretchen will never have a husband.

Will never have a family of her own.

She will never get out into the world again.

And being wrinkled and gray sounds like a picnic compared to being twenty-seven years old and so hideously deformed that children run screaming in the opposite direction.

This is her life, right here.

Isolated from the world.

The irony is that she has been living just as Mallory Eden had apparently lived these past five years, and less than fifty miles away.

Mallory, like Rae, had been a prisoner of the past, forced to hide from strangers' prying gazes.

Would she return Gretchen's phone call?

Would she dare to confront the woman whose life she had ruined?

Would she agree to pay for a consultation with Dr. Reed Dalton, the plastic surgeon whose fees were astronomical, but who had told Gretchen that there's hope . . .

Hope she had long ago given up.

Would Mallory Eden spend the hundreds of thousands of dollars it would take to reconstruct Gretchen Dodd's face again?

That would remain to be seen.

For now, Gretchen can do nothing but wait.

And stare out the window.


"Ms. Eden? Somebody's here to see you."

Mallory looks up at the young police officer, the one who had been stationed at the back door.

"Who is it?" she asks, setting her glass of iced tea on the table and standing.

"It's me." Pamela Minelli steps into the kitchen.

Her pretty, chubby face bears the evidence of too many tears and too little sleep, and her blond hair is matted, as though it had gotten damp in the rain that had ended earlier, and Pamela hadn't bothered to brush it.

She's wearing a pair of baggy sweatpants and an immense sweatshirt that must belong to her husband, the way the sleeves hang over her hands. The oversized clothing gives her a little-girl-lost appearance.

"Where are the kids?" is all Mallory can think of to say to her neighbor.

"They're home, with my mom and dad. I reached them in Maine last night and they drove down to be with us."

"That's good."

Pamela nods.

"How are you?" Mallory asks after an awkward moment of silence.

She knows the question is a mistake as soon as it's out of her mouth, but she can't take it back.

There is a flicker of anger in Pamela's red-rimmed eyes, and then, surprisingly, it vanishes.

She doesn't lash out, doesn't say, "How the hell do you *think* I am?"

She just shrugs and says, so quietly Mallory can hardly hear her, "Surviving. So far."

Mallory nods.

Pamela stares at her muddy tennis shoes.

Mallory tries to think of something to say, something that isn't trite or hurtful or depressing.

Her mind is a blank.

"Where's Harper Smith?" Pamela asks suddenly, looking up.

"He went home to get some sleep."

"How long have two been seeing each other?"

"Oh . . . we're not . . . we're not really seeing each other. I mean . . . he's a friend."

"Oh."

Silence.

Then Pamela sighs.

Mallory looks out the window over the sink, at the sky that has gradually been clearing all afternoon.

Pamela clears her throat.

Mallory glances up at her.

"I just want you to know," she says at last, looking Mallory in the eye, "that whatever Frank is responsible for doing to you, he never meant to hurt you. You've got to talk to the police, tell them that he never—"

"He attacked me!" Mallory cuts in, anger transforming her hands into fists clenched tightly at her sides. "He broke into my home. He—"

"But he didn't know who you were. He didn't—"

"He sent me a card that said 'I know who you are,' " Mallory retorts.

"But he didn't realize that you were Mallory Eden. He thought you were just some porn actress trying to hide your past. He never stalked you in California, and he never tried to kill you. He never—"

"How do you know?" Mallory cuts in angrily.

"Because he told me." Pamela's voice is quiet, but her blue eyes are blazing as they bore into Mallory's face. "He admits to what he did last night, and to watching you over the past few weeks, but he says that's all there is to it. And I believe him. I can't have him go to jail for a crime he didn't commit. I know he's telling the truth."

"How can you say that?" Mallory is incredulous at this woman's need to deceive herself, to believe a lowlife like Frank Minelli. "How can you listen to anything that comes out of a man who—"

"Because he's my husband. The father of my children. They need their father. You've got to tell the police that—"

"The police are conducting their own investigation of Frank. I've already talked to them. I've told them everything I know."

"You don't have proof that he was the one who was stalking you, who shot you . . ."

"He was in California five years ago, at the exact time I was being stalked. Are you saying that's a coincidence?"

"That's exactly what I'm saying." Pamela lifts her pudgy chin with conviction. "I met Frank five years ago. I know what he was like. He wasn't some psycho who went around stalking movie stars, killing dogs, shooting people as they slept."

"And yesterday, if someone had asked you if he was a psycho who prowled around spying on unsuspecting women—ransacking their houses, sending frightening letters, trying to rape them— what would you have said?"

Mallory's words hang in the air.

For a moment she and Pamela Minelli stare at each other, and Mallory is certain that the fury she sees in her neighbor's gaze is mirrored in her own.

She wants to shake this foolish woman who refuses to face the truth about her husband. Who insists on defending him even now, after what he's done. Who actually expects Mallory to stick up for him, to tell the police that he's not responsible for what happened in California.

Finally, Pamela breaks the eye contact, turning away.

She walks out the door without another word, and Mallory watches her cross the driveway and the yard, seemingly oblivious of the questions hollered by the hordes of reporters camped out in the street.

Brawley had gone to the airport on impulse, bought the plane ticket on impulse—without waiting to hear from Mallory first.

Only now, when he's sitting back in his seat, his head turned toward the window and the view of LAX disappearing below, does he stop to think about what he's done.

His destination: T. F. Green State Airport in Rhode Island, via New York City.

He paid full fare for the last-minute first-class ticket, putting it on his one credit card that wasn't maxed out.

It's pretty damn close now.

But he doesn't want to think about the serious debt he's amassed over the past decade in an attempt to keep himself in designer clothing, and visible on the L.A. scene.

Nor does he want to think about the fact that he no longer has a job. Not after calling his boss this morning and saying he needs a few more days off from his job driving rich celebrities and out-of-town businessmen around in a stretch limo.

"I gave you last weekend off so you could do all those interviews," his boss had groused. "You can't have this weekend too. You know I need you this afternoon and all night."

Brawley had tried to explain that he needed the time because his ex-fiancée had been found alive, which his boss must have known. No one with a radio or television set and a pair of functioning eyes and ears could not have known about Mallory Eden turning up in that rinky-dink Rhode Island town.

But his boss didn't care.

His boss had told him not to bother coming back.

*No problem*, Brawley thinks, turning abruptly away from the window as L.A. disappears beneath a bank of smog.

He won't need to come back.

Not if he has Mallory.

Mallory . . .

And her money.

She'll get him out of debt.

Hadn't she always been happy to throw him a few hundred, even a few thousand here and there?

Well, maybe not *happy*.

But she had done it, if only to keep him quiet and out of her hair.

Now, after living alone for five years, she might be glad to see him . . .

To let bygones be bygones.

To pick up where they'd left off, back when she was a nobody.

Then again, she might not.

And if she doesn't . . .

"Can I get you something to drink?" asks a pretty flight attendant, stopping in the aisle beside his seat.

She's smiling at him, not in the way first-class flight attendants smile at all their passengers, but in the way a woman smiles at a man she wants.

Brawley smiles back even as he notices a slight space between her front teeth. And her eyes, while they're a nice shade of blue, are set a little too close together.

"I'll have a sparkling water," he tells her, keeping his voice pleasant.

"No cocktails for you this afternoon?"

"No, thanks."

He needs to keep his mind clear for what lies ahead.

Becky leaves the bathroom and hurries back down the hallway of the rooming house, moving with unseeing eyes past the jagged holes in the pea-green plaster and the water stains on the wall outside her room.

The door is ajar, just as she left it, and Gerry from down the hall is sitting dutifully on her bed.

"Did she call?"

Gerry shakes her head.

"You were here the whole time, waiting by the phone?"

"Ain't that what you tol' me to do? An' you owe me another buck fifty for doin' it."

Becky sighs and dutifully digs into the pocket of her worn jeans to produce three quarters, four dimes, and five nickels. She thrusts the change into Gerry's outstretched hand.

"Next time you need me to come down here to listen for your phone, you're gonna give me five bucks," Gerry says after shrewdly counting the coins twice. She walks out the door. "I ain't no answering service, you know."

"I know. Thanks for helping me out."

She closes her door and looks at the phone sitting silently on the dilapidated table by the lone window.

"Ring," Becky commands. "Ring. Now."

Nothing but silence.

She scowls.

She doesn't know why she's expecting Mallory to return her phone call now.

She hadn't done it years ago, when Becky had tried to reach her through the office of that fancy Hollywood agent of hers.

"Whom may I tell Ms. Eden is trying to reach her?" the agent's snooty secretary had asked.

"This is her mother. Becky Baxter," she had said.

Then, realizing her daughter wouldn't recognize the last name she had taken from the long-dead junkie who had briefly been her husband, she had amended, "Becky O'Neal. Tell her it's Becky O'Neal."

"And where can you be reached?" the dubious-sounding woman had asked.

She'd had no number to leave.

She had been living on the streets of Chicago.

So she had hung up.

And, falling back into a drug-induced haze, she had forgotten about Mallory Eden.

At least, for a while.

Until Elizabeth had gotten herself into trouble.

Elizabeth . . .

Becky Baxter's second-born daughter.

Two daughters, two chances.

The first child, she had quickly given up on, handing her over to her mother, Vera, to raise.

But the second . . .

She hadn't wanted to make the same mistakes with the second child.

The second child she had raised herself. First, with very little assistance from the father, a no-good husband who finally got himself killed on the streets when Elizabeth was still in diapers. And after that she'd gone it alone, taking handouts where she could find them, turning tricks to support her child—and her own drug habit.

In the end, what she thought had been a mistake had turned out to be the best thing she could have done—giving her firstborn to Vera.

And what she had thought had been a responsible decision— to keep her second born with her—had turned out to be a serious error.

The child her mother had raised had grown up to be a modern-day princess.

And the child Becky herself had raised had grown up to be a lying, scheming junkie.

*Just like me.*

It isn't a new thought, but it disturbs Becky now as deeply as it always has.

She isn't proud of who she is or what she's done.

Still, it's too late to change some things. . . .

But not others.

Becky O'Neal Baxter, old before her time, will never erase her past, and she will never make amends with her mother.

Vera—who, Becky is certain, went to her grave despising her only child—isn't coming back.

Elizabeth, poor Elizabeth, who had OD'd at seventeen, isn't coming back either.

But . . .

Becky thinks of her other daughter, who has been in hiding for the past five years . . .

And calling herself by her dead sister's name.

Maybe it's not too late with Cindy.

Mallory.

Whoever she is.

*She's still your daughter.*

*You're still her mother.*

*She might need you now, with everything that's going on . . .*

*And she might not.*

*But you sure as hell need her, especially now that you're clean and ready to live a normal life. She owes you. If it weren't for you, she wouldn't have even been born. It's time for payback.*

*Will she agree?*

Her gut twists as she stares again at the phone that refuses to ring.

Mallory picks up the phone when it rings, even though it's almost midnight and she had almost fallen asleep.

"It's me," Harper's voice says quietly in her ear, intimate as a lover's whisper.

*It's me.*

Casual words that are used by people who have been together a long time, people who expect each other to call, to be there.

Not by two people who barely know each other.

And yet . . .

"Hi." Mallory's own voice sounds strangely breathless. She props herself on her pillows.

"Were you asleep?"

"Are you kidding?" She stifles a yawn.

"Are the reporters still stalking you?"

"The last time I peeked out the front window, there was an army of them in front of the house."

"What about the police?"

"They're still here too, keeping an eye on things."

"Keeping an eye on you."

"I guess. Not because I'm in any danger . . ."

She has to say it, has to hear the words so that maybe she'll actually start believing that they're true.

"But because of the press. I know." Harper sighs. "They're swarming around me too. I'm keeping my phone off the hook— do you still have my pager number?"

"I think so," she says vaguely.

She doesn't want to tell him that she tucked the scrap of paper into her wallet for safekeeping. Just in case she needed something . . .

Him.

"Good. If you have to reach me, use that," he says. "Anyway, I was offered half a million to tell a tabloid what you're like in bed."

She sucks in her breath. "Oh, no . . ."

"I told them that if I knew, *they'd* be the last ones I'd tell."

"Thank you." She shakes her head ruefully, adding, "I'm sure half a million dollars would come in handy for you."

"Nah," he says, and she smiles.

"What are you going to do, Mallory?"

His question catches her off guard.

"What do you mean?" she asks.

"About this. Everything that's happened. Are you really going back to L.A.?"

"Who said that?"

"Some reporter on television."

"I haven't given a statement to anyone. I haven't talked to anyone about my plans," she says, her temper flaring.

Then she catches herself, sighs. "I don't know why I'm so surprised. I guess I'd forgotten what it's like to live like this. You have no idea what Hollywood is like—what my life was like before I came here."

He's silent for just a moment too long before saying, "No, I guess I don't."

She contemplates that.

Then she says carefully, "You know, Harper, it isn't fair. I just realized that you probably *do* know. Because every detail of my whole life is being aired on every television network. By now you must know my grandmother's maiden name and that I once fainted at junior high cheerleading practice because I'd been on a liquid diet for a week." She takes a deep breath. "But I don't know anything about you."

He doesn't answer right away.

And when he does, it's with a question.

"What is it that you want to know?"

The smile is gone from his voice.

"Just the basics," she says, frowning.

Wondering what he has to hide.

Wondering if she was wrong when she decided—well, almost decided—to trust him.

"The basics? I was born in Oregon; my parents' names are Terry and Joe; I have an older sister."

"Are you close to her?"

"Not anymore."

"What about your parents?"

"I haven't seen them in a long time."

"Oh. So you lived in Oregon before you moved here last year?"

"No."

"Where did you live?"

"Why does it matter?"

Taken aback at the ire in his tone, she retorts, "Because I'm curious. You know everything about me. Hell, *everyone* knows everything about me, and—"

"That has nothing to do with me though," Harper cuts in. "And before you were splashed all over the six o'clock news, you didn't tell me anything about yourself."

"But you know why I didn't! Because I feared for my life!"

"I know. And did you fear me?"

The question catches her off guard. She hesitates.

She hasn't told him that she had suspected him of being the stalker. She had told the police, but not Harper, what Frank had said about him resembling a wanted fugitive from California.

Now that it's all over, she doesn't want to admit to the man who risked his life to save her that she had thought he was the one who was trying to kill her.

"You don't have to answer that," Harper says abruptly. "You don't need to. You obviously were afraid of me."

"I was afraid of everyone. Can you blame me?"

"No," he says simply.

"Well, then . . ."

"Look, I was wrong to try to force you to open up to me," he tells her. "I don't even know why I tried."

"Why did you?"

"Maybe because . . . when I met you, something just . . . clicked."

He's silent for a long time.

And so is she, thinking about what he's said.

She decides to take a chance for a change. To open up just a little. To tell him what she's feeling.

"I know what you mean," she says softly. "It clicked with me too."

"I haven't been with a woman in a long, long time," he says in a muted voice, almost as though he hasn't heard her. "And when I saw you, I just . . . there was something there. Something I knew I should ignore. But I didn't want to. I couldn't."

*But why?* she wants to ask. *Why did you want to ignore it? I had a good reason not to want to get involved.*

*But what was your reason?*

Mallory wishes that he were there in front of her instead of on the phone. That she could see his face, look into his eyes, know whether she should ask those questions, because she would be able to tell exactly how he feels about her . . .

How she feels about him.

Right now she's confused. Torn between wanting to reach out to him, to trust him . . .

And wanting to shut him out, leave him behind.

Along with everything else that's connected to her existence in Windemere Cove.

"What are you going to do now?" he asks abruptly, as though he's read her mind.

"I don't know. I guess . . . I guess I'll go back to L.A.," she tells him softly, wanting him to make her take it back, to stop her from talking, stop her from going.

He is silent.

She goes on, feeling her way blindly, recklessly making plans, because she has to do something, say something.

"I'll get in touch with my agent and see about getting back to work. And I'll stay with my friend, Rae . . . she'll help me until I can get settled again."

Still, he's silent.

"I guess I should go as soon as possible, to get away from the press," she fumbles on. "I mean, I know they'll be pestering me wherever I am, but at least in L.A., everyone's used to it. There, you can hide. Here, the police seem kind of befuddled by what's going on."

"What about security?" he asks abruptly.

"What about it?"

"Are you planning to hire bodyguards?"

"No," she says quickly without pausing to consider it. "I'm through with that. I've spent too much time being afraid. First I had bodyguards watching over me every second, and then I spent five years hiding in this tiny house, terrified to set foot outside. I'm through with that," she says again more forcefully.

And she realizes she means it.

*No more bodyguards.*

*No more fear.*

"So," he says slowly, "you're going back."

"I'm going back."

She tells herself that she can't wait to be back in sunny L.A., back in Malibu, where she'll find another house nestled in the cliffs, where she'll once again be able to walk on the beach and feel the salty wind in her hair, feel free, feel . . .

Safe.

"When are you going?" Harper asks.

She hesitates, just for a moment, hoping he'll utter something, anything to change what she's about to say. What she *has* to say.

He's silent.

Waiting.

"As soon as possible, like I said. Probably tomorrow, if I can get a flight," she tells him, trying to sound breezy, even eager to move on.

Trying to sound as though some part of her hasn't just inexplicably died.

"After all," she hears herself add in one last attempt to get him to stop her, "there's nothing to keep me here in Windemere Cove."

"No," he agrees, his tone flat. "I guess there isn't."

# chapter

# 12

Manny happens to look up, out the front window, just in time to see the long black stretch limousine pull up at the curb. In front of it and behind it are two police cars with their lights flashing.

It can mean only one thing.

His heart starts pounding as he stares at it, watching as the uniformed driver steps out and goes around to the door facing the house.

He opens it.

Manny holds his breath.

A pair of bare legs appears.

Then a hand, reaching up to take the outstretched hand of the driver.

Then, at last, a woman emerges from the dark interior of the limousine.

Manny slowly releases his breath at the sight of a real live movie star.

This isn't Elizabeth, this beautiful woman moving slowly toward the house, her long legs carrying her in a casual, almost lazy manner.

So different from the way Elizabeth had moved—always quickly, as if she were in a hurry to get someplace—or get away.

This woman is wearing Elizabeth's clothes—Manny remembers those wide-legged black shorts that almost look like a skirt, and that white sleeveless blouse. But before, she had never worn the blouse tucked into her waistband, with the top two buttons undone. And she had always worn the shorts with sneakers, never with a pair of strappy black sandals that show her bare toes, painted with red nail polish.

And her hair . . .

It's . . .

Well, it's *big*. All high on her head and loose around her face and flowing down over her shoulders. He never knew she had so much hair.

She's wearing makeup too. And earrings.

And a pair of black sunglasses—but then, Elizabeth had always worn sunglasses.

But that's the only thing that's familiar about the woman who is walking up to the front porch, carefully sidestepping the rotting boards that Manny tried, but failed, to fix.

She rings the doorbell.

Manny is unable to move, but the sound brings his grandmother from the kitchen, where she has been making egg salad sandwiches for lunch.

She opens the door, makes an exclamation.

Still, Manny is frozen.

He just sits on the couch, suddenly feeling miserable.

He listens as Elizabeth says, sounding just like her old self, "Hello, Mrs. Souza. Is Manny home?"

"He's in the living room, watching television. Manny! Manny! Get in here!"

Manny forces his legs to the floor, to carry him into the front hall, where the beautiful woman is waiting, not seeming to notice that his grandmother is just standing there, gaping at her with her mouth hanging open.

"Manny! Come here!" Elizabeth kneels on the worn linoleum floor and holds her arms out to him.

Finding himself forcing back a sob that has come out of nowhere, he goes in to them, allows himself to be enveloped in her fierce embrace.

"You even smell like a movie star," he says when she finally releases him.

She makes a sound that's either a laugh or a choked sob; he can't tell which.

"So you know," she says, "about me."

And he nods.

"I saw you on TV all day yesterday," he tells her. "I'm really sorry about what that bad man tried to do to you. But he's in jail now, isn't he?"

She nods, reaching out to brush some hair out of his eyes.

Then she turns to his grandmother, who looks flustered.

"Do you want egg salad?" Grammy asks in her thick Portuguese accent.

"No, thank you. I'm on my way to the airport. If I could just talk to Manny alone for a few minutes . . ."

She's on her way to the airport.

Her words sink in as he absently watches his grandmother leave the room, returning to the kitchen, where Manny's grandfather loudly wants to know what's going on.

"Where are you going? Back to Hollywood?" Manny asks, turning back to Elizabeth.

She nods.

"I figured you would. There aren't any other movie stars living in Windemere Cove."

She smiles faintly.

He notices that her lips are outlined in dark red lipstick; it makes them seem a lot fuller than before. But he's not sure whether he likes the way she looks. It's almost too perfect, too . . . fake.

She asks him in a low voice, "How have your grandparents been since you got back? They haven't hurt you, have they?"

He shakes his head, wanting to ask her if she's still going to help him do something about his mother but afraid to open his mouth.

Now that he knows who she is, he can't believe she had ever offered to help him with his problem. She had so many problems of her own.

"Manny," she says, suddenly taking off her sunglasses and looking into his eyes. "I want you to know that even though I'm leaving town, I'm not abandoning you."

How long has he been wondering what her eyes look like behind those dark glasses?

Now he knows. They're a light brown color, like warm honey, the biggest, prettiest eyes he's ever seen—and it isn't just because of the way she's outlined them in some smudgy dark pencil, or because of the mascara that makes her lashes longer. It's the expression in them, the way she's looking at him . . .

Like she really cares.

"I've spoken to several police officers about your case, and they're going to be coming over to talk to you and your grandparents. I don't want you to be afraid of them, Manny. They're going to help you. And so am I."

"But you're going away."

He sees a flicker of sadness in her expression.

"I'll still help you," she says. "I'll be in touch with you, and I'll make sure nothing bad happens to you. Okay?"

He nods, wanting to believe her.

"And maybe," she continues, brushing another piece of hair from his face, "I'll fly you out to California to see me. Would you like that?"

He nods again.

So part of his dream is actually going to come true.

But what about the rest?

The part about her being his mom?

*That's the impossible part*, he reminds himself.

"I have to go now, Manny," she tells him, straightening up again, checking her watch.

"Thank you for making my costumes," he says, swallowing hard over a lump in his throat. "Rhonda dropped them off for me yesterday."

"You're welcome. I . . . I wish I could come to your play next week, Manny. I'd love to see you perform."

"It's okay," he says with a shrug.

"As soon as I get to Los Angeles, I'll call you with my number."

"Are you going to your house there? The one they showed on TV?"

"No," she says quickly. "That isn't my house anymore. I'm going to be staying with a friend of mine. I haven't been able to reach her to tell her I'm coming, but I'm sure it'll be fine with her. So I'll call you from her house as soon as I can."

"Okay," he says in a small voice.

"I really will be there for you, Manny," she says, looking first into his eyes, then over her shoulder at the limousine driver outside, who's standing at the curb by the car with his legs spread apart and his hands clasped in front of him.

"I know . . ."

"And I want you to call me if you need me. Just because I'm in Los Angeles doesn't mean I won't come if you need me. Okay?"

He nods, staring into her eyes, trying to memorize what they look like.

And then he realizes that they're all shiny. . .

And she's crying.

She pulls him into her arms, holding him close against her so that he can feel her heart beating.

He lets his own tears spill over, unable to stop them. He cries so hard that he's making loud, gasping noises, clutching her tightly around her neck, never wanting to let go.

Then she says in a strangled-sounding voice, "I've got a flight to catch. Be good, Manny. I'll be in touch."

One last squeeze, and she's gone—out the door, down the stairs, and into the car.

Still sniffling, Manny steps out onto the lopsided porch. The windows of the limousine are tinted; he can't even get one last glimpse of her.

He waves anyway, in case she's watching.

Waves as the limousine and the police cars start up and drive away.

Waves until they have disappeared around the corner.

Only then does he believe that she's really going—that she's really *gone*.

Only then does he wipe at the tears that are still trickling down his face, and softly call, "Good-bye."

Brawley Johnson steps out of the rented car on Green Garden Way and stares down the street at the small white Cape Cod.

He would have known it's the right house even if he hadn't seen it on the news the day before; press vehicles and satellite trucks are parked directly in front of it, and there's a throng of reporters and other people milling about in the street.

He moves toward them, vaguely disturbed by the notion that they almost appear to be . . . disbanding.

What's going on?

Can he possibly be too late?

If only his flight into New York hadn't been late last night . . . too late to catch the last connection to T. F. Green.

If only it had been easier to find ground transportation once he'd landed first thing that morning. But there hadn't been a cab, and the car rental place had been a nightmare. And then, once he'd rented a car and gotten on the road, he'd found himself hopelessly lost. He'd missed the exit off 95 in Providence and was halfway to Boston before he realized what had happened.

And now he's here at last, at the house where Mallory has been living for five years . . .

Five years of him thinking she was dead . . .

And something tells him it's too late.

He approaches a man who's loading camera equipment into the back of an open van.

"Is this where Mallory Eden is?" he asks the guy, a scruffy type in ripped jeans and a goatee.

"Not anymore" is the terse reply.

Brawley's stomach turns over. "What do you mean?"

"You just missed her, man. Left in a big stretch limo, police escort and everything. She's out of this burg."

"What? Where did she go?"

The guy flashes a sarcastic expression. "Hmm, let's see. Big movie star. Now, where would she go?"

"Are you telling me that she's on her way back to L.A.?"

"That's my guess. She didn't stop to consult me. I spent the whole night driving down here from upstate New York just to get a look at her."

Brawley narrows his eyes. "You a fan?"

Again the sarcasm. "Yeah, right. That's why I have all this camera equipment. I'm a reporter, man. Like everyone else hanging around here."

"Newspaper?"

"Uh-uh. *Eyewitness News.* How about you?"

Brawley shifts his gaze away from the now-deserted house, glancing absently at the man beside him.

"Actually, I'm an old friend of hers," he tells him.

"Of whose?"

"Cin—Mallory Eden's."

"Yeah, right."

"I'm serious."

"Come off it."

"Look, I don't care whether or not you believe me. My name is Brawley Johnson. I was engaged to her a long time ago."

The guy frowns. Adjusts the visor of his baseball cap so that it faces forward, shading his face from the sun. He peers at Brawley, then nods. "You know, that name is familiar. Brawley Johnson. Weren't you on some TV show last week, talking about Mallory Eden?"

"I was on a couple of them," Brawley informs him, straightening his shoulders.

"Yeah? Would you mind talking to me for a few minutes? I'd like to get some tape ... and my producer's over there ... hey, Bob? Can you come here for a minute?"

Brawley hesitates, thinking about it.

*Eyewitness News* from upstate New York?

It's really no decision.

"Hey, where are you going?" asks the reporter as Brawley strides away toward his rental car. "Just let me ask you a few questions, man."

"Who is he?"

"Why do you want to talk to him?"

Brawley hears the buzz among the press.

He breaks into a run.

So does the *Eyewitness News* reporter.

So do the rest of them, scrambling pell-mell to interview him despite the fact that they have no clue who he is.

Brawley, who spends five hours a week with a personal trainer, is into the rental with the engine started before the out-of-shape East Coast tribe reaches him.

He speeds down Green Garden Way, heading back in the direction he came: the airport.

Mallory breathes a sigh of relief once the airport security guard has deposited her inside the private airline club, the heavy door closed firmly behind her, blocking out the trickle of reporters who managed to catch up with her at the airport.

The place is Sunday-morning deserted; she glances around and sees that there's a man reading a newspaper in one corner and a well-dressed couple chatting quietly in another.

Nobody seems to notice or care that she's Mallory Eden.

Or maybe they don't recognize her, with her hair still dark and the extra pounds padding her once-skinny figure.

What had she been thinking when she got ready to leave that morning? Why had she worn all this makeup and hairspray; why hadn't she put on a pair of jeans and a T-shirt?

*Because if you're going to go back, you might as well do it right,* she reminds herself.

*You can't hide anymore.*

*You don't want to, remember?*

She thinks of Harper Smith and lifts her chin defiantly.

If he wanted to stop her from leaving, he could have. He could have called, or come over to her house, and told her . . .

What?

What could he—a virtual stranger, or so she's trying to convince herself—have said that would make her change her mind about going?

One word, actually.

*Stay.*

If he had said it, she would have done it. At least, for a little while. Long enough to collect her thoughts, to make rational decisions about the future . . .

Long enough to get to know him better.

But Harper Smith hadn't said anything but "Good-bye."

And "Good luck."

A perfectly appropriate farewell, coming from a man she'd known for only a few days.

Even if he did save her life.

Even if he did make her wonder what would have happened between them if she didn't have all this . . .

"Baggage, ma'am?"

She looks up, startled, to see a pleasant-faced female airline employee looking down at her.

"Excuse me?"

"Do you have any baggage that needs to be checked?"

"Oh . . . no. No, just this." She holds up the small carry-on bag at her feet, the one that holds her money and some toiletries, a change of clothes.

The same bag she'd brought with her from her old life.

The bag had cost more than most people in Windemere Cove made in a month.

If the airline employee recognizes her, or if she thinks it's strange that someone would fly across the country without luggage, she doesn't let on.

Once she's alone again, Mallory turns her attention to the telephone sitting on the table beside her.

She has to call Rae.

Collect, she realizes . . .

Because she doesn't have a credit card.

She doesn't have a lot of things she'll need now that she's going back to the real world.

She reaches into her pocket for the sheet of paper the cop had handed her yesterday, the one with all the names and phone numbers on it.

*Flynn Soderland.*

*Brawley Johnson.*

*Rae Hamilton.*
*Gretchen Dodd.*
*Becky O'Neal.*

Of them, Rae is the only one she's tried to reach. Last night, and this morning. After getting constant busy signals, she had concluded that her friend's phone was off the hook.

Was it because Rae doesn't want to talk to her?

No, of course Rae wants to talk to her. Rae had called, had left a number.

Mallory figures that under the circumstances, there's only one other reason that Rae's phone would be off the hook.

She must be getting barraged by the press.

She supposes she could have tried to reach Flynn. He would be glad to let her stay at his place.

But with Flynn, things were touchy before she left. Because of his drinking. She had actually threatened to fire him over that.

It seems like it had happened in another lifetime . . .

And it had

But with Flynn, you never knew. He might be carrying a grudge. And if not, he might want to talk business right away. Try to convince her to audition again.

She isn't ready for that.

She isn't ready for any of this.

But she'd told Harper Smith she was going back to L.A., and so she will.

She just isn't ready to face . . . everyone.

Not Flynn.

Certainly not Brawley.

And not Gretchen . . .

Poor Gretchen.

Mallory notices for the first time that the telephone number she'd left had had a Connecticut area code.

She vaguely remembers now that Gretchen had grown up in New England.

Funny, after living in Rhode Island for all these years, it had never occurred to her that her former assistant might be close by.

She should call Gretchen.

And she will.

But not yet.

Her eyes flit over the last name on the list.

*Becky O'Neal.*

She will never call the mother who beat her, who abandoned her, who came back only when she needed money.

*I will never, ever call you. Never.*

Swallowing hard, Mallory forces thoughts away from her mother, her gaze back to Rae's name and number, which she hasn't tried in over an hour.

And then, taking a deep breath to steel her nerve, she begins to dial.

"Is it true that you're Mallory Eden's mother?"

"Have you spoken to your daughter in the past twenty-four hours?"

"Were you aware that she hadn't really committed suicide?"

Becky O'Neal Baxter puts her hands up in front of her eyes, trying to shield them from the glare of the camera lights gathered at the foot of the steps in front of the old rooming house.

She clutches the railing for support, wishing she had stopped to comb her hair before coming out to see what all the fuss was about, wishing she were wearing something other than these holey jeans and the size small T-shirt that hangs like a sack on her bony frame.

"I . . . can you ask one question at a time?" she asks timidly, glancing around at the clamoring reporters.

They pay no attention to her request, continuing to shout questions at her.

Confused, disturbed, she turns away, wanting only to escape back to her room, to wait by the phone . . .

The phone that hasn't rung.

Somebody grabs her arm and says in a low voice that's somehow easier to hear than all the shouting, "Mrs. Baxter, I'd like to talk to you privately."

She turns to see a very pretty female reporter standing there.

"If you'll talk to me," the reporter says, "I'll see that you're reimbursed for your time."

"Reimbursed . . . how?"

"Why don't you let me come inside with you, and we'll talk about it?"

Becky O'Neal thinks it over.

And as she does, she notices the woman's big diamond ring and her fancy shoes and expensive-looking suit.

"Okay," she says, and holds the door open to let the reporter inside.

Harper blinks as he steps out of the white clapboard congregational church and into the bright morning sunshine on Pine Street.

All around him, people of all ages, dressed in their Sunday best, are chatting and calling greetings with the easy familiarity of small-town folks who have known one another forever.

He's an outsider here, the only outsider, it seems, in this tiny New England town . . .

Now that Mallory is gone.

Maybe that's what had drawn him to her, he thinks as he walks down the wide wooden steps and turns right, heading down the sidewalk toward Center Street.

Maybe he sensed that she, like he, didn't belong here, that she wasn't a part of the Yankee network of families that stretches back generations. That she had come from a far-off place, forced to forget her past, to start over . . .

Just as he had been forced to do, after—

Out of habit, his thoughts skitter away, some built-in defense mechanism keeping him from remembering the details of what had happened back in Los Angeles.

Instead, he thinks of how drawn he'd been to Mallory, of how certain he'd been that he'd seen her someplace before.

Now, of course, he knows where it was—he had realized the moment he discovered her true identity.

Not that he's told her why she looked so familiar.

Telling her would force him to reveal too many details of his past in L.A.

The shade-dappled, tree-lined street is quiet now that he's left behind the social hubbub of the church. He walks past the big, old white houses with their white-spindled porches and gables and fluttering flags. In the distance he can hear lawn mowers and children playing and, as always, the lapping waves of the bay.

The ocean, of course, is what drew him to this coastal town. He has always loved to watch the churning sea, to contemplate its vast expanse, to breathe its briny scent, to feel its salt spray and brisk wind on his face.

He had grown up in a fishing town on Oregon's craggy coast, a town hauntingly similar to this one, a town where majestic old sea captain's mansions and lighthouses perched on misty headlands, overlooking the vast, cold sea.

And though he had willingly left it behind long ago, he had missed it.

He just hadn't realized it until the cold gray day late last summer when, driving up the New England coast in search of a place he could call home, he had happened upon Windemere Cove.

He had known instantly that he would stay, even before he checked further and found that it met the requirements he had set. Rentals were plentiful and cheap, and there weren't very many locksmiths in the area.

Harper's father had been a locksmith by trade, though he'd always said he was a fisherman first, where it counted—in his heart. He had built a decent local business in that small Oregon town, generating enough income to feed his family and enough freedom to allow him to take to the sea every now and then, to sail out over the waves, cast a line, and wait for a catch.

Harper had never liked fishing.

Had always been too restless to simply sit and wait for something to happen. Even though that was what his life was about, though, in that tiny Oregon town. Waiting.

When he graduated from high school at last, his father, who had taught him the locksmith trade over the years, had expected him to take over the business.

But Harper, in the tradition of all rebellious firstborn sons, had had other ideas.

His father hadn't said much when Harper had told him he was leaving. But his mother had cried, begged him to stay. Told him how proud his father would be if he would just stay for a while, just give the business a try. Even his sister had tried to talk him into it, had threatened never to talk to him again if he left.

He had left for Los Angeles that June, and his sister had kept her promise.

But Harper had never looked back. Never allowed himself to feel guilty that his father couldn't add "and Son" to the sign hanging over his shop.

It wasn't until last year, when Harper suddenly found himself in trouble, adrift, that he had realized he needed to fall back on the trade he had reluctantly learned so many years before.

The double irony: that he would never be able to tell his father how grateful he was.

His father had been dead for five years by then, killed in a fishing accident during a coastal storm.

And yet despite—or maybe because of—that, Harper had continually been drawn to the sea.

He had lived in Venice Beach when he first arrived in L.A., and then later, as he moved up in the world, in the once-again-fashionable Santa Monica. Always, he had needed to be near the pounding surf, needed the familiar, constant presence of the sea.

When he moved here, alone and troubled and trying to forget, he had thought that was all he needed to make it into home. Just to be near the water, as he always had been.

But he had discovered he needed something more.

That's why he had started going to church again. He hadn't attended since he was a boy. Back then he had complained every Sunday morning when his mother dragged him out of bed and made him slick back his hair and put on ironed clothes. He had fidgeted through services as he imagined all the things he'd rather be doing.

But lately he has found himself drawn to the familiar rituals of organized religion, has found himself searching.

Maybe searching for comfort, and maybe for some meaning to what happened in Los Angeles.

Then he met Elizabeth—Mallory.

And something about her touched some innate part of his soul.

Made him want to reach out.

Made him realize that he may need in his life something more meaningful, more comforting than the sea, and the church.

Something he had already found . . .

And lost . . .

Once before.

He doesn't want to take a chance again.

Doesn't want to care about a world-renowned celebrity whose life is filled with complications he doesn't need.

And yet . . .

He does care.

And he's worried about her.

He needs to protect her . . .

Although, from what, he hasn't a clue.

Her stalker is behind bars.

And anyway, she's gone, off on her own, back to L.A.

She has told him, in no uncertain terms, that she doesn't want to be coddled. That she can take care of herself. That she isn't afraid anymore. That she doesn't need him.

*But what if I need you?* he wonders, kicking a pebble in his path, watching as it skips across the cracked concrete and disappears over the edge, into the grass.

# chapter

# 13

"Mommy?"

Pamela stirs, feeling something wet jabbing into her face.

She opens her eyes and sees that it's the corner of Hannah's blankie, which has most likely been in her mouth or in the toilet.

"Wake up, Mommy."

Pamela rubs her eyes, sees that she's on the couch.

Her parents slept in the master bedroom, she remembers.

And Frank . . .

Frank's in jail.

"Where Daddy is?" Hannah asks in a small voice.

"Daddy's . . . at work," Pamela tells her. Her voice comes out raspy.

She glances at the clock, exhausted. And no wonder. She just fell asleep an hour ago. She was up all night with the baby, who was running a temperature. Must be that summer cold that's going around.

Pamela wouldn't have slept even if Jason had though. How could she sleep after what had happened with Frank?

"Hannah eat now," her daughter says, tugging on her arm.

Pamela sighs wearily, closing her eyes. "Hannah, please. Not yet. Just give Mommy a minute to—"

"Hannah eat now!"

A flash fire zaps through Pamela's veins. "You little brat!" she hollers, grabbing her daughter's arm and shaking her. "Don't you dare act like this now! Don't you dare!"

"Pamela!"

She turns to see her mother in the doorway, wearing a robe and a disapproving expression.

"Is that any way to talk to a two-year-old?"

Pamela sighs, wanting her mother to go away, wanting Hannah to go away, wanting everyone and everything to just go away and leave her alone.

She gets up off the couch, stalks away, down the hall.

"Where are you going?" her mother calls after her, above Hannah's wails.

*Where are you going?*

*Back in time,* Pamela thinks wistfully. *If only I could go back in time. Back to when Frank and I first met. Back to sunny California, and walking on the beach, and wearing a bikini . . .*

"Pamela?" Her mother raises her voice. "I asked you a question."

*Where are you going?*

"I have to get out of here for a day or so, Mother. Maybe longer."

"You can't just leave! Where would you go?"

"I don't know," Pamela snaps. "Someplace. Anyplace but off the deep end. And that's where I'm headed if I stay."

"Please hold for Martin de Lisser."

Flynn inhales sharply, clutching the phone against his ear. When it rang so early on a Sunday morning, waking him from a deep and dreamless sleep, he had expected to pick it up and hear Mallory's voice.

Now, as he holds for the famed director, he sits up in bed and struggles to organize his booze-scrambled thoughts.

At least he's alone, he realizes, after glancing, with some trepidation, at either side of the rumpled king-sized bed.

Last night is an unpleasant blur of smoky nightspots in West Hollywood, of throwing cash around and flirting wildly with alluring young men. Of trying to forget that he's come to a crossroads in his life, now that Mallory Eden has resurfaced and changed everything.

*Everything.*

His head is pounding and his mouth dryer than the miles of desert between here and Vegas.

Vegas . . . he had toyed with the idea of taking off and driving to Vegas at some point last night. He even remembered getting on the freeway, heading east toward Interstate 15.

Luckily, he had realized that he was too drunk to drive all the way to Vegas.

He fumbles on the nightstand for the glass of water he always takes to bed with him; it isn't there.

He can't even remember driving home last night, much less getting ready for bed. He must have—

"Flynn?"

"Hello, Martin."

"I heard the news."

Of course he's heard the news. Flynn has known this call would be inevitable, wonders why it hasn't come sooner.

De Lisser tells him in the next breath.

"I was hiking up north all day yesterday, out of contact with civilization."

Flynn frowns, wondering why a high-powered player like de Lisser hadn't brought a cellular phone along.

Again, his question is promptly answered, almost as though de Lisser is reading his mind, a disconcerting notion.

"I like to be out of contact with civilization every now and then," the director confides, "because I need to clear my head. Especially at the beginning of a new project. Especially at this point in my career."

"I know what you mean," Flynn says, wondering, as he rubs his throbbing temples, whether his own head will ever be clear again.

"So," de Lisser says, "Mallory Eden."

"Yes," Flynn acknowledges.

And then, because the director seems to be waiting for him to add something more, he says, "I'm very shocked and excited about the fact that she's alive."

"You and the rest of the world," de Lisser says dryly. "Have you spoken to her?"

Flynn absently folds the edge of the satin bedsheet back and forth in his fingers, wondering whether he should lie.

"Actually, not yet, but I was . . . out of contact myself for most of yesterday and last night."

"I see."

If the director is wondering why a big star like Mallory Eden wouldn't promptly call her agent under circumstances like these, he doesn't say it.

Nor does Flynn dare to betray his own uncertainty.

Why hasn't Mallory called?

What if she doesn't come back to L.A.?

What if she doesn't come back to him?

He can't ignore that it's a distinct possibility. Can't forget how she had threatened to fire him that last summer, when both their lives seemed to be falling apart around them.

Everyone will be expecting her to be his client once again, but what if she no longer wants him? What if she wants a fresh start with someone else?

"Her first project," de Lisser announces, "is going to be my film."

Flynn nods. He has been anticipating this.

Still, he has to ask . . .

"What about Rae?"

De Lisser lets out a low, almost mocking chuckle. "Why would I want a Mallory Eden imitation when I can get the real thing?"

"We don't know that Mallory is planning to return to acting," Flynn says, intending a gentle reminder.

But it comes out rather sharply, and de Lisser is silent for a moment afterward.

Then he says somewhat icily, "I suggest that you find out, Flynn, at your earliest convenience."

"I'll do that . . ."

"And," de Lisser continues, "I suggest that if she isn't inclined to return to acting, you do your very best to convince her."

"I will." Flynn clears his throat. "And . . . what should I tell Rae in the meantime?"

"Why do you need to tell her anything? She's an intelligent woman. She'll figure out where she stands, if she hasn't already."

In other words, Rae will be *out* if Mallory should decide she wants *in*.

And if Mallory doesn't want *in*—

Or want Flynn—

Or want to return to acting—

Then *Flynn* will be out.

Left again to the bleak, mundane existence of an aging retiree. A has-been.

*Just last week you were retired. And you didn't feel that that was a fate worse than death,* he reminds himself.

But now that he's had another taste of that heady, high-powered tinseltown status, he simply can't allow himself to sink back into oblivion.

If he loses the strategic foothold he's gained by his association with the most influential director in town, he knows what he'll have.

Nothing.

Nothing but the booze and the gambling and the one-night stands that were almost the death of him once in his life.

"Frank," his lawyer says, swooping into the small meeting room and shaking his hand. He's chewing gum, as always, working it rapidly in the front of his mouth. "How are you doing? Hanging in there?"

"What do you think?" He glowers at Stan Bauer, but the attorney doesn't seem fazed.

"I have news for you," he tells Frank, whose heart lurches.

"What news?"

"She's gone."

"Pamela? Oh, Christ, I knew she wouldn't—"

"Not Pamela. Mallory Eden. She left for the airport an hour ago, to fly back to Los Angeles."

"But . . . how can she just pick up and leave?"

Bauer shrugs. "She'll be back, I'm sure, to testify against you. "

"Oh, *that's* good news." Frank buries his head in his handcuffed hands for a moment, then looks up at his lawyer. "She has to tell them that it wasn't me in L.A. That I'm not the one who stalked her there, who shot her."

"Look, Frank, she's not going to do that. She—and everyone else—thinks you were the one. She never got a good look at whoever shot her, and there's circumstantial evidence pointing to you as the—"

"I didn't do it. You've got to let me talk to her. I've got to tell her that it wasn't me!"

"Calm down, Frank. I know you're upset about this. But we'll straighten it out."

"She's the only one who can straighten it out. She has to convince them that it wasn't me."

"First we have to convince her," Stan says calmly, still chewing his gum. "Pamela went over there and tried talking to her yesterday."

"What happened?"

"I don't know, but it wasn't good."

"Christ."

"Don't get all worked up, Frank."

"You've got to get me out of here, Stan."

"I know. I'm working on getting them to set bail. Like I told your wife last night, I plan to get you out of here by the end of today. Just hang in there."

Frank shakes his head sullenly, hating Stan, hating Pam, hating Mallory Eden most of all.

"I have a collect call from Mallory; will you accept?"

Rae's heart leaps into her throat.

"I'll accept."

There's a click, and then her old friend's voice is on the line, asking, "Rae? Are you there?"

She swallows, sits down, hard, on a chair.

"I'm here," she manages to say.

"It's me . . ."

"I know . . ."

And somehow all she can think of is Mallory's ghost. How frightened she's been, for five years now, that Mallory's ghost would come back to haunt her.

"Well . . . I guess I have some explaining to do," Mallory says, sounding nervous.

"I guess you do," Rae agrees softly, and bites her lip to keep it from trembling.

"Pardon?"

She forces her voice out again, louder this time. "I guess you do have some explaining to do, Mal," she says.

"I'd like to do it in person, if that's okay with you."

"That's . . . fine."

"Good. My flight is boarding. I'll be landing at LAX this afternoon."

"Do . . . you want me to meet you there?"

Mallory exhales, her relief obvious. "Would you?"

"No problem. Just give me a minute to find a pen, and I'll write down the information." Rae crosses to the kitchenette on shaky legs, fumbling in the drawer for a pen and something to write on.

"This is so damned strange, Rae."

Mallory's comment startles her. "What do you mean?"

"Here we are, making plans to meet, like nothing ever happened. Remember how you used to meet me at LAX sometimes when I was on my way back from location? Remember how we'd go straight out to the beach so that I could feel like I was home again?"

Rae is still, staring off into space. "I remember."

"Listen, would it be all right . . . would you mind if I stayed with you awhile?"

"Sure," Rae says after only the slightest hesitation. "Sure, it would be fine."

"I know it's weird of me to ask, but I really have nowhere else to go."

"It's okay."

"Thank you. But, Rae . . . would you do me a favor? Would you not tell anyone that I'm coming?"

Rae falters for only a moment before saying, "I won't."

"Thanks. I knew I could trust you. God, I have a lot to tell you, Rae. And I know you must have a lot to tell me." Mallory sounds nervous, chatty. "I watched you on *Morning, Noon, and Night* . . . you were terrific."

"That's . . . thanks."

"And I don't even know if you're married—"

"Married?" She chuckles humorlessly. "God, no. Never even came close."

"Still have a one-track mind, huh? Totally focused on career?"

"Absolutely."

"I don't even know what you're working on these days."

*I was about to replace you, Mallory.*

Imagine if Rae blurted that out.

But of course, she won't.

Mallory will find out about that soon enough.

*And what about you, Mallory? What are your plans? Are you coming back to acting?*

Rae longs to ask the question, to put an end to the awful suspense. But that, too, will have to wait.

She clears her throat, blindly grabs a white paper napkin from the holder on the counter, and holds the pen poised over it.

"Okay, Mal," she says, "I'm all set to write down your flight information. Go ahead. . . ."

"The next flight to Los Angeles departs in fifteen minutes, connecting through Denver," says the short, stout woman at the airline reservations desk at T. F. Green State Airport. "We have plenty of seats available, but you'll have to hur—"

"I'll take a one-way ticket," Brawley cuts in brusquely. "First class."

"All right, sir." The ticket agent's fingers fly over her keyboard.

He raps his knuckles impatiently on the countertop, looking around anxiously, hoping for a glimpse of Mallory. She's nowhere in sight, of course.

She'll be down by the gate, getting ready to board.

This is the first flight to Los Angeles from Providence today; it has to be the one she's taking.

And she has to be in first class.

As soon as he boards, he'll request that his seat be changed so that he can be next to her.

He smiles faintly despite his impatience, imagining her surprise when she sees him.

She'll probably—

"I just need your credit card, then, sir."

He nods and pulls it from his wallet, shoving it into her outstretched hand.

Mallory will probably do a double take when she sees him.

She'll get that startled expression she used to have when he would unexpectedly show up to meet her on the set of her first movie—

Her first *real* movie, after calling herself Babie Love for Jazz Taylor's low-budget porn film.

Back then, when she was on the road to becoming a legitimate actress, and he would show up on the set, she would be all surprised. Pleasantly surprised. At least, that was what she said, although sometimes he wasn't so sure.

Especially later, looking back, after she'd dumped him.

That was when he started to wonder if maybe she was a better actress than he'd given her credit for being.

If maybe she was acting like she cared about him, when all along she was using him. Even back in Custer Creek.

Using him to impress all her friends, who had thought it was cool for her to be dating an older guy . . .

Using him to prove a point to her grandmother, who thought she could keep Cindy locked up and obedient in that old farmhouse, like a prisoner.

And still, she'd had the nerve, later, when she was Mallory Eden and she no longer needed him, to accuse *him* of using *her*.

She had actually said—

"Sir? There seems to be a problem. This isn't going through."

He blinks, then frowns at the ticket agent who's interrupted his thoughts. "What isn't going through? The ticket?"

"The credit card. It says you've exceeded your limit."

"Damn." He fumbles in his wallet. "I must have given you the wrong one. Try this."

She takes the card he hands her.

He watches, again thrumming his fingers on the countertop, watching intently as she attempts to make the transaction.

"I'm sorry," she says at last, handing the second card back to him. "I'm getting the same thing."

"Something must be wrong with your machine," he says angrily, glancing at the clock. "I'm going to miss this flight if you don't—"

"There's nothing wrong with this machine, sir," she cuts in.

He hates her dumb, round, ugly face and he hates the way she's looking at him from behind those dumb, round, ugly glasses.

"Try this card," he says, tossing another one at her. This one, he knows, is maxed out. But he's starting to feel panicky, like he'll do anything—*anything*—to get onto that plane with Mallory Eden.

The woman bends to retrieve the card, which has fallen to the floor. She turns to glare at him before inserting it into the slot on her machine.

"What was that look for?" he demands, leaning toward her.

She ignores him, pressing buttons.

His blood boils.

The clock ticks.

The plane is going to leave without him.

Mallory is going to leave without him.

"I'm sorry, sir," she says smugly. "This one won't go through either."

"Then you must be doing something wrong! What the hell are you doing? You're going to make me miss my plane!"

"Don't you yell at me!" bellows the woman.

"I have to get on that plane!" Brawley hollers. "Do you understand me? I *have* to get on that plane!"

"Yes, Ms. Dodd, we did forward your message to Mallory Eden," says the harried male voice who answered the phone at the Windemere Cove police station.

"Isn't there any way you can give me her number?" Gretchen asks him, frustrated.

"I'm sorry, even if I were able to do that, it's too late to reach her here in town."

"What do you mean?"

"I understand that she left this morning for Los Angeles."

"I see." Gretchen hangs up the phone without another word.

She narrows her eyes, sitting absolutely still, her hand still resting on the receiver.

So. Mallory Eden doesn't have a care in the world. She's going back to her charmed life in Hollywood . . .

Obviously with no intention of returning Gretchen's phone call.

Obviously not caring that her former loyal assistant is doomed to live life as a reclusive freak.

*Damn you, Mallory Eden,* Gretchen thinks as bitter tears spill from her eyes and trickle over the scarred red flesh that had once been her cheeks.

*I'm going to make you listen to what I have to say. I'm going to make you look at this face, and then look me in the eye and tell me you won't help me.*

She crosses to her closet, opens it, and looks at the sand-colored Coach luggage sitting there, a gift from Mallory on the one-year anniversary of Gretchen's employment.

She hasn't touched it in five years.

But now she reaches down, picks it up, and carries it over to her bed, to start packing.

Becky shifts her weight on the edge of her bed, watching the cameraman pack his equipment into a big bag, and waiting for the pretty lady reporter to get off the phone, where she's talking in a low voice to someone—her producer, Becky thinks she said.

It turns out the lady's name is Laura Madison and she works for some local television program. She spent an hour talking to Becky, and the cameraman filmed the whole thing.

Becky's going to be on TV.

Maybe she shouldn't have told the lady so much. About how sorry she is for the way she'd treated Cindy back when she was a little kid, and how she'd run off and just left her daughter that way, never calling or coming back to see how she was.

And maybe she shouldn't have told them about Elizabeth either.

But the lady seemed to have known about her being dead from drugs and all, though she'd been surprised when Becky said Elizabeth had tried to get her sister to help her. The reporter had asked Becky about it, and Becky had told her how Elizabeth had called Mallory up and told her who she was, and how Mallory had agreed to fly her out to Los Angeles.

Elizabeth had even stayed in Mallory's movie-star mansion for a while. And she'd tried to get Mallory to let Becky come too. But Mallory wouldn't even speak to Becky on the phone. She said she didn't want anything to do with her.

"She turned her back on her own mother?" the lady reporter had said, shaking her head in disbelief.

"She turned her back on her sister too," Becky had said, caught up in her memories. "She kicked Elizabeth out of her house one day. Put her on a plane back to Chicago, not caring that she had no place to go. Didn't even send Elizabeth her stuff. Elizabeth came back without her purse, without her ID, without anything. That's how bad her own sister treated her."

"What a shame," the lady reporter had said.

She seemed so sympathetic, Becky had kept talking. Telling her how Elizabeth had OD'd not long after that. And how she, Becky, had tried to get through to Mallory to let her know. How she had figured maybe Mallory would want to come to Chicago to be with her.

But all Mallory had done was arrange for the burial to be paid for. That was it. Her own sister was dead, her own mother was grieving, and she hadn't even seemed to care.

"Okay," Laura Madison is saying into the phone, "I'll get back to you with the details. Thanks, Shawn."

She hangs up and looks at Becky.

Becky can tell by her expression that she's excited about something.

"Did you ask them about my reimbursement?" Becky asks. "For doing the interview?"

"We're going to give you something even better," the reporter says.

"Something better than money?"

Puzzled, Becky frowns.

What could be better than money?

"Becky," Laura says, "how would you like to be reunited with your daughter—maybe even tomorrow?"

"But ..." Becky frowns. "She's in Rhode Island, isn't she?"

"Actually, it's been reported that she's on her way back to Los Angeles. We're trying to confirm that."

"But ... how would I get to Los Angeles?"

"We would fly you there, Becky. We would make all the arrangements for you to come face-to-face with the daughter you haven't seen since she was a little girl. What do you say?"

Becky's jaw falls open.

Her mind spins.

"Becky? What do you think?"

A broad grin spreads slowly across her face. "I think I'd like that," she tells Laura Madison. "I'd really like that a lot."

*What are you doing?* Harper asks himself as he dashes through the quiet departure terminal.

*You can't do this.*

But he's already doing it.

He's already there.

And the next flight to Los Angeles leaves in less than one minute.

Mallory Eden is on that flight. He's certain of it.

He leaps over a pile of luggage somebody's left in an aisle, and skirts around a flight attendant pushing a passenger in a wheelchair.

Gate 7 ...

Where the hell is Gate 7?

Glancing around wildly, he spots it.

The waiting area is deserted except for an airline employee who's just closing the door leading to the jetway.

"Wait!" Harper hollers to her, breaking into a sprint.

She looks up, startled.

"I need you to stop that flight!"

"It's already taxiing out onto the runway," she tells him, glancing around, as though nervous about his intentions. "What seems to be the problem, sir?"

"I just ... I had to talk to someone who's on that plane."

"I'm sorry, sir."

Out of breath from his mad dash, he strides over to the window, looks out at the 737 that's preparing for takeoff.

Then he turns back to the airline attendant, who is still watching him warily, as though poised to summon security.

"Do you know when the next flight leaves for Los Angeles?" Harper asks her breathlessly.

"We don't have another one until this evening, but I believe that Delta has a West Coast connection departing early this afternoon."

He doesn't even bother to stop her, just turns and makes his way back toward the terminal and the reservations desk.

# chapter

## 14

"Mallory?"

"Rae?"

"My God." Mallory opens her arms and pulls her friend into them. Suddenly tears are streaming from behind her dark glasses, trickling down her cheeks to dampen Rae's silk blouse.

Her friend doesn't seem to mind.

"I can't believe you're really here," Rae tells her, finally pulling back and looking at her.

Mallory nods, unable to speak, her throat choked with emotion as she takes in the changes the years have wrought in this once dear and familiar face.

Her friend had looked the same from a distance a moment ago— same impeccably styled blond hair, same svelte figure, moving along through the gate area in the same hurried stride.

But up close Mallory sees that Rae's eyes are edged with a faint network of lines, that there are bags beneath them, marring her perfect complexion.

Rae looks older. World-weary.

"We should get out of here," Rae says hurriedly, casting a furtive glance around.

Mallory does the same, aware of the bustle around them as other passengers emerge from the jetway. But people are scurrying by undistracted, as if they haven't bothered to notice the two long-lost friends greeting each other at the gate.

And Mallory realizes that no one has recognized her—yet.

The anonymity she had enjoyed during the long plane trip— mostly spent sleeping off a week's worth of exhaustion—has carried over. Because no one is thinking of Mallory Eden as a brunette with an hour-glass figure.

Still, if the local press has been tipped off and is awaiting her arrival, it's only a matter of time before they spot her, dark hair and all.

"Did you tell anyone you were meeting me here?" Mallory asks Rae, trying to quell a rush of uneasiness.

"You told me not to, and I didn't. Did you tell anyone I was meeting you?"

"Who would I tell?" Mallory asks.

Rae shrugs. "I don't know. Is there someone . . ."

"There's no one," Mallory says firmly, shoving aside thoughts of Harper. "I've been alone for five years. There's no one to tell— about anything I do."

"Except me," Rae says, flashing a smile that almost reaches her shadowed eyes. "Now that you're back."

"Except you. I've really missed you, Rae."

"I've missed you too, Mallory," her friend says, her tone hollow.

Mallory knows how hurt she must be, knows she should say something, should attempt to apologize, somehow, for the way she had left. For allowing Rae to believe she was dead for all these years.

But there will be time for explanations later.

Plenty of time.

"Let's go, then," she tells Rae, slinging her bag over her shoulder, eager to get out of there. She can't help feeling like a target, out there in the open.

Rae snaps into action, turning toward the main terminal with an efficient air. "Did you check any luggage?"

"Are you out of your mind? First of all, there's nothing I'd want to bring with me from there that wouldn't fit into this carry-on bag . . ."

*Five years, and there's nothing to leave behind,* she thinks ruefully.

Not material possessions anyway.

Again she shoves aside thoughts of Harper.

And Manny.

"Second," she continues, "I can't wait to just get out of here, before the press sniffs me out."

"They've already sniffed me out," Rae says, leading the way along the concourse. "That's why I've had my phone off the hook since yesterday."

"That's what I figured," Mallory says.

" 'No comment' wasn't sitting too well with anyone, so I decided to be out of reach for a while, at least so I could get a decent night's sleep. But this morning I figured I'd better put the phone back on the hook, in case you were trying to call."

"I'm glad you did. Where are you living anyway?"

"Burbank," Rae says briefly. "I've been renting a condo there for a year. But we're not going there."

"We're not?"

"There was a horde of reporters camped out in front of my building this morning. I snuck out the back way. We can't go there."

"Where are we going?" Mallory asks uneasily.

Maybe she shouldn't have come back so soon. Maybe she should have waited a little longer, until the fallout settled, until the worldwide curiosity had waned.

"Where are we going?" Rae flashes a smile. "You said it yourself. Remember?"

"What did I say?"

"That whenever I used to pick you up at the airport after you'd been out of town for a while we would go—"

"Straight to the beach," Mallory says with a grin.

"Right." Rae slings a limber arm over Mallory's shoulders. "I was thinking we'd really shake the press off our trail . . . maybe drive up to Big Sur for a few days. We can be there late tonight. I made a reservation at the Treetop Inn."

The Treetop Inn . . .

That's the isolated resort hotel where the two of them had spent so many relaxing weekends. Mallory closes her eyes and pictures the rambling hotel, perched high above the pounding Pacific surf.

"You made a reservation? You didn't use your own name, did you?" she asks Rae.

"Of course not. I used Amy Abernathy, of course."

Mallory smiles. The name had always been her travel alias. "I can't believe you remembered that."

"How could I forget. It'll be perfect, Mal. We'll be anonymous, bum around . . . just like old times."

Big Sur . . .

The isolated wooded stretch of rocky California coastline is the perfect place to hide temporarily while she adjusts to the dizzying changes—and to once again being Mallory Eden.

"Oh, my God, Rae, Big Sur sounds fantastic. You"—Mallory gives her friend a squeeze—"are a lifesaver."

\* \* \*

Flynn refills his glass from the bottle of gin, then reaches into the dwindling bowl of cut-up limes and plucks one out. He sloppily squeezes the green rind so that the tart juice trickles over his fingers before dripping down into the gin, then plops the whole wedge into the glass with a splash, and dunks his hand in to rinse it off.

He licks his fingers, takes a sip from the glass, and then a gulp, appreciating the way the citrus flavor mellows the liquor's sting. He leans back in his chaise and sighs.

He's merely having a civilized cocktail or two, simply relaxing on a hot summer Sunday afternoon by the pool.

He's not guzzling cheap rotgut straight from a bottle, the way a lowlife drunk would. No, sir.

His glass is Wedgwood crystal; his gin is top-shelf stuff. He's clean-shaven, his thinning hair neatly combed. The music piped over the stereo speakers is classical. Pachelbel's *Canon in D*.

And as soon as he finishes guzzling this drink, he's going to try calling Rae again.

He'd reached her about an hour ago. She'd sounded rushed. Breathless. Like she was on her way somewhere.

He had asked her if she'd heard from Mallory, and she had said she hadn't.

But he wonders if she was lying.

If she was protecting Mallory, for some reason.

He has heard the rumors that Mallory left Rhode Island, that she was flying to Los Angeles.

Why wouldn't she have gotten in touch with him first?

There's only one reason that Flynn can think of.

Mallory doesn't want to see him.

She doesn't want him to be her agent anymore.

He takes another big swig, finishing what's left in his glass.

The gin burns going down, and when he's swallowed it, he looks at the bottle again, contemplating another drink.

Just one more . . .

No, he decides grimly, standing and starting, on unsteady feet, for the house.

He has to go find Rae.

And Mallory.


"Ladies and gentlemen, this is your captain speaking. Those of you seated by the windows will have a great view of the Grand Canyon in just a few minutes."

Harper is in a window seat.

He stares absently out at the cloudless sky, not caring about seeing the Grand Canyon.

Not caring about anything but the fact that in just a few hours he's going to be landing in Los Angeles.

The city he'd sworn he'd never return to.

The city he had left abruptly just a little over a year ago . . .

After the funeral.

Carolyn's funeral.

Carolyn Rutherford.

The woman whose life had been entrusted into his hands.

He had failed her. Failed her miserably.

And all because he'd fallen in love with her.

As a security specialist, he had been well aware of how risky it could be for a bodyguard to become emotionally involved with the person he was assigned to watch over.

And he had known the moment he laid eyes on Carolyn, a slender blonde with a throaty laugh and a provocative gleam in her dark eyes, that he was hopelessly attracted to her.

She knew it too. She later told him that.

He, who had always been a ladies' man, who had vowed never to settle down, had told himself that she was no big deal.

And Carolyn, who had always loved a challenge, had made it her mission to seduce him . . .

To prove that what sizzled between them was more than lust, and that maybe they should *both* consider settling down—together.

He should have refused the assignment.

Lord, why hadn't he refused the assignment?

Because the beautiful heiress was in danger, and he had been cocky enough to need to be the one who kept her safe.

Her father, Cyrus Rutherford, a billionaire computer software wizard, had been the victim of a thwarted kidnapping attempt just weeks before hiring the security firm that employed Harper. Convinced that his entire family was at risk, Rutherford had been willing to pay any price to keep them safe.

Especially Carolyn.

The youngest of his four grown children. The free spirit who had insisted on moving from the family compound in Carmel to Los Angeles. Bent on "just having fun," as she put it, she frequented seedy after-hours nightclubs, socialized with an eclectic crowd, lived alone in an isolated beach house.

Her father had believed that her imprudent behavior would get her killed, so he had hired a bodyguard.

Little had Cyrus known that it was her bodyguard who would get her killed.

Harper will never forget the grieving billionaire's words to him when he had tried to attend Carolyn's memorial service.

"How dare you try to set foot in this chapel," he had said, meeting Harper at the door, glaring at him with tormented eyes. "You murdered my daughter as surely as if you'd fired that gun yourself."

And he had been right.

Harper had been asleep in Carolyn's bed the night the kidnappers had broken into her house. Asleep, after a steamy bout of lovemaking.

He'd never heard the two men who swept into the bedroom and brazenly grabbed Carolyn . . .

Never heard them—until it was too late.

Until her muffled scream woke him, sent him fumbling for his gun.

Only he couldn't find it in the jumble of rumpled clothes beside the bed.

The two men had panicked; one of them had shot at him, but missed.

That was when Harper had tried to be a hero.

More gunfire had erupted, and Carolyn had been caught in the cross fire.

Harper, seeing that she'd been struck in the head, had screamed. "Noooo . . ."

Sometimes that scream echoes back to him.

He had sunk to his knees in the pool of blood soaking the white bedroom carpet, had taken her into his arms, had moaned her name, told her not to leave him.

But she had died right there, as the retreating footsteps of the two kidnappers faded away to mingle with the pounding surf.

And so he had left L.A., left the profession that had once filled him with a sense of power—a sense that he was actually helping people, keeping them safe.

And he had struggled to create a new life in Windemere Cove, a life he had vowed would be lived in isolation.

He had hurt too many people.

His parents.

His sister.

And Carolyn.

Every meaningful relationship he'd ever had.

That's why he should never have allowed himself to fall for Elizabeth. But the attraction had struck him like lightning this time too, sparked by the nagging idea that he had seen her someplace before . . .

Now he knows where.

At the Academy Awards ceremony the March before she'd disappeared.

She had been there with some big-name actor, and he had been on security detail at the Shrine Auditorium.

He had heard the crowd getting all worked up, had watched as the cause of their excitement stepped onto the red carpet.

Mallory Eden, the famed, beloved actress, had arrived.

And at that moment, as she stood there, poised and smiling for the zillions of screaming fans and cameras and reporters, gazing around at the throng, their eyes had collided.

It couldn't have been for more than a second or two, but she had seen him.

And he had felt an electrifying surge of attraction.

It was easy enough to dismiss in the next moment as her eyes drifted past him and she moved away, down the red carpet on the arm of her date. What red-blooded man in the world could lock gazes with a screen goddess like Mallory Eden and not feel a stirring in his loins?

Still, the moment had never really left his consciousness. Not if the memory had been triggered the moment he heard her tortured voice saying her name to Frank Minelli in that darkened house on Friday night.

That long-ago, fleeting connection to her had come to him in a flash . . .

Along with the knowledge that she was in danger, and he had to save her.

He hadn't stopped to think when he went hurtling into that shadowy room to grab her attacker.

Not about the wisdom of making his presence known to a man who might have a gun . . .

And not about what had happened to Carolyn.

All he knew was that she needed him; Mallory needed him.

Just as all he knows now is that he needs her.

There's a click of the public address system, and then the captain's voice is once again booming through the cabin. "Well, ladies and gentlemen, there's that view of the Grand Canyon I promised you. Truly amazing, isn't it?"

And Harper thinks that the only thing that's truly amazing is that he let Mallory Eden leave town without telling her exactly how he feels about her.

But this time, for the first time in his life, it won't be too late.

Gretchen stares out the window at the sprawling Grand Canyon below, but not because it's "truly amazing," as the pilot described it. She isn't even seeing the scenery beyond the layers of glass.

She's been staring absently out the window ever since the plane took off from T. F. Green airport.

Anything to shield her face from the curious, or pitying, or horrified stares from the other passengers.

The big, broad-brimmed hat and oversized sunglasses she wore in the car and in the airport hadn't provided nearly enough camouflage. She had heard people gasping as she passed, and several small children started crying at the sight of her. Her rage had grown with every step she had taken toward the departure gate.

Damn Mallory Eden for not returning her call.

Damn her for leaving Rhode Island.

Damn her for forcing Gretchen to venture out in public for the first time in five years.

By now, her mother will have returned home from work. She'll see that the Chevy is missing from the driveway, and when she goes inside, she'll find the note Gretchen wrote her.

The note telling her not to worry; that Gretchen had some business to attend to, and that she'll call or come home in a few days.

Of course, her mother will worry anyway. She's been a nervous wreck ever since Gretchen's father dropped dead of a heart attack ten years ago, a few days after Gretchen had moved to Los Angeles.

*Sorry for putting you through this, Mom,* Gretchen says silently as the Grand Canyon fades into the distance. *But I have to take this chance.*

She closes her eyes and rests her forehead against the window, telling herself that Mallory Eden will agree to help her.

She has to.

She *has* to . . .

How many times had she said to Gretchen, "Remind me that I owe you a big favor"?

She'd said it when Gretchen had hunted all over Melrose Avenue to find the perfect shade of a chiffon floral scarf to match an outfit she was wearing to a charity luncheon.

She'd said it when Gretchen had driven Mallory's dog, Gent, all the way up to that Big Sur resort that Mallory and her friend Rae were always going to, just because Mallory had decided she missed her pet.

She'd even said it whenever Gretchen drove the long way to work so she could stop at a Santa Monica bakery and pick up a couple of the low-fat chocolate muffins Mallory loved.

*Remind me that I owe you a big favor, Gretchen.*

*I will, Mallory,* Gretchen thinks grimly, digging her nails into the palm of her hand. *Believe me, I will. . . .*

"Well, you can't have him!"

"The hell I can't! He's my kid!"

Manny winces at the shrill voice that belongs to his mother, and hugs his knees more tightly against his chest, listening to the argument. Though it's taking place all the way downstairs, in the kitchen, every word is loud and clear.

"We're going to talk to the police about you, so don't you go thinking you can—"

"What do you mean, talk to the police about me?"

"We're going to tell them to make sure you stay away from Manny."

"You can't do that. He's my kid!"

"You just want him because you're jealous that he was spending time with that movie-star lady," Manny's grandfather accuses. "Until he started hanging around her, you never cared what the hell he was up to."

"Hell, I didn't know she was a movie star until yesterday. But she had no business trying to take over my kid! If she wants him, she has to talk to me about it. She has to pay."

"Pay?" Manny's grandfather yells. "You want to sell her your own son? I knew you were rotten through the core, but—"

"Rafael, calm down," Manny's grandmother cuts in. "You're getting all red in the face. Calm down. Your heart . . ."

"Do you hear what our daughter is saying? She wants to sell her own son!"

"Well, that woman can't just have him! You can't just take somebody's kid away."

"He's not yours anymore. You signed your rights away to us a long time ago, remember? When he wasn't more than a baby. You never wanted him."

Manny's stomach does a flip-flop at his grandfather's words. So his mother signed her rights away. Why should that take him by surprise? Anyway, he should be happy to find out that she has no legal claim to him. . . .

"And at least the movie star tried to help him! That's more than you ever did." That's Manny's grandmother talking, her voice shrill and her accent thicker than usual, the way it always gets when she's angry.

"I don't have to listen to this. I want my kid. Where is he? Manny!"

"Get back here! Get back here! You can't take him!"

Tears fill Manny's eyes at his grandfather's fierce words. How had he ever doubted that Gramps and Grammy loved him enough to keep him? They won't let her take him away. They won't.

Manny huddles on the floor in the corner of his room, trembling. What if they can't stop her?

Several sets of footsteps are pounding rapidly along the downstairs hall toward the stairs.

Grammy is crying now, yelling, "Stop it! Don't go up there! Leave him alone!"

"Get back here!" Gramps hollers again. "Don't you dare—"

His words are cut off abruptly with a gasp, and a moment later Manny hears a loud thump.

"Rafael!" Grammy shrieks. "Rafael! Oh, God, Rafael! It's his heart! It's his heart! Do something! Call 911! For Christ's sake, he's your father! Call 911! Please!"

Manny's hands fly to his mouth and he squeezes his eyes shut, paralyzed in horror, listening as he hears his mother's footsteps racing back toward the kitchen.

He half expects to hear the back door open and slam, but then her voice can be heard on the telephone, calling for help.

At the foot of the stairs his grandmother is wailing. "No! Rafael, don't you leave me! No!"

And still Manny can't move, can only sit motionless, listening, longing to somehow end the nightmare.

*Elizabeth*, he thinks, tears streaming down his cheeks. *If I ever needed you in my whole life, it's now.*

*But you're gone.*

*You're gone forever.*


Rae's car phone rings as she's steering onto the Ventura Freeway. She glances at it, then at Mallory.

"Are you going to get it?" Mallory asks.

"Should I?"

"Do you think it's some reporter?"

"I don't know how they'd get this number," Rae tells her. "Only a handful of people have it."

"Go ahead and answer it, I guess," Mallory says with a shrug.

Rae picks up the phone, propping it between her ear and shoulder and steering the car into a center lane as she says, "Hello?"

"Rae, it's me."

"Flynn . . ." Rae glances at Mallory, who's shaking her head.

Mallory mouths, "Don't tell him I'm here."

Rae nods. "How are you?" she asks. She glances in the rearview mirror, noticing a blue compact car moving into the same lane some distance behind her. Wasn't that car behind her on the freeway on the way to the airport earlier?

"*Where* are you? I've been trying to reach you at home, on your cell phone . . ."

"I wasn't carrying it with me." She glances again at the car. A truck has entered the lane in front of it, and it's out of her view.

"Where are you?" Flynn asks again.

"On the freeway."

"Have you heard from Mallory?"

Rae tightens her grip on the steering wheel. "No," she lies. "I haven't."

"I haven't either. I just heard on the radio that she's supposed to be flying back out here."

He's slurring, Rae realizes. He's been drinking again. Damn.

"She may already be in town," he goes on. "I figured she'd contact you or me."

Rae nervously reaches down to adjust the volume on the radio. "Well, she didn't call me."

"Rae, look out!" Mallory screams in the seat beside her.

Rae glances up through the windshield, sees that the car in front of her has slammed its brakes on.

She swerves into the next lane, narrowly avoiding a collision.

"That was her!" Flynn's voice accuses in her ear. "That was Mallory's voice. She's with you, Rae."

"Flynn—"

"You lied to me. How could you lie to me, Rae? After what I did for you, setting you up with de Lisser?"

"Flynn—"

"Bring her over here, Rae," he commands churlishly. "I need to talk to her."

"I can't, Flynn. We're . . . we're getting out of town for a few days." She glances at Mallory.

Mallory's face is pale, watching her.

"Where are you going?" Flynn wants to know.

Rae hesitates, stares out the windshield, looks again at Mallory. Mallory shakes her head.

"I'm not sure," Rae tells Flynn.

"Tell me, Rae!"

"Flynn, I have to go."

"Rae—"

She disconnects the line.

"I'm sorry for making you lie," Mallory says. "I just can't see him right now, Rae. I don't want to see anyone yet. I need time."

"I know."

"Oh, God. I feel sick inside. Hiding from Flynn . . ."

"It's okay, Mal"

"Was he angry?"

"He'll get over it." Rae keeps her gaze focused on the traffic.

She remembers to check the rearview mirror after a moment, and sees that the blue compact car is nowhere in sight. It must have been her imagination.

Becky O'Neal feels like a movie star as she steps into the terminal at LAX.

Lights and cameras are everywhere, all of them aimed at her.

And so are the questions . . .

So many questions.

"Have you been in contact with your daughter since she turned up alive?"

"Why did you abandon your daughter?"

"Is it true that you're clean?"

"How long has it been since you last did drugs?"

Becky glances at Laura Madison, who looks calm. She takes Becky's arm and leads her through the crowd, following two important-looking men in suits. They go down a long hall and through several doors, into a private lounge area.

"I need to make a call," Laura tells Becky as they sit on two chairs off in a corner. "Then we'll go out to the limo."

"Limo?"

Laura smiles. "Sure, Becky. In exchange for giving us the exclusive on your reunion with your daughter, we're making sure you get there in style."

"Where *is* Cindy? Is she waiting for me?"

"She's not waiting for you, no. We're going to surprise her, remember? Everyone likes surprises."

Becky nods. She remembers how little Cindy had loved the big, brightly colored plastic blocks she'd given her for her first birthday. Her little face had lit up and she'd clapped her chubby hands together in glee, squealing at her mama, holding her arms up for a hug.

But today's surprise would be quite different.

Today Becky's daughter might not be so eager to smile, to hug her.

*I can't take any more rejection from her,* Becky tells herself, tensely clasping her trembling fingers with the opposite hand, watching but not listening as Laura Madison talks on the phone.

*If she hurts me today, in front of Laura and all those cameras, after I traveled so far to be with her . . .*

Becky clenches her jaw and tries to stop the trembling.

"Okay," Laura says, hanging up her cellular phone and turning to Becky. "We've got Mallory heading north up the coast."

It takes a moment for Becky to focus, and even when she does, she doesn't quite understand what Laura's talking about. "What do you mean?"

"We had someone trailing an old friend of hers on the hunch that Mallory might have contacted her for a rendezvous. It paid off. The friend picked up a woman at the airport a few hours ago, coming in on a flight from Rhode Island. The passenger didn't look like Mallory from what our reporter could see, but nobody's seen her in five years, so we're assuming it's her."

"Did you tell her I'm here?"

"No—remember? It's a surprise, Becky." This time Laura

sounds impatient, and not as pleasant as she had been the whole flight out here.

"I'm sorry. I just . . . I guess I forgot."

"Let's go. We have to get on the road."

"But how do we know where we're going?"

"I told you. We have someone on Mallory's trail. We'll keep checking in with them until we get a destination."

"Okay."

Laura sure is smart. Becky would never have thought of looking up Cindy's old friends in case her daughter had called one of them. She doesn't even know who Cindy's old friends are.

Her own daughter, and she knows nothing about her life from the time she was two years old.

Except, of course, for what Elizabeth had told her when she'd visited her sister in Los Angeles.

And that wasn't much. Elizabeth was so far gone most of the time that she hadn't noticed or conveyed many details.

Becky has spent too many years wondering about her mystery daughter.

And now she's about to come face-to-face with her at last.

Gretchen closes the hotel room door behind her and lets out an audible sigh of relief. She tosses the keys to the rental car onto the table between the two beds and perches on the edge of one of them.

She made it.

She's back in Los Angeles.

And she's finally alone again, away from strangers' gazes.

The flight was hell, and so was the endless wait at LAX for a rental car. Thank God the hotel is right across from the airport, so she didn't have to deal with traffic on top of everything else.

Now all she has to do is figure out where Mallory would have gone once she landed in L.A.

At least she had remembered to bring her old Filofax, the one from her stint as Mallory's assistant. The one that lists all of Mallory's friends and business associates.

It had been packed away in a box in the attic, along with the rest of her belongings her mother had had shipped back to Connecticut after the accident.

Gretchen had never bothered to unpack anything. She hadn't

wanted reminders of that fleeting golden life she had lived on the West Coast.

But that morning she had hurriedly dug through first one carton, and then another, until she found the Filofax. She had left the rest of her stuff—the designer clothes and stacks of head shots and textbooks from her acting classes—strewn all over the attic floor.

The first call she places is to Rae Hamilton.

She, if anyone, will know where Mallory is. The two were inseparable.

Rae's line has been disconnected.

It figures.

Not everyone is going to be in the same place they were five years ago, Gretchen reminds herself. But some people are bound to be.

Flynn Soderland is next.

Her heart leaps when she hears a click and then his voice, but she realizes then that it's just voice mail.

Well, at least his number hasn't changed.

Gretchen hesitates, uncertain whether to leave a message. She decides against it, opting instead to try his cellular phone, on the off chance that that number, too, has remained unchanged.

The line is answered almost before it finishes one ring.

"Yeah, this is Flynn."

"Flynn Soderland?"

"Who is this?"

She hears the distant sound of traffic, horns honking. He's on the road somewhere. Is Mallory with him?

"This is Gretchen Dodd," she says, struggling to keep her voice from wavering. "I'm Mallory Eden's former assistant, and—"

"Mallory's assistant? Has she called you?"

"No." Her hopes sink. "You haven't heard from her either?"

"She hasn't called me, no. But she's with Rae Hamilton. They're heading out of town."

Gretchen's heart is pounding. "Where are they going?"

"I have no idea. They wouldn't tell me. Rae says Mallory needs a few days to herself."

He's slurring his speech, Gretchen notices. She suddenly remembers that Flynn had always had a drinking problem. In fact . . .

Jeez, how could she have forgotten that?

Mallory had been thinking of firing him that last year, Gretchen recalls, after he got into drunken public arguments with business associates.

Details come rushing back at her, triggered by the sound of Flynn's voice, and being back in town.

She is seized by a sudden torrent of longing for her old life. Christ, how glorious it had felt to be a part of that fast-paced, high-powered, scandal-ridden world. She squeezes her eyes closed against the flood of memories.

"Listen," Flynn is saying sloppily, "you wouldn't know where they might be headed, would you? The two of them used to go off together on those long weekends all the time, remember?"

"I . . . I really don't remember that, no," Gretchen says, trying to stay focused on the conversation.

*Where would Mallory and Rae be headed?*

Again she is transported back over the years, back to the old days as Mallory's assistant.

"They always went up to Big Sur," Flynn says, "and I'll be willing to bet that's where they're headed now."

*Big Sur,* Gretchen thinks. *Yes, that's where they always went.*

"In fact," Flynn continues, "I'm on my way up there myself. But do you know where I should start looking? I can't seem to remember the name of that hotel Mallory loved so much. It's on the fringes of my mind, but it keeps evading me."

"Uh, I can't tell you what it was, Mr. Soderland." Gretchen stands and paces the narrow aisle between the hotel room's two double beds, eager to get off the phone.

"You don't know?" Flynn asks, sounding disappointed.

*Of course I know. But, like I said, I can't tell you.*

"I'm afraid not," she says aloud.

"Well, if you think of the place, would you give me a call back?"

"Sure I will. And if you see Mallory . . . tell her I'm looking forward to connecting with her again."

"I will. . . . What was your name again?"

A prickle of anger darts through her. He doesn't even remember her name, and she had practically talked to him daily when she worked for Mallory.

"It's Gretchen," she says curtly.

*Gretchen Dodd . . . you old drunk.*

"That's right. I don't know why I can't remember anything today."

*Probably because you're wasted.*

"Hey," he says abruptly, as if he's just remembered something. "You're the one who got hurt. Didn't you? When that flower arrangement blew up in your face?"

"Yes" is her terse reply.

"I forgot all about that. How are you? You got pretty banged up. It was your legs, right?"

"My face."

"Are you okay now?"

"I'm fine now," she says crisply, careful not to walk all the way to the end of the aisle between the beds, where she might catch a glimpse of her reflection in the full-length mirror on the back of the bathroom door.

She bids a quick, terse farewell to Flynn Soderland and hangs up the phone.

So Flynn suspects that Mallory and her friend Rae are headed toward Big Sur.

And Gretchen knows how to find out for sure.

*Her* memory is sharper than ever.

All she has to do is flip through her Filofax to the T's.

She starts dialing.

"Good evening, Treetop Inn," a voice greets her a moment later. "How may I help you?"

"I 'd like to confirm a reservation," Gretchen says, the years falling away so that her voice is an echo of her long-ago efficiency.

"Certainly. May I have the name, please?"

"It's Abernathy. Amy Abernathy."

"One moment while I check, please."

Gretchen clutches the phone to her ear, her vacant gaze darting around the silent, impersonal hotel room.

If this isn't it, she'll have to go back to the phone book and start calling other contacts. The trouble is, if Mallory's with Rae, she probably hasn't called anyone else. The two of them pretty much kept to themselves when they were together.

And if they aren't at the Treetop, then Gretchen has no idea where—

"Hello? Yes, your reservation is confirmed, Ms. Abernathy. And I do have your credit card approval for late arrival this evening, so you're all set."

"Thank you very much," Gretchen says, smiling as she hangs up the phone and picks up the keys to the rental car.

*  *  *

Harper is stuck in traffic on the San Diego Freeway.

Not that it matters.

He has no idea where he's going.

No idea how to begin looking for Mallory.

He figures he'll find a hotel somewhere by the beach, settle in, and wait for her to surface.

It shouldn't take long.

He isn't the only one looking for her.

The press has apparently worked itself into a frenzy. He saw reporters and camera crews all over the airport when he landed, and as soon as he turned on the radio in the rental car, he heard a deejay offering free tickets to a Nine Inch Nails concert to the first listener who calls in an accurate Mallory sighting.

In the meantime, Harper is sitting in traffic, wondering why he had ever thought living in Los Angeles was a good idea.

Sure, the beach is great . . .

But there's a beach in Windemere Cove too. And no traffic.

No smog either, he thinks, glancing out the window at the indistinct night sky.

He thinks about all the other negative aspects of living here.

The high rent.

The earthquakes.

The crime.

The—

He jumps in his seat, startled by a faint tone coming from the vicinity of his waist.

His pager.

Somebody is paging him.

Can it possibly be . . .

He pulls it from his belt loop and glances at the number displayed.

It's an unfamiliar number; the area code is 408.

Where . . . ?

*It's in California, he realizes.*

The area code for Carolyn's family's compound up in Carmel.

They wouldn't be calling him, of course—for all they know, he's fallen off the face of the earth, and none too soon for them.

Harper knows nobody else living in that area code.

Can it possibly be Mallory, trying to reach him?

Is she somewhere up the coast, in trouble, waiting desperately for him to call this number?

He glances out the windshield at the cars in front of him. He glances in the rearview mirror and sees nothing but a sea of traffic behind him too. He's boxed in. At a standstill.

Without a phone.

Mallory checks her watch one more time.

It's been a half hour since she had impulsively tried to page Harper, and he still hasn't called her back.

*Maybe he doesn't want anything to do with you now that you're gone,* she thinks wistfully as she flashes one last glance at the pay telephone before turning away.

The only phone for guest use at the inn is tucked away in a dark nook of the rustic lobby, around the corner from the registration desk and the comfortable seating area by the stone fireplace.

The place is fairly deserted at this hour on a Sunday evening. As she passes through the lobby, Mallory spies a lone man sitting in front of the floor-to-ceiling windows, a sketch pad on his lap.

She frowns.

What can he be sketching at this hour?

There's nothing to see out the window but velvet, starlit sky.

Yet in the morning, Mallory knows, the view will be dazzling.

She walks slowly back along the corridor, shadowy with its dark, rough-hewn cedar walls, toward the second-floor suite she and Rae are sharing. It, too, has a spectacular vista of the ocean, as do most rooms in the inn.

The Treetop sits on two hundred secluded acres atop a sheer cliff that rises more than a thousand feet above the foaming white surf. There are several sun decks, lush flower gardens, and a series of trails through deep thickets of redwood and pine that emerge periodically at majestic clearings high above the sea.

Mallory tells herself, as she mounts the staircase at the end of the hall, that she has to relax. She's been on edge all day.

*Hell, you've been on edge for over five years,* she reminds herself.

Being there at Big Sur with Rae is the soul-cleansing she so sorely needs. She can finally forget about the nightmare of the past, the . . .

But what about the stalker?

What if it wasn't Frank?

She had called the Windemere Cove police station before trying

Harper just now. They reported that Frank is still in custody, and hasn't confessed to stalking her in California.

That was what had triggered her to call Harper's pager.

For some reason, she had thought that if she could just hear his voice, she might be able to put to rest the nagging sense of uneasiness that has dogged her ever since she touched down in L.A.

*What if it wasn't Frank?*

*What if whoever was after me five years ago is still out there someplace?*

*What if he's been watching, and waiting to strike, and . . .*

She shudders and picks up her pace, arriving at the top of the stairs and turning the corner. She hurries past the row of closed doors until she reaches the end of the hall.

Two quick knocks, and the door is promptly thrown open by Rae, who's wearing a pair of light blue silk pajamas. She looks cool, comfortable, and stylish, as always. But her eyes are troubled.

"My God, you don't know how worried I've been," she says, stepping aside to let Mallory into the suite. "Where have you been? I thought you were just going to call the police back in Rhode Island and come right back."

"I was, but . . . I decided to take a short walk around."

She isn't ready to share her thoughts about Harper yet—not even with Rae. Nor does she want to tell Rae about Manny, whom she had also intended to reach—until she realized it's well past midnight on the East Coast. She'll call him tomorrow.

"You were walking alone, in the dark?" Rae looks dismayed.

"I just strolled out to see the calla lilies in the garden. It's been so long since I've been here. I just couldn't wait to look around a little bit. It hasn't changed."

"Well, don't forget we're going hiking on the trails first thing in the morning. You'll be able to see everything better then."

"I can't wait."

"Did you get ahold of the police?"

Mallory nods. "They said he still hasn't confessed."

"To stalking you five years ago?"

"Right."

"What if he doesn't?"

"They'll try to prove it was him. He was in Los Angeles at the time." She shrugs.

Rae is watching her. "Do *you* think it was him?"

Mallory hesitates, then nods. "After the way he attacked me the other night, yes. He's sick. I just hope he doesn't somehow get away with all of this."

"Don't worry, Mallory. They'll get him to confess. Or they'll find the evidence to convict him. And then this whole nightmare will be over."

*But will I ever feel truly safe again?*

"Just try and put the whole thing out of your head if you can," Rae suggests.

"Good idea." Mallory yawns and starts toward the sleeping area off the rectangular sitting room with its homey couch and chairs. "I think I'll go right to bed. I'm exhausted."

"Are you sure?"

She turns at the unexpected sound of disappointment in Rae's voice.

That's when she notices the two glasses of red wine on the low oak coffee table, and the sea breeze wafting through the open door leading to the secluded balcony.

She realizes that Rae had planned on the two of them sitting out there, drinking wine until the wee hours, the way they always had when they came up here.

"I thought . . . I mean, we have so much catching up to do," Rae says, sounding hesitant. "I guess I'm just eager to hear about everything, not just what you've been doing alone in Rhode Island for all this time, but about your plans for the future. I mean . . . I don't even know whether you've decided to go back to acting."

Mallory hesitates in the doorway, looking from the waiting wine to Rae's face, which looks slightly wistful.

For a moment she considers sitting down for a nice rambling conversation, unwinding over a glass of wine, reestablishing the old intimacy with her dearest friend.

But then she realizes that she's simply too bone tired to think straight. All she wants to do is fall into bed and sleep for hours, without intrusive thoughts of the past—or the future.

"I'm sorry, Rae," she says reluctantly. "I'm exhausted. I'll be more in the mood to chat tomorrow. But thank you for all you've done. You . . . you've saved me."

"It's no big deal," Rae tells her, flashing a brief smile. "I'm really tired too. Let's just go to sleep. But I'm going to wake you up at dawn for that hike."

"You do that," Mallory tells her with a grin before going into her room and closing the door.

She changes into one of the nightgowns she had purchased that afternoon when she had Rae stop at a shopping mall along the way. She needed everything—pajamas and clothes and undergarments and shoes and jackets, even toiletries.

In the adjoining bathroom she swiftly brushes her teeth, washes her face, and runs a brush through her hair. Her face in the mirror is lined with shadows, testimony to what she's been through these past few days.

Hell.

*You just need to sleep,* she tells herself. *Everything will be better in the morning.*

She climbs into the mission-style bed and sinks gratefully into the downy feather bed cushioning the mattress.

But she doesn't fall asleep right away, despite her fatigue.

For a long time after she hears Rae's bedroom door close next door, she lies awake in the unfamiliar bed, listening to the distant crashing of the waves. . . .

And telling herself that there's nothing to fear.

Frank Minelli is a continent away.

*But what if it wasn't him?*

*What if it was someone else?*

*Someone who knows where I am?*

She remembers the way Rae had seemed to be keeping an uneasy eye on the rearview mirror during the drive up here. As though she were making sure they weren't being followed . . .

Or as though she thought someone was trailing them.

When Mallory asked her about it, she said she was just being cautious, keeping an eye out for the nosy press.

*And that's probably all there was to it,* Mallory tells herself.

Probably.

# chapter

# 15

Harper has driven the winding highway up the coast only once, with Carolyn, on the way to her parents' home in Carmel. But that had been in his trusty Ford Explorer, in the daylight. And even though Carolyn, daredevil that she was, had urged him to step on the gas, he had taken the curves slowly and cautiously. She had complained that it had taken them twice as long to get there as it did when she drove it alone.

Now, in the middle of the night, in an unfamiliar rental car, feeling almost numb from exhaustion, Harper finds himself practically creeping along the road through the thick mist drifting off the sea.

Several times he's had to pull over so that tailgating headlights can shoot past him. Anyone driving that fast on a road like this must be in a real hurry to get someplace . . .

Not that he isn't.

He just wants to make sure he gets there alive.

Ever since he pulled off the freeway, got to a phone, and dialed the number that had paged him, he's been filled with a sense of urgency . . .

Because he's about ninety-nine percent certain that it was Mallory who called him.

The man who answered his call had told him he'd reached a pay phone at the Treetop Inn in Big Sur. He was a guest who happened to have been in the lobby, heard it ringing, and picked it up.

Harper had swiftly gotten the inn's main number from directory assistance and called it, intending to find out whether there was anyone registered by the name of Elizabeth Baxter or Mallory Eden.

But he had gotten the inn's answering machine, telling him to try back tomorrow morning.

Just as well. Harper doubts that she would be using either of those names.

But he's certain she's there.

He's certain, because the closer he gets to Big Sur, the more anxious he feels. It's almost as though he can sense her presence. She's nearby, waiting for him, needing him.

*This is lunacy*, he thinks, stifling a yawn and noticing that the sky in the east is showing the first twinges of pink.

*You flew all day and drove all night, chasing a woman you barely know, a woman who might not want you to find her . . .*

But she had paged him.

It *had* to have been her.

Unless it was a wrong number . . .

It *could* have been a wrong number.

Harper sighs, blinking his weary, strained eyes, struggling to stay focused on the narrow road that snakes ahead, tracing the rocky coastline above the sea.

Just a few more miles to the Treetop Inn.

A few more miles, and he'll know.

*But I know already.*

*She's there, and she needs me,* he thinks, staring out into the night.

Gretchen turns off the car engine and is instantly aware of the hushed night sounds filtering through the darkness outside.

Crickets, and a rustling breeze that stirs the stand of redwoods overhead, and distant waves crashing on rocks.

She stares out the window at the sky in the east, where a faint, milky sign of dawn is creeping through the trees.

Then she glances at the dark building looming at the end of the narrow, gravel-covered lane. The Treetop Inn looks deserted, not a flicker of light spilling from the shuttered windows.

Someplace inside, Gretchen is certain, Mallory Eden is sleeping.

Is it a deep, peaceful sleep, the kind of sleep that has evaded Gretchen for so many years?

Or is she tormented by nightmares, thrashing restlessly in her hotel bed?

Gretchen leans back against the headrest and sighs.

She's exhausted.

Not just from the long flight and the endless drive up the coast on a fog-shrouded mountain road.

She's exhausted, too, from the months, the years, of loneliness. Of resentment. Of bitter hatred.

And helplessness.

Until now, there was nothing she could do about her situation. No vent for her anger, no hope of changing what her life had become.

Gretchen closes her eyes, yawns.

When daylight arrives, she'll confront Mallory Eden.

For now . . .

Sleep.

Manny jerks upright and rubs sleep from his eyes at the sudden sound of a voice nearby.

*Where am I . . . ?*

Oh.

The hospital.

Sitting on the uncomfortable couch in the tiny lounge. His grandmother is beside him, just as she has been for hours, rosary beads and a wet handkerchief clutched in her hands.

When he looks at her, he sees that she's looking at someone else.

A man wearing one of those blue surgical jumpsuits is standing in the doorway. His eyes, behind his round glasses, are serious. Manny realizes this is the doctor, and that he's finally come to them with news about Gramps.

"Mrs. Souza? Would you like to speak to me in private? Without . . ." He glances toward Manny.

"I want to stay," Manny speaks up, holding his grandmother's hand. "I want to hear."

He can't leave her alone now. Not the way his mother had. After calling 911, she had simply left, scurrying out the back door like a rat dodging a broom. There was no one but Manny to ride with his grandmother in the ambulance to the hospital, no one but Manny to try to convince her that everything is going to be okay.

When, of course, it isn't. Nothing is ever going to be okay again.

"Mrs. Souza . . ." the doctor says.

His grandmother heaves a shudder and a little moan, as though she knows what's coming.

And then the doctor is speaking quietly, professionally.

About Gramps.

About how they tried, but they couldn't save him.

Manny's arms are squeezed around his sobbing grandmother, tears are gushing from his eyes, and he can't think of anything to say.

Not to her.

Not to the doctor who told them Gramps is dead.

Desperately, he longs for someone to come and put comforting arms around him, to make it better somehow.

*I need you, Elizabeth. I need you so bad . . . .*

*Please, Elizabeth, please call me.*


Becky opens her eyes, wrenched out of her restless sleep as she has been countless times since she went to bed.

She yawns and wonders what time it is.

Sitting up in bed, she reaches over toward the bedside table. Her fingers strike the unfamiliar surface hard and she winces, then feels around until she finds the lamp and turns it on, illuminating the small hotel room.

The clock says that it's four thirty-nine A.M.

Too early.

Laura had arranged a wake-up call for six.

With a sigh, Becky leans back against the plump pillows, leaving the lamp on so that she can look around the room.

Laura had said she was disappointed with the accommodations, but that it wasn't easy to find something in Monterey on such short notice.

But never in her life has Becky stayed anyplace so luxurious.

In addition to the bed, table, and clock, there's a little table with two chairs, a telephone, and a television set with a remote control.

Becky hasn't watched television since the old days, growing up with Vera. How her mother had loved to sit and watch her programs. She used to talk about the actors and actresses as though she knew them personally. Lucille Ball and Fred MacMurray and Eva Gabor . . .

Becky sighs, putting Vera out of her head.

Of course she won't go, the stubborn old bag. She's there, telling Becky that she's just like her father, Vera's ex-husband, Ralph, who had run off and left them when Becky was a baby. Becky had his drab brown hair and thin lips and scrawny frame, and his wild, foolish streak, too, according to her mother.

"If you don't settle down and straighten out, young lady, you'll never be anything but a loser, like your father."

How many times had Becky heard that, growing up?

One time too many.

And that one time was the night before she took off for good, telling herself she never wanted to see her mother again. Vera had ripped into her for going out to a high school dance, breaking her curfew, and wearing "sleazy" clothes and makeup.

"What kind of a mother are you?" Vera had demanded. "What kind of example are you setting for that daughter of yours?"

"What kind of mother are *you*? " Becky had lashed back. "I'm taking my baby and I'm leaving."

"Go ahead. Get out. But you leave that little girl here with me," Vera had said. "No sense throwing two lives away."

Becky had realized, in that instant, that her mother wouldn't care if she left. She would probably be glad to get rid of the daughter who was a constant reminder of the husband she loathed.

She had planned to take little Cindy, just for spite. But then she thought better of it. Realized she could have a lot more fun on her own than she could dragging a kid around the country.

Cindy.

In a few more hours Becky will be seeing her again.

It's been such a long journey.

Not just the two flights yesterday—the first on that jumbo jet from Chicago to Los Angeles, the second on a prop plane from Los Angeles to San Jose—followed by a boring drive down the coast with Laura and the film crew.

But it isn't just the past twenty-four hours that have seemed so endless.

She's been waiting her whole life, it seems, to reclaim her first-born.

When Laura had told her last night that it was too late to go down to where Mallory was staying, Becky had been devastated. But then Laura had explained that it would be better to get a good night's sleep, to collect her thoughts so she'd be fresh for the reunion in the morning.

Now morning is almost here.

Now she'll know whether her daughter is going to forgive her this time . . .

Or reject her again.

Whether she's going to start paying back what she owes Becky, who, after all, brought her into this world.

*You owe me, kid. All I need is to get my hands on some cash, I'll have a chance to really turn my life around. You've got to help me.*

Becky draws a deep breath, lets it out, and stares, brooding, into space.

Flynn shivers in the chilly predawn mountain air, vaguely thinking he should probably have put up the top of the Jaguar. He had left it down hoping that the cool breeze would help keep him alert, help knock some of the booze out of his system.

But maybe that's not such a good idea—to let the buzz wear off. Maybe he needs a little something to help wake him up, he decides foggily.

He reaches toward the passenger seat beside him and feels around for the flask he'd thought was there.

Or did he leave it behind when he'd stopped at that bar for a couple of drinks a few hours ago?

Fuzzily, he tries to remember the last time he saw it.

He remembers now that he'd carried it out of the bar with him, after bribing the bartender to fill it with single malt scotch.

"I hope you're not getting behind the wheel in your condition, bud," the guy had said as Flynn walked out of the bar.

But he had known damn well that Flynn was going to drive away.

After all, he'd come in alone, and the bar was in the middle of nowhere, some rinky-dink town south of Morro Bay, where Flynn had stopped to gas up and quench his thirst with a couple more drinks.

But he's fine to drive.

He's made it all this way, hasn't he?

Has managed to keep the Jaguar between the lines even when he has to squint to make out the blurred, winding path ahead.

He'd actually considered stopping for the night after leaving the bar. But there's nowhere to stop on this lonely stretch of highway.

And anyway, he's eager to find Mallory. To talk to her about her future. *Their* future. As a team.

Never mind that he has no idea where she is. How many hotels can there be in Big Sur? He'll find her.

"You can't hide from me, Ms. Eden. I'll find you," he says aloud, taking one hand off the wheel to shove a cigarette into his mouth as he steers around a curve.

The tires hit the right shoulder and for a moment he struggles with the skidding car, just missing the rock ledge running along the road.

Then he regains control.

Close call.

*I need a stiff drink after that one. Christ.*

Shaken, he slows his speed, peering through the fog that seeps onto the road. He lights his cigarette, takes a deep drag. Another.

Then, frustrated, he presses the gas pedal again. No need to drive like somebody's grandmother.

*I've been driving roads like these for years,* Flynn thinks as he expertly guides the Jag around a narrow hairpin turn. *And this is a great car. No problem. Just . . .*

Where the hell is that flask?

He feels again on the seat beside him. Nothing.

It must have rolled onto the floor.

Keeping his left hand on the wheel, he shoves the cigarette between his teeth as he leans forward and moves his right hand along the floor mat in front of the passenger seat, his fingers clawing for the familiar hard metal rectangle.

Nothing.

Maybe it rolled under the seat.

He reaches his hand underneath, straining to stretch far enough back to find the flask.

The sound of a car horn startles him.

Sitting up, he looks through the windshield and sees that he's drifted across the line into the oncoming lane.

And a pair of headlights is bearing down on him from around a sharp curve.

Panic seizes him.

He instinctively steers off the road to avoid the car.

Too late, he realizes he chose the wrong side of the road.

The left side.

He's airborne the next instant, the Jaguar sailing off the edge of the cliff.

For a moment he feels as though time has stood still, as though he is somehow hovering in midair in that car over the raging Pacific Ocean, hovering on the narrow threshold between life and death.

Then he's falling, swiftly, through the black void.

A bloodcurdling scream of anguish . . .

An explosion of bone-shattering pain . . .

And then . . .

Nothing.

"Good morning, Mal. Rise and shine!"

Rae's singsong voice invades Mallory's slumber and she stirs reluctantly, resisting, wanting to slip back into her dream.

Because in the dream she and Harper had been on a sleek sailboat together, rocking gently on the calm blue sea. The sun was beaming down and Harper was standing solidly behind her, his strong arms wrapped around her, and she was utterly at peace . . .

Except that it wasn't real.

Harper isn't here.

And now she's opening her eyes, and she's in her bed in a suite in the Treetop Inn.

Rae, standing in the doorway, is looking pulled together as usual. Her hair is damp and combed back from her face and she's wearing a crisp white sleeveless blouse, khaki shorts, and hiking boots.

"I already took my shower," she says cheerfully. "Your turn. And then we'll hit the trails."

Mallory groans and burrows into the blanket. "Already? Can't I sleep in? I'm so tired."

"Come on, Mal, you know how much you've always loved this time of day up here."

"I like any time of day up here."

"Yeah, but at this hour we'll have the trails to ourselves."

Rae is right.

Mallory throws off the covers and grumbles all the way to the shower.

As she stands under the hot spray, yawning and stretching the muscles in her exhausted body, she slowly comes fully awake.

And as she does, she realizes that the sense of trepidation from yesterday hasn't waned over a good night's sleep.

The anxiety is still there, making her tense despite the steaming stream of water gushing over her.

There's something wrong, something she can't quite put her finger on.

And Mallory can't help feeling as though the day ahead isn't something to look forward to . . .

But to dread.

\*   \*   \*

She's so close.

After so many years, Mallory Eden is actually here, actually within reach.

*All you have to do is—*

But not yet.

It isn't time yet.

*Not now, in the wee hours of the morning, when you're too exhausted to think clearly. You need your wits about you. You need to rest, so that you'll be ready when the time comes . . .*

*If* the time comes.

That would depend on Mallory.

*Your destiny is in your own hands, Mallory. You don't have to die. I don't want to take your life . . .*

*But I will if I have to.*

Tomorrow will come soon enough.

And slowly, like the fog seeping off the waer and snaking around the silent inn, sleep steals in . . .

Bringing, as always, violent nightmares.

Nightmares about a long-ago August night, and a gun clutched in trembling fingers that pulled the trigger, a split second too early . . . or was it too late?

A moment earlier, and the bullet would have sailed past Mallory, close enough to scare her, yet leave her unharmed.

A moment later, as Mallory started to crouch to protect herself, and the bullet would have struck her in the head instead.

But she had been hit in the stomach, a flood of wet crimson soaking her pure white cotton nightgown as she lay motionless on the bed.

And then there was the uncertainty . . .

*Did she glimpse your face?*

*Did she know it was you who shot her?*

The agonizing hours of waiting for her to regain consciousness, your own fate hanging in the balance with hers.

And then, exhilaration.

*She never knew. She never saw you. She never suspected . . .*

And she still doesn't.

Maybe she will never have to know.

Or maybe, tomorrow, she'll discover the terrible, shocking truth . . . in her dying moments.

# chapter
# 16

With Rae right behind her, Mallory steps out onto the porch of the inn and is startled by the sound of someone calling her name.

"Mallory! My God, you look different. I've been waiting for you."

Gasping, she spins to see the figure of a woman striding toward her from the small gravel parking lot alongside the winding drive.

Her eyes are momentarily blinded by glare from the rising sun. All Mallory can see is the woman's silhouette, and that she's wearing a broad-brimmed hat.

"Who is that?" Rae asks in a low, nervous voice.

"I don't know . . ." Panic slices through Mallory. Should she turn and run?

She couldn't if she wanted to. Her feet are rooted to the wide board floor, her body frozen as she stares at the approaching stranger.

"It's me, Mallory," the eerily familiar voice calls as the woman draws nearer. "Remember me? You're not the only one who looks different."

Mallory is trembling now, bracing herself for whatever is going to happen next. She takes a step backward, bumping into Rae, who steadies her with two strong hands on her upper arms.

Suddenly the woman steps out of the glare and her face comes into view.

Mallory gasps at the hideous sight in front of her.

"My God. It's Gretchen," Rae whispers.

Mallory nods, speechless.

The once-beautiful face of her assistant, framed by matted blond hair, has been mangled beyond recognition. Where there should be smooth white skin, there is mottled red and pink and purple scar tissue.

"Look what you've done to me, Mallory." The words are slightly muffled, coming from a stiff, mutilated mouth that barely moves as Gretchen speaks.

"Gretchen, I didn't do this to you." Mallory is incredulous. "I didn't—"

"When you faked your death and disappeared, you doomed me to the life of a freak. I needed you, and you weren't there."

"I was there. I called you in the hospital; I paid for your treatment."

Gretchen gives a bitter laugh. "You think that was all I needed?"

"What . . . what else did you need?"

"I needed money to pay a surgeon to fix my face, Mallory. The kind of money a normal human being doesn't have. Only a movie star has that kind of money."

Mallory fumbles for something to say.

"I would have helped you if I could, Gretchen. If I had known . . ."

"Help me now."

"I . . ." Her thoughts are whirling. All she has left in the world is the cash in the zippered pouch up in the suite. Everything else went to set up the foundation when she "died."

"Gretchen, I don't have any money now."

"Oh, please," she scoffs, coming closer so that they're separated only by the flight of steps leading up to the porch. "How can you not have money? What have you been living on for the past five years?"

Mallory falters, glances at Rae, who is simply staring at Gretchen, her expression a mixture of disbelief and pity and, yes, anger.

"I need your help, Mallory," Gretchen says again, putting a foot on the bottom step.

"She can't do this," Rae mutters. "You don't owe her anything."

Mallory opens her mouth, uncertain what she's even going to say. "Gretchen—"

The word is interrupted by the sudden sound of crunching gravel on the drive.

Mallory glances up to see a long black limousine pulling toward them, trailed by a blue van.

Her heart pounding, she clutches the railing for support and watches as both vehicles draw to a stop and the back door of the limo opens.

A woman she's never seen before in her life climbs out and waves. "Mallory Eden? I have a surprise for you!"

At the same moment, several men spill out of the van, camera equipment in their hands, all of it trained on Mallory.

"My God," Mallory breathes, shaking her head to clear it.

Is this a nightmare?

It has to be.

This can't really be happening.

"It's the press," Rae murmurs. "I *knew* someone was following us yesterday."

The woman calls some instructions to the camera crew, then turns back to the limo, and Mallory realizes that another person is stepping out.

At first the figure is unrecognizable. A stranger. And then she speaks.

"Cindy? It's me. Mama."

That voice, those words, slam into Mallory like a falling piano.

She shrinks back, away from the haggard woman who is moving toward her, away from Gretchen, who is still poised at the foot of the stairs as though she might advance at any moment.

"Rae," Mallory says, turning to her friend for support. "God, Rae, help me."

"Come on." Rae grabs her hand and pulls her into the inn, slamming the door. "Let's go."

Mallory's feet leap into action, following Rae a few steps through the still-deserted lobby, and then through a door leading to a corridor running the length of the building.

"They'll think we've gone back to our room," Rae says breathlessly, pulling her along. "But we won't."

She opens another door, and Mallory realizes what she has in mind. This is the passageway to the back garden. The door at the end opens into a small courtyard edged with lush, blooming foliage.

Rae pulls Mallory across the cobblestones, through a hedge, and onto a short path. It winds away from the inn through a dense thicket of pine trees, ending at a rocky, wooded incline where the wilderness trail begins. Wisps of morning mist hang in the air, making it impossible to see beyond the trees.

"Are you ready to go on that hike?" Rae asks, wearing a wry smile.

Mallory nods gratefully, unable to find her voice.

They scramble forward, disappearing into the fog-shrouded forest.

"What's going to happen now?" Manny asks his grandmother, who is sitting at the kitchen table, a cup of tea in front of her. Her eyes are red and swollen, and Manny knows his must be the same way.

"I don't know," Grammy says, shaking her head slowly. She reaches a gnarled hand for the cup, starts to lift it, and sets it down with a plunk, sloshing tea on the table. "I'm going to lose the house now. We'll have to move."

"Where?"

"There's that senior subsidized housing over in Warwick—but I don't know . . ."

When she doesn't finish, Manny prompts. "You don't know . . . what?"

"I don't know if they allow children there. If they don't, we'll think of something else."

He swallows hard. "Or," he says miserably, "I could go with her."

"With who?"

"You know . . . my mother. If she wants me so bad, she can take me."

"Manny," his grandmother says gruffly, "you're not going anywhere with her. She signed away her rights years ago. And if she tries to take you again, we'll go to the police. I don't think she will though. Now that Rafael—" She breaks off, tears filling her eyes again.

"But, Grammy," Manny says, "what if you can't take care of me on your own? Who's going to help us? There's no one . . ."

*Now that Elizabeth is gone,* he thinks bleakly.

And despite her promises to keep in touch, he knows he can't count on her. She's a world away. Pretty soon she'll forget all about Manny.

*But I'll never forget you,* he tells her silently. *And I'll never stop wishing that somehow, you could have been my mom.*

Gretchen stands in the lobby of the inn, motionless, listening for the sound of running footsteps belonging to Mallory and Rae.

But all she can hear, drifting in the open window, is the sound of Mallory's mother outside.

She's hysterical, ranting, shrieking. "Cindy! You come back here to your mama! Don't you turn your back on me again. Don't you make me come looking for you. This was your last chance...."

And, of course, the cameras will be focused on the pathetic figure; maybe the reporter in her expensive designer suit will even be doing a subdued voice-over, shaking her head sympathetically at the tragic scene: a mother offering too little, too late, and a daughter who can't find it in her stone-cold heart to forgive.

None of that has anything to do with Gretchen.

And she has no intention of being captured on film, a hideous human monster adding to the drama of Mallory and her mother's plight.

Here, in the shadows of the sleeping inn, she simply stands, her ears trained, waiting . . .

A creaking floorboard somewhere nearby rewards her.

She moves stealthily through a doorway and down a hall, then stops and listens again.

Nothing.

But she won't move.

She won't give up until she and Mallory Eden are face-to-face once again.

Mallory stands at the very edge of the land, the toes of her new hiking boots flush against the rocky dropoff.

Gulls swoop overhead. The air is scented with pine and salt and flowers. In front of her is nothing but vast azure sky, dazzling with sunshine that's already burned off the early morning fog. And below—straight down, a sheer drop—is the foaming surf of the Pacific Ocean.

She can't help being reminded of another time, another place, when she had stood, very much like this, poised high above white, thrashing water.

She leans her head back, closes her eyes, and breathes deeply, then, hearing a footstep behind her, she spins around, startled yet careful not to lose her footing.

"Sorry . . . did I scare you?"

It's only Rae, who had gone into the underbrush along the trail to answer nature's call.

"I'm just jumpy," Mallory tells her, and glances back at the view.

"Don't worry. We've covered miles. They'll never find us up here. They're probably still looking for us back at the inn."

"But we have to go back sooner or later."

Rae doesn't reply to that.

"I can't believe my mother is here," Mallory says after a moment. "I can't believe she thinks she can show up with some reporter and a camera crew and expect me to . . . can't believe it."

"I'm assuming you haven't had any contact with her since your sister died?"

Mallory shakes her head. Rae knows the whole story, of course. She had witnessed Elizabeth's visit, had seen how Mallory had struggled to establish some bond with her half sibling. But how did you bond with a lying, wasted, selfish junkie?

Elizabeth had stolen money from Mallory, had embarrassed her in front of her friends, had nearly OD'd in the guest room. Mallory had thrown her out the day she'd come home to find her living room filled with drug paraphernalia and spaced-out strangers—and several valuables missing.

"I'm having a party, sis," Elizabeth had slurred.

When Mallory had tried to kick people out of the place, her sister had flown into a rage, slamming things around, breaking furniture, finally putting her fist through a plate-glass window.

Mallory had paid for her emergency room treatment and tried to force her into rehab. When Elizabeth had refused, she had bought her a ticket back to Chicago. One way.

"What was my mother thinking?" Mallory asks Rae, shaking her head and staring at the sky. "Did she expect me to welcome her into my life with open arms? I can't do that. She beat me, Rae. And then she left me."

Her voice is tight. She can't look at her friend.

But Rae knows. She knows every detail of Mallory's past. About her teenage mother running off. About Mallory's guilt over leaving Vera, and about Vera's sudden death. And about Brawley . . .

Brawley, who had smothered her with everything but love.

"Everybody in my life has always wanted something from me, Rae," Mallory says bleakly, her gaze on the horizon. "Everyone except you. Even Gretchen now . . ."

"I know. She's a mess."

"All this time since I left L.A., I've been trying not to think about her. Not to wonder . . . But now I know. I have to help her."

"Mallory . . . how?"

"Like she said . . . I have to pay for a surgeon. Someone who can do something about her face."

"Do you have that kind of money?"

"No. Not anymore. But I can get it."

"How?"

"You know how." Mallory sighs and watches a gull swooping up off the water, arcing across the sky. "I have to come back. I have to start acting again."

But even as the words spill out of her mouth, she regrets them. She doesn't want to go back to being Mallory Eden. She doesn't want to live the rest of her life that way, surrounded by opportunistic hangers-on, and the press always probing.

"Are you sure?" Rae asks quietly.

Something in her tone causes Mallory to turn her head, to look at her friend. She can't read anything in Rae's expression, and her eyes are concealed by black designer sunglasses.

But Rae knows her so well. Rae must sense that the decision isn't an easy one. That she has doubts . . .

But what choice does she really have?

She owes Gretchen . . .

And what about herself? She had worked so hard to build a career . . .

Anyway, she had always loved acting—the actual art. Just not everything that went with it.

But maybe this time it will be different. Maybe this time she can avoid the Hollywood hoopla.

Besides, what else is there for her? Where else is there?

Her thoughts dart fleetingly to Windemere Cove. To Harper. And Manny . . .

"God, it's gorgeous," Rae comments suddenly, looking out over the majestic scenery. "I haven't been up here since you . . ."

She trails off.

Mallory shifts uncomfortably and looks at her friend, wishing she could see her eyes.

"Since I supposedly killed myself," she finishes for Rae, who nods and looks away.

"I'm sorry, Rae. I'm so sorry I did that to you. I know how

furious you must be, that I put you through all that. But . . . if there was anyone I considered telling, it was you."

"Why didn't you?"

Mallory longs to see what's in Rae's eyes, needs to discern whether she's more angry or hurt. Then she wonders if it even matters. Rae has always been a loyal friend. Her only loyal friend.

She'll get over it. Maybe she already has.

"I didn't tell you," Mallory says carefully, truthfully, "because I didn't want to put you at risk. I was afraid that whoever was after me would turn to you, thinking you might know something. Or that if you knew I was alive, you wouldn't truly seem like you were grieving."

"What you're saying is that you didn't think I was a talented enough actress to pull off the role of the grieving friend."

Mallory frowns, surprised at Rae's brittle tone. "That's not what I meant, Rae."

"Come off it, Mallory. Of course it's what you meant. You never thought I could act. Neither did Flynn. Nobody in this town ever thought I could act."

"Rae, come on . . ."

"But I did it. I pulled it off."

"Pulled what off?" Mallory feels as though she's missed part of the conversation. Where had this tension, this resentment come from?

"I played the grieving friend for five years," Rae is saying. "And do you know what? I'm the best goddamned actress anyone ever saw. I deserve an Oscar for that performance."

Mallory stares at her in disbelief. "What are you talking about, Rae?"

"Do you actually think I mourned the loss of someone who stole every role I ever should have gotten?"

There's a rushing sound in Mallory's ears, blood pumping to her racing heart, panic surging through her veins, disbelieving questions roaring through her mind.

In shock, she can only stare at Rae, feeling as though she's seeing a stranger.

She looks like Rae—perfectly coiffed despite the long hike, her clothes unrumpled, her bare arms and legs tanned and lean and muscular, her makeup in place.

But Rae wouldn't talk like this. Rae wouldn't say . . .

"If it weren't for you, I would have made it, Mallory." Her

voice is carefully modulated, the way it always has been. Clear enunciation, East Coast Ivy League inflections and all.

The stranger looks like Rae, and she *sounds* like Rae.

But her eyes . . .

They're still hidden behind the dark glasses.

And Mallory wonders what she would see in them if she could.

"Rae, I don't know what you're talking about," Mallory says, her voice trembling. "I tried to help you."

"You never tried to help me. You stole every opportunity I ever had. Nobody ever looked past you to see me."

"I can't believe you're saying this. I never knew you had so much anger—"

"You never knew me at all. You never bothered to try to know me. It was always about you, Mallory. All of it. The focus was always on you."

"That's not true! I cared about you. I asked about your life, about your feelings. You were my friend. But you never wanted to talk about anything personal. You never talked about yourself."

Rae gives a wintry laugh. "That's because my life was about hating you."

"This is—" Mallory breaks off, shakes her head. Her stomach is churning, her mind swirling. "You didn't always hate me, Rae."

"In the beginning, maybe I didn't. Until you kept getting in the way. It would have been so simple if you hadn't been in the way, Mallory. You should have listened when I tried to get you to leave."

"What are you talking about? You never—"

"When I sent those letters. And made the phone calls. Do you know how hard it was for me to get that voice box for my phone so that you wouldn't recognize that it was me? I had to date an asshole of a sound technician just to get access to that equipment. But did you listen? No."

The impossible, appalling truth is creeping over Mallory like a killing frost.

"It was the perfect plan. And I never realized how well it would work. I knew that all I had to do was scare you into fading away—"

"It was *you*." Mallory's voice is barely a whisper. "*You* were the stalker. You tried to kill me. Oh my God. Oh my God . . ."

"I never tried to kill you, Mallory. You killed yourself, remember? At least, that was what I thought. Very clever, faking your death that way. Anyway, I had no intention of killing you. I just wanted to scare you. And it was so easy. You gave me access to every part of your life—even the keys to your house. You trusted me."

Oh, God. Mallory remembers the way Rae had first insisted on coming to stay with her after what happened to Mallory's dog.

*Being alone isn't healthy . . . I'm coming over.*

"You killed Gent," Mallory says incredulously, desperately wanting Rae to deny it.

But Rae is nodding, her mouth curling into a grim smile. "I never liked that dog. He smelled. He slobbered all over my clothes."

"I was heartbroken over what happened to him. And you were the one who sent those flowers that blew up in Gretchen's face. And you broke into my bedroom with the gun. . . ." Mallory wraps her arms around herself, trying somehow to shield herself from the terrible knowledge "My God, Rae . . . how could you . . . ?"

"I had only planned to shoot you in the legs," Rae says matter-of-factly. "But you woke up and moved at the wrong moment. I never meant to hit you in the stomach. And I was sorry about that . . . I mean, I know you always wanted children. That was what you should have done in the first place. Gone back to Nebraska, married a farm boy, and had a bunch of kids."

Her voice is mocking now.

*This can't be happening.*

*This is a nightmare.*

"I knew that as soon as you were gone, it would be my turn, Mallory. I never thought it would take five years for it to happen, but that doesn't matter now. It's finally happened."

"What's happened?" Mallory can't stop shaking. Her hands are icy; her teeth are chattering.

"The new Mallory Eden. That's me. I've finally taken your place. It's my turn now. And I won't let you get in the way," she bites out, malice dripping in every word.

Mallory realizes, then, that this isn't a nightmare. She's really here; Rae's here. It's actually happening.

*But it must be a joke,* she tells herself, trying to quell the panic that is rising inside of her.

*She's playing a joke.*

*She has to be playing a joke, except . . .*

Rae has never been the type to play a joke.

*So? You haven't seen her in five years. Maybe she's changed. . . .*

Seized by a dire need to believe the impossible, Mallory reaches out abruptly and grabs Rae's black sunglasses, swiftly pulling them away from her face.

The unmistakable madness she sees in Rae's ice-blue eyes as they bore into her own confirms that this is no joke.

"Rae," Mallory says urgently, suppressing a shudder and flinging the sunglasses to the rocky ground, "you need help. I'll make sure that you get it. You need—"

"The only way you can help me is to kill yourself again, Mallory. But this time, do it for real."

Mallory follows Rae's gaze downward, to where her own shoes are inches from the edge of the precipice. Beyond the edge, twelve hundred feet straight down, are jagged rocks and the raging sea.

"Rae, no," Mallory says raggedly. "I'm not going to do it. You know I'm not. I have no desire to kill myself."

*I want to live. I want to go back to Windemere Cove. I want to be with Harper. I want to take care of Manny. They need me. I need them.*

The realization that all at once she knows where she belongs is lost in a sudden jolt of fear as Mallory takes a step backward, away from the cliff—and feels Rae's cold hand clamp around her arm.

"You don't want to live, Mallory. Not after everything you've been through. Your mother showing up, and Gretchen . . . It's too much for you to bear."

"No," she says, bewildered, looking into Rae's steely gaze. "Rae, you don't know what you're doing."

"Sure I do. I had no idea they were going to show up here when they did, but I have to say, everything's fallen into place nicely."

"What do you mean?"

"Witnesses. Your mother, Gretchen, the reporter, the camera crew . . . I have all those witnesses who saw how distraught you were when you ran away from them. No one who saw you would doubt that you were so unbalanced, so upset, that you came up here and killed yourself. It's even the same method you supposedly used five years ago—jumping all that way into that deadly water. It's perfect."

"I'm not going to kill myself."

There's a faraway expression in Rae's eyes as she talks on, seemingly murmuring to herself. "I'll tell them that I brought you back to the room when we left the porch, but you escaped when I wasn't looking. That I came out here to find you, but it was too late."

"Rae, this is crazy."

*You're crazy.*

"I'll tell them that all last night you were threatening suicide, and I was trying to console you."

"Rae . . ."

"Go ahead, Mallory," Rae says, her eyes snapping back into focus, zeroing in on Mallory's face. "Jump."

"I'm not going to jump."

Rae shrugs. "Then I'll have to push you."

In one abrupt movement she releases her grip on Mallory's arm, then shoves hard against her back with both hands.

"No!" Mallory shrieks, struggling to keep her footing.

"Yes!"

"No!"

It's too late.

Mallory feels herself losing her balance . . .

But then, instead of a terrifying, prolonged drop toward the sea, she instantly finds herself jarred by painful rocks beneath her.

She's been knocked to the ground at the very edge of the cliff. She looks up, dazed, and sees Rae standing above her, smirking.

"Oops, you missed. Good-bye, Mallory," Rae says cheerfully.

"No, Rae . . . don't do this . . ."

"I have no choice." Rae bends toward her, giving her a mighty push.

Mallory resists, squirming under Rae's hands, scratching at the rocky slab beneath her . . .

But there's nothing to grab on to.

And then her legs are flying over the edge into nothingness, and she's clawing frantically for anything that will stop her, and there's nothing, nothing, nothing . . .

Until her hands latch on to a chunk of rock jutting from just beneath the top of the ridge.

Loose stones are still raining from above, falling past her toward the distant sea, too far below for their splashes to be heard.

And despite the momentary reprieve, Mallory knows it's over. She can't hold on.

Still, she swings her dangling legs toward the rock wall in front of her, searching vainly for a toehold in its sheer face.

"Well, look at you." Rae's voice sails down from above. "You really are something. You know, I think it's time you had a choice in this matter. Do you want to hang there for a while and think about how eventually your arms or that rock are going to give way and send you to your death? Or should I give you a hand

and get it over with for you? After all, dying is inevitable either way. Which would you prefer?"

Mallory grits her teeth, fighting to hang on, unable to look up at Rae or reply. She looks down, desperate to find a toehold, and catches a glimpse of the rocky, foaming sea far below, waiting to swallow her battered body.

*No! This can't happen! I'm not ready to die . . .*

"No answer? Well, that's rude." Rae's shadow looms over her. "I'll just be merciful and give you a hand, then. It's too cruel to let you suffer this way. After all, even animals are put out of their misery."

She feels Rae's fingers brush against her own and braces herself for what's coming.

*Please, God, let it be fast—*

There's a sudden scrambling sound, a high-pitched shriek above her, and then something swooshes past, just missing her.

Mallory knows what has happened even before Rae's scream travels upward and then fades as her body hurls toward the sea.

She lost her balance. She fell. Rae fell over the edge. Rae's going to die.

*And so am I,* Mallory realizes.

Her shoulders and arms burn with the exertion of being contorted, of supporting her entire weight. She will never have the strength to pull herself up over that cliff. There's no hope for her. She might as well let go . . .

*But I can't just give up . . .*

*I don't want to die . . .*

*Please . . .*

But her strength has run out. Her hands are slipping from the rock, and this is it . . .

Except that she's falling up, not down.

How can that be?

"It's okay, I've got you."

And then she realizes that someone's strong hands are on her wrists, that someone is pulling her up, up, up, over the edge.

And then she's on the ridge again, lying like a rag doll on the sun-warmed rocky ground, her eyes open and staring overhead, where a gull is banking against the deep blue sky.

For a few moments she's too stunned and exhausted to move; she can only lie there, panting and thankful.

Then she feels gentle hands stroking her hair, and strong arms pulling her close.

"God, Mallory, if I hadn't gotten here in time to stop her . . ."

"Harper," she murmurs, dazed, turning her head and looking into those clear green eyes.

"I've been looking all over that trail for you for hours now," he says, his breathing as labored as her own. "I heard her voice before I reached the clearing."

"She's . . . is she dead?"

Harper nods grimly.

"You pushed her?"

"No. She lost her balance when she was trying to make you let go of the rock. Maybe because she heard my footsteps behind her, but . . . oh, Mallory . . ."

He pulls her closer still, and his lips come down over hers in a sweet, lingering kiss. Her heart rate, which had just begun to slow, accelerates again.

Then he pulls back, and she shakes her head in wonder. "Am I dreaming this?"

He smiles and shakes his head.

"But what are you doing here? You're supposed to be back in Rhode Island."

"I couldn't stay there without you. There's so much I have to tell you—"

"Me too—"

"But all of that can wait," Harper says softly, running a fingertip down her cheek. "There will be plenty of time for talking."

"I know . . . there's just one thing I want to tell you now."

"What is it?"

"I'm coming home."

He frowns slightly.

"To Windemere Cove," she tells him.

"For good?"

"Yes. It's where I belong."

*With you.*

*And Manny.*

*The three of us together . . . maybe we can be a family.*

But she doesn't say any of that. As he said, there will be plenty of time for talking. And for . . .

Other things.

Harper grins.

She laughs. Hard.

"What's so funny?" he asks, watching her.

"Nothing. I'm just . . . happy. For the first time in—maybe ever. It just feels good to laugh."

He joins in.

And the ripples of their exhilarated laughter mingle with the ageless harmony of calling gulls and the breeze rustling the trees and the rhythmic, crashing waves of the ocean.

# epilogue

Wearing her nightgown and a bulky oatmeal-colored wool sweater several sizes too big, Mallory stands on the rocky cliff above the crashing ocean, her eyes trained absently on the horizon. The sky is still faintly streaked with pink from the sunrise, and the water is dotted with silhouettes of early morning fishing boats.

She wraps her arms around herself, hugging herself against the September chill in the salt wind that whips off the water.

September.

Again.

Time for the days to grow darker and shorter, for the flowers to die and the leaves to fade and fall, and the water and sky to meld in a drab shade of gray.

Time for so many things to end . . .

And for some to begin.

She hears a footstep behind her and gasps, jumping backward, away from the edge.

Then she spins around, sees who it is, and relaxes.

"Sorry to scare you," Harper says.

"It's okay."

Maybe it will never go away, the memory . . .

Of Rae.

And what she did.

And how she died, her body battered but not lost in the churning Pacific.

But the memory has faded, some, in the thirteen months since it happened.

And it will continue to fade.

Because Mallory won't let it haunt her forever. She has other things to think about now. Better things.

She smiles at Harper. His hair is sleep tousled, his face tinged by the shadow of a beard. He's wearing a flannel shirt and navy sweatpants, soft, rumpled clothing that makes her want to step into his arms and snuggle her face against his warm chest.

So she does.

And as he holds her close, he says, "I brought you something."

"Coffee?" She lifts her head hopefully.

"It's brewing in the kitchen. I brought this."

She frowns. "The newspaper?"

He hands it to her, folded to an inside page.

And then she realizes what it is. "Oh . . ."

"It's an excellent review," he says as she scans the article, topped by the headline *She's Back, and Better Than Ever Before.*

"They liked the movie," Harper goes on. "Liked de Lisser. *Loved* you."

She nods faintly, reading.

*. . . In her first role since her career was suspended, Mallory Eden is, in a word, dazzling. Her ravishing looks are more serene and womanly than before; she is, if possible, even more stunning as a brown-eyed brunette than she was as a blue-eyed blonde. She dazzles us, as always, with effervescent humor in the comic scenes, while her serious moments are tempered with a quiet inner strength that wasn't there before.*

"You have no idea how proud I am," Harper says, behind her, encircling her waist with his arms. "I know how hard it was for you to do this film. I know you didn't want to."

"I had to."

She leans her head back against his shoulder and closes her eyes momentarily, thinking back over the months of emotional trauma and media frenzy and intense longing to be someplace other than on the set of Martin de Lisser's latest movie.

To be right here, in fact . . .

On this high rocky ledge overlooking the Atlantic.

Behind her, in the distance, looms the house she bought with part of the money she got for doing the film. The rambling old three-story home, covered in weathered gray shingles and skirted by a wraparound porch, isn't grand or enormous. But it's right on the water, and it's plenty big enough for Mallory and Harper . . .

And Manny, who has a whole two-room suite with a bath in a corner of the second floor . . .

And his grandmother, who's perfectly content in the small efficiency apartment above the garage, overlooking the large vegetable garden she planted this summer.

"Is he still sleeping?" Mallory asks Harper, who nods knowing, of course, who she means.

"I'm going to wake him when I go inside. We're going fishing. I don't suppose you feel like coming along?"

She considers it. She's still jet lagged, having flown in from the premiere in L.A. just last night.

But fishing with Harper and Manny . . .

That sounds like heaven.

"I'd love to come," she tells him.

"Good. I'll go get Manny moving and put the coffee into a thermos."

She smiles, watching him head toward the house.

Then she turns back to the article, scanning the part that discusses Martin de Lisser's past film credits, and her own.

. . . *We can only wonder what is next for this multifaceted actress who has proven with this comeback that she is well worth the reported thirteen-million-dollars she was paid for this film* . . .

"Twelve million," she murmurs, shaking her head.

Enough to buy the house . . .

And pay for Gretchen's plastic surgery . . .

And buy a small condo in Chicago to ensure that Becky O'Neal will never be forced to live on the streets again.

She knows that isn't what her mother had had in mind, but it's the best she could do for a woman who wasn't there when she should have been.

Maybe someday Mallory will change her mind, will be able to give Becky O'Neal more than a roof over her head and small monthly checks to cover her living expenses.

And maybe not.

She certainly won't change her mind about Brawley Johnson. The big oaf had the gall to come begging for another chance at a relationship—and for money. Seemed he'd dug himself in a little too deep with his credit cards. And according to him, she owed him, after the way she'd dropped him when she made it big.

She sighs and turns away from the ocean, begins to walk slowly toward the big gray house in the distance.

It's a far cry from the Malibu mansion she had once called home.

Different, too, from the small white Cape Cod tucked at the end of Green Garden Way.

She had driven by the place a few weeks ago, feeling nostalgic. A young family is living there now, and she was happy to see the place looking lived-in, the front yard littered with tricycles and sand shovels and toy trucks.

As for the house next door . . .

There was a for sale sign on the lawn.

Harper, who had bumped into Pamela Minelli one day in town, had told Mallory that she and her children were moving up to Maine, where her parents have a house. She filed for divorce from Frank shortly after he was released from prison, and he had moved to California to live again with his brother.

Mallory has almost, but not quite, forgiven him for what he did to her that night. After all, if it hadn't been for him, she might still be living alone behind tightly drawn blinds, constantly looking over her shoulder.

Thankfully, those haunted days as Elizabeth Baxter are over.

And so is Mallory Eden's career.

She did the de Lisser film because she had to. Because twelve million dollars was too much money to turn down.

It was enough, with careful investing, to ensure a sizable monthly income so that she will never have to work again.

Manny's college education is paid for . . .

As is the Hawaiian honeymoon she and Harper will take next month, after they are quietly married by the justice of the peace with only Manny as a witness.

That seems fitting, that it will be just the three of them, since his adoption will become legal that same day.

Mallory gives the newspaper article one last glance as she reaches the screen door at the back of the house.

*She's Back, and Better Than Ever Before*

Oh, well.

She tucks the paper under her arm.

They'll figure out soon enough that the de Lisser film was her swan song . . .

Her way of letting go of one dream to make way for another.